LEE

NO MAN'S CHATTEL

Merchant's Largesse Books

No Man's Chattel
Merchant's Largess Books
Copyright 2019 by Lee Swanson

Cover art and design by Kerrie Robertson,
Kerri Robertson Illustration, Inc.

First Edition
ISBN-13: 978-0-578-44431-4 (paperback edition)
ISBN-10: 0-578-44431-3

Books>Historical Fiction>Medieval

Historical Notes

From the 12th to the 17th Century, a loose confederation formed by the merchants of primarily northern German cities provided an important cultural and economic link between the principal ports of northern and western Europe. Known as the Hansa, the league's ships plied the waters of the Baltic and North Seas, transporting goods as varied as furs, wax, timber, salted cod, wool, and cloth to the markets where highest demand brought the greatest profit. Throughout much of its history the Hansa centered on the Baltic city of Lubeck, while the most important centers of foreign exchange were London, the Flemish city of Bruges, Bergen in Norway, and the Principality of Novgorod in Russia.

At no time was this truer than the fourteenth century, which saw Lubeck and its sister-cities enjoy a near monopoly of the trade of Northern Europe. Even the powerful monarchs of England deferred to the Hansards, granting the Germans commercial and legal privileges that sometimes exceeded those of their own subjects. This preferential treatment infuriated local merchants and sometimes resulted in violent confrontations; yet, the trade treaties with the Hansa continued. The flow of goods into and out of the country was too important to risk even a temporary disruption, let alone an embargo that could last for years.

Consequently, some of the Hanseatic merchants of the fourteenth century grew tremendously wealthy and politically powerful. These were men who participated almost exclusively in the conduct of long-distance trade. They constituted a privileged class, consisting of a relatively small number of families interlinked through shared ventures and matrimonial connections. The Kohl and Revele families central to the plot of this novel are fictional representations of this privileged class.

These magnates jealously guarded the influence, prestige, and privileges they had attained. A comprehensive set of regulations was established by councils of aldermen that controlled both the commerce and conduct of the individual merchants. Enforcement was strict and punishment was harsh. Nonconformity was not tolerated and could result in the banishment of the offender from the Hansa forever.

Women, of course, played no direct role in the commercial aspects of the Hansa in the fourteenth century. As with the remainder of medieval privileged society, their primary importance was almost wholly as matrimonial pawns and guarantors of the continuation of familial bloodlines.

Certainly, it seems possible some women may have played a more active role in the actual mercantile tasks of a Hanseatic family, albeit in a behind-the-scenes role. But would some be unsatisfied even with that rare concession?

And that, dear reader, is where our story begins. . .

For Karine, may we always journey the road less traveled together

Chapter 1

"God's blood, man, mind that rope! If that cask falls, the master will have your bollocks for breakfast!"

The foreman added a sharp cuff for emphasis to the side of the head of the youthful offender, who reluctantly turned his gawking gaze away from the tall, auburn-haired girl looking out the second story window. With a somewhat rakish smirk, the boy turned his attention back to the block and tackle, lowering the barrel of salted codfish from the fourth-floor storeroom far overhead.

Christina shook her head in mock disapproval, although she was secretly pleased by the young workman's attention. Alf was a pleasant enough lad, but he was learning the hard way there was a time for work and a time for play – and this definitely was not the time to be flirting with one of Master Thomas Kohl's daughters.

To a casual observer, the frenetic activity of the laborers and servants outside the red brick building would have appeared chaotic; each hefting, hoisting, pushing, or pulling a seemingly endless supply of goods from the cavernous storage areas on the third and fourth floors of the house onto the train of wagons. Christina was aware, however that, just like an army of ants, every individual knew his role in safely loading the barrels, boxes, and crates, having performed these tasks repeatedly throughout the year. For if there was one thing a man living in Lubeck understood, it was the loading and unloading of trade goods.

She noticed white froth bubbling from the nostrils of the

lathered dray horses as they rested while the wagons were being laden, testimony to the considerable weight of the loads being transported from the massive merchant house on Engelsgrube to the quay on the river Trave at the end of the street. Although the distance was not great, the combination of the unseasonably warm day, the heaviness of the goods, and the number of trips needed to fill the large hold of the cog had sapped the animals of much of their reserves of strength. Luckily for both the beasts and the tired, sweaty men, this was the last of the cargo that needed to be stowed.

I'll sneak down to the stable later to help groom and feed the horses, she decided, knowing they would be much more enjoyable tasks than helping her mother ensure tonight's festivities were perfect.

She stretched sensuously, feeling the heat of the sun's rays on her face and linen-clad arms. *How good the sun feels after such a cold and wet summer,* she exclaimed to herself.

Christina was suddenly shocked from her reveries by the pain of a hard pinch on the soft skin of her left upper arm. She whirled about, only to discover the smirking face of her older sister Margarete staring up at her in disapproval.

"I should have known! Everyone attending to their work, except for you, who'd rather hang out the window flaunting yourself to the workmen like a common whore. By the Holy Virgin, Christina, you must be such an embarrassment to Father and Mother. You certainly are to me! How happy I will be to leave Lubeck, if only to get away from you!" She coughed delicately into her handkerchief, wiping the corners of her mouth primly afterwards.

"Not half as happy as I will be to see you go!" Christina retorted angrily. "I hope your new husband in London beats you every day and twice on Sundays!"

"Well, if he does you won't be there to see it. I'll be an important lady living in a fine stone house, with obedient servants to dress me in beautiful gowns. And where will you be, darling Sister? Still here in Lubeck, that's where. Spreading your legs for fat George Muller, bearing him litters of fat little piglets that reek as badly as him!"

Christina flushed, her temper threatening to overcome her good sense. She had no doubt she could best her sister in any physical confrontation, as she could since she had begun to tower over Margarete when she had turned thirteen years old. Now, nearly four years later, she was a good six inches taller than her oldest sibling. She was also heavier, faster, and a far better fighter. *Margarete has one final thrashing coming before she sails away to her new, wonderful, life and it is about to happen right now!* She thought with rising ire.

"Christina! You leave your sister alone this instant!" her mother's voice unexpectedly commanded. "Your father will be the laughing-stock of the city if his eldest daughter shows up for her marriage feast appearing like she's been in a street brawl."

Christina glanced toward the carved oak doorway, her eyes meeting those of her mother, whose steely glare confirmed there would be no toleration for even the slightest disobedience. Christina's anger continued to simmer, but she dutifully lowered her head submissively.

"As you wish, Mother," she muttered, knowing it was useless to try to pin the blame for their argument on her sister.

To her parents, Margarete could do little wrong, *especially now*, Christina thought somewhat petulantly. Margarete's forthcoming marriage to the son of the chief alderman of the German merchant settlement in London would forge an enviable economic alliance for the family;

consequently, the elder Kohls' customary preference for her older sister was intensified by the honor and wealth inherent in her upcoming match. Or at least that's how it seemed in Christina's mind.

"Thank you, Mother," Margarete said coyly. "I know how difficult it must be for you and Father to be cursed with such a willful and ungainly child as this."

She patted her sister's cheek in mock affection as she walked serenely toward their mother. She spun gracefully to flash a triumphant smile at Christina, then turned back toward their mother.

"Mother, would you please send Anna to my room with a glass of honeyed wine? My throat feels far worse today."

She demurely curtsied, and disappeared into the hallway, followed closely by her doting mother.

Although Christina had barely felt the disdainful brush of her sister's hand as she passed by, it had caused her to dig her nails deeply into her clenched fists to keep her anger under control. *Why does she have to be so mean to me, especially now? She's getting everything she wants: marrying a wealthy husband and becoming mistress of her own home. Well, she can have those things, if that's what she wants!*

Yet, in her heart, Christina knew she was in some ways jealous of her sister. Not necessarily of her upcoming marriage, the thought of trading her subservient role in her father's home for that of being the dutiful wife of someone she had never met caused her to shudder with revulsion.

No, she thought to herself, *what I envy is the opportunity to adventure across the sea, to behold strange and wondrous sights far beyond the city walls of Lubeck.* To do that even once would almost be worth submitting one's self to a loveless marriage based solely on familial advantage.

But not quite, she admitted to herself. For if there was one thing of which Christina Kohl was certain, it was that she craved her independence even more than adventure.

Well, there's little enough chance for either, she thought sourly.

She knew her father was making discreet enquiries of some of the other merchant patriarchs of the city, those with marriageable men in their families. At the thought of the term "marriageable," she unconsciously spat vituperatively on the wooden floor then, guiltily, hurriedly wiped it away with the hem of her gown. To her father, any male between twelve and seventy would suffice for his second daughter. *Oh yes,* she added sarcastically, *and as long as he has a good family name and a large bag of silver Hohlpfennige hidden under the bed.* After marrying, she could look forward to a life that went unchanged from day to day, its monotony broken only by yearly trips to the birthing chair. *Damn you, Father,* she hissed between her teeth, then spat once more on the oak floorboard.

This time, she left it uncleaned.

Her dark mood unabated, she ascended the stairs, the soles of her leather shoes making a sharp, staccato slap with each step. She thrust open the door to her room and threw herself onto her bed. Although the last thing she wanted to do was attend a feast in Margarete's honor, she knew she had no choice in the matter. She stripped off her worn day-gown and chemise, then poured water from the ewer on the table into the adjacent large earthenware bowl. She picked up a small bit of soap and washed herself thoroughly, reveling in the refreshing sensation of the cool water on her hot skin.

After drying herself with a length of coarse linen cloth, she picked up her most prized possession, a small Venetian looking glass that had been a gift from her father. She viewed her nude body critically, thoroughly unimpressed by what she saw. Her hair was mousy brown, neither the honey-gold of that of her sister, nor the exotic, raven-colored locks of her mother. Her face was angular, with a high forehead and aquiline nose. Inquisitive brown eyes stared back at Christina from under a delicate brow. Her skin was unmarred by the pox but, almost in retribution for having this one good feature, was dappled with a myriad of light brown freckles. She tilted the mirror downward, disappointed in the breath of her hips. A quick glance at her small, pert breasts, flat stomach, tufted nether-region, and well-muscled legs completed her frank self-assessment. Combined with her tall stature and broad-shouldered frame, she was handsome rather than beautiful, although Christina would certainly have thought she was neither.

A knock on her door broke her from her reverie. As it began to slowly open, she flew across the room, throwing all of her weight against its inner surface. It slammed shut with a loud bang, accompanied by a sharp yelp of pain from the other side.

Recognizing the voice instantly, she opened the door a crack and guffawed as she saw the lanky young man struggling to raise himself from the floor. As he lifted his head, she peered into a face that almost perfectly replicated the image she had appraised in the mirror a few seconds before.

"What are you trying to do, Christina, kill me? If I would have put my head through the door, it would have been cracked like an over-ripe melon."

"If you'd have put your head through the door, you'd have seen me naked; which would have been the last thing you saw before my foot would have cracked your head like said over-ripe melon!"

She glared at him with an expression of pure homicidal malice then, unable to keep a straight face any longer, she began to giggle uncontrollably.

Trying to retain whatever dignity he still possessed, Frederick Kohl rose from the floor gracefully, although rubbing his bruised backside unconsciously somewhat diminished the desired effect.

He looked at the sliver of his older sister's face and, bowing deeply, stating, "Please forgive me, sweet Sister, for my thoughtless transgression of milady's privacy."

He lifted his eyes and gazed at her in grave supplication before he too erupted into laughter.

He wiped merry tears from his eyes, then said, "I am sorry, Christina, but Father just dismissed me so I could dress for tonight. I was wondering If, before getting ready yourself, you had enough time to . . ." He let his words trail off but peered at her hopefully.

Christina's mind raced as she considered his offer, weighing the pleasure of spending secret time alone with her brother against the trouble in which she would be should she arrive at tonight's feast late. She decided she would hazard her parent's anger against herself; however, she could not chance placing her brother in her father's ill favor as well.

Not wishing to risk being persuaded to change her mind, she said grumpily, "Well, it's easy enough for you to think you have enough time, but things are more complicated when you're a woman. Now get out of here! I'll be lucky not to be late as it is, standing here prattling with you and not a stitch on me yet!"

He laughed once again and then his eyes turned grave. He said, "I know there really isn't enough time, but it's just that we have so few hours together before I leave for London with Father and Margarete. Oh Christina, I'll miss you so much!"

Christina was both surprised and moved by her brother's sudden burst of affectionate emotion. She too felt deeply wounded by Frederick's impending departure for, unlike the emotional gulf that separated her from her sister, she and her brother were bonded by deep friendship as well as blood. That was why she couldn't chance him incurring their father's wrath, particularly just before the long sea voyage to England.

Her tone softened as she said, "You know I will miss you just as deeply, dear Brother. If we arise early, might we get in some sport before Father requires you in the morning?"

His immediate grin brought warmth to her heart as no one else could. They agreed to meet as usual at very first light in the old warehouse on Fischergrube their father used for the storage of timber from the east as well as other bulky goods. She then shooed him away and, closing her door, returned to the task of readying herself for the evening's festivities. She found it hard to concentrate, however, as her attention was divided between what she must do and what she longed to do. Her heart beat faster at the thought of being alone with her brother, amplified by the real danger of being unexpectedly discovered. *Father would punish Frederick severely*, she thought, *but I would be thrashed within an inch of my life and sent to a convent!* Despite the risks involved, however, she knew she would not avoid a final clandestine assignation with him.

Christina spent considerable time combing her long hair since she would wear it unfettered, as befitting a maiden. She then opened the large wooden trunk adjacent to her bed and retrieved her new, white linen smock. Pulling it over her head, she next laid aside the woolen stockings she had favored over the recent period of cold weather and selected a pair of very light linen. Sitting on her bed, she pulled each up over her knee, securing them with woven strips of blue wool to serve as garters. Next came her favorite low-cut leather shoes with the little straps across the instep.

She arose and went to a wooden bench, where her mother had laid a new dark green *gunna* or, as Margarete had informed her in her damnably superior, officious manner, a kirtle, as it was called in England. Her friends envied Christina for the frequency with which she was provided with new clothing. *One of the few advantages to being so tall is that you your mother and older sister's hand-me-downs don't fit,* she thought happily.

The warmth of the night air persuaded Christina to forego wearing an outer garment as the great hall of the *Rathaus* was only a few minutes' walk away. *Besides,* she thought, finally getting somewhat excited at the thought of the feast, *I plan on dancing every dance, so there is no way I'll get cold!* Wrapping her best leather girdle low about her hips and attaching her purse, she felt she was finally ready to go.

With growing eagerness, she hurried down the stairway, almost forgetting to don pattens before exiting the building. Although it had been a warm day, the streets were still quite awash in mud and filth after the recent rains. *The last thing I need to do is ruin my best shoes,* she thought carefully. *Besides, who would want to dance with someone leaving a slimy trail of mud and horseshit in her wake?*

As soon as she entered the hall, she began searching for Frederick. She spotted him within a few seconds, the same amount of time it took for him to see her. He waved to her excitedly and began to work his way through the crowd of people that loitered between them. Before he could reach her side, however, the call was given for the meal to begin. An orderly procession began to the tables, with everyone standing respectfully until the aldermen took their seats at the high table.

As was customary, the Kohl family occupied one of the tables closest to the high table. Thomas, of course, did not sit with his family, seated as he was with the rest of the aldermen. Christina's mother had relinquished the honor of sitting at the center of the table to Margarete, a gesture Christina felt was excessive. *Well*, better her than me, *Christina thought with satisfaction, at least I don't have to sit next to him!*

The "him" she referred to was Kurt Ziesolf, whose emotionless face gazed straight ahead as if carved of stone like one of the gargoyles that stared down from the eaves of the holy *Marienkirche*. The man had served her father for as long as she could remember. She no longer screamed if she encountered him unexpectedly and ran in the opposite direction as she had when she was small. Nor did she cry as she had when Margarete had told her their father would make her marry the man.

Although she was no longer irrationally frightened by Ziesolf, she couldn't help but shudder at the sight of him. An angry red line traversed his face diagonally. The part to the left functioned normally; however, the part to the right was frozen, the skin sagging and the eye milky-white and unseeing. His inhuman appearance strengthened her comparison of the man to one of the grotesque stone effigies on the church.

Gossips in town attributed his disfigurement to wounds he had received while on crusade against the Ests, some even claimed he was a disgraced knight of the Teutonic Order; however, none of them would repeat this rumor in front of the man. For Kurt Ziesolf was also said to be the best swordsman in all of Lubeck, no one would dare to incur his ire. Most of the men in the city wondered why such a man was not in the employ of a nobleman, even the emperor himself would surely have a use for a seasoned warrior of his great ability. Yet, when they queried her father about why Ziesolf remained in his employ, he would smile mysteriously and tell them they would have to ask the man himself. *To date, no one has been inquisitive enough to do that*, Christina sniggered to herself.

The evening was proceeding far better than Christina had originally hoped. The musicians playing in the gallery could barely be heard over the raucous cacophony of the myriad of animated conversations. Soon, each course began to arrive in turn, presented of course to the high table first. Her mouth began to water as she saw many of her favorites appear: baked herring with sugar, roast coney, breme in jelly, swan neck pudding, damsons in fine syrup, almond crème, hot apples and pears with sugar candy; she ate until she felt as if she would burst. *Can I risk even one of the almond tarts?* she considered guiltily, trying hard to resist her urge to indulge in further glutinous abandon. Surprisingly, she saw Margarete had barely touched her food. *Ever trying to be the fine lady*, Christina thought contemptuously, grabbing two tarts in spite.

Christina's thoughts were interrupted when she noticed a silence descend upon the room. She glanced toward the high table to see her father had risen and was looking out over the rest of the hall. His gaze eventually fell upon his wife, who nodded encouragingly. He cleared his throat and began to speak.

"Good people of Lubeck, I am happy to welcome you to this evening of laughter, good food, and sweet Rhenish wine. The betrothal of one's daughter is always a time of great joy, as it is with that of our sweet daughter, Margarete."

Christina's eyes flew involuntarily heavenward. Her father continued, "Yet, her marriage is even more cause for happiness to our family, because it represents a new alliance, linking the Kohl's fortunes to those of family Revele. Soon, our warehouses in London will be filled not only with our goods from Novgorod; furs, amber, and honey; but, Revele cloth from Bruges as well. Our family's prosperity will be assured, guaranteed by the watchful eye of the chief alderman of the German merchants of London, Johann Revele himself. For his good fortune will mean our good fortune, as well as that of his son Albrecht and our daughter Margarete.

Two days hence, with God's good grace and favorable weather, we will begin our voyage to England. But Margarete is not the only member of my family who will be traveling to London with me.

Frederick, my son, will be apprenticed to my younger brother, Gerhardt, who represents my business interests in England. There, Frederick will expand on what he has learned from me. He will also be able to form a strong alliance with the family that, up to now, has been our chief rival in the city, the Reveles. He will then have the knowledge and connections of both Kohl and Revele, preparing him well to become my successor as head of family Kohl. So, drink, my friends, drink to Margarete as well as Frederick, may they both represent Lubeck well!"

Thunderous acclaim echoed throughout the hall. Not only were the Kohls one of the wealthiest families in Lubeck, but also one of the most popular. The remainder of the evening passed in merriment as each attendee drew pleasure from the Kohl's happiness and bounty. Everyone made their way to congratulate Margarete, who surprisingly for once did not seem to be enjoying the attention. Instead, she seemed distracted, often turning away from a well-wisher, even while he or she spoke.

How rude, thought Christina, *if I acted in such a manner, Mother would box my ears. Oh well, I'm not Margarete, I guess.* She crossed herself and murmured, *thank the good Lord for that!*

Although Christina was pouting a bit because of the attention being paid to everyone else in her family, her spirits immediately lifted when the tables were moved back to make way for dancing. She was overjoyed when she heard the music for the first dance, which would be the *Springtanze*, her favorite. This was followed by an *estampie.*

Soon she was lost in a sea of movement, negotiating each step with a lightness and sense of balance that belied her large stature. She glimpsed to her left and noticed Margarete had also joined in the dancing. *I knew she couldn't play Miss High and Mighty all evening,* Christina thought, grinning widely.

Suddenly, the music from the instruments ground to a discordant halt. Christina, who was in mid-step, glanced about in an irritated manner. She then saw her parents bending over a still figure collapsed amid the dancers. She drew closer and saw the prone figure was Margarete. She ran to her mother's side just as her father lifted her sister gently into the air.

"She's probably just had a bit too much to eat and drink," he reassured his wife who waited anxiously at his side.

"Father, no," Christina blurted, pulling anxiously at his sleeve. "She hardly touched her food and she drank no more than one cup of wine, if any at . . ."

"Be quiet, Christina!" her mother scolded. "Oh, by the Virgin's tears, please stop bothering your Father and let us attend to your sister."

Mechtild Kohl's hand moved to gently stroke her eldest daughter's hair from her face. She inhaled sharply and drew her hand away from the young woman's forehead, exclaiming, "Dear Lord, Thomas, she is burning with fever! We must get her into bed."

Weakly, Margarete's eyelids fluttered open. "What happened to me? I remember I was dancing and now I'm in Father's arms. Why is there no music? Oh, I feel so cold, please hold me closer, Father." Her eyes flew open wide as she erupted into a fit of spasmodic coughing.

Her father commanded, "Christina, if you want to be of help to your family, run to the Hospital of the Holy Spirit and fetch one of the healers for your sister. Hurry now!"

Christina sped away, all animosity toward her sister forgotten. Beating furiously on the door, she soon awakened one of the brothers who listened intently to her excited plea for assistance. He bid her to remain and left, only to return a few minutes later with a grey-haired monk who readily agreed to accompany Christina to the Kohl home. Upon their arrival, she showed Brother Udo to Margarete's chamber and stood quietly in the background, unconsciously seeking the strength of Frederick's hand in fear for her sister's life. Her parents thanked the monk for venturing out so late at night and moved away so he could examine their daughter.

Margarete was conscious and considerably more lucid then she had appeared at the hall. To Christina's surprise, she was sitting up in her bed.

Margarete thanked Brother Udo for coming but chided her family for being overly concerned about her well-being. Yet, one could easily discern the paleness of her skin, the thin glistening of sweat on her brow, and the dark circles that had begun to ring her eyes. Margarete had bid her mother to pile her bed high with blankets despite the warmth of the evening. It was readily apparent to everyone in the room the young woman was seriously ill.

Their mother shooed her husband, Christina, and Frederick from the room as Brother Udo began the examination of his patient. Together they waited outside the room, worry and impatience in equal measure. Approximately an hour later, the door opened and Brother Udo appeared.

Before Thomas Kohl could ask, he said, "It appears your daughter is afflicted with a fiery and moist humor in her lungs. Although this in itself is common in women and young people, whose bodies are by nature moist and hot, she also complains of catarrh and pleurisy. Most seriously, she told me she has suffered from these maladies for at least two weeks."

"If you wish her to have any chance to recover, you must do the following. For the next three days, steam your daughter with a moist dressing of oil, hot wine, and soft wool pads, especially the right side of her chest and throat. Also, apply compresses of wax, cypress oil, and ground mustard to her body. She must continue to eat to conserve her strength, soft-boiled eggs and broth of *ptisane* with fish sauce and pepper will be best. Most importantly, she must take mead infused with rue, bitter almonds, hyssop, and polygony every day on an empty stomach. Your daughter is very ill, but these treatments may, God and the good Virgin willing, give her a chance to live."

At that, Christina's mother sank to her knees and bowed her head in sobbing prayers. Brother Udo gazed at her with troubled, yet compassionate eyes. He placed his left hand lightly on her shoulder while making the sign of the cross with his right. The other members of the Kohl family looked on silently, not knowing what to do to help either Margarete or her despairing mother.

Breaking the silence, the monk murmured, "God be with you all," and nodded toward Thomas Kohl, who accompanied him down the stairs.

Shortly thereafter, the loud thud of the substantial front door closing echoed like a death knell throughout the house.

Mechtild Kohl rose to her feet. Her sense of purpose and strength belaying the helplessness she had displayed only a few moments before. She stared in the direction of her two younger children, a faint smile of determination fixed upon her full lips. "There is nothing either of you two can do right now to help your sister. I will stay with her myself. Frederick, go to your bed. You must help your Father tomorrow with the final preparations for your voyage. Christina, waken Anna and have her come to me immediately. Then, to bed with you as well." Frederick obeyed his mother's bidding immediately, departing for his chamber with a troubled expression of deep concern etched into his handsome features. Christina tarried, considering whether to ask if she might help her mother care for her sister rather than Anna.

Just as she was about to volunteer, her mother turned sharply and said, "Can you not even do this, Christina, as you are told? Do you hate Margarete so much you wish her to die?"

"My God, Mother! No!" Christina cried out and fled the room swiftly.

She wept as she ran up the stairs to the maids' room in the loft, confused as to whether her tears were predicated upon anger against her mother, concern for her sister, or both. She pounded on the door until it was opened a few seconds later by a clearly exasperated Anna.

Thrusting her head through the narrow crack with which she held the door open, the woman muttered, "Are you unaware it's the middle of the night, child? What is it that you want?"

Still standing in the hallway, Christina summarized what had transpired earlier that evening concerning Margarete

Imperiously, Anna uttered a single word, "Wait," and closed the door emphatically, leaving Christina standing in the middle of the hallway, unsure what to do next. Although Anna was only a servant, Christina had always felt intimidated by the humorless and overbearing woman. This feeling was intensified by the close relationship the maid shared with Margarete. Consequently, even though she felt disinclined to follow Anna's order, she was somewhat compelled to do so. *Well, thank God, I'll soon be rid of both of them*, she thought, remembering Anna was accompanying her sister to London. She immediately felt badly, however, guiltily remembering her sister's perilous condition.

Suddenly, the door flew open. Christina's startled look changed to one of happiness as, instead of the expected Anna, a girl burst through the doorway. "Trudi!" she said as she hugged Anna's younger sister. Normally, they would have exchanged pleasantries or even jokes, habitually sharing an easy relationship unaffected by the difference in their social class. Both had been born in the house in the same year, trusted confidants from their earliest recollection. Tonight, however, there was no place for frivolities or shared secrets. Christina hurriedly told her friend about Margarete's condition but, before she could finish, Anna elbowed both younger girls aside, purposely striding down the hallway and beckoning impatiently for Christina to follow. Christina ran after her, waving farewell to the younger maid as she rushed to catch up with the older.

They hurried down to the second floor, Anna turning toward Margarete's door. She instructed Christina to go to the spice cabinet and collect the ingredients Brother Udo had specified. She would then meet her in the kitchen. A few minutes later, Christina delivered the spices to Anna, who dismissed her with an absent-minded wave of her hand as she set to work making the compresses. With no further tasks to attend to, Christina went to her room. She stepped inside and moved to light a large candle next to her bed from the stumpy taper she held in her hand. A soft glow permeated the room. She opened the shutters on her window, allowing the cool evening breeze to ease the heavy, thick atmosphere of the room. She sat down on the side of her bed, head bent and tears running in salty rivulets down her cheeks.

Lord, please forgive me for my wickedness, she implored silently. *I've asked you so many times to make horrible things happen to Margarete but, now that something has, please realize I never meant what I said. I do love my sister, even when she's unkind to me. Please God, I'll try to be a better Christian, just help Margarete get well again!*

Not knowing what else to do, Christina undressed and got ready for bed. As soon as she was under the covers, her eyelids began to droop and the tension in her body began to subside. Soon, she fell into a troubled sleep, her concern for Margarete relegated to fodder for vague and distressing nightmares.

Chapter 2

Christina awoke with a start, a fine sheen of sweat glistening on her milky white skin. Temporarily disoriented, she was caught in a netherworld between reality and the deceptively tangible world of her dreams. Her room was dark, warm, enveloping; she snuggled deeper beneath her covers until she felt consciousness begin to once again slip away. It was then that she noticed the faintest contrast of light on the horizon. She groggily questioned herself as to the significance of this portent of the impending dawn.

She was suddenly wide awake. She leapt from her bed and stood on the cool wood of the floor. In a panic, she once again peered out the window, this time making a more careful calculation of how much time she had available before sunrise. Her assessment calmed her somewhat as she realized she had sufficient time to complete her customary morning ablutions. A trip to the chamber pot was followed by a quick wash and a stubborn comb through of her tangled hair. She dressed herself somewhat haphazardly, *well, I won't have them on very long anyway,* she thought with a grin, excusing herself for her inattentiveness. She grabbed the bundle from her trunk she had packed the previous day and silently slipped out of her door and into the hallway.

She crept through the house as quietly as possible, cursing herself for unthinkingly putting on her shoes instead of tiptoeing out in her bare feet. Despite the soft scuffing of her leather shoes along the floorboards, no one arose to question her as to why she was about so early or what it was she was carrying. Christina tarried just long enough in the lower hall alcove to retrieve the massive key to the warehouse door. Moving more swiftly now, she closed the kitchen door behind her and stepped out into the yard, relieved she had once again been able to leave the house undetected.

She consciously controlled her pace as she walked the short distance to the warehouse. Too fast or too slow would certainly draw attention, perhaps even an inquisitive greeting. She knew that, if she was questioned, the subject of her early morning foray would certainly be a topic of conversation among the merchant wives of Lubeck.

Damned gossips, Christina thought to herself, *worse than a bunch of gaggling geese!* Consequently, she kept a measured, purposeful gait, which was excruciatingly difficult as she wanted to sprint all the way to the warehouse and her imminent rendezvous with Frederick.

The building soon loomed directly ahead of her. She cast a furtive glance about her to ensure no prying eyes were gauging her movements. Satisfied, she placed the key in the hole and twisted. Christina entered and was immediately met with a rich medley of fragrances from a variety of woods in various stages of seasoning. Oak, pine, larch – each had a particular scent her discerning sense of smell identified with ease.

Although the cavernous room had no windows, the young woman was able to move purposefully to the wall of the building fronting the river, assisted through the dark passageways both by the bit of light entering the room through the door she had left open and the memory of previous covert visits to the building. Soon, she reached her destination. She flung the massive loading doors open and her senses were overcome by the blinding glare that flooded the warehouse from the dazzling morning sun skimming across the river.

"I was beginning to think you had forgotten about me."

The quiet voice behind her spoke in English, rather than in its customary middle low German dialect. The words startled her momentarily, causing her muscles to tense, then slowly relax as she realized who it was that had spoken. She turned and saw her brother emerge from the shadows, a happy, anticipatory grin spread across his features.

She matched his broad smile with one of her own.

"Christ's Blood, Frederick, you gave me a fright. Do you have to lurk about like a damned cutpurse?" Christina replied in English as well.

"Well, someone has to give you a fright to teach you a lesson. What if it had been a couple of loutish churls sleeping off a head full of beer you'd disturbed? Are you so eager to lose your virtue that you take no care for your safety?" he asked, half seriously.

Christina snorted, then laughingly replied, "The day I can't handle two hungover rogues figuring to stretch their yards at my expense is the day I'll begin to take caution, brother!" the musicality of her lilting contralto voice belying the ferocity of her words.

Frederick sighed and bowed in mock tribute. Even though her brother was only being playful, Christina felt her ire rise, she hated being teased, even by him.

A little too harshly, she asked, "How did you get in, by the way? The door was still firmly locked when I arrived."

"We all have our secrets," he said mysteriously. Then, gesturing toward the large bundle she carried, he asked, "For instance, what have you there, Sister?"

Her irritation evaporated as suddenly as it had appeared. She could never stay mad at Frederick for long.

"Oh, a bit of a surprise for you, darling Brother," she said, a bit enigmatically herself. "Wait here for a few minutes – and no peeking, damn you!"

She shook her finger at him in warning and disappeared behind a substantial stack of old casks. Dropping her load, she efficiently shed her gown and chemise, shivering slightly as the cold, dank air caressed her naked skin.

A few moments later, Frederick heard his sister clear her throat. He turned around and was shocked by what he saw. Christina stood before him, her feet and lower legs bare. The rest of her body was clad, however, but not in what was to be expected of a young woman. Instead, she was dressed in a faded green gambeson, the quilting torn in places and tufts of padding protruding from the holes. Even more shocking, she had donned a pair of overly large braes, held about her slim waist with a tightly cinched leather belt. A pair of thick gloves completed the ensemble. Try as he might to resist, the young man was suddenly overcome with laughter at the sight of his sister, his raucous guffaws reverberating throughout the room.

Christina flew across the room and backhanded her brother with considerable force. He stumbled rearward, catching himself before toppling unceremoniously on his backside.

"Ow!" he yelled involuntarily, rubbing his stinging jawline. "All right, I'm sorry!"

His apology temporarily forestalled a continuation of Christina's physical attack. The rage in her eyes was unabated, however.

"I only wanted to surprise you, you bastard! I thought you'd be happy, but what do I get instead? Your ridicule. Damn you to hell, Frederick!"

She wheeled about, hot tears springing unbidden from her eyes as she started to return to her impromptu dressing room.

Frederick ran forward and placed his hand on his sister's shoulder, an action requiring considerable courage in light of her previous attack. She turned but withheld any further violence for the time being. "Christina, I truly am sorry, I was just so taken aback. I had never seen you attired so and, and . . . the clothes do not fit you very well," he continued diplomatically.

Her right hand shot forward and grabbed him by the throat. Her grasp tightened threateningly, then fell away as she began to giggle. Cautiously, Frederick began to laugh as well, joining his sister's mirth but careful not to surpass its intensity.

Frederick's face sobered as he said, "Well, did we come here to laugh like buffoons or to train? We've already wasted enough time."

Christina's eyes flashed, but now in excitement rather than anger. The young man reached behind a coil of rope and drew out the two old falchions they had used so often during the past three years, first in play and then in more earnest pursuit. Christina had discovered them one day in an old trunk on the top floor of their house.

She and Frederick had smuggled them out of the house, spending hours in the old warehouse clashing them together, engaging in mock combat against imaginary Livs, Rus, and Saracens. When Frederick turned thirteen, however, the timbre of their swordplay dramatically changed.

Almost every day, Frederick spent an hour or two under the tutelage of Kurt Ziesolf. Their father believed it was just as important for a merchant to know how to defend himself as it was to master tabular accounting. Consequently, Frederick soon learned there was more to swordplay than simply clanging the blades about. During these sessions, the old knight also taught the young man to speak and understand English so he would not be at a disadvantage when he reached his apprenticeship. Frederick was a quick study in both disciplines and his prowess grew daily in each. He loved his time spent with Ziesolf, but the man had other duties as well, leaving his student's desire for more practice unquenched. It wasn't long before Frederick was once again vying with his sister in mock combat, only this time imparting the skills and knowledge of the master swordsman to his middle sibling as well as his newly learned language. Like so many other things in their lives, his interests were mirrored by her own, and surpassed by her proficiency.

Up to this point, her dexterity had been hampered by the bulk and ungainliness of her female attire. *Long skirts are not so good for following through on a thrust,* she remembered ruefully, recalling tripping and falling on her face, followed by Frederick's blade whacking down hard across her buttocks. Those were two things she swore she wouldn't allow to happen again.

Her household duties had not required her to go to the fourth-floor storeroom until two days prior. Her father had ordered her to bring down a small box of raw amber that would become part of the cargo of *der Greif,* the broad-beamed cog that would carry her father, sister, and brother to England. She found the box next to the dusty trunk where the falchions had been stored. *There could be anything in there,* she thought to herself. *I wouldn't have noticed a pearl the size of a quail's egg, all I could see were the blades.* She peeked surreptitiously about, then opened the trunk once more. Disappointingly, the remaining contents appeared to be just a collection of old clothes. It was only upon holding them up that she realized their true nature. She wrapped the gambeson tightly around the braes and tucked them under her arm. She picked up the box of amber and walked quietly down the two flights of stairs. She peeked around the corner of the hallway to ensure no one was there. Seeing it was empty, she hurried to her room and hid the illicit garb under her bed before carrying the box of amber downstairs to complete her assigned task.

"Hey, are you still asleep or what?"

Christina broke from her reveries to see Frederick's impatient face before her, one of the falchions held forward in his hand.

"Oh, I'm very awake, Master Kohl," she said, grabbing the proffered hilt of the weapon and flashing her brother a wolf's smile.

She leapt back and swept the blade through the air to test the sword's weight, even though she knew its balance by heart. She then settled into her guard, circling slowly to her right with measured steps. The sunlight that reflected from her blade danced across the dark walls of the warehouse. The loss of warmth from her bare feet and lower legs went unnoticed as she placed her full focus on the opposing blade.

Suddenly, Frederick's sword thrust forward in a smooth, snake-like fashion. Christina flicked her wrist in an easy parry. *You'll have to do much, much better than that*, she thought smiling to herself.

He stepped back, raising his sword in mock salute. Christina lunged, closing the distance between them in a flash. Her falchion swept in a high arc, the flat of its blade striking her brother's upper arm powerfully.

"Christ's blood, Christina! That hurt!"

Unexpectedly, her brother's words elicited a wave of angry emotion.

"For God's sake, Frederick, you're a man – act like one. This is no longer play, Brother. The next time you hold a blade in your hands your life may depend on it! Now, fight, damn you!"

Her ferocious words were matched by the glint of tears in her eyes.

Shocked at his sister's sharp rebuke, Frederick's face hardened, all signs of merriment disappearing. The tenor of their circling became completely serious.

He attacked again, a repeat of his earlier leisurely thrust. Exasperated, Christina again moved her sword to parry. Her blade met only air, however, as he spun his body inside her guard, crashing his elbow into her left bicep then moving lithely outside her striking distance.

She involuntarily gasped as a shock of pain coursed up her arm.

"When fighting for your life, Sister, the sword is only one of your weapons," he muttered sarcastically through tight lips.

Ignoring the growing soreness in her arm, the corners of Christina's mouth rose into the slight semblance of a smile. She gave a curt nod of her head, acknowledging her comeuppance but taking care to maintain her distance slightly outside the range of his blade.

She now pressed the attack with a series of swift slashes that were each met by her brother's high parry. He gave ground slightly as she stepped up the intensity of her attack. The sharp metallic clang of weapon on weapon filled their ears. Sweat began to ooze from their bodies as the heat of their exertions surmounted the chill of the early morning air.

As he countered her next slash, however, he twisted his wrist, causing the blade of her weapon to slide down the length of his, trapping it on his crossguard. He pushed her backwards, using his slightly greater strength and weight to his advantage. She stumbled a few steps in reverse, then regained her balance. Frederick, however, had used the instant of her vulnerability to close with her. The point of his falchion now poised motionless an inch from her stomach.

"Hold!"

The inflection of command in that single word froze the sibling combatants. They spun involuntarily toward the source of the voice. There, nearly filling the large doorway, stood Kurt Ziesolf. He appraised them impassively; Christina could not discern whether he was angry, bemused, scornful, or all three.

Ziesolf said tersely, "Get your clothes on, girl. Frau Kohl needs you immediately. Come with me young master, your father wants you as well."

As Christina turned toward her makeshift dressing room, the man continued, "Leave the falchion, you'll have no further need of it."

She spun angrily, a caustic retort balanced on her tongue like a hawk ready to fly from its aerie. Meeting the steely stare from Ziesolf's good eye, however, she felt the wisdom of choking her words back down. Leaning over, she felt some immature satisfaction in allowing the weapon to fall from her grasp a few inches from the floor, construing the small clang of the metal on the stone as a minute victory of sorts.

When she emerged clad in her womanly attire, she was alone in the storehouse. The falchions, Ziesolf, and her brother had disappeared. Only now did she truly consider the consequences of her actions. These varied in severity depending on whether Ziesolf confided what he had seen only to her father or if the story spread to the aldermen, clergy, or the tavern-goers of the city. If her transgressions became common knowledge, it would ruin the good name of her family. *Oh, sweet mother of Jesus, who will place trust in a merchant who can't even manage his own daughter?* She thought miserably.

She drew a deep breath and, after securing the door after her, proceeded to walk home briskly. *No*, she told herself firmly, *Ziesolf's allegiance to Father is absolute. He would never do anything to shame him.* The realization of this fact cheered her immensely. Her improving mood darkened, however, when she began to consider the very real consequences of her father's ire. *No chance of escaping a beating*, she concluded ruefully. She gulped involuntarily at the memory of the willow switch smacked repeatedly across her bare buttocks when she was ten for stealing cakes from her own kitchen. If that was a measure of the punishment meriting the crime, she took small solace in the knowledge her father could not legally kill her.

Suddenly, an even worse thought crossed her mind. *He could send me to a convent!* The thought of spending the rest of her life in a tedious state of prayer and contemplation was worse than a thousand imagined beatings.

All too soon, her house stood in front of her. She offered a prayer to the Holy Virgin for forgiveness of her sins, crossed herself fervently, and entered. She was greeted with a resounding silence.

In a timorous tone, she called out, "Mother?"

The sudden rustle of skirts rushing down the stairs startled her. She was quite surprised to see that, rather than her mother, it was Anna swiftly approaching.

"Where have you been, girl?" the maid asked sternly.

Christina was confused as to how to respond to the question. Certainly, Ziesolf had reported what he had seen to her father. She was certain the elder Kohl had shared the news of their family's disgrace with his wife, but had Anna learned of Christina's blasphemous behavior as well? If so, was the servant seeking to get her to add to her list of sins by lying as well? But, if Anna was still ignorant of what had occurred, Christina certainly didn't want to be the one to enlighten her. *Bollocks, this is making my head hurt!* She moaned to herself. Christina glanced up to meet Anna's dark scowl.

"Has God finally seen fit to cut out that sharp tongue of yours? Don't just stand there like an idiot!

Go to your mother immediately!"

She doesn't know, Christina thought with relief, then asked, "Uh, where is she?"

She hoped against hope it was her mother that was to punish her and not her father.

Anna glared at her with an astonished expression on her face which then, surprisingly, softened. "She is with your sister, child, go to her now." She beckoned with her hand toward the stairs.

Christina flew up the stairs. *Oh, sweet Mary, Mother of Jesus, I've forgotten about Margarete! But she had been feeling better after getting home last night and Brother Udo had prescribed draughts and compresses. Perhaps it's just Margarete seeking attention. It certainly wouldn't be the first time,* she thought. The growing hard knot she felt in the pit of her stomach told her otherwise, however.

She opened the door softly into a room silent save for her sister's labored and ragged breathing. As she approached the bed her mother, who was kneeling by the its side, turned her head. Christina was shocked by her appearance. Her fine features were drawn and haggard. It seemed she had aged ten years overnight. Her eyes were glazed and appeared unseeing. She turned slowly back toward Margarete, her hands clasped in fervent prayer.

Christina moved to her mother's side, kneeling as well. If she had been surprised by the appearance of her mother's face, she was absolutely appalled by that of her sister. Margarete's skin had a blue tinge, save for the circles of near black around her eyes, which were rheumy and bloodshot. Her lips and the skin around her nose were cracked, rife with open sores stained by phlegm. If Margarete had not been lying in her own bed, Christina would have had difficulty recognizing the haughty and beautiful woman she had known her entire life.

The door opened again and her father, accompanied by a priest, entered. Guiltily, Christina's thoughts returned to her earlier fears of punishment. One glance at Thomas Kohl revealed that, even if her father knew of what had transpired at the warehouse, he had no care for discussing it at this time. Deep concern for his elder daughter was etched on his face, a glint of moisture reflecting in the corners of his eyes.

Christina felt profoundly ashamed she had in that instance thought about herself rather than the plight of the young woman lying on the bed.

Thomas Kohl placed his hand firmly on his wife's shoulder, beckoning her to rise. She shook her upper body violently in abject refusal of what she must know was now inevitable. He gently placed his hands around her waist and brought her to her feet. As she came erect, her body arched and she emitted a long wail of pure despair. Christina rose as well, moving to her parents' side as the priest began the rite of extreme unction.

When he had finished, her father bade Christina to show the priest from the house. She accompanied him down the stairs, thanking him as he went out the door. As she began to close it, however, she saw Frederick sprinted up the street. He rushed inside and hugged her closely, wetting her face with the tears flooding from his eyes.

"How is Margarete, Christina? Father only told me she was seriously ill, then sent me to tell the captain of *der Greif* to ensure all the cargo was properly stowed, but that the plans to sail may be changed. I ran here as soon as I had delivered the message. How is Margarete, Christina?" he repeated.

She gazed gravely into his eyes then slowly shook her head from side to side. His chin quivered as he fought to hold back his emotions. Christina took his hand and they ascended the stairs together. They sat outside their sister's room, holding silent vigil for what they knew must certainly come.

Shortly after Compline, the door to Margarete's room opened. Her father contemplated his two remaining children and sadly nodded, her mother beside him, deeply in shock, stared ahead unseeingly. They proceeded to their chamber, the door closing softly behind them.

Chapter 3

It was three days after Margarete's body had been placed in the crypt of St. Mary's Church that Christina was summoned by her father to the hall of their home. As the family was still in deep mourning, she was puzzled by the formality of her father's request, which had been relayed by Anna rather than said to her by Thomas Kohl himself. As she walked down the stairs, a sickening thought crossed her mind. *Oh, no! I've completely forgotten about what happened at the warehouse but, apparently, Father hasn't. Please, Sweet Jesus, let him have some mercy on his only remaining daughter!*

Walking into the room, Christina was relieved to see her parents both seated there. Her father appeared as he always had, perhaps with a few more lines of worry draw across his forehead. Her mother had seemingly recovered from the death of her only child somewhat as well. She still appeared abnormally aged but had regained her previous composure completely. The most distinctive difference was in her mother's demeanor, however. Whereas she had previously seemed enthused with the joy of life, she now appeared to be resigned to enduring her remaining years on earth as a crushing burden. Although Christina was saddened by her mother's melancholy, she was unable to offer any relief. Margarete had been her joy and delight.

Her father bade her to sit. Puzzled and still slightly frightened, she complied. *At least he didn't tell me to bend over the stool,* she thought thankfully. He stood, cleared his throat, and began to speak.

"Christina, your sister's death has been a terrible loss for our family. She was your mother's first child and, as you must know, held a special place in her heart." He glanced down at his wife briefly, then continued. "We all mourn her loss, even you I think."

Her father's words stung Christina deeply. *How can you possibly doubt the love I felt for her, Father? Although we didn't really understand each other, we were sisters after all.* In her heart, however, she now wished she had never spoken so many harsh words to Margarete or thought so many evil thoughts toward her.

He continued, "Even though our mourning period for her will last for many more months, that does not mean we will spend all of our time in prayer. Trade is our city's lifeblood and it will continue with or without our family."

Christina nodded, but was uncertain why her father was stating something so apparently obvious. "Therefore, *der Greif* will sail on the next favorable winds. Your brother and I will depart for England as planned." He hesitated slightly before continuing. "Christina, we know you are a good child. Too headstrong and often disobedient at times, however. Although you have little skill with a needle you do have a quick head for figures, which is also important to the efficient running of a household."

Her father's itemization of her virtues and flaws made Christina feel as though she were a cargo being appraised. His next statement removed any doubt in her mind that that was exactly what was happening. "The death of Margarete has resulted in a deep loss to our family; however, it has equally created a problem for our business. Your sister's marriage to Albrecht, the son and heir of Johann Revele, was vital to our plans for a trade alliance. Without a linking of the families, there is no strength to the agreement, it may be broken at any time. This must not be allowed to occur. That is why, Christina, you will marry Albrecht Revele in Margarete's stead."

Christina sat stupefied. *I, journey to London and marry in Margarete's place? Become a wife to a man whom I have never met? I can't, I won't, I . . .*

Her discordant thoughts overwhelmed her. She gawked upwards to see her father still standing before her, the attempt of a smile on his face struggled against an expression of mounting impatience.

"Well, say something, girl, instead of sitting there gaping like a codfish caught in a net."

"I...I...I can't! Don't make me do this, Father!"

The shock on Thomas Kohl's face was immediate, but soon transformed into a look of dark anger. He now looked as though he was ready to administer the beating she had feared before.

Her mind raced, trying to form words to a more coherent response that would not trigger the back of her father's hand across her face.

"What I mean, Father, is that it seems sinful, marrying a man who was betrothed to my sister, especially with her dead only a little over a week. Certainly, the Church cannot approve."

His anger somewhat abated by the ecclesiastic bent of her argument, he replied, "Your consideration of the morality of the act is admirable, Daughter, even if it is quite unlike you to do so. Your fears are unjustified, however, as I have already spoken with the bishop on the matter. Clearly there was no consummation of the union; therefore, Albrecht Revele is free to marry as his family wishes."

Her principal argument dashed, Christina thought then, hesitantly, began again.

In a small voice, she said, "But…but Father, I am not Margarete. She was beautiful and well-mannered and delicate, while I am … well, I am only me. Why would a man who had been promised Margarete be willing to accept someone like this?"

She gestured with her hand down her body, lowering her gaze toward the floor.

He mulled over her words for a few seconds before saying, "Yes, there is truth to what you say. You are considerably less than what Revele had bargained for. I'm afraid he will insist on renegotiating the dowry, and certainly much to our disadvantage. This sometimes happens, I'm afraid. After all, a merchant can't expect to get top prices for a cog full of herring when the buyer was expecting cod, can he?"

He chortled momentarily at his joke, then continued. "It is settled. You have little time for preparations, so begin immediately." He turned and walked from the room.

With desperation clearly etched on her face, Christina now turned her gaze toward her mother.

It was now Mechtild Kohl's turn to stand prior to beginning to speak. "I have already commissioned new gowns and shifts to be made for you, Christina. It is a pity you could not take those that were made for your sister, but there is no way they could be altered to fit someone of your size. I hope you appreciate the extra cost to the family. Hopefully, they will be ready by the time you depart. Otherwise, they will have to be sent afterwards. To be sure, you will need to pack a trunk with what clothes you already have."

Christina was mortified. *Oh, I can imagine how pleased my new husband will be. A big horse for a wife instead of beautiful Margarete. And clad in worn shifts that are mostly too small. What an impression I will make,* she thought sarcastically. Her mother continued, "I am sorry, but there will obviously be no wedding feast. It would be improper to hold a celebration so soon after the funeral. You may, however, sort through the gifts that were given to poor Margarete to see if there is anything you may find useful."

Even from the grave you get your spite, Margarete! Christina thought maliciously. She immediately felt ashamed of her spiteful thoughts, vowing to atone for them at her next confession.

Her mother's hand touched her cheek in a slight caress.

Christina's eyes rose and her mother said, "I know you are not prepared for this, child. You must, however, do your best to be a good wife. Even if your life is not happy, God in his mercy may see fit to reward you with many sons. They will become a credit to the family and the business, you will become a credit to the family and business. Just as your dear, sweet sister would have, had she lived." Her mother's hand fell from Christina's face and she hurried away, trailing soft sobs behind her.

Christina stood, walked to the door, and went outside. The conflicting emotions warring inside her required physical activity to abate. She began to walk briskly down Engelgrube street; however, her brain neither noted her surroundings nor had an inclining of her destination. Her mind was solely focused on unraveling her own feelings about her father's astounding pronouncement.

Her thoughts, which were usually so incisive, now moved as if through jelly. *Less than an hour ago, I was a young maiden. Now I am betrothed. I am to leave Lubeck, my family, and the people I have known all my life, probably never to return. How can this have happened?*

She knew the answer to this question of course. Her sister had died, and now she was Margarete's replacement. *Plain and simple, isn't it?* she thought.

But her sister's impending marriage had seemed different somehow. Whereas Margarete's engagement had been the subject of great joy, Christina's seemed more like a trade transaction, a contract coldly negotiated without a tinge of emotion. Even the announcement she would have no wedding feast before her departure emphasized the fact this was solely the consummation of a business agreement. *Even the parents of a lowly peasant girl will scrape together enough food and drink to host a wedding meal; however, my family, one of the wealthiest in all Lubeck, do not see fit to arrange one for me*, she thought dejectedly.

She did understand it would be unseemly for her family to host a celebration during their time of deep mourning, but could her departure not be delayed a matter of a few months? *No, of course not. "Der Greif will sail on the next favorable winds,"* her father's words reverberated in her mind. *Whether you, my second-best daughter, fucking likes it or not!* She added miserably.

Oh yes, I almost forgot, Christina, she addressed herself in her mother's voice now. *You may rummage through Margarete's things like a common ragpicker, taking what you want. No thank you!* Her angry thought then gave way to shame. *Please forgive me, Margarete. I'm taking away your new life and husband. I won't take your possessions as well.*

Hopefully, I won't inherit my curse of a husband who beats me every day and twice on Sunday either, she thought without humor.

She abruptly halted, noticing her surrounds for the first time. She stood in front of the newly erected *Katharinenkirche*, the church of St. Catherine of Alexandria. She went inside and offered a heartfelt prayer to St Catherine, the patron saint of unmarried girls.

After a while she began the walk back home. She had considered the thought of running away. She was enough of a realist, however, to know that a life as a wife of a wealthy merchant, regardless of whether he beat you or not, was still preferable to becoming a whore or a washerwoman. Few other alternatives seemed to exist for a woman striking out on her own, so Christina began the painful process of reconciling herself to her fate.

At least I have the adventure of a sea voyage to look forward to, she reasoned, *as well as a huge and exciting city to explore. Although Lubeck holds nearly 15,000 souls, I have been told London has over five times as many people. But will I even be allowed outside the house? Of what interest will the city be if I am to be imprisoned within the four thick stone walls of my home? Of course, the extent of my freedom will be determined by Albrecht Revele, my husband.*

The last two words rolled off her tongue clumsily, *my husband*. Christina was not naïve enough to think her father would have allowed her not to marry. No, if the match to the Revele heir had not presented itself, an agreement would have been reached with one of the prominent families of the city, probably that of one of the other aldermen. She shuddered as she considered the list of eligible bachelors from among the group. Some were old enough to be her grandfather, others sniveling idiots or overbearing bullies. *Of course, there are some who are very appealing*, she blushed at the recollection of the outline of Caspar Vogelsank's shapely leg beneath his closely tailored hose. But the odds were definitely in favor of a choice being made from the former group rather than the latter.

So, at least my husband-to-be is only a few years older than I am, she considered judiciously. *His family is wealthy and of high precedence. I suppose it could be far worse,* she admitted grudgingly, her spirits rising a bit.

In the distance, she saw the figure of her brother quickly approaching. He stopped directly in front of her, hopping from side to side with excitement, a toothy grin creasing his face. Since it appeared as if he might throw decorum to the wind and grab her here on the street in a massive embrace, she moved first, proffering her hand. *After all, I am soon to be a married woman*, she told herself primly.

He took her hand, kissing it fervently. Rather than releasing it, however, he continued to hold the hand, shaking it vigorously.

"Oh, Christina, I am so glad!" He blurted.

His grasp was beginning to cause her hand to ache. She used her other to gently but firmly free it from his hold then replied formally, "Thank thee, Brother."

She grinned herself, though more as a response to Frederick's enthusiasm than in shared happiness for herself.

He stepped back and scrutinized her appraisingly. "But are you not pleased?" he inquired.

She thought a moment then replied in an uncommitted tone, "Yes, I believe so."

"But why not?" he implored. "Don't you realize we are both going to London, that we will be together!"

She was shocked she had not considered this factor when she had been weighing the merits of her impending marriage. Being able to see the beloved brother she had thought would disappear from her life forever was worth almost any hardship.

With laughter in her voice that was now completely genuine, she said, "Oh, yes! Of course, Frederick, of course! We will be together always!"

Disregarding propriety, she grabbed her brother, holding him in a close embrace. Let the disapproval of Lubeckers be damned, she was not going to lose her brother!

Begging her pardon, Frederick broke free from his sister, stating their father had tasked him with an errand to the market square. Her spirits much more buoyant than when she had left, Christina re-entered the house.

Closing the thick oak door behind her, she was startled to see the figure of Kurt Ziesolf waiting impassively outside the drawing room. She had not seen the man since he had come upon her and her brother in the warehouse. It was readily apparent that he, for his own enigmatic reasons, had refrained from telling her father about finding her attired in men's clothing. He surveyed her with his one good eye without a hint of emotion on the functional side of his face. Christina was uncertain as to what to say but realized she must say something.

She walked hesitantly toward the man, stopping a few feet to his front.

She began, "I…I must thank you most profusely, sir, for maintaining my secret. I know…"

His movement forward surprised her, causing her to cut her words off in mid-sentence. She grew alarmed as he reached out with both hands, grabbing her firmly by the shoulders. He lifted her off the ground as easily as if she were made of feathers. The man then placed her down in a profile stance, sweeping his foot beneath her skirts to force her back leg into a wider base.

He then moved back to a couple of feet to her front, examined her up and down, and nodded slightly.

In his raspy voice, he said, "Better girl, is it not? Men will almost have the advantage in strength and weight. If you square up before them, you're always going to find yourself on your ass. Except it will only happen once, then you'll be dead and you'll have no need to remember next time, understand?"

Christina nodded her head mutely, shifting her weight to gain better balance. *He's right, of course,* she thought in self-disgust. *How could I have been so stupid?* Now I have another thing to thank him for. As she opened her mouth to begin, he raised his gnarled right index finger to his lips, simultaneously shaking his head slightly from side to side. He then dropped the hand to his side and resumed the stiffly erect pose he had held when Christina entered the room. Realizing their discourse was over, she backed away and ascended the stairs.

Later that night, she snuggled under the coarse linen of her bedsheets, considering her earlier meeting with Ziesolf. Not only was she still amazed he had not told her father, but that he had also shared the experience of his sword-craft. *What had prompted him to do either?* the question turned over in her head repeatedly. Unable to discern the man's motivations, her eyelids began to droop heavily. Within seconds she was fast asleep as the most pivotal day to date in her young life came to a close.

For the next four days Christina seemed to be the center of attention, a role to which she was completely unaccustomed. Now that she had tasks before her, Mechtild Kohl regained much of the liveliness she had lost after Margarete's death. She seemed to be everywhere, clearly the mistress of every facet of housewifery. She critically examined each piece of Christina's clothing before deciding whether it should be placed in one of the trunks going to London or into the rag bin. Holes in hose were given to Trudi or Anna for mending, frayed cuff seams on her gowns were picked and re-stitched, and embarrassing stains on her chemises were openly discussed, leaving Christina somewhat mortified, before being bundled off for scrubbing or discard. There seemed so little time and so much to accomplish. Grudgingly, she acknowledged she would have been incapable of completing her preparations for the journey had it not been for her mother's capable presence.

Christina was somewhat taken aback by the feeling she had taken on a newly elevated status among the citizenry of Lubeck. Burghers and their wives who previously would have acknowledged her presence with a disapproving frown, if at all, now smiled at her, nodding their heads, and wishing her well. This made her feel awkward, as she felt she had nothing to say to these elders other than a self-conscious "thank you."

Worse yet was that her friends treated her somewhat deferentially, no longer rising to points of argument that would have previously resulted in mirthful slaps that left a lasting mark or playfully pulled hair. Nor was their laughter raucous and uninhibited, instead somewhat polite and restrained. No one even belched or passed wind in front of her. She felt strange and, in some ways, out of place and unwelcome.

Is this what happens when a girl gets married, she questioned herself angrily, *everyone treats you like you're about to start scolding them or giving them a job to do? Can't they see I'm still the same person as before? I don't care if I am going to be a married woman, there will definitely be more to Christina Kohl then running a household, suckling babies, and making sure her husband's socks are mended!*

A guilty thought popped into her mind. If I am to have any sort of control over the remainder of my life, I must start now. The self-assertiveness she had professed moments ago now seemed to melt away, replaced by a sense of dread. She had sought to avoid what was sure to be an inevitable confrontation with her mother. With the day of departure imminent, she knew she could delay no longer.

She walked from her room to the hall, finding her mother purposefully re-packing one of Christina's trunks to fit in a new kirtle that had just arrived. Frau Schmidt was not necessarily the best seamstress in Lubeck, but she certainly was one of the quickest. Although the dark green wool of the fabric was certainly warm, the garment was definitely staid and rather old-fashioned. *Well, at least it's one new thing in my trousseau,* she thought optimistically, though inwardly fearing her wardrobe might be a source of embarrassment upon her arrival in her new home. She sighed, knowing there was nothing could be done about it now.

Breaking from her reverie, Christina saw her mother was regarding her questioningly. Knowing she must broach the subject now, if she was ever to, she said. "Mother, I will be leaving in a matter of days."

Mechtild Kohl nodded, unsure why her daughter was stating the obvious.

Just say it, damn you! She told herself vehemently, disgusted with her own lack of nerve. She began again. "Mother, I will be leaving any day now. I wish to thank you for everything you have done to help ready me for the journey. I could never have completed my preparations without you."

Her mother blushed and lowered her face, but Christina could plainly see the words she had spoken had pleased her. *Well, that's about to change,* she thought sourly.

Although I trust your decisions completely, mother, I must ask you to send Trudi to accompany me, rather than Anna."

Her mother peered at her again, only this time incredulously. Laughing, she said, "You foolish girl, are you serious? You must have someone of experience to help you establish your new household, not a silly little goose who knows even less than you do! Don't be absurd, the matter is settled. Anna is to go. By the way, do not forget to have her pluck your eyebrows. How can you be presentable to your new husband with two furry caterpillars perched above your eyes?"

In an even but firm voice, Christina replied specifically to her mother's decision, ignoring her direction completely, "No, please. It will be unbearable in London by myself. Trudi is my friend, we will learn about how to run a household together." "Absolutely not, Christina. You will thank me for this decision later."

Christina searched her head frantically for an argument that would sway her mother to change her mind.

The best she could do, however, was, "This is to be my house; however, I am afraid instead it will be Anna's. She has told me what to do all my life. She slapped my hand or switched me when I disobeyed her. To have Anna with me would be as bad as..." She stopped abruptly before she said it.

Her mother's expression clouded, her earlier pleasure completely supplanted. "Be as bad as if I were there?"

Her mother finished Christina's ill-conceived sentence. An awkward silence ensued, neither woman knowing what to say next. Finally, Christina just turned and walked back up to her chamber.

Her silence could not be construed as a submission to her mother's decision however. It meant quite the opposite. Very rarely was Christina rendered speechless; however now, when she was bubbling over with anger, could definitely be characterized as one of those instances. *I absolutely will not have that bitch Anna telling me what to do for the rest of my life,* she fumed. *Even if she says nothing, she will still fix me with that disapproving expression of hers. If she gets on the ship, I'll shove her into the sea in the dead of night! I'd rather have no maid at all rather than her!*

There must be a better means to get rid of Anna than drowning her, she thought, admitting this solution was a bit too drastic, even for her. She wracked her brain for an alternative, then suddenly remembered a prank she had played on Margarete when they were younger.

I'm sorry, Sister, for that and all the other mischief I visited on you, she reflected remorsefully. Her feeling of guilt did not extend to Anna, however. She set out purposefully for the store room on the fourth floor. She knew exactly what she needed and where it could be found.

Two days later she stood on the quay, her thoughts solemnly mulling over the fact this was to be her final hours in the city of her birth, perhaps never to return. Her eyes took in the pirouetting gulls, their greedy cries harsh and discordant as they fought over the cod spoil a fishing boat had swept from its deck into the Trave. She barely noticed the damp smell peculiar to dockyards everywhere, having grown accustomed to its sickly scent her entire life. She wondering if her new home would ever feel as familiar.

"Halloo!"

Frederick's happy shout from the deck of *Heiligen Maria* interrupted her contemplation. She glanced up to see him waving at her frantically, a wide grin traversing his face. He would not be traveling aboard *der Greif* with Christina and her father, instead sailing on the slightly smaller ship he was now helping ready for sail.

She eyed each of the two ships that would be conveying her family to England. They varied very little in design. *Der Greif* stretched one hundred feet from stem to stern and about twenty feet in the beam, *Heiligen Maria* was of similar proportions, only its hull was about ten feet shorter. Both drew a depth of about ten feet of water. Their hulls were constructed clinker-style, made of oaken planks that overlapped each other like the tiles of a roof. The single sail meant they were relatively easy to handle and moderately fast, capable of four to five knots with a good wind. They were solid, dependable ships that served as the lifegiving blood that ran along the arteries of the Hanseatic trade routes.

To Christina's experienced eye, the decks seemed absolutely awash with people. In addition to each ship's regular compliment of approximately a dozen sailors, her family's party added an additional seven members. It was the other members of the sailing party that drew Christina's interest, however.

Because of the tremendous value of the cargo being transported and the need to safeguard the members of his family, her father had hired a troop of Hamburg mercenaries for the voyage. They were mostly sullen, dangerous looking men, their somewhat filthy personal appearance contrasting sharply with the state of their weapons that gleamed with the clear evidence of recent use and good maintenance. They were the sort of men Christina would take care to avoid on the main streets of Lubeck, let alone in the side alleys.

Even as she appraised them, she saw two of them were gaping at her as well. The taller of the two, a heavily muscled bear of a man with a nose permanently displaced to the left, leered at her obscenely. His mouth parted, letting his fat tongue protrude through his semi toothless grin to slowly lick his lips obscenely. He fondled his crotch simultaneously, then gave her a knowing wink.

Although Christina was far from prudish, his overtly sexual gestures shocked her greatly as she felt color rising to her face in a flaming blush. The heat in her cheeks was matched by her fury. She was left clenching her fists in frustration, however, as she couldn't decide exactly how to respond to the man's affront. *Well, I can't very well challenge him to a fight, can I?* she thought sardonically.

She was obviously unarmed and, even if she had been, it was probably unwise to make an enemy of one of the very men who her father had paid good money to protect their family during the voyage. *Damn his eyes!* She seethed, momentarily unsure of how she would retaliate toward the lout; yet, absolutely certain that she would.

Suddenly, she saw Kurt Ziesolf approach the man, an uncharacteristic trace of a smile fixed on the good side of his mouth. The offender glanced toward Ziesolf, the initial expression of alarm on his face melting somewhat into an uneasy smile to match that of the man approaching him. Even though the mercenary was tall, Ziesolf exceeded his height by at least three to four inches. Still seemingly amused, the old knight came closer, catching the man seemingly casually by the arm and leaning forward to whisper something in his ear.

As she looked on, it was clear to Christina Ziesolf was tightening his hold on the man's bicep. The man's face suddenly contorted into a rictus of pain and fear. As Ziesolf eased his grip, the mercenary glanced again toward Christina. This time, however, he lowered his head in deference, touched the knuckle of his right index finger to his forelock, and swiftly departed to find a less dangerous pastime. Without even a glance toward Christina, Ziesolf also turned away, returning to his previous tasks.

Although she knew she should be grateful for Ziesolf's intervention, she instead felt a nagging irritation at his characteristic male presumptiveness. Her ire slowly changed to a sick feeling at the pit of her stomach. *What the hell are you doing, Christina?* She asked herself. She had spent the first sixteen years of her life being told what to do by her father. Now, a man she had never even met would rule her for the rest of her days. Even here, in the short period of time between masters, a man had usurped her prerogative. *Damn them all*, she thought fiercely, hot tears rolling unbidden down her cheeks. She swiped at them roughly. *You and I*, she nodded in the general direction in which the old knight had gone, *will one day come to an understanding that I can take care of myself. And you*, she fixed her gaze on the offending mercenary who had now busied himself coiling a length of rope, *are going to find an aching arm is the least of your problems.*

"Christina!"

Well, she thought, *at least sometimes I get my way.* She turned around to see Trudi hurrying up the quay with a large bundle in her arms. Her mood lifting immediately at the sight of her dear friend, she smiled and waved back in response.

By the time the plump blond girl caught up with her mistress, she was completely out of breath. She bent over, taking in breaths of air in huge gulps.

After a few seconds, she lifted her still red face and said, "I'm so sorry for being late, but I was waiting for Frau Stein to complete your new surcoat, the red and yellow one. Oh, Christina, it's absolutely lovely! You will look so beautiful in it!"

"Oh sure, polished up like a new tin tankard just waiting for a man to take his first deep draught from it!" Christina remarked sarcastically, her sour disposition still not completely evaporated.

Trudi gazed at her quizzically for a moment, then broke into a giggle.

She said, "I went in to give my final farewell to Anna, but she was on the chamber pot again. Oh, sweet Jesus, Christina, her bowels were voiding like a waterfall! I couldn't help but feel sorry for her, so I helped her back into bed. She seemed absolutely green! So, I gave her a little kiss on the forehead and ran out of the room as fast as I could. I almost retched before I could get the door open, the smell was so awful! I was so glad to get out of there, and now I'm going with you!"

Although her mother had been very suspicious at the maid's sudden malady, she was simply left with no alternative. She could not send an already ill woman on a sea voyage, so Trudi had been informed she was going in her older sister's stead.

Christina felt somewhat ashamed upon hearing Trudi's graphic description of Anna's condition. After all, liberally dosing Anna's food with flax oil over the last few days had been guaranteed to beset the older maid with rampant flux. *It was the only thing I could think of,* she thought to herself as a means of excuse, *but I just couldn't endure being shackled to her for the rest of my life. Maybe she shouldn't have been so hateful,* Christina recalled the innumerable swats, slaps, and pinches she had been dealt by Anna when she was younger. *Besides, she'll recover, but not before we have already left.*

She listened again to the gulls' discordant chorus. *Perhaps they are telling me goodbye,* she imagined. *More likely cursing me for all my sins,* she smiled humorlessly. She turned back in the direction of the only home she had ever know and offered a brief prayer. *Loving Father, protect Mother and keep her safe. Yes, and Anna as well. Please allow me to one day return and find them safe and happy. And us as well,* she added as an after-though, her appeal encompassing her father, Trudi, Ziesolf, the crew of the ships, even the man who had gestured obscenely at her. She crossed herself hurriedly then, taking a first resolute step forward, began her new life.

Chapter 4

At Sea, October 1309

Christina awoke from her nightmare with a start. Although she was wet with perspiration, she shivered uncontrollably at the recollection of screaming faces outlined by a background of fire and water. The most shocking of these was that of her sister, Margarete, whose dead eyes glared at her accusingly in contrast to the loud howling she emitted from her ruined mouth. Christina shook her head violently to rid her brain of the terrible image. Gradually, her thoughts began to focus as her senses supplanted the horrid images of her dream-world with those of reality.

She felt soft skin next to hers and reached out, caressing its warmth. A contented sigh was emitted in reply. Despite the near darkness, she could faintly discern a cascade of blond hair falling scant inches from her eyes. As the figure snuggled closer, an arm fell delicately across Christina's stomach, its hand extending upward to cup her right breast. She closed her eyes, somewhat guilty at the unexpected pleasure she experienced from the sensuousness of the caress. Suddenly, the flap to the heavy canvas enclosure that defined her temporary cabin was flung open and brilliant early morning light caused her eyes to immediately begin to water.

"Christina, you and Trudi must get up now!" Her father's habitually calm voice now quavering noticeably.

She glanced down and was relieved to see she and her maid were both still covered in the heavy furs under which they had slept. She then turned to her father to ask why it was necessary to come out on deck. *It's not like we actually have duties, you know,* she grumbled to herself. After all, they had rarely been permitted to leave their quarters since leaving Lubeck eight days prior. Christina's father had told her he did not want to have the crew distracted from what they were supposed to be doing to ogle at two young women. *Well, not much chance of that*, she thought sardonically. Ever since Ziesolf had upbraided the ruffian at the dock, whose name Christina had since learned was Reiniken, the men aboard the ship had avoided eye contact even during the rare times she and Trudi had been permitted to leave their area of the stern castle. Why…" her question trailed off as she saw her father had already disappeared.

Oh, hell, she thought, *I'd better go see what's happening.* She was irritated by the urgency in his voice requiring immediate activity on her part; yet somewhat relieved she had an excuse not to ponder the significance of her dream. She shivered, partly from the cold she felt as she threw back the furs that covered her near-naked body and in equal measure from the ominous portent of her unbidden vision.

Trudi groaned, feeling the damp chill begin to permeate her body as well. The two women hurriedly completed the most basic of ablutions, dressed, then exited their once cozy nest. Christina blinked as her eyes slowly adjusted to the intensity of the sunlight. A strong breeze blew from the east and she could feel the ship cutting through the water. The sky overhead was beautiful, the few clouds painted in hues of pink. *Was this what he had wanted. to show me, a lovely sunrise?* She shook her head in disbelief. *If there is one thing I know about my father it is he has no sense of the romantic. It must be something else.*

As she took in the panorama of the ship's deck, she quickly realized something had changed from the repetitiveness of the previous seven mornings. *Is it because it's so early in the morning?* She asked herself, considering whether she had somehow missed this part of the shipboard routine previously. The tense mood among the sailors and mercenaries, however, alluded to the fact their present circumstances were far from ordinary. Although five crewmen were performing the normal task of adjusting the huge square sail, just about everyone else was at the starboard rail.

Jostling one of the men aside to make a space beside her father, Christina asked, "What is it?"

Thomas Kohl lifted his right arm and pointed toward the horizon far out on the Kattegat. She squinted her eyes tightly into the intense sunrise. Slowly, she began to discern several small shapes on the water emerging from a low, grey, fogbank in the far distance.

"Are they islands?" she asked naively.

"No, not islands," he replied. "Ships."

Christina surveyed the sea more closely, this time perceiving the uniformity of their shape. She wondered whether it was her imagination or could she now discern sails.

"Are they other merchants?" she asked hopefully, not wishing to consider the other, deadly, alternative.

"No." her father's terse reply was enough to confirm her fearful suspicions.

It would have been impossible to grow up in Lubeck and not have heard the stories of the pirates who infested the Baltic trade routes traveled by the Hanseatic merchants. Often, they were only a single craft manned by a few desperate men. Even then, they were frequently able to overcome an unwary cog's crew. There were other, more menacing, stories of a vast armada under the command of a pirate king that ravaged any ship or ships who sailed the waters he claimed as his own. Killing the crew or selling them into slavery, they added the vessel to their fleet, making it even less likely for the next victim to escape.

Those are only old wives' tales, Christina reassured herself, *meant to keep scared children from straying too far away from home.* Peering again into the distance, she wished she believed that were true.

Oh, dear Lord, where's Frederick? She thought suddenly, frantic with worry. She ran to the prow of the ship and was relieved to see *Heiligen Maria* a few hundred yards ahead of *der Greif.* She scanned the deck for a glimpse of her brother but could not see him. She thought of yelling to him but was certain even her hearty voice would not be able to be heard at that distance. Unexpectedly startled, she felt a hand grip her arm tightly. She turned to see Trudi staring up at her with fear in her eyes.

"One of the men said there were pirates chasing us! I'm so scared, Christina. I wish Anna had come instead of me!" the young maid blurted.

"Don't worry, Trudi. The other ships, if they are pirates at all, are very far away. Besides, we have trained fighting men aboard as well as the sailors. The pirates are in for an unpleasant surprise if they're foolhardy enough to attack us. We have nothing to fear."

Christina hoped her voice didn't betray her own doubts about her confidence in her statements

She heard approaching footsteps that made a clunking sound against the sturdy oak planking of the deck. She glanced toward the sound and saw her father, lines of worry again etching his forehead like plough furrows through loamy soil.

She said to Trudi, "Go tidy up our sleeping quarters. We can't let the rumor get to my future husband that his new wife favors living in a pig sty, can we?"

She flashed what she hoped was a confident and reassuring smile at her maid. Trudi tried her best to match her mistress's self-assured expression with one of her own but could only manage a slight upturning of the corners of her mouth. She did as she was told, however, and wobbled off toward the stern.

Turning back, she asked her father, "Is it true, Father? Are they pirates?"

"Probably so," he admitted grudgingly, not wishing to alarm his daughter but knowing she would want the truth. "We cannot be certain until they're closer, a circumstance we will try our hardest to avoid."

"Surely we would be able to defeat them in a fight. We have the mercenaries, let them earn their pay."

"We have counted at least seven ships. Even with our extra men, we will be outnumbered at least two to one." "

Can we turn back, return to Lubeck?" she asked hopefully.

"No, that would be a mistake, Daughter. They would have the benefit of the wind, while we would have to tack for hours. We would be even more likely to become their prey if we did that."

His mention of the word "prey" evoked images of a pack of wolves devouring a helpless deer.

Her mind racing to help her father find a way to extricate them from their grave predicament, she said, "How about running the ship ashore? We would have a chance to run away before they could catch us, we might even be able to find some help."

He smiled grimly and replied, "They have chosen the position well to spring their trap, Christina. We have open water to our right and miles of submerged sand banks to our left. We would need a knowledgeable local pilot to get to shore, one of which we do not have. Otherwise we will most certainly wind up aground, even more helpless to defend ourselves. The only answer is to continue forward and hope to beat our way around Jutland before they catch us. We can then see if they have the stomach to follow us into the North Sea."

"How far away do you think they are?" she asked deliberately.

"Between two and three leagues."

Having a good head for figures, Christina quickly calculated the chance they could outrun their pursuers. What she came up with was not heartening. The best speed their two ships could make was about six knots. Barring a freakish change to the brisk easterly wind that now filled their sails, she concluded a conflict with the pirates was inevitable. Scrutinizing her father's somber face, she saw he had come to the same conclusion.

Before she could speak, he said, "Now, Christina, you must do exactly as I say. You and Trudi must go to your quarters and stay there. No matter what you hear, you must not come out. When whatever happens is finished, I will come and get you. Do you understand you must obey me?"

Having little alternative, Christina nodded her head.

"Now go. We must prepare to defend the ship and I have no more time to waste talking."

He walked purposefully toward the captain of the mercenary force and began speaking earnestly.

Christina returned to the stern castle, not really knowing what else to do other than what she had been told. Trudi was halfheartedly attempting to clean the small space. She moved to embrace Christina who, distracted, pushed her away thoughtlessly. Upset, the maid returned to her tasks with tears flowing freely down her cheeks. *Oh, for the love of Christ,* she thought, irritated by Trudi's emotionality; yet, feeling guilty for denying her any comfort.

Here we are, penned up like pigs for the slaughter. What are we supposed to do, wait patiently until some lout with salt herring on his breath comes to rape us? Well, if he does, he's going to find a surprise. I'll bite his balls off before I let him hurt Trudi, her earlier exasperation now supplanted by a feeling of fierce protectiveness. She now reached out and grabbed the servant girl, hugging her fiercely close.

"I'll be damned before I let anything happen to you!" she told the girl with a determined voice.

Overwhelmed by her mistress's concern, Trudi held her head tightly to the bosom of Christina's linen cotelette. A small sound behind her caused her to whirl about fearfully.

At the canvas flap stood Ziesolf. He said, "Take this," proffering a large cloth wrapped bundle to Christina.

She took it, realizing the content immediately upon unconsciously gauging its weight. While the man stood in silence, she quickly removed the cloth to reveal the falchion he had taken from her days prior at the warehouse. She fitted her hand around the hilt and held the sword up to eye level, examining the blade critically. Whereas the blade had previously been so dulled it could not have even cut goat's cheese, it now gleamed with a finely ground edge whose sharpness was indisputable. She gazed up at Ziesolf, her earlier feeling of helplessness dissolving as her lips curled into a wolf's grin.

Seeing her expression and sensing its meaning, Ziesolf nodded and said, "If they get past us, you must make a decision. If you decide to fight, you will probably be killed. If not, you will undoubtedly be raped and beaten. But even then, you may be killed afterwards. If not, you will probably be taken to the slave markets or kept by the man who took your maidenhead. Not very good choices," he admitted soberly before departing as swiftly as he had appeared.

Despite their desperate situation, Christina felt empowered now she held the familiar weapon in her hand. *Let him think I'm just going to cower here, waiting until the battle is over before doing anything,* she thought spiritedly. *When the fighting comes, I'm going to be in the thick of it!* Knowing her father would certainly not approve of her plan of action, Christina placed the falchion in the corner before returning to the deck.

Although she was disobeying his earlier order, Christina's father was too busy to enforce it. She went again to the rail and stared toward the east. The approaching ships seemed somewhat nearer, but she was unsure whether it was because they were actually getting closer or if it was an illusion created by the receding fog. *No, their sails are taking on a definite shape,* she concluded.

She felt compelled to stay there, silently willing their pursuers to get no closer. She recognized this was wishful folly, however. Whether they escaped or were caught would have nothing to do with her supplications; only God, the weather, and the skill of the respective crewmen would determine their destiny.

All around her, men sharpened weapons that were already finely honed, placing them where they could easily be reached when needed. Two mercenaries armed with large crossbows stood in the ship's topcastle, keeping keen watch on their opponents' progress. *Well, for better or worse, it seems we are as ready as we can be.*

I wish I could be with Frederick, her train of thought wandering. *I hope he's not scared.* Knowing Frederick as she did, she didn't think so. The captain of the other ship was Georg Muller, a long-established merchant in Lubeck who was one of her father's most trusted associates. *I know he is in capable hands, but his own father is not there to look after him. Nor Ziesolf. Nor his big sister,* she added unhappily.

The remainder of the day was emotionally and physically draining for everyone on board *der Greif. There are only so many times you can sharpen an axe, only so many times you can trim the sail to gain even the most miniscule advantage from the wind, only so many times you can peer over the side to see the slow but steady encroachment of the other vessels. It's like time is refusing to move,* she thought exasperatingly.

By late afternoon the other ships were close enough for Christina to discern tiny figures clambering aboard them like dung beetles on a fresh cowpat. *A few hours ago, the ships had been that size*, she observed, bringing her hands together closely. Now, she had to double the space between them to encompass the profile of the largest ship.

It had long ago been confirmed there were seven vessels in total, none superior in size to *der Greif* and only one nearly as long as *Heiligen Maria.* None would be a match for the two vessels singly, and probably not as a pair. At more than a three to one advantage, however, the Hansa ships were clearly over-matched.

As the sun began to near the horizon, the wind shifted perceptibly to the northeast. The temperature dipped and the sky prematurely began to darken. The sea, which earlier had been nearly smooth, became choppy. Soon swells appeared, rocking *der Greif* gently, then more insistently, from side to side. A squall line developed in the distance behind the pirate ships. Older sailors began to exchange knowing glances, some even breaking into a relieved grin.

Christina immediately inferred the cause of their lightened mood. A cog had several excellent attributes, one of which was the height of its freeboard. This made it very seaworthy in rough water. The smaller craft of the pirates were not so lucky and risked the very real danger of being swamped. In the best of circumstances, the entire pirate flotilla would break off their chase. If not, even if the smallest of their craft turned back it would help even the odds. Everything now depended on the boldness and determination of their attackers.

Over the next hour, Christina kept a constant watch on the race between the ships and the impending storm. To her chagrin, she saw none of the other vessels had left the pursuit. They were so near now she could discern the features on the pirates' faces. She started to count their numbers in an attempt to figure the odds that faced the Lubeckers. Intent on her self-appointed task, she did not notice the approach of her father. His hand on her arm spun her around roughly. She started to speak then thought better of it when she saw the anger on his face.

"Christ's Holy Nails, Christina! Can you not ever do what you are told? If you don't get in the stern castle and stay there, I'll have you trussed! Now, go girl!"

Christina realized she could not directly defy her father's command. She walked toward her quarters, pushed back the flap, and entered disconsolately. Trudi looked at her with questioning eyes. Christina said, "They're still coming," the simple statement telling all. The two young women sat down, each deep in her own thoughts.

I can't just stay here like a dumb cow waiting to be slaughtered, Christina thought sourly. *I'm strong and I'm fast and I may not be the best with a sword on this damned ship, but I'm certainly not the worst! They need me!* Her father's order was clear, however, and he had made it clear he would not tolerate any disobedience. *But he's wrong,* she thought, *I've got to do something!*

Suddenly, a bold thought occurred to her. She asked Trudi, "Have you returned those garments to Father that he asked you to mend?"

Surprised at such a mundane question being asked in their current circumstances, Trudi stammered, "Uh, what? Well, no. Sorry, Christina. Do you wish to have me do it now?"

"No. That's fine, Trudi. I have something else for you to do. Get the scissors from the trunk, you're going to cut my hair."

Her maid gazed at Christina dumbfounded, as if she'd asked her to sing a song or do a little dance. *Surely, she jests!* Trudi thought. The fierce expression in her mistress's eyes conveyed she was completely serious. Trudi rummaged in the trunk until she found them.

Turning to Christina, she asked, "Where do you wish me to cut?" Christina replied, "Here," indicating just above her shoulders.

The maid was so surprised she dropped the scissors. "But you'll appear to be a man, milady."

In shock at Christina's request, she lapsed into a formal voice, one she never used with her mistress. "That's the idea," Christina said. "Just get on with it."

Trudi began, cutting long lengths of auburn locks and letting them fall to the floor. Tears filled her eyes as she had always believed Christina's hair was one of her most beautiful features. When she had finished, she gawked at her mistress with surprise, almost as if she had seen her like this before.

"Now, help me get out of these clothes and into Father's."

When they had finished, Trudi stood back to examine the transformation of her mistress. Although the clothing was ill-fitting, it very successfully concealed the truth about her sex. Thomas Kohl had been slender as a young man; however, an ample table had added several inches to his girth in middle age. Consequently, his tunic hung loosely about Christina's upper frame, completely concealing the swell of her small bosom. On the other hand, his braes were quite a tight fit around her hips and were almost comically short on her long legs, an effect accentuated by her bare feet. Despite the shortcomings of Christina's garb, a casual observer, especially one whose attention was fixed on fighting for his life, would readily believe it was a young man who stood beside him and not Thomas

Kohl's daughter.

"How do I look?" Christina asked.

"Like a man, like… like…" Trudi stammered.

Suddenly, a roar of thunder filled the air outside their canvas walls. Several men shouted and the ship gave a perceivable lurch. A drumbeat of rain began to tattoo the canvas separating them from the world outside. Christina wanted to rush on deck to gauge the approach of the pirate vessels, caution held her back. *If Father sees me, he'll go mad,* she thought. *He'll have me tied up to keep me out of the way or, worse still, put under guard with a man whose loss the defense of the ship can ill afford.* Even though it was killing her to remain inside, she knew she could not risk discovery until the heat of battle drew everyone's full attention.

Her tension was palpable and she began to sweat despite the chilly air. She wiped her face but remained focused on the flap of canvas directly in front of her face. The roar of the wind, the incessant rain, and the intermittent rumble of thunder made the shouts of the men on deck unintelligible, leaving Christina vexingly ignorant of how close their attackers' vessel had come.

Suddenly, the noise of the storm somewhat abated and she heard, "Get down!"

This was instantaneously followed by the unmistakable "thunk" of a crossbow quarrel imbedding itself deeply into oak wood. The wind then began to shriek once more and any attempt to discern the progress of battle was lost. She only knew she had not yet heard the unmistakable clang of blade on blade; consequently, she knew it was not yet time for her to enter the fray. She sat still, sword in hand, worried, but without fear. Yet, that was not to say she had no doubts. *I've never killed a man, nor even injured one, not counting the scrapes I've given Frederick. Can I really do this?* she thought in sudden panic.

Without warning, the hull of the ship suddenly heeled over to starboard. *It must be their grappling hooks! Well, if I'm going to do this, the time is now!* She mumbled to herself.

"Pray for us!" Christina yelled to Trudi then, without hesitation, she ran on deck.

She halted, mesmerized by the scene that unfolded beyond her.

As she had suspected, their ship had been grappled on the starboard beam. The heavy seas, however, made it difficult for the pirates to secure the two vessels together and their hulls rhythmically crashed together like the tolling of a church bell. A second ship had worked its way to port and was attempting to get close enough for its crew to board *der Greif* as well. Christina cast a swift gaze ahead only long enough to see *Heiligen Maria* was similarly engaged.

A wounded man cowered beneath the starboard bulwark, seeking to avoid another of the lethal quarrels such as the one that protruded from his shoulder. A couple of others had not been so fortunate, their bodies lying about the deck oozing red. She was relieved to see none of the wounded or dead figures appeared to be her father.

She was shaken from her inaction by the triumphant cries of the crew of the starboard vessel, who had finally succeeded in lashing the two ships together. The fighting became fiercer as they attempted to get on board *der Grief*, swords and axes seeking to counter the frantic thrusts of boat hooks that sought to keep them at bay. Soon, one and then another closed with the Hansa men and heavy steel sought out flesh, blood, and bone.

One of her father's mercenaries was being beat back, two pirates slashing at him simultaneously. He parried desperately, the only thing saving him was that they kept getting in each other's way in the small space of the crowded deck. Without conscious thought, Christina leapt forward, extending her falchion beneath the mercenary's right elbow and thrusting into the stomach of one of the pirates. Even though a falchion is primarily a slashing weapon, the broad point could do tremendous damage to soft tissue. She took another small step forward, driving her weapon deeper into the man until it found the bone of his spine. *Remember, straight back and into guard,* she told herself, cleanly disengaging her weapon as her target crumpled to the deck, crimson already beginning to soak the front of his tunic.

The surprise of seeing his fellow pirate's swift transition from on the attack to mortally wounded temporarily distracted the other man and he gaped down at the soon to be corpse. The mercenary suffered no such compulsion, however. His sword swung in a heavy arc. Unopposed by a counter, the blade cut deeply through his opponent's shoulder, half-severing the man's head. The mercenary raised his left fist into the air toward her in a brief salute of thanks. His eyes and sword stayed to the front, however, ready to defend the ship against the next onslaught of attackers.

She had no time to reply, however.

Just as she was about to move forward to fight at the side of the man she had saved, she heard the clatter of a grappling hook seating itself into the portside railing. The men on the starboard side of *der Greif* were certainly hard-pressed, but they were holding their own. This left few defenders to man the other side, however. She sprinted to the left veering to where she saw the grapnel biting deeply into the oak. An immediate course of action formed in her head.

She swung the falchion down over her head with all her strength, as if she were chopping a tree. The dense blade sang through the air, biting completely through the rope attached to the hook. It recoiled harmlessly into the water, leaving the cursing men aboard the attacking ship to glare at her hatefully as they pulled it back.

Christina's sudden appearance had surprised the pirates. They were determined, however, to not be thwarted again. An intermittent discharge of crossbow quarrels peppered the side of the ship, forcing Christina and the six men who defended that side to hunker down below the railing for cover. Two, three, and then four more grapnels were thrown. Unable to stand, she could not create enough force to cut through the ropes connecting them to the other ship. She knew the pirates would be aboard *der Greif* long before she could saw through them. All that was left to do was wait for them to begin boarding, then cut them down as they came.

She didn't have to wait long. She heard them before she saw them, cursing and shouting in an effort to bolster their own spirits and destroy those of their opponents. Moving into a half-crouch, she was surprised to see a man's hand appear, grasping the rail to pull himself aboard. Her sword flicked out and the hand kept coming forward, although it had been cleanly separated from the wrist to which it had been attached a second before. *Well, that's one of the bastards we won't have to worry about again,* she thought with a brief twinge of satisfaction. Rising to her full height, she refocused her attention immediately as several more of the pirates pushed forward to take his place.

Christina realized keeping their foes from boarding *der Greif* gave her and her fellow defenders the best odds of survival. *Keep them in front of you, girl,* she said to herself, as she raised her sword to parry a wicked looking axe being swung at her head by a burly pirate. The force of his blow rang through her blade, nearly paralyzing her arm. She stepped lightly to her right, however, and the axe continued its downward motion, throwing the man off balance. The numbness in her sword arm not yet subsided, she took the hilt of her weapon in both hands and swung the falchion in a tight arc that ended at the back of her adversary's neck. She had no time to celebrate her victory though, as she saw the man to her right fall, his guts spilling onto the deck from a deep slash across his belly that had almost cut him in two.

With their perimeter breached, she knew it was only a matter of time before they were overwhelmed. The pirates would swarm onboard and their superior numbers would allow them to single out and surround the Hansards, stabbing and slashing at undefended sides and backs. Two pirates climbed over the length of undefended bulwark, as if wishing to confirm her prediction. Christina wanted to rush over to engage them before they found their balance on the deck; however, her attention was diverted to another adversary approaching from her front.

Suddenly, she heard the clang of steel on steel to her right, immediately followed by a fearful scream dissipating into a choked gurgling sound. *What the hell?* She thought, *there were only pirates there a second ago*. Unable to chance a glance to her side as she engaged her next opponent, she only hoped the obviously dying man she heard was not another of the ship's defenders.

Her sword arm still ached terribly and that, plus her growing fatigue, forced her to give ground. A pirate gained the deck, the first of their adversaries to plant both feet in the area Christina was defending. He was a huge brute, towering over her by at least half a foot. He grinned at her from a mouth peopled with blackened, broken teeth. His huge blond beard was fouled with spittle and remnants of food and drink. He was attached to a massive two-handed sword before him at guard, its length making it impossible for her to even hope to reach a vital organ with her own blade. *My only hope is to be faster than him*, she thought desperately, *there's no way I can even begin to match his strength.* But she had no quickness left. She was exhausted. She realized her death was imminent and, although she had no thought of embracing it passively, knew there was little she could do to stop it.

The giant's grin, however, turned to a look of bewilderment. His grip on his sword loosened, allowing it to fall to the deck with a heavy thud. Slowly, he dropped to his knees, then followed his weapon to lie supine on the deck. It was then she noticed a gory blade being withdrawn from behind the man's arm. Following its length with her eyes, she glanced up to see Ziesolf, his customary emotionless expression fixed on his face.

"Don't let them get onto the deck," he said in his customary, gruff voice. "That's not good."

He then spun around, his sword a blur as it moved through the air, neatly decapitating a head that had unfortunately chosen that time to appear above the side of the ship. Hot red blood shot into the air from the unseen neck below. Ziesolf then moved away to defend what previously had been an unprotected length of deck.

Anger rose in Christina. *Does he think I'm stupid? Of course, I'm not going to let them on the deck, at least not if I can help it. What does he think I've been doing here anyway?* Exhausted, she fought back tears that threatened to cloud her sight.

Damn you! She cursed herself. *There's no time for self-pity now!*

The slight respite had given her new strength. Her sole purpose in life now was to cut, slash, parry, and thrust. It became automatic as her body adjusted to the attack of each new foe. The driving rain had long since thoroughly soaked her. The heat of her exertions kept her from feeling the cold, however.

Why are they so determined? She asked herself. It was not like the stories of pirates she had heard secretly eavesdropping on discussions in her father's study. It had seemed consensus among the merchants the rogues usually only chose to attack craft that were weakly defended. There were too many ships sailing the route along the Kattegat to risk taking casualties. Better to cut off an attack if their quarry was too well protected and wait for an easier victim.

So, why are they still coming? She asked herself again. She risked a glance to her right and was shocked to see there were only two defenders remaining, besides herself and Ziesolf. What was happening on the starboard side of the ship she had no way of knowing, as she was not foolhardy enough to turn her back to see.

Two more of them crested the through-beams in front of her. *Thank God for the design of this ship,* she thought as she moved forward wearily. *If cogs weren't designed with such a high freeboard, they could have rushed us at once. At least this way we've had a chance.* The man to her right moved to join two of his fellows who were worrying Ziesolf.

Although she wished she could repay her father's man for his earlier assistance, she knew she couldn't take on two attackers at once, especially not as fatigued as she now was.

She concentrated instead on the one who had sprung as lightly as a cat to the deck before her. In place of a sword or axe such as the other attackers she had faced had carried, she saw the man before instead carried two long daggers. Perhaps lured into a false sense of security by the greater range of her weapon. She thrust her falchion forward, throwing her slightly off-balance. The pirate used both daggers in unison to neatly catch her blade, forcing it upward and over his shoulder. He extricated the weapon in his right hand and swung it toward her in a tight arc. She abruptly felt an intense flash of pain move across her lower ribs. She wanted to double over to ease the ache but realized that would be the last thing she would ever do before dying. Ignoring the wound, she stepped backward swiftly. Somewhere, a horn was blowing, but for what purpose she had no time to fathom. Her opponent grinned at her from beneath his jaunty red cap and gave a mocking salute. She grimaced and assumed her guard as best she could. Exhaustion, blood loss, and pain threatened to overwhelm her.

She stubbornly fought back the urge to close her eyes, to surrender to the siren's call of sleep. Oddly, she felt she was missing something important. It was only then she noticed her blade extending into open air. No pirate stood before. *Where has he gone?* She murmured to herself in amazement She cautiously approached the bulwark. Although the grapnels remained firmly imbedded in the oak planks, the ropes attached to them had been severed and were hanging harmlessly down the side of the ship. Gazing over the water, she was surprised to see the once churning sea was now perfectly tranquil. The rain had also subsided at some point unbeknownst to her. She heard the large square sail overhead flapping lazily, the ship having shifted almost directly into the wind. In the distance, she saw the pirate ships tacking away rapidly off their beam.

She gripped the side of the ship for support, nearly too weak to stand. She saw Ziesolf rapidly approaching, his arms extending. *Oh, Sweet Jesus! Is he going to embrace me?* she thought, almost laughing aloud at the thought. *Imagine, the least emotional man I know overcome by …*

Her thoughts were cut off at the shock of suddenly hitting the cold waters of the Baltic Sea.

She convulsively gasped for air, her lungs taking in a draught of seawater at the same time. Christina's arms flapped wildly. Her mind tried to coalesce around a single question but failed to focus even that much. Beginning to lose consciousness, she felt herself ascending. But whether it was to safety or to heaven she really couldn't tell.

Chapter 5

She fought for her life, her sword cutting deeply into flesh that yielded no blood. As she sank her blade deeply into the man who faced her, she was horrified to realize it was Frederick, her beloved Frederick, whom she was killing. *I've no time to mourn!* She thought to herself hysterically, turning her weapon swiftly on a shadowy figure approaching from the left. Reacting without thought, the point of her falchion penetrated deeply into the chest of her next victim, her father.

As he crumpled his mouth silently formed the word "why?" before he too dropped to the floor.

She turned around to find another menacing figure standing before her. She sliced across its belly, leaving a gaping wound. Instead of organs, however, a mass of charnel worms plopped to the floor.

"You! It's your fault! It's always your fault! How can I go to my new husband appearing like this? You always ruin everything!"

Christina gawked at the rotting face of her sister, who issued forth a heartrending scream before falling away as well.

Now it was Ziesolf face, so close she could feel his hot breath on her face. She tried to bring her sword around to parry the blow she knew was coming, but he held her arms too tightly. She struggled to get free but could not.

Slowly, she stopped resisting and opened her eyes.

Despite the dimness, she could see she was in one of the makeshift cabins on *der Greif*, but not her own. Ziesolf knelt beside her, still holding her arms in a firm grasp. Seeing reason return to her face, he let her go; whereupon, she brought her right hand up to slap to slap the side of his face with a resounding crack. Before she could deal another blow, however, he caught her arms once more, this time not relinquishing his restraint.

"You rutting bastard!" she yelled, her ire overcoming the good sense to know she should not be insulting such a man. "You threw me into the goddamned water! I could have drowned!" "It was necessary," he replied as calmly as if he were telling her to close the door.

"What do you mean 'necessary? I could have drowned!"

"No, you couldn't. I saw you swimming like a herring when you were young."

Christina's face flushed with embarrassment. She had taken great care in sneaking to the Trave the summer she was ten to immerse herself in the luxuriously cool waters of the river. *How had he known?* she asked herself. She imagined him watching her little naked body moving lithely through the water and blushed again.

He continued, "Besides I was ready with the boathook the minute you went in. We hauled you out almost before you got wet."

"But why?" she asked, bewildered by the unfathomable rationale for his seemingly contradictory actions.

He contemplated her for a few seconds before answering. *There's something wrong here*, she thought, a rising panic causing her to struggle to get to her feet. As before, however, he held her down, albeit this time more gently.

"What's happened? Tell me now," she cried.

He began, "It was a hard battle, as you yourself know, Mistress Christina."

Her lips started to form a sarcastic retort, but she left it unsaid as the import of his words hit her. *That's the first time in my life he's called me anything but "girl,"* she thought in amazement.

"You fought well, perhaps very well. It might be that your sword was what turned the fight in our favor. Who knows?" he shrugged his shoulders.

When did he have time to watch me? Christina mused to herself in astonishment. *Throughout the battle, he faced one, two, even three of the pirates. Could he be the reincarnation of Odin, the one-eyed king of the old gods?* She thought, only partially in jest.

"It was a hard battle," he repeated, "and many men were lost. If the weather is reasonable, I think we have enough of a crew left to limp our way to England."

Where is he going with this? her feeling of dread beginning once more.

"What I mean to tell you is this. We were able to defend ourselves successfully, but those on board our other ship were not. They were overwhelmed by their attackers. When the pirates' ships sailed away, *Heiligen Maria* went with them."

Tears immediately overwhelmed Christina's eyes. "Oh, Sweet Mother of God. What of Frederick?"

"There is no easy way to say this. The men on board that vessel were brave, they knew what would befall them should they be captured. The fact the ship was taken means most, if not all, were killed. What remains, if any, will be sold in the east, in Rus, as slaves. If your brother is not one of the former, he is most certainly one of the latter."

The sickness in the pit of her stomach threatened to overwhelm her. Her head spun and she felt she was again about to lose consciousness. After a minute or two the world slowly began to stabilize.

She wiped her eyes. There would be no more tears. Frederick was gone and she would never see him again. This was now a certainty such as the sun rising in the east each morning. She held the pain she felt in the loss of her brother deeply now in the depth of her heart. *I will mourn him, but not here, not now.* "And?" Her voice was steady now.

"When I saw you fighting, hair cut short and dressed in man's clothes, I asked myself from whence you came. But the fact you were killing pirates was a good thing, so I ignored you for a while, being rather busy myself. When we had beaten off their attack, however, I regarded you again, only to still be confused. How had a boy I knew was on the *Heiligen Maria* suddenly appeared on our deck?

I turned to see that ship sailing away, Frederick Kohl either dead or a prisoner. If I had believed in witchcraft, I would have crossed myself. Instead, I looked at you again. It was then that I guessed the truth. I threw you over the side of the ship so others wouldn't come to the same conclusion."

"But it will be very easy to prove I'm Christina and not Frederick," she protested the absurdity of the men confusing her with her brother.

"But that is what we do not want to do." He gazed at her steadily, as if willing her to discern the import of his words.

"But...but...that's silly! How long did you expect me to keep up this sham? Until I have to squat to make water, maybe? Besides, don't you think my father knows the difference between his son and his daughter?"

She almost laughed at him, only the depth of her respect for the man swayed her from doing it aloud. Ziesolf fixed her with another grave expression.

"Get dressed and come with me." He walked toward the flap of the canvas, then turned and, indicating a pile of clothing in the corner, added, "Wear those."

She pushed the heavy furs that had been covering her away and arose from the pallet. She suddenly realized she was naked. *Did he...?* She gasped, her face burning a bright crimson at the thought he had stripped her sodden clothes away himself. *Well, there's nothing I can do about it now, but I vow I'll make him pay later for the liberties he has taken!*

Christina took stock of her condition as she painfully dressed. Her limbs felt leaden, she had barely enough strength to lift her arms. Ugly yellow and green bruises contrasted distinctly with her otherwise pale skin. The wound she had received to her ribs had been cleaned and neatly stitched together. *All in all, I'll live*, she thought, taking scant solace in the fact her life would henceforth be without her brother.

Now fully clothed, Christina followed Ziesolf out onto the deck. She shielded her eyes against the sun's glare to see the squall line rapidly receding into the horizon. A faint breeze had arisen, causing gentle wavelets to caress the waterline of the ship. The pleasantness of the weather, however, drew a sharp contrast to the horror littering the deck. What few able-bodied men who were left made rudimentary attempts to succor the wounded, whose screams and whimpers filled the otherwise silent tableau. Sliced flesh was bandaged and a broken arm splinted, but there was little more that could be done. Fortified wine was poured down the parched throats of the dying as well as those likely to live in the hopes it would alleviate their agony, if even just a bit. The dead lay everywhere, for the time being unnoticed and uncared for.

Christina hurried to catch up to Ziesolf, who continued to stride purposefully toward the bow of the ship, seemingly unaffected by the carnage he passed. *Where is he taking me now?* she wondered. He stopped at the set of steps leading up to the forecastle, motioning her ahead with a nod. Uncertain as to what she would find, she ascended. As her head crested the upper deck, she was shocked to find her father lying supine on the deck timbers. One of the crew knelt beside him, adjusting a bandage on his arm that still seeped blood through the cloth. It was not this wound that drew Christina's attention, however, nor the one that caused her to draw a sharp breath of alarm.

Thomas Kohl had received a terrible blow to his head. Although it was not bleeding openly, it was evident: blood was pooling beneath the skin and bloating it to a dark purple. It was also possible to see a slight depression in his skull despite the swelling. He groaned softly as he hovered on the edge of consciousness.

She moved to embrace him carefully, aware he may have sustained even more injuries that were not so apparent. Christina murmured, "Father, Father," repeatedly.

The eyelids of the gravely injured man fluttered open for a second, then closed. In a barely discernible voice, he whispered, "Frederick, my son is that you?"

Before Christina could speak, she felt a hand grip her shoulder, firmly turning her body about. She saw Ziesolf silently nod his head affirmatively. She pushed his hand away roughly, angered at his apparent desire to have her deceive her father even as he lay mortally injured.

"Frederick?" The merchant cried out again, this time slightly louder and more insistently.

What should I do? She thought, torn between the truth and her faith in Ziesolf's absolute loyalty to her father.

Finally, she replied in a low voice, "Yes, Father, I'm here. It's me, Frederick.

"My son," he began, gripping her arm with what little strength he could muster. "...Pirates...too many...betrayal...Christina safe?"

Although his words were disjointed, she inferred their intent. She felt a lump arise in her throat, a portent of emotions that threatened to engulf her. *He asks about me! I do matter to him!* "Yes, she is here as well," she finally responded with a half-truth.

"Protect her, Frederick. Treachery...too many...treachery...remember what I told you! My words...London...beware treachery!"

He tried to raise himself, gripping Christina tightly and pulling himself upward through sheer force of will. The most he could manage, however, were a few inches. His gripped loosened and he slumped back to the deck, his exertions costing him his consciousness.

Again, she felt Ziesolf's hand on her shoulder; however, this time more gently. Christina rose and stood aside as two of the few able-bodied sailors remaining bent down and lifted her father, maneuvered him carefully down the steps, and toward his cabin in the stern.

As she moved to follow, Ziesolf said, "Leave him be. Give him rest. It is in God's hands now."

Christina looked on helplessly as the men carried her father into the stern castle. *First Margarete, then Frederick, and now Father. Ever since he announced Margarete's*

marriage, calamity has befallen our family. Am I to be next?
A chill rose up her back that had nothing to do with the
weather. She realized her father's words had been disjointed;
yet, they conveyed a clear air of warning.

She stared at Ziesolf. His face was etched with caution, a
silent warning that she was to speak softly so their
conversation could not be overheard.

She asked, "Could you make any sense of my father's
words? What did he mean 'treachery' and 'betrayal'? Who
could have betrayed us and why?" "I don't know," he
admitted, slowly shaking his head in a negative manner. He
pondered the question for a moment before continuing.
"Money has the power to subvert men's loyalties, causing
them to break even the most sacred of sworn bonds. And
who has more money than the great merchants of the Hanse,
of whom your father and his competitors are among the
richest. So, we might ask ourselves who would stand to gain
should your father and his heir die? The answer: Any of
them, all of them! But who specifically? Only your father
and brother know for sure."

At the mention of Frederick, Christina again felt an icy
stab of dread pierce her heart. *He is alone,* she thought, *at
the mercy of desperate men made angry through the loss of
their shipmates as well as one of their prizes.* She hoped what
Ziesolf had said was true, that even the most savage of pirates
would recognize Frederick's worth as a prisoner to ransom.
*Perhaps his value will shield him from the worst of the
pirates' fury.* She would not even consider the possibility he
was anything but alive. She broke from her fearful musings
to notice Ziesolf was continuing to speak.

"The pirate attack was very strange, I think. It was almost
as if they knew our course and the time of our passage. If

they had not been lying in wait for us, in just the right position, they would have never caught us. It seems they knew about us in advance."

"That in itself is not so peculiar," he shook his head seemingly in doubt. "There is always someone hanging about the docks who is willing to trade information for a silver *Hohlpfennige* or two. But it is the actions of the pirates after they spotted us that is so unusual. First, even their smallest ships sailed into the storm to pursue us. They could have easily been swamped, their crews drowned. Although they are murderous scum, they cowardly choose to take very few chances. Why would the men in the two knarr take such a risk, especially to attack such large and well-defended prizes? It makes no sense! But they did attack, and kept attacking, despite their losses. They only stopped…" He paused, then his jaw dropped slightly.

"They only stopped when?" Christina repeated his words.

"When your father fell."

Oh, Good Lord! she thought. *Could it be they were not seeking plunder after all and that, instead, they were seeking to kill Father? Who could it be who would plan such a thing? Whoever it is,* she vowed grimly, *they will pay for the harm they have caused to my family!*

"Are the men trustworthy?" she waived her hand to encompass the ship. With the threat of betrayal from an unknown quarter so real, she felt she had to narrow down the possible sources.

"Aye. Those who survived defending you, your father, and his cargo," His terse reply carried a veiled rebuke. The crew and hired men had proven their loyalty with their blood.

She shrugged her shoulders in exasperation. "I'm sorry, but I had to ask. It seems there is not much we can do then, except to pray for my father's rapid recovery and to remain vigilant."

"There is something more we must do," he stated matter-of-factly.

She peered at him quizzically.

He continued, "You must continue to pose as your brother. Until we know for certain who it is who is plotting the death of your father, it must seem his heir is capable of controlling the family business. If your father recovers…"

"When he recovers!" she interjected harshly.

"When he recovers," he corrected himself for her sake, "He will take his rightful place and he will decide how to repay those who sought to harm him. You can then again become Christina. Until then, however, for your father's sake, you must remain Frederick."

She scrutinized his face, uncertain as to what to do. It seemed so ludicrous she should attempt to present herself as a man; yet, she also understood the dangerous position in which her family now found itself. Her father grievously injured, her brother captured, who could save their family if not her?

And certainly, not as Christina, she thought. *No man would strike a bargain with a woman, it probably wouldn't even be legal,* she added ruefully. *I don't have to keep up the charade forever, only until Father is better.* She grinned slightly. *Imagine what a beating I will get for this! But best to worry about that later.*

She still had reservations, however. "Are the men so stupid that, one minute a girl is aboard then, the next, it is a boy? Yes, they saw you rescue what you say is a boy from the water, but do you not think even one will ask what happened to the girl?"

He replied, "They all heard your father order you to stay in the stern castle twice. They also know you to be both disobedient and willful. So, when I say you fell overboard, they will say it was your own fault."

She was shocked at Ziesolf's appraisal of the men's casual reaction to her supposed fate.

The bastards, she thought, somewhat hurt by their anticipated lack of compassion over the terrible end of such a nice young girl as herself.

"Besides," he continued, "Sailors are a superstitious lot. It would seem to make sense to them that, one Kohl in the water, and one Kohl out. Combined with the fact the men on *der Grief* had no opportunity to get to know your brother, I think they will have no real reason to doubt who we say you are."

I think they would probably not doubt anything Kurt Ziesolf tells them, she thought, *regardless of how absurd it sounds.*

"Alright," she said, perhaps a bit too hastily. "I'll do it."

Ziesolf gave a quick nod of approval and descended the forecastle to supervise the reorganization of the ship's crew so they could get underway.

Alone for the first time since awakening that morning, she was surprised to notice the sun was beginning to fade below the horizon. *Has the entire day really already passed?* She asked herself incredulously.

It was then that a tremendous sense of fatigue engulfed her. She walked across the deck toward the stern of the ship, fighting hard to keep from collapsing with each step. Upon entering her quarters, Christina was enveloped by Trudi's fierce hug which, although very affectionately given, was more painfully received.

"Ouch! I'm just as happy to see you as you are me but, if my ribs were not already cracked, they certainly are now!" Christina complained, wincing as she spoke.

Trudi loosened her grip a bit, but only slightly, burying her face into her mistress's shoulder and saying, "Herr Ziesolf told me about what happened to your brother and father. Oh, it's all so terrible! He also ordered me to treat you as if you are Frederick. But, you're a girl, Christina! I'm so confused!" She began to sob noisily.

Trudi's emotional outburst threatened to elicit a similar reaction from Christina. She felt tears well up in her eyes but fought them down angrily. *First, if I am supposed to pass myself off as a man, the last thing that needs to happen is for one of the crew to pass by and hear what sounds like two silly women bawling their eyes out,* she scolded herself. *It makes no sense to give the sailors cause for suspicion. Second, crying isn't going to bring Frederick back or heal Father.* The thought of the two men she held dear in her life caused the lump in her throat begin to swell once more. *For the love of Christ, Christina, get a grip on yourself!*

How would Frederick act at a time like this? Christina suddenly questioned herself. She began to pat the maid awkwardly on the back then, pushing her away slightly, brushed her lips chastely against her cheek. Trudi glanced up with a startled expression on her face, then kissed Christina fully on the lips.

It was now Christina's turn to react with surprise. Trudi flashed a half-hearted smile and in a still slightly broken voice said, "If you are to make people believe you are a man, you have to think like one. Do you remember when my aunt Agnes died? I was absolutely heartbroken. Well, that nice stable-boy Manfred tried to comfort me and I cried into his shoulder just as I did to you now. The next thing I knew his hands were up the back of my skirts and grabbing my buttocks! I kneed him so hard in the bollocks he couldn't ride for a week!" With the telling, she seemed to regain her spirits somewhat and gave a little laugh.

Christina was shocked. *How could a man be so crass as to take advantage of someone else's suffering?* She felt depressed, a state heightened by her sense of loss and need for sleep.

"I need to sleep, Trudi," she said, beginning to lower herself to the invitingly comfortable pallet stretched before her on the deck.

"Not here you don't, Master Frederick! I'll not be having my virtue besmirched by allowing a handsome young man to share my bedchamber. And so soon after the loss of my dear, sweet mistress? Have you no shame, sir?"

Trudi could not hold her look of indignation long before breaking into a wide grin.

Shit! Christina thought, beginning to anger, then realizing that Trudi, despite her joking manner, was actually right.

I can't sleep here. The men would certainly question Thomas Kohl's son and heir flagrantly bedding one of his household's servants, which it would readily be assumed to have happened. I can't chance bringing discredit to our family at a time like this, she thought miserably.

"I agree," Christina said soberly. "Ziesolf believes a very real threat exists to our family, Trudi. For some reason I don't really understand, he thinks we are in less peril if I pose as Frederick. All I know is Father trusts him; therefore, so must we."

She stooped to pick up a thick black bear skin. "I am going to sleep in Father's cabin. That way I can check on him during the night. Isn't that what a dutiful son would do?"

Trudi regarded her for a second, then stepped forward and embraced her mistress once more, whispering, "Please be careful, Christina. There may be more danger here than even Ziesolf suspects."

The maid loosened her hold and Christina departed to spend the night with her father, restless dreams, and troubled thoughts.

Christina awoke the next morning not quite so certain if the events of the previous day had been real or imagined. In the nearly complete darkness of the cabin, she could imagine Trudi's warm, soft body lying only inches from her. Soon, she would go out on deck and try to spot Frederick on the *Heiligen Maria*, perhaps catching his eye to respond to her frantic waves with one of his own.

Her idyllic imaginings were quickly dispelled, however, as soon as she became aware of the sound of her father's shallow, belabored breathing nearby. She groped around in the dark to find the flint and steel she had left on the small table next to her father's pallet. She lit the beeswax candle stub and, in turn, used that to light the lantern that hung overhead.

As light began to flood the room, Christina was appalled by her father's appearance. The swelling over his damaged skull had increased, causing his face on that side of his head to become misshapen. The purple blood that pooled under his skin contrasted with the dark circles around his eyes and the whiteness of his skin below the wound. His eyelids fluttered sporadically, revealing unseeing, bloodshot eyes.

His lips were arid and cracked, covered in dried spittle. It was clearly evident his condition was life-threatening.

Why can't you just wake up? She beseeched him silently. *I don't know what to do! You said there was a betrayal, but I don't know by whom or why. Ziesolf believes it is better that I pose as Frederick for now, but I can't believe that is what you'd have me do. What would you have me do? Oh, Father, please!*

She gaped at him helplessly, realizing her father could not help her. In frustration, she dug her fingernails deeply into the palms of her hands, not noticing the drops of blood that fell to the floor. *No, he cannot help me, at least not now. I must make these decisions myself.*

She had spent much of the night thinking about Ziesolf's plan for her to assume Frederick's identity. *It would be impossible to do such a thing in Lubeck, but in London?* No one had ever met either her or Frederick, so it would be impossible for someone to spot the small differences in their appearance.

The same thing held true for their voices. Frederick's voice was easily recognizable in the *Marienkirche* choir, his tenor notes almost heavenly in their purity and beauty. In contrast, people likened Christina's attempts to sing to those of a lowing cow begging to be milked.

But can I pass myself off as any man, not just Frederick? What does a man do that I cannot? He eats, drinks, belches, and shits, any of which I can do as well as any man, she thought frankly. She tried to think of the young men she knew in Lubeck and their mannerisms. Perhaps some were a bit coarser by nature than she and her friends, but some were not. She imagined the same would be true in London. *Besides, if I act a bit unusual, they will just think I am some stupid*

foreigner. I just have to remember not to try standing to piss!
Or try to fuck, she added, grinning.

At that thought, her mood sobered. *There is one other important matter to consider before I decide to agree to this masquerade. Do I really want to give up my identity as a girl?* She gazed across at her father and thought optimistically, *It may not be forever. When he recovers, I can go back to being Christina and pick up my life just as if this never happened.*

She knew the truth was very likely to be far different, however. Her father's condition was critical. Even if by God's kind intervention he did recover, it could be months or even a year before he regained his full strength. *It would be more likely he will remain an invalid or even feeble-minded considering the severity of the injury to his head,* she thought emotionlessly. *No, this decision must be considered as if it is going to be final.*

Is it right to give up my marriage, a contract father thought to be in the best interests of both our family and the business? She thought a moment then shook her head slightly. *But not necessarily in mine,* she added sadly. *After all, the arrangement had been made between Thomas Kohl and Johann Revele, and then for Margarete and not for me. No one asked for my thoughts then, but it seems by the grace of God I do have a say so now.*

Margarete had been excited by the prospects of a large manor, an important husband, a future family of handsome boys and beautiful girls. But that is her, not me. I have no desire to be a brood mare, even if I am kept in a fancy stable. Besides, she admitted to herself, the thought of her future husband fumbling about the cleft between her legs held little appeal. The one Lubeck boy she had allowed to touch her there had been seized by a compelling need to see how many fingers he could stick inside her. It had hurt, been a little frightening, and it took a hard punch to his nose to make him stop. She perceived scant advantage in enduring a similar act for the rest of her life.

Instead, I have an opportunity before me that few, if any women, have ever had. I have a chance to make my own decisions, to control my own destiny. Even if I am only to live like this for a short while, it will have been worth it. I will be free.

Content now the path she was taking was one she had truly chosen and not one selected for her, she washed, dressed, and, perhaps with a bit of swagger in her step, walked from the cabin to begin her first day as a man.

Chapter 6

Ziesolf was already on deck, standing alone at the forecastle. He gazed straight ahead, as if his good eye could discern what lay before them all the way to London and perhaps even after. Hearing her footsteps behind him, he turned and appraised her critically.

"Is everything to your liking?" she asked sarcastically.

"No," he replied gruffly. "A man would never wear that belt so low. It is intended to hold up your braes, not show off your big ass. Men don't have large, rounded hips, don't draw even more attention to yours by slinging your belt across them."

Stung by his rebuke and his (hopefully) unintended slur on her body's proportions, she made quick adjustments to her clothing and stepped back for his reappraisal.

He stared her in the face and said, "Christ's bollocks, are you going to turn red every time someone mentions the word 'ass'? What about 'cock,' or 'balls,' or 'tits'? How do you expect to pass yourself off as a man when you blush every time someone speaks?"

She looked Ziesolf squarely in the face and said evenly, "Well, what would you do if someone talked about your little worm of a cock or tiny *kugeln*? Wouldn't you be embarrassed as well?

"No, I'd knock him on his ass and then take my cock out and waggle it in his face to show him it is not so small after all. Since you obviously cannot do the latter, you must learn how to do the former. For the rest of the journey, I will teach you how to defend yourself."

Christina's ire rose immediately. "How to defend myself? In case you've forgotten, it was only yesterday that I not only defended myself, but this whole damned ship as well! Did you count the men who died under my blade? No? Well I did. Five of those bastards aren't drinking ale tonight, thanks to me!"

Ziesolf stood impassively, waiting for her outburst to end. When she paused to take a breath, he said, "Yes, you fought well, but I already said that, didn't I? Must we begin each day with me giving you a compliment? What a waste of a fine morning!" He began to walk away.

"Wait! Please!" Christina's anger dissipated. *If I am going to make this work, I am going to need this man,* she realized. *I can't afford to let my feelings or pride get in the way of whatever he offers to help. And what young man in Lubeck would not have jumped at the opportunity to train with such a warrior?* "Please," she repeated. "I'm sorry. Please teach me."

"First," he began, paying no heed to her apology or her actions that had necessitated it. "We will work with the dagger. If the last man you faced, the one with the knives, had not heard the recall horn, he would be drinking ale in a tavern, sharing a laugh with his friends about the stupid boy who couldn't parry a blade thrust!"

Christina fought against the reddish glow she knew was beginning to rise in her cheeks at Ziesolf frank appraisal of her helplessness against the last pirate. He reached inside his cloak and threw her a long dagger. She caught it deftly, hoping her skill in catching the weapon would negate him berating her again over blushing.

He took an identical blade into his right hand and said, "Now, do as I do."

"Wait," she said again. "I need to take off my shoes first."

"Of course," he said, saluting her slightly with his blade.

As she bent down, however, she felt a hard kick to her buttocks. Losing her balance, she tumbled over unceremoniously, falling flat on her face on the oaken planks. Infuriated, she raised herself to her hands and knees, then another kick sent her back down as before. She felt a knee between her shoulder blades pin her down, then a thumbnail drag slowly and painfully across her throat.

"Two mistakes, each would have cost you your life. If someone is angry enough with you to attack you with a knife, why in God's holy name would you think they would wait for you to take off your shoes, comb your hair, or have one last draught of ale before they tried to cut your throat? Second, even if by some miracle they didn't spill your guts on their first pass, they wouldn't pass up a second invitation to do so. Why didn't you at least try to defend yourself instead of giving me your back a second time?"

Ashamed, Christina had no answer. She heard the hoot of a short, derisive snort somewhere toward the stern of the ship. She knew it was one of the mercenaries or crewmen who had witnessed her pitiful ineptitude. She started to form a sharp retort in her throat only to let it die unsaid. *He was right,* she admitted, acknowledging her unseen critic, *that was pitiful.*

To Ziesolf she said, "May we continue?"

She felt the pressure on her back lift. Instead of rising to her hands and knees, however, she twisted her body around to face her opponent as she rose. She held her dagger in front of her, ready to parry an impending attack.

"Better," he said.

She regained her feet, keeping her eyes steadily fixed on his weapon. She feinted a jab toward his stomach, then turned the blade over and brought it in an upward slash toward where she anticipated his knife arm to be moving. Instead, he used his left arm to push hers harmlessly outside his body. He followed through with an elbow to her ribs that caused her to exhale in a loud "whoosh." As she involuntarily doubled over, he hooked his foot behind her heel, sending her unceremoniously on her backside once more.

In her anger, Christina's first reaction was to throw the knife at her instructor, but then thought better of it. *I'd probably miss anyway*, she fumed in frustration. Instead, she brought her knife up defensively and slowly regained her feet.

Ziesolf studied her for a few seconds, as if waiting for her to make an angry comment. *I won't give him the satisfaction,* she thought.

She waited for him to speak. When he did, she was surprised to hear, "That was a very clever move, Frederick. Many men would have been tricked by your feint. A slash across the muscle of their knife arm, as you were attempting to do, would have rendered them helpless. So why didn't it work this time?"

"Because you're the best fighter in the world, maybe?" Her comment was dripping with sarcasm.

He paid no attention to the mocking tone in her voice. "Not the world probably, but certainly on this ship," he said matter-of-factly. "Your feet were planted firmly on the deck, that's why."

"But, if I don't brace myself, you just push me over!" she protested.

He lowered himself to the deck, took a seat, and motioned for Christina to sit beside. She hesitated, wary in case this was a ploy designed to make her lower her guard.

Surmising the rationale for her hesitation, he said, "Wary. Yes, that it is good." He then patted the planking beside him.

Christina moved to the man's side and took a seat, confused as to why. *I hope it's not another lecture,* she thought.

Ever since she was a young child, Christina had hated to listen to long explanations. She remembered several times when her mother had been trying to explain how to do a task and her attention had wandered. It was only when she received the inevitable slap that her focus returned to what her mother was trying to tell her.

Oh, dear God, she thought suddenly, turning immediately and staring at Ziesolf in rapt attention. She hated to imagine the penalty for woolgathering while Ziesolf was speaking.

"You must listen carefully to what I am about to tell you," he began in a low voice. Christina successfully resisted the urge to roll her eyes toward the sky. "You are a big, strong girl and you have much natural talent as a fighter. You are also tough and fearless and that is very good as well."

He now had her undivided attention. *Compliments are always nice to hear,* she thought.

He continued. "But you will never be as strong as most men you are likely to fight. They will almost certainly out-weigh you and be hard and brave as well. That said, you are almost certain to lose any straight-up fight that you fight on their terms."

Christina's mouth began to form words of protest. He cut her off with a wave of his hand.

"That does not mean you will lose, only that you will if you attempt to match your opponent's power. To win, you must instead rely on your speed and your brain. Even though you have never fought before with a knife, you devised a very clever move. What's more you did it in the heat of combat. That was very smart. But when you allowed your opponent to close with you, that was very dumb. You let me take away your advantages and allowed me to make use of my weight and strength – my advantages. Do you understand?"

Christina nodded her head gravely. *This certainly makes sense.* "Can you teach me to fight this way?" she asked.

Ziesolf replied, "When I was on crusade in the Holy Land, one of the infidels surrendered to us, claiming he had found the truth in the word of Our Lord Jesus and wished to convert to the Christian Church. He told us he was a warrior, but we knights laughed at him because he was such a small man. How surprised we were when we found none of us could best him with any weapon. He moved with the speed of lightning and he was as hard to find with a blade as smoke. This man, Muhammed Ibn Al Kindi, shared much about his fighting style with me. These things I will now teach you, if you are willing to learn that is."

Without hesitation, she replied, "Yes, I would like that very much."

"Most men are taught to overwhelm their enemies in combat, to use brute force to hack and chop until their foe has no power left to resist. You have little chance of winning such combat. Instead, you will learn to be quick and avoid your opponent's blade unless you are certain to mark him at no risk to yourself. This may mean you will only score a light wound instead of one that kills, but that is what you must do. Sooner or later, he will grow impatient and try to rush at you.

Then, when he is off-balance and careless, that is when you must strike the telling blow."

Christina inwardly groaned. She knew patience was definitely not one of her strongest attributes. *How am I supposed to fight like this when I am the one who wants to rush to the attack even more than my enemy?* She felt like telling Ziesolf, "No." It was demeaning to fight in such a cowardly manner; yet, in her heart she realized his frank assessment of her was true. Consequently, she instead muttered, "I'll try."

The next hour was one of the hardest of her life. Ziesolf punished her again and again for pressing the attack or allowing herself to come within his reach in a clench. He proved repeatedly what he had told her: that she could not overcome his size and strength. She felt battered and well imagined the colorful hues of the multiple bruises she knew were progressively covering her body.

With the passing time, however, she began to learn Ziesolf's hard lesson. She started to step backwards and evade her opponent rather than move to meet his advance. She stayed on the balls of her feet, maintaining a perfect balance that allowed her to shift her weight instantly, evading his thrusts and slashes with increasing ease. She became acutely alert for small openings in his defense, darting in to take a nick here and a cut there; yet, never committing long enough to become a target herself. *If we weren't fighting with shielded daggers, he'd be bleeding in a dozen places by now,* she thought with satisfaction. She permitted a slight smile to curl her lips. She backed away, waiting for him to leave another opening for her flashing blade to find.

Instead, he let out a mighty yell and rushed forward, his dagger extended before him like a knight's lance. Christina was completely taken by surprise and stumbled backwards, tripping over a small coil of rope. Once again, she found herself on her back, completely at the mercy of Ziesolf. The point of his sheathed dagger pushed hard between her breasts, painfully preventing her from rising back to her feet. Her own knife lay where she had dropped it, well out of reach.

"So, what advice do you have for me if I find myself in this situation?"

"Hope you have recently been to confession so your sins have been freshly absolved," he answered with a stern expression. "I told you your opponent will eventually grow tired of dancing with you and seek to overwhelm you with his attack. This is what I told you would happen and this is what I did. Yet, you were still not ready. It should be me down there with your dagger at my heart instead of the other way around. You also missed taking advantage of three openings I gave you to wound me. You must not waste such opportunities or you will be very dead."

Christ's Nails! she blasphemed, *he was giving me those openings, allowing me to score on him!* She felt depressed. She had thought she had actually penetrated his guard. "So, shall we begin again?" she said, desperate to do better.

"No," he held out his hand to help her back to her feet, "That is enough for today. We will begin again tomorrow. You will be sorer, but hopefully a little wiser, yes?"

She wanted desperately to say "No," but recognized the ache and fatigue that permeated her body. *He's right,* she admitted grudgingly, *any more and I won't be able to stand for a week, let alone train tomorrow.* She thanked him and turned to go to check on her father's condition. Ziesolf went back to scanning their course ahead, almost as if he was seeking to speed their progress through the sheer force of his will alone.

She found her father laying just as she had left him. She moistened his lips with a sponge dipped in wine, allowing a bit of the liquid to trickle down his throat. *There is little else I can do,* she thought hopelessly. She gazed over at the small table in the corner of the cabin and spotted her father's book of accounts. Although her father's feelings about the place and duties of women in society were very traditional in most things, he was firm in his belief that, not only should his son learn to read, write, and do calculations, but his daughters as well.

As a result, Christina easily made sense of the concise Latin phrases and numerical entries written in her father's neat, precise hand. There were pages giving the prices and particulars of goods dispatched, others listing receipts of cash and goods, as well as another in which a running total of the balance was kept. She looked at her father and shook her head sadly. She realized she had another important task before her.

Thank you, Mother, she thought gratefully. Although Margarete had displayed little interest when their mother had shown them her account book listing ground rents and other domestic transactions, Christina had been fascinated. The fact her mother could tell her how much the family had spent on butter for ten years running amazed her daughter. Christina had eagerly asked to be shown everything and her mother readily complied, happy her younger daughter, who exhibited very little enthusiasm for any other women's duties, was so interested in managing the home's accounts. Consequently, as Christina studied the ledger, she began to grasp the extent of the Kohl family business.

As the days passed, Christina's world revolved around daily bouts of training with Ziesolf, time spent practicing her English, perusal of the family account record, and tending to her father. She felt her body begin to harden from the exertions of rigorous daily training with sword, knife, and even unarmed combat. Once, after being thrown to the ground over the hip of Ziesolf for the third straight time, she spit a bit of blood out of her mouth and turned to her teacher with anger flashing in her eyes.

"It's funny, but I have seen many youths grow into manhood in Lubeck who were destined to take over their family businesses. They spent their days in the taverns trying to get under the skirts of the barmaids, not getting thrown about by some sadistic old man. Tell me, is this really necessary or are you just amusing yourself at my expense?" she asked sarcastically.

"If it was fun throwing a clumsy ox about, I would rather be standing in a nice sunny field to do it," he replied evenly.

Christina leapt to her feet and rushed Ziesolf in a fit of blind rage. He easily sidestepped her attack and, for the fourth time, flung her to the ground. This time she stayed down, panting and groaning, but otherwise silent.

"You are not like other men," he said bending down, his voice barely above a whisper. "Most fights do not end in death. There are far more little squabbles in which a punch or two are thrown, someone is wrestled to the ground, he yields, and then all is as before. There are very few men who never lose such a fight. But you must be one. All it would take is for your opponent to find breasts where he was expecting none, or a void in your crotch where he was punching, and your ruse would be over. What if you are bleeding or knocked senseless? Some well-meaning fellow might try to dress your wounds and discover your secret as well."

Christina listened in silence, now realizing the precariousness of her deception.

"Therefore, you must never lose. Ever," he said simply. He offered his hand, helping her to her feet.

Her training continued. When they were three days from arriving in London, however, this routine was abruptly altered. Christina awoke and, as had become custom, went to tend to her father. Surprisingly, his eyes were wide open. Her momentary surge of happiness was short-lived, however, as she found he had taken his last breath sometime during the night.

She gently laid her head upon his chest and began to sob. *I wish I had been a better daughter to you, Father,* she lamented, recalling the many the times she had been disobedient and willful. *Even if you had no reason to be proud of my before, I hope that what I am planning will do so now.*

After what seemed an eternity, she rose from her father's side and covered his body. She finished dressing and, after taking one last glimpse back, went out on deck. As had become customary, Ziesolf stood on the forecastle anticipating their course.

Whether through an inference from the expression on her face or some other form of prescience, he said simply, "I am sorry for the loss of your father. He was a very good man"

Christina stared at him helplessly, tears streaming down her face. "I should have done more, I should have helped him get better!" "His fate was certain, it was only a matter of time. I have seen younger, fitter men with such a wound. Always they died, without exception."

"Why didn't you tell me!" She shouted, wanting to beat her fists into his chest in punishment for his deception. "I…I could have been prepared for…to see him…." Her voice trailed off.

"It would have served no purpose. He was beyond your help. Would you have felt better, watching him slowly die and knowing there was nothing you could do about it?"

She turned away in frustration and grief. *He was right,* she admitted to herself, but it still felt as if her heart would burst.

"What now?" she asked simply.

He seemed surprised at her question. "Why, we continue as we planned, what else? You are now the master. House Kohl is now your responsibility."

She brushed away her tears and gazed at him wearily. *Do I even want this now? Always before, I thought I was helping Father, that one day he would be well and I could go back to being Christina. But not now, not ever.* "Could I not just marry Albrecht Revele? This deception seems so pointless now."

Ziesolf glared at her and, for the first time she could recall, anger clouded his face.

"So, do you want so much to dishonor your father's memory?"

She gaped at him in shocked silence, stung by the venom in his words.

"Your father spent his lifetime building House Kohl into one of the great merchant families in Lubeck, in all of the Hanse. And now, with his body barely cold, you wish to throw it away, to give it to another family, glorifying their name while that of your father fades from memory. And why? Is it because you are afraid because you are only a girl, or is it because you like the idea of a cock in your quim?"

Christina had never heard Ziesolf speak like this, had never had any man speak to her this way. She stepped forward and slapped him hard across the face.

He accepted the blow without flinching, a trickle of blood beginning to seep from the corner of his mouth. Unexpectedly, tears began to flow from his clear eye and roll noiselessly down his cheek.

"Nearly thirty years ago, I was still a young man in years; yet, old in experience as a warrior. After the fall of Acre, I and a few of my fellow knights returned north, determined to defend Mother Church against a new foe, the Samogitians. We had been taught these pagans had no right to exist. Unless they accepted the cross, they were as sheep infected with disease that must be destroyed to save those in the flock that are healthy. We believed Christ himself would fling their foul souls into hellfire.

The lands these human beasts inhabited was a trackless wilderness of dense forests, mosquito-filled swamps, and unnavigable rivers. We did not battle as we had in Outremer, no lines of armored knights facing mounted Saracens. Instead, we fought sharp, bloody skirmishes, our small patrols suddenly attacked by dozens of screaming savages who fought with the axe, the club, even their bare hands.

It was during one of these patrols that I was dismounted and captured by these heretics. For months, I was starved, beaten, and tortured until I was no more than an animal myself. Eventually, I was traded to a man of Rus', who took me to the great city of Novgorod. There, he kept me in chains outside his house, as if I were a dog. As the weather grew colder, I reconciled myself to the fact I had not much longer to live and made peace with God as best I could.

That was when I heard a voice, a German voice! I called out as best I could. I was not sure he would hear me or, if he did, he would understand me. The only sounds I had made during the entire time of my capture were groans and screams, and these through the ruined face you see before you now.

But he did hear, he did understand. This man was your father, one of the *sommerfahrer,* the merchants who traveled to Novgorod to trade in the summer. He was young then, of course, and not nearly as wealthy as now. He asked the Rus'ian what he wanted in trade for his captive. The man laughed and said four bolts of Flemish cloth! This was the ransom of a nobleman and I, as far as your father knew, was only a penniless wretch who spoke some German. Yet, he paid the man without haggling, the only time I have ever seen him agree to a trade without bartering. After that, he took me to the German compound, the *Peterhof.* He fed me, clothed me, and took me back to Lubeck with him. I have been by his side ever since.

I am sorry for what I said to you, they were angry words and should not have been spoken. I do not have a family, but perhaps your father was my family, Frederick was my family, you are my family.

Your father and sister are certainly dead, your brother probably so also. I do not want the same to be true of you. Your father mentioned treachery, but "by whom?" you asked. Who would have more to gain from the deaths of your father and brother than the husband of Christina Kohl, who would gain all the property and chattels of his new wife? A handsome dowry could be expected from such a family as the

Kohls, but how much better would it be to gain their entire holdings?"

Christina had listened spellbound as Ziesolf had related his tale. Her ire rose, however, as he disclosed his suspicions about the Reveles. *It makes a great deal of sense,* she thought, *but could the Reveles really be so avaricious as to seek to murder Father and Frederick so ruthlessly?* She was not sure. *Ziesolf had no evidence of their treachery, but was it plausible? Yes.*

"Mistress Christina?" He asked, attempting to regain her attention. "I am sorry, Herr Ziesolf, but Christina is dead. Now it is only I, Frederick, who is left to carry forth the name of Kohl."

Chapter 7

Arrival in London, October 1309

Item: On October 12th, in the Year of Our Lord 1309, Master Thomas Kohl died from wounds received in bravely repelling a pirate attack on the vessel *der Greif,* bound from Lubeck to the English city of London. Eternal Rest Give unto Him, O Lord.

Recorded this day under my hand, Frederick Kohl

Christina closed the account book with a heavy sigh, her gaze resting on her father's signet ring that now rested on her finger instead of his. She cried no more tears; her eyes had been emptied over the past two weeks. For the first time in her life, she felt truly on her own. She knew Ziesolf was available to advise her, while Trudi was always ready with an encouraging smile and a warm cuddle. It was not the same, however. Despite her independent ways, she had known she always had her father or her mother to guide her, to forbid her from doing foolish things. Now she knew her ultimate counsel was to be her own.

With landfall estimated in less than two days, she realized there were several tasks that needed her attention. She dreaded one more than the rest. *I know I have the responsibility to write to Mother to tell her what has occurred, but, how can I? How do I even begin? And what do I tell her?* These thoughts raced through her head, eliciting no answers, just more questions.

I want to tell her the truth, Father dead, Frederick missing, and I alive. But what if someone else reads the parchment? I would be found out and exposed. This, I cannot risk, she thought to herself unhappily. Picking up the quill, she instead related how the ships had been attacked, resulting in the death of both Thomas and Christina Kohl. At the end, she signed the missive in her bold hand, "Your Devoted Son, Frederick Kohl,"

In her time of grief, will mother notice the message is written in my handwriting, and not that of Frederick? She wasn't sure. She had thought of dictating the letter to Ziesolf, claiming her hand had been injured so she herself could not write. In the end, she had decided to write it herself. *This at least provides a chance Mother may infer the truth.* It was the best she could do without risking the discovery of her deception.

With the letter to her mother written, Christina moved on to her next task. As a young child, some of the happiest days she could remember were when her father had returned to Lubeck from his trading voyages. He always brought back an unusual gift for each of his children from his travels and, being the most impatient of the three, Christina found the waiting time between the arrival of his ship in harbor and when he burst through the door of his house to be agonizing.

"Can I go to wait for him at the dock? Please, Mother, please!" she had begged.

"No, Christina, he will be home when he is ready."

"But why doesn't he come right away? Why must he always make us wait? It is so mean of him!"

Mechtild Kohl had given her daughter a stern look, stilling any further complaints.

She then said, "Your father must first always check the ship's cargo before he comes home. He must know the condition of each item exactly so he may negotiate the best price from his buyers. His reputation would be ruined if he misrepresented the quality of his goods. Would you want your father to be thought of as a cheat and a liar?"

Christina had solemnly shaken her little head. Even at six years old, a child in Lubeck knew being thought of as dishonest was one of the worst things that could happen to a family. After Thomas the Baker had been accused of selling underweight bread, he and his family had been shunned by other townspeople.

Eventually, they had had to leave Lubeck. Christina certainly did not want that to happen to their family. So, after that, she had sat squirming and fidgeting, but always waited silently for her father to come home.

She opened the main hatch in the deck and carefully descended into the dank hold. Although *der Greif* was a stalwart vessel, the musty smell permeating the air was indicative sea water had somehow found its way into the cargo area.

Christina got down on her hands and knees and thrust her small lantern into as many nooks and crannies of the hold as she could access. To her immense relief, she found no signs of pooling water that could, over time, seep into the wooden containers that held the sundry commodities being transported to London.

She next inspected the ropes that held the crates and casks in place. Despite the storm and the attack, she noted nothing had been displaced. She next made an examination of each individual container, albeit a somewhat cursory one, to determine its condition.

She was disappointed to find the seams of one crate, containing a hundredweight of beeswax, had loosened, exposing slivers of its gleaming contents. Christina made a mental note to ask one of the sailors to bind the box together with rope to ensure that, when it was being carried onto the wharf in London, it would not completely split open and spill its contents. *Well, if this is the worst damage, I should consider myself lucky,* she thought. *At least the fur casks seem undamaged*

After examining her father's account book, Christina knew *der Greif's* cargo was extremely valuable: Prussian beeswax, honey, and amber were among the items that would command the highest prices from the English merchants who would purchase the contents of the hold. By far the greatest profits, however, would be from the twenty barrels containing the fur of a tremendous number of one small animal, the northern grey squirrel. These had been procured by her father's agents in Novgorod Rus', where they had been sorted according to quality, place of origin, and the degree and manner in which the pelt had been dressed. The furs were then bound into bundles of forty pelts and packed into casks of from five to ten thousand skins.

According to her father's accounts, the hold of *der Greif* contained nearly one hundred and forty thousand of these squirrel pelts. Furthermore, two of the casks held only *meuvair puratus*, or the white belly fur of the squirrel that had been trimmed from the grey. This premium fur could fetch four pence per pelt. Consequently, her father estimated the total value of the furs at approximately ten thousand, four hundred silver marks, a princely sum. *Even after shares are paid to Father's partners, shipping costs are assessed, and the loss of Heiligen Maria is accounted for, there should still be a considerable profit,* she though with some satisfaction. To Christina, however, the loss of her father and brother were debits that could never be balanced by monetary gain.

As Christina began climbing up from the hold, she was surprised to see the sun had set and the sky was rapidly darkening. A hand reached down to her from above. She gladly took it and was hoisted bodily to the deck. When she twisted around to thank the man who had helped her, she was taken aback to find it was Reiniken, the man who had insulted her on the dock in Lubeck. He gawked at her slightly quizzically for a second, then let out a loud guffaw and clapped her thunderously on the back. The force of his blow nearly sent her sprawling. Barely managing to keep her balance, she turned back toward the mercenary, fearful he had seen through her disguise.

Although his reply once would have angered her, she was instead greatly relieved to hear him say, "Goddam, lad, you better be careful lurking around in the dark from the rest of these lewd bastards! They'll be plugging you in your rear vent if you don't start growing some chin hair soon!"

He laughed loudly at his own joke and moved to help one of the sailors who was making a slight adjustment to the sail.

She stared after him. Her shocked expression slowly transformed into a wide grin as she realized that, rather than being an affront, his coarse joke had been a sign of acceptance. *There is no guile in this man,* she thought to herself. *If he had even the slightest doubt about my true identity, he would have confronted me openly and directly.* Relieved her disguise had held up, she set off to complete duties of her own.

A day and a half later, Christina caught her first glimpse of England. Peering off the starboard beam through a relentless light rain, she saw the steel grey of the water become increasingly punctuated by brown blotches of land. These became increasingly more distinct as they traveled on, eventually separating into more recognizable landforms. Then, they disappeared altogether and there was again only water to every side.

As the sun dropped low on the horizon a flurry of activity caught her attention. Crewmen scurried aloft to furl the great, square-rigged sail. The anchor splashed into the sea and the ship came to rest, riding easily on the relatively calm water.

With a look of exasperation set on her face, Christina searched out Ziesolf, finding him at the forecastle scanning the waters on the lee horizon. "Why are we stopping?" she demanded.

"We have arrived," he replied mildly, still peering out over the sea.

She was confused. She rotated around slowly, straining her eyes in all directions to discern a bit of land that might confirm the man's observation.

Finding none, she turned again to Ziesolf, her staring eyes demanding a more thorough explanation. "We have arrived," he repeated. "We are in the estuary at the mouth of the London River. We wait now for the morning tide which will assist us up the river to the city."

She shook her head in disbelief. When *der Greif* had sailed from the Trave into the Baltic, the opposing river banks had seemed almost close enough to touch. Now, Ziesolf was telling her they were further than the eye could see.

"How far," she began in amazement, "how far is it across the estuary?"

"About eighteen miles," he murmured distractedly, turning to again survey the rapidly darkening waters.

Christina gulped, finding it almost incomprehensible the mouth of the river could really be so wide. Realizing the man desired no further idle conversation, she pivoted away and walked aft, musing ruefully this was only the first of many surprises that undoubtedly awaited her.

As she exited her small cabin in the morning, she was again nearly blinded by the intensity of the brilliant morning sunlight. All traces of the previous day's pervasive rainclouds were gone, replaced by a dome of unsullied azure so intense it made her shield her eyes with her hand. As she strode forward on the deck, she became aware the ship was moving once again. She glanced left and then right, amazed they no longer existed in the midst of an endless watery expanse. Instead, rolling hills of green formed clear boundaries to each side. It was evident to Christina that, while she had slept, the ship had made good progress up the Thames.

Christina moved to the forecastle where she sat on the railing to comfortably observe the unfolding panorama. By early afternoon, the herons, grebes, and swans who had been their companions on the river were being increasingly replaced by a variety of water craft ranging from small one-man boats to ocean-going hulks that dwarfed even *der Greif*. At times, a few of her shipmates would wave to the men on a particular vessel who would bellow "hallo" in response. Alternatively, certain ships would be greeted with particularly rude gestures and shouted insults, which were responded to in kind. Regardless of whether the others were represented as friend or foe, neither they nor *der Greif* deviated from their chosen course in the slightest.

As the day turned toward evening, she noted with some alarm a thickening haze in the distance. She turned and asked one of the crewmen making a slight adjustment to the sail whether this should be a cause for a more cautious approach up-river. The man straightened from his task and, wiping sweat from his eyes, peered ahead to see to what Christina was referring. He chuckled and said, "That be London, young sur. We're getting close."

"Is there a fire in the city?" she said, concern evident in her voice as she imagined the seriousness of a conflagration that would darken the sky to this degree.

"Aye," he replied," about twenty thousand of 'em!"

He laughed, touched his forelock, and went back to work.

Christina felt embarrassed by the naivety of her question. This was quickly forgotten as she marveled at the idea of so many people living together, they could cloud the sky from the fires in their homes. *It seems almost a sacrilege that the work of man can obscure that of God*, she though involuntarily crossing herself. Her theological musings were soon forgotten, however, as they rounded a final bend and the city of London unfolded before her eyes.

How can so many people exist in one place? She murmured to herself totally awestruck. There were now literally hundreds of boats on the river, across which spread an enormous whitewashed bridge that was surmounted by a series of buildings several stories tall. Beyond the docks and quays, solid rows of structures were arranged like waves spreading inland parallel to the river. Her mouth gaped wide open in wonderment.

"It happens to everyone," said a voice from behind her.

She turned to see Ziesolf, who had appeared noiselessly.

"I have seen many cities in my life; Cologne, Novgorod the Great, even Constantinople. None affected me like my first time here. London seemed like more than a collection of wood and stone, almost as if it is a living creature. A beast that will devour one who is not careful, Christina."

She glanced away from the great sight before her. She rose and matched her gaze with that of the man before her. He continued, "I have trained you as best I can. Combined with your speed and natural talent, you are the match of most men in a fight, regardless of the weapon. Now, however, you are entering a battle where your only weapon is your brain. Your opponents now are other merchants, who will use every ruse to deceive and cheat a competitor, especially one as young and inexperienced as you. I will support and guide you as best I can, but I cannot speak for you."

She nodded her head solemnly at his words. She had never lacked in self-confidence, but now a series of nagging self-doubts sent waves of panic through her body. She fought a sudden irrational urge to run to the cabin and hide beneath the furs.

"Most importantly, your true nature must be concealed at all costs. Even the slightest doubt in someone's mind that you are not a man could be catastrophic. If a challenge is made, you are lost. You will be imprisoned or even executed for disguising yourself as a man, an act viewed as unnatural and contrary to both the laws of man and of God. Your ruse must be perfect, always perfect. Do you understand?"

"Of course, I do," she responded brittlely," You've told me so many times. But what choice do I have now, except to follow through with this absurd scheme? One which you convinced me of, I might add!"

Her eyes flashed angrily at the man who stood before her. *Such a grave appearance on his face!* she thought. "You, a grown man, taking advantage of a poor naïve maiden to embroil her in your immoral plots!" she added with all the venom in her voice she could muster.

Shock involuntarily spread across Ziesolf's face, which immediately fell away as Christina's fierceness dissipated into a grin punctuated by a series of low giggles.

"Mark what I said," he said harshly.

As he turned away, however, she discerned that even this most stoic of men must have a sense of humor as a wisp of a smile appeared on his tight lips.

Soon after, the crew of *der Greif* moored the ship on a section of quay dominated by hulks and cogs of what she surmised were other German lands. Some of what their crews were saying was easily understandable while the words of others, though tantalizingly familiar, were almost incomprehensible. This served as a reminder to Christina she was in an alien land and that she must observe carefully and learn quickly if she were to survive. Most importantly, she must do nothing that drew undue attention or interest.

The majority of the men would remain on *der Greif* with only Ziesolf and two of the surviving mercenaries accompanying Christina and Trudi ashore. As the small party stepped onto the quay, Christina peered back at the ship that had been her home for the past weeks. She choked back tears as she recalled the terrible things that had occurred during the voyage: the loss of her brother and the death of her father, whose body now lay preserved in a cask in the hold. She felt a hand touch her shoulder, urging her forward. She straightened and turned, fully aware she had no time right now to mourn the past and that her attention must be fully set on the future.

Within minutes, she was totally disoriented, realizing she could not find her way back to her ship's mooring if her life depended on it. Although the street they walked upon was quite wide, it was absolutely inundated by a diversity of people she had never before witnessed. *The noise of this many different tongues must surely rival the tower of Babel,* she thought, resisting the urge to cover her ears with her hands.   Some were dressed in brilliantly colored velvets, satins, and damask, some in practical woolen and linen garments, while others were clad only in rags or were nearly naked. Here and there a stray dog or pig darted among the waves of humanity that somehow progressed along the streets. Her feelings of claustrophobia were heightened by the terrible stench that issued forth from the grayness beneath her feet. Although at times she could perceive she was walking on a solid stone surface, at others she strode along in a slurry of mud, animal dung, fish and animal remains, and vegetable refuse.   She felt an involuntary desire to reach out for Ziesolf's hand to keep from being swallowed into this miasma.

In time, she became more used to her surroundings and was able to discern individual voices through the noise that had threatened to deafen her. She took the opportunity to glance at the shops that bordered the street. *Such a variety*, she thought, her mouth agape. *Pelterers, fishmongers, and fullers stood side by side with apothecaries and spicemongers. Every conceivable thing is for sale here.* Christina wanted to tarry, to explore this mad, wonderful world, but knew Ziesolf would never continence a delay. *Not now perhaps, but certainly later,* she promised herself.

Eventually, they came to a street quite a bit wider than its predecessors. After a few hundred feet, Ziesolf stopped and motioned toward an imposing timber-framed structure on the left-hand side of the street. Gazing in that direction, Christina observed that a series of shops ran along the ground floor; a goldsmith, a parfumier, an apothecary, and a spice merchant. *No smelly fuller or tanner plying their trades here,* she noted with satisfaction.

In the center of the run of buildings stood a stone entrance arch blocked with a pair of substantial wooden gates reinforced by strong, wrought iron straps. Ziesolf approached the right gate and, taking the rope that hung to its side in hand, pulled down sharply. Immediately, the sound of a large bell pealed sonorously from inside the compound. They waited. A few minutes later, the gate opened and a frowning, middle-aged man appeared, dressed in rich livery.

"God be with you, Peter," said Ziesolf with a slight inclination of his head.

"Hail fellow, well met, Herr Ziesolf," the man replied, his previously disapproving gaze now one of warm greeting.

He quickly appraised the composition of their group, seemingly somewhat surprised by what he saw.

Recovering his composure, the servant bowed slightly and motioned for the party to cross the threshold. Walking forward they entered a large courtyard, bounded by a series of storage buildings on the left, stables and workshops to the center, and domestic structures to the right. The cobbles of the courtyard were exceptionally clean, especially compared to the layers of filth on the streets through which they had just passed. A number of men went busily about their tasks, although they also cast surreptitious glances at the strangers in their midst with interest.

Ziesolf motioned for the two mercenaries to remain outside. Following Peter, he, Christina, and Trudi walked up a flight of broad stone steps, through a stout door, and into a screened passageway that then opened onto the main hall of the manor house. Christina stood still, momentarily frozen in amazement. She estimated the room to be approximately thirty feet wide and twice that in length. Craning her neck upward, she saw the intricately carved beams of the roof arches rose at least forty feet above the stone floor. Diffuse light entered the room through a bank of large windows that were glazed with thick panes of translucent, slightly greenish glass. To the sides of the large central hearth, brilliantly colored wall hangings hung above benches covered in thick cushions. The wealth of the owner was apparent everywhere she looked. *Even the wealthiest burghers in Lubeck have nothing to match this,* she thought, impressed by what she saw. *It is nearly as large as the hall of the Rathaus!*

Engrossed in her appraisal of the room, Christina was surprised by the sound of a door closing. Three figures had appeared at the end of the hallway. The two younger women to the sides were clearly servants, easily identified by the contrast in dress to the central figure who was opulently attired in a cotehardie of thick green brocade over a blue kirtle of what must be extremely fine silk.

It was easy for Christina to infer this figure was the mistress of the house, Matilda, her aunt. In contrast to her exquisite garb, however, she wore a simple lead pilgrim's pendant suspended from a leather thong about her neck, signifying that, at some time in her life, she had made the arduous and peril-filled journey to the Holy Land itself as a penitent.

Perhaps the most striking aspect of the woman was not her dress, but her size. She was so tiny, she seemed absolutely consumed by the rich fabrics she wore. Combined with the tranquil benevolence of her expression, she seemed to be more like a figure in a religious painting than a living person.

As the women walked toward them, Christina was fascinated by the way her aunt seemed to float above the floor, rather than taking steps along it. When they neared, Ziesolf bowed deeply while Trudi made a respectful curtsy. Absentmindedly, Christina nearly followed Trudi's lead before catching herself and making a clumsy bow. *You long-eared ass!* She chided herself angrily. *You nearly gave yourself away in the first minutes we're here.* Her self-incriminations were interrupted, however, as her aunt began to speak.

"God be with you all, Herr Ziesolf, and welcome once again to my husband's home."

What an odd way to phrase a greeting, Christina mused to herself. Not 'my home' or 'our' home, as her mother would have welcomed guests to their house in Lubeck. Instead the woman's words made it seem as if she had no claim to the house at all. *How strange.* Although her aunt spoke German, her pronunciation and inflection seemed a bit peculiar to Christina. *Perhaps it is the customary way of speaking here in England.* Christina began to fear people here might find her speech even more foreign, drawing their attention to her words in the same way her interest had been piqued by those of her aunt.

It was apparent her aunt knew Ziesolf from his previous trips to London with her father. It was also obvious that, with her father's absence, she assumed he was the ranking member of their group and not the bumbling youth or what was clearly a servant girl. Her feelings a bit hurt, Christina thought about correcting the woman's erroneous assumption. Observing Ziesolf had said nothing, however, she decided to follow his lead and remain silent. *For now, at least*, she thought with a bit of satisfaction.

The woman continued formally, "I hope your journey was a pleasant one." This jarred Christina, but then she realized the woman had no way of knowing the terrible occurrences that had transpired. "Herr Kohl is not home at present. I have sent a servant to let him know you have arrived, however. For the time being, may I offer you food and drink?"

Suddenly realizing she had not eaten since before noon, Christina prayed Ziesolf would accept the woman's offer.

She was greatly relieved when he said, "We thank you for your gracious hospitality, Frau Kohl. It has been a long journey and we have important news for your husband, both business and personal."

Her aunt nodded gravely then made a slight gesture to her women, one of whom then moved noiselessly from the room through a door into what Christina assumed to be the buttery or the pantry.

Frau Kohl then said, "I will leave you to your repast now as I have other duties to which I must attend. Hopefully, my husband will return shortly. For now, fare thee well."

At that, the other maid spun on her heal, opening the same door through which Christina assumed they had entered. With practiced grace, her aunt disappeared further into the house, followed closely by the maid. The door clicked shut and they were alone once more.

Soon, the first maid appeared with a goodly platter of bread, cheese, and meat and set it down at one of the tables at the end of the hall. She exited, but quickly returned with a jug of beer and three earthenware cups, then departed again. Christina ate voraciously, raising her gaze periodically to view with interest the pewter and silver tableware conspicuously displayed in her uncle's aumbry. *If my father were here, would we be drinking Rhenish wine from those silver cups instead*? she wondered idly. *No matter*, she decided judiciously, taking a long draught from her cup. *The quality of the beer is excellent.*

Suddenly a magnificently garbed, portly figure appeared from the passageway leading to the exterior, followed immediately by three younger men. As they approached, Ziesolf and Trudi stood and repeated their previous gestures of obeisance. At the same time, Christina rose and executed (what she felt at least) was a bow worthy of an imperial courtier. "God be with you, Ziesolf," her uncle said. Christina was somewhat chagrined he did not extend his greetings to her. "I have been expecting your arrival for a few weeks now, but better late than never I suppose. Is my brother in the solar, or is he still at the quay?" An awkward silence momentarily ensued. Annoyed, Gerhardt Kohl continued, "Well, spit it out man, or have you lost your tongue?" Ziesolf paused momentarily, then said, "I am sorry milord, but the news I have is hard to speak. We were attacked by pirates in the Kattegat and one of our ships was lost. Unfortunately, the life of my master, your brother, was taken as well."

Gerhardt's face blanched as he slowly comprehended the import of Ziesolf's words. He moved unsteadily to his chair at the high table and sat down heavily. He remained silent with his head in his hands for a few moments.

"Wine!" he said eventually, raising his head somewhat.

One of his men hurried off to the buttery, returning quickly with a jug. He reached inside the aumbry and drew out a gilt silver-embossed mazer, which he filled and sat before his master. Her uncle drained the bowl in one gulp, then motioned for another. Taking this in hand, he took another drink, then regarded Ziesolf.

"It seems there is much we need to speak of then, Ziesolf. Let us adjourn to the solar where we may discuss matters more comfortably. I will send one of my wife's maids to attend to your girl. Richard," he turned to one of the young men, "See to the needs of the boy there."

"Come boy," the man identified as Richard spoke briskly to Christina.

"Milord," Ziesolf interjected. "Pardon me, but I believe the young sir should accompany us instead. May I introduce you to your nephew, Frederick." "ah, yes," her uncle seemed momentarily lost in thought. "The young man who is supposed to be apprenticed to me. Well then, come along, Nephew."

They walked through the doorway through which the women had disappeared earlier. Gerhardt Kohl called for one of the maids, instructing her to gather up Trudi and take her to the servant's quarters deeper within the house. While her uncle attended to this, Christina glanced about the solar with interest. After the great expanse of the adjacent hall, the solar seemed almost diminutive by comparison. Upon examination, however, Christina realized the room was not so much small as it was intimate and inviting. A small fire warmed the room and a row of windows allowed the setting sun to infuse the room with a golden glow. Rich tapestries hung from the remaining walls while the floors were covered with thick rugs. Two chairs and a number of benches and stools provided ample seating. There was no bed in the room, alluding to the presence of separate chambers for sleeping somewhere in the house. Fresh sprigs of lavender set about the room filled it with a pleasant odor. Clearly, her uncle was a man who enjoyed his comforts.

Gerhardt settled into one of the chairs, proffering the other to Ziesolf. Ignored, Christina chose a comfortable looking embroidered cushion set upon an ornately carved wooden bench close to the fire. For the next half hour, Ziesolf provided a succinct account of their voyage, interspaced by her uncle's questions. Ziesolf left nothing out, save for details that pertained to the loss of Frederick and her deception.

Nearly lulled to sleep, Christina grew attentive with a start when she heard Frederick's name mentioned. She suddenly realized their journey was no longer the focus of the conversation, but rather her.

Her uncle turned to her and said, "So Nephew, I am very sorry for the loss of your father, but life must move on you know. As he and I agreed, I will take you on as an apprentice. You will live here, learning and working as one of my apprentices, until one day you may become a merchant in your own right."

He turned back to Ziesolf, having nothing more to say to what he believed to be his nephew.

In those few words, her fate for the foreseeable future had seemingly been decided. Christina had imagined she and her uncle would negotiate, to establish a working partnership similar to that which he had had with her father. To dismissively be relegated to the position of an apprentice would not only be demeaning, it would also be impossible. *How long could I live in close quarters with a group of boys before someone noticed I never bathed, never swam, never took my shirt off to work bare-chested in the hot summer sun? How long before someone noticed I did not take my cock in hand to see who could piss the farthest?* She doubted she could maintain the ruse for a week, let alone the years her uncle would string out an apprenticeship.

She also realized this would mean her father's share of the value of *der Greif's* cargo would simply be apportioned to her uncle. Similarly, any of her father's other goods stored in London and perhaps even elsewhere would default to her uncle as well. *No,* she resolved, *unless I say something now, I am lost!*

Christina slowly rose to her feet. She stood silently for a moment until her uncle noticed her, his face assuming an expression of surprise. Ziesolf regarded her as well, his implacable expression impossible to discern.

"Herr Kohl," she began in a formal manner, "I thank thee for your kindness, both in offering to take me on as an apprentice as well as honoring the arrangement you made with my father, may God rest his soul. I cannot, however, agree to accept this position in your house."

Her uncle's expression widened into one of amazement. "And why is it you find it necessary to refuse my kindness?" He queried.

She replied in an even tone, "Because, with the death of my father, I am the heir to his holdings, a Hanseatic merchant in my own right. I cannot hope to oversee this business successfully while also serving as an apprentice. Consequently, I must decline your offer."

Her uncle's previous appearance was supplanted by one of growing ire. His ruddy, round face became even more crimson and his eyes narrowed into mere piggish slits. His hands clenched involuntarily. Then, angry words exploded through his thick lips.

"Ungrateful whelp! You, a merchant? You should be ashamed to even imagine yourself as such. You know nothing, a fact your father must have realized when he begged me to consent to accepting you as an apprentice. Now, he is dead, his body hardly cold, and you deny him one of his final wishes. Your overweening pride disgraces his memory."

He next turned angrily to Ziesolf, "Did you tell him these words to say?"

Ziesolf raised his gaze, stared the angry man in the eyes and replied, "No, my lord. They are his words alone."

"You're a damned liar!" Gerhardt shouted, slamming his fist on the arm of his chair for emphasis.

Ziesolf rose to his full height. Again, he gazed directly into the man's eyes with his one good one; however, this time he had to look down as he towered over Gerhardt by nearly a foot. He spoke softly. "I care not, Herr Kohl, whether you believe me untruthful, each man may have what thoughts they will, answerable only to God and his own good conscience. When he speaks these words aloud, however, he is also answerable to those whom he may offend."

Her uncle appeared confused and more than a little frightened by the other man's thinly-veiled threat.

Kohl spoke hastily, "I am truly sorry, Herr Ziesolf, for my angry words. They were said in haste, without prudent consideration. I did not mean to besmirch either your honesty, nor your honor."

Ziesolf gave a curt nod, tacitly accepting the man's apology, then sat back down in the chair. Gerhardt remained standing, however, focusing his angry attention back on Christina.

"You, your men, and your girl will now leave my house forever. If you so desire, have the body of my brother sent to me and I will ensure he has a proper Christian burial. If not, dispose of his body as you will, adding one more ignoble act to those you have already committed."

Gerhardt took satisfaction in noting how his last words pained Christina and at the tears that formed in the corners of her eyes.

"I will send my men to offload your cargo, bringing it here to my warehouse until it can be further disposed. You may then sail your ship back to Lubeck or off the edge of the world for all I care." He stood implacably, waiting for Christina and Ziesolf to leave.

Christina stood her ground. "And my share?" she queried.

"Ah, yes. What riches await to be thrown into the lap of our newest merchant brother?" Gerhardt said sarcastically. "Very little, I am afraid. By the time the loss of the other ship, due to my brother's negligence I might add, is deducted from the profits, you can consider yourself fortunate if you are not mired in debt. The goods were destined for my storerooms, and that is where they shall be taken. No amount of impudence from you will change that." "Then I will plead my case before the aldermen," she said simply. Gerhardt snorted. "You, before the aldermen? Why do you think they would even agree to listen to you, let alone believe you over me?"

"Because I am in the right and possess the documents to substantiate my claim. I possess a sealed copy of the contract establishing a partnership of the type known as *wedderlegginge* between my father and his investors for the fitting out of the two ships and purchase and disposal of the movables contained therein. In this type of partnership, as you well know, each partner is only responsible for the original amount invested and profits, or losses, are shared in proportion to the capital invested. This agreement has been duly recorded in the *Niederstadtbuch* in Lubeck and will certainly validate my entitlement."

Christina drew a quick breath and continued, "I am very sorry, uncle, that our first meeting should end with such discord between us. I must now see to procuring a place to store my goods as well as make inquiries concerning their sale. I now say farewell, and God keep you." She again executed her courtly bow, turned on her heel, and trod purposefully toward the door. Without looking, she heard Ziesolf follow her lead.

Before she reached the door, however, she heard her uncle say, "Wait . . . please." With curiosity, she turned.

Gerhardt continued, "I . . . I am sorry. Please forgive me for speaking so harshly. The suddenness of your visit and the news of my brother's death have caused me to act shamefully. Your knowledge of commercial law is surprising in one so young, Frederick. Your words reflect well upon you, young man, as well as your willingness to defend yourself against someone whom you believe is committing a wrong against you."

Her uncle was smiling, yet in a way that made her slightly uncomfortable. "Even when the person you are arguing with is your elder, as well as an alderman himself."

Christina smiled wanly back at him, not knowing whether she should apologize or take the man's words as a compliment. For now, she said nothing.

"I will have rooms prepared for you, of course if that is what you wish?" Gerhardt's tone was now almost differential.

Although Christina accepted the offer of lodging, her unease increased. She thought she had done well in presenting her arguments to her uncle, but she was under no illusion they had been so brilliant as to convince him to drop his claim so readily. *Even though we are blood relatives, I do not trust him entirely. Better to be on guard and later find my suspicions baseless than to be ruined through misplaced confidence in this man,* she warned herself.

Later, as Christina walked toward the room where she would be sleeping, she encountered a tearful Trudi waiting for her in the hallway.

"Oh Chris . . . I mean Frederick," changing her words as she remembered she was not to call Christina by her true name. "I hate it here! The other women won't even talk to me, they just ignore me as if I were only a block of wood. They just left me in a little room and shut the door! I'd rather be back in the cabin on the ship than here. Can't I stay with you? I can sneak in later and leave before anyone rises in the morning. I'll be very quiet, no one will even know I'm there! Please!"

Although she knew she would have to say no, Christina was strongly tempted to agree to Trudi's mad plan. As the tears rolled down the maid's plump cheeks, Christina could feel her own eyes begin to cloud. She began to feel uncontrollably weepy as the pressure of the day's events seemed to hit her all at once. She thrust the door to the room open, grabbed Trudi's hand and dragged her inside.

As soon as the stout door shut behind them, the emotions pent up inside Christina suddenly let loose as if a dam had burst. Trudi's tears stopped at the shock of Christina's emotive breakdown. Then she let loose as well, holding Christina's waist tightly and burying her face into her taller mistress's shoulder.

After a few minutes, their sobs began to subside. Christina pushed Trudi gently away. She glimpsed down into the deep blue eyes of her devoted maid, eyes that were now tinged with red. She placed her hand under Trudi's chin and, raising her head slightly, kissed her tenderly upon the lips. The maid's body stiffened slightly, then she attempted to pull Christina closer, her moist red mouth greedily seeking that of her mistress once more.

Christina gently, but insistently, pushed her friend away. She was seriously tempted to succumb to the temptation of Trudi's suggestion. She knew in her heart; however, she could not permit herself be drawn into an act that might imperil her situation in a dangerous new way.

"My dear, sweet Trudi. I love you as much as if you were my very own sister, but I cannot risk my position, which is precarious enough as it is, by agreeing to what you suggest. Even if my disguise as a man is not uncovered, I would be accused by my uncle of bringing debauchery into his household. It will be difficult enough to convince the alderman of my rights as a German merchant without also having to defend myself against an accusation of overt sinfulness. Do you understand?"

Trudi nodded slightly, but she was agreeing out of a desire to please and not because she was convinced.

Christina heaved a tired sigh then went on. "One recognized as a Hanseatic merchant enjoys great privileges and nowhere is this more so than in England. A Hansard is exempt from customs duties, others are not. A Hansard's disputes are handled in a German court, others are not. I cannot risk expulsion from the Hanse by befouling the good reputation of my uncle's house. While I am sure such things do occur, and are disregarded in the homes of others, I do not trust my uncle sufficiently to risk it here."

Christina's head hurt terribly. It seemed as if the entire day had been spent arguing and trying to convince other people they were wrong and she was right. She had to bring this discussion to a close before her brain exploded.

"Besides, we will not remain here forever. When I have sold the cargo, I will search for a house of my own."

Trudi's mood seemed to lighten at the thought of soon leaving Gerhardt Kohl's house. Wasting little time, Christina shooed her maid out the door and to her own room. Absolutely exhausted, she fell fully clothed onto the bed, too weary to do anything else. She drifted off to sleep, her mind troubled by thoughts of what additional problems and pratfalls she may encounter on the morrow.

Chapter 8

Christina awoke the next morning with a feeling of cautious optimism. *Today will be a time for moving forward,* she vowed to herself. Having reached an understanding with her uncle the day prior, she believed she could now set about contacting the English merchants with whom her father had made tentative arrangements for the purchase of *der Greif's* cargo. When that was accomplished, she could begin to make inquiries for the purchase of wool and finished cloth to fill the ship's hold for its return journey to Lubeck. *Perhaps I might even be able to bargain with my buyers for a direct exchange for English goods at a more favorable rate,* she mused. She looked forward to the challenge of besting the other merchants, almost as if it were a game instead of a livelihood.

What then? She thought to herself. *When I have arranged a cargo for der Greif, what about me? I could return to Lubeck on the ship, confess my deception to my mother, and go back to being Christina.* This held no allure for her she realized. Instead, she envisioned a life where she could make her own choices, not those dictated by her mother or a husband. *I will have my own house, with storerooms of my own arranged around a paved courtyard. I will be respected in my own right and, perhaps, someday I may even be asked to become an alderman.* A smile spread across her lips as she dreamed about her future. *But that is then and this is now*, she pulled herself back to reality. *This first thing I need to do is get out of bed!*

She vaulted to her feet and quickly began dressing. Suddenly, her spirits dampened as she realized she had another unpleasant task to perform. *I must request an audience with Johann Revele to inform him the marriage between our two families is now impossible. That, not only one daughter of Thomas Kohl has died, but two.* She wondered how he would take the news. *In good humor*, she hoped, although she pessimistically felt there was scant chance of that.

Christina went down the broad, highly polished wooden stairs and into the small family dining room. Her uncle, who was seated at the table examining a number of documents strewn before him, bade her to join him.

As she was seating herself, he gathered the parchments into a somewhat tidy pile and said in a jocular manner, "Good morning, my boy. Did you sleep well?"

She answered in the affirmative and he directed the servant who was attending him to bring her food.

As the servant scurried away to fulfill her task, Gerhardt asked, "So, Nephew, what plans have you for the day?"

"I had thought to contact the merchants who are to purchase *der Greif's* cargo, to arrange a time when they might inspect the goods. Then, when they have completed offloading the ship. I thought I might begin to procure goods for the return voyage." Christina hesitated, then added, "I must also seek a meeting with Herr Revele, to inform him the marriage between his son and my sister, sisters, is no longer possible."

"Really?" his round face abruptly shone with interest. "And why is that?"

Christina suddenly realized she had neither told her uncle about the death of her sister but had also said nothing about her own sham demise while at sea. She briefly summarized how Margarete had died, then launched into a more embellished tale of her own death.

He eyes narrowed as he asked, "Why did you not bring her body as well as that of your father to London?"

"I wish with all my heart we would have been able to give my sister a Christian burial; however, her body was lost at sea during the fighting," she lied glibly.

"But were you not on the other ship, or possibly even in the water yourself, when your sister was lost?

How can you be certain she was not taken alive by the pirates?"

"Because my maid saw her fall into the water during the thick of the battle. No one else noticed as they were too busy trying to stay alive themselves. She must have been weighed down by her clothes as she disappeared beneath the water and never surfaced."

Christ's blood! She fumed at herself. *The last thing I need is for my uncle questioning Trudi to see if my story matches with hers. I have no doubt about her loyalty, but little confidence in her ability to withstand my uncle's interrogation. As soon as I leave here, I'll find her and make sure she knows what to say.*

She realized her uncle was speaking once more. ". . . sorry for the loss of your sister. It seems tragedy has befallen you doubly, nephew. If it would be of service to you, if you can provide me the names of the merchants your father had arranged to purchase your goods, I can send a man to set a meeting time. I can also send word to Herr Revele, if you wish of course," he said with the same disconcerting smile that had bothered her the day before.

Although she was hesitant about allowing her uncle to become too far involved in her affairs, she decided to accept his offer as she realized she had no way of knowing where the men she sought might be located. She provided him with the names of the English merchants and he left her to find the man who would deliver her messages. She finished her meal and left to find Trudi.

After ensuring Trudi could somewhat accurately attest to the tale she had told her uncle, Christina went outside to the courtyard. Already the day promised to be a hot one, compounded by little breeze finding its way through the surrounding structures. She approached a man who was repairing the tongue of a wagon, asking him if he had seen Ziesolf. The man shook his head without lifting his face from his work, gesturing instead toward two men conversing outside one of the storage cellars.

As Christina walking toward them, she noticed one was Richard, the young man who had been in the company of her uncle yesterday.

She said to him, "Good day to you, Goodman Richard, how fare thee? Would you know the whereabouts of the man who was with me yesterday, Herr Ziesolf?

The other man laughed and poked Richard in the ribs. Richard turned to her and said harshly, "do I appear to be, a nursemaid? If you have lost your man, perhaps you should put a collar about his neck and chain him somewhere where you might find him more easily. Now, away boy, and bother busy men no more!"

Christina's blood began to heat and she was just ready to challenge the man's impertinence when she saw Ziesolf come through the gate and into the courtyard. Marking Richard as a knave and someone to avoid in the future, she fixed him with, what she hoped was her most contemptuous scowl, and walked to meet Ziesolf.

"Is there something wrong?" he asked.

"No. Nothing," she responded curtly

Although he cast a curious glance toward the two men with whom Christina had been talking, Ziesolf said nothing further on the topic. Instead, he reported, "Everything is as it should be aboard *der Greif*. The guards I posted last night are still in place and most of the other men are sleeping off the ill effects of their first night in port in weeks." "Good," she replied. "I have sent word to those who are to purchase our goods. Hopefully, I can complete a swift sale."

Ziesolf raised the brow over his one good eye and asked, "How exactly is it you sent word?"

"My uncle offered to contact the English merchants on my behalf. Why? How else was I supposed to notify them we had arrived, knock on every door in London until I found them?" she answered sarcastically, still smoldering from Richard's impertinence.

The two men at the other end of the courtyard glanced their way in interest.

Ziesolf lowered his voice so it was barely audible to Christina.

"You now have presented your uncle with the opportunity to say whatever he wants to your buyers, perhaps informing them in advance they are no longer trading with Thomas Kohl, but his inexperienced boy instead. I have no trust in a man who, in one instant, is ready to throw his kin out of his house, while he swears he has your best interest at heart in the next. This may well have been a very serious mistake, girl."

Christina flushed bright red and hissed, "If I am to make a permanent life here, I will have to place a bit of my trust in others besides you, Herr Ziesolf. Other than you, who would imagine the entire city of London is plotting against them?"

He studied her carefully, then replied simply, "Your father."

He paused a moment, then said, "I will be at the ship."

He turned and left.

Does he have to find fault with everything I do? Perhaps I should just rip out my tongue, providing reason for him to speak in my stead! Anger passed through her body in waves. *Sooner or later, I have to stand on my own feet. I am not so prideful I believe I am perfect. If mistakes are made, so be it. I will learn from them and know better in the future,* she rationalized.

She re-entered the house in a foul mood. It had only just begun to abate when her uncle entered the solar.

"Good news," he proclaimed rather formally. "I have received word from the skinner Master William Shipton he would be delighted to meet with you at your ship early this afternoon to inspect your cargo of furs and, should you come to an agreement as to their purchase, arrange their swift conveyance."

Christina's mood lightened considerably. This was the best news she could hope to receive. Although the hold of *der Greif* held many marketable commodities, the cargo of furs was far and away the most valuable. She tried to keep the excitement from her voice as she thanked her uncle.

"I am only too happy to help. I hope this is the beginning of a relationship that's warmth is rivaled only by its profitability."

"As do I," she responded. *I have clearly misjudged you uncle,* Christina thought, a bit ashamed of her earlier reservations concerning his motives.

Her uncle sat down at the table, returning to the documents he had been examining the previous evening. Although the meeting was still a few hours off, Christina was too eager to wait patiently. She said farewell to Gerhardt and departed for the waterfront. As she left, he gazed at the door through which she had just passed, a hard look fixed on his face that offered no hint of his earlier friendliness.

Christina concentrated hard on retracing her steps from the previous day. If anything, the streets seemed even more crowded, more raucous, and to smell even worse in the heat of the day. Frustratingly, she lost her way a couple of times, but was quickly able to return to her course without too much of a delay.

Soon, she was relieved to find herself back at the river. Turning downriver, she found *der Greif* moored where they had left her the previous day.

She thought about climbing on board but decided against it. *I'm sure Ziesolf will be there, ready to tell me something else I've done wrong. To hell with him!* She thought; however, even thought of receiving another admonishment failed to deflate her buoyant mood.

Instead, she gazed along the waterfront with interest. Upriver from her ship, she saw a massive hulk resting heavily in the water. *It must be nearly a hundred lasts!* She thought, impressed by its hold capacity of almost two hundred tons. *One day I will have a fleet of these ships, traveling the seas between all of the great Hanseatic kontors; Bergen, Bruges, Novgorod, and, of course, London.*

She turned to survey the view in the opposite direction and saw two men hurrying up the quayside toward her.

"Hail, fellow," one said, "Might you know where I might find Master Kohl?"

"If you desire Master Thomas Kohl, I am grieved to say he rests now with the angels. Should you desire Frederick Kohl, his son, I am he."

"Good day to you then, Master Kohl. I am William Shipman. I apologize for my early arrival but, as other business brought me to Thameside this morning, I found it convenient to impose on your good graces to conduct our business sooner rather than later."

"Yes, of course," Christina replied, bothered by a vague feeling she had somehow been maneuvered into a disadvantage.

Once on board the cog, Christina called to a couple of the ship's crewmen to hoist one of the barrels of pelts onto the deck. With the help of a few of their fellows they were finally able to heave the heavy container from the hold. One of the sailors stood the barrel upright on the deck and used a prybar to remove the head, revealing a mass of gleaming grey fur.

Christina breathed a silent sigh of relief as a musty smell wafted into her nostrils. *Thank God*, she thought. If water had somehow found its way into the cask, or if the pelts had been improperly cured, the furs would have molded and been absolutely worthless. The distinctive smell of decay was not present, however. This was a very good sign the pelts' value was undiminished.

At a slight nod from Shipman, his servant carefully began to unpack the barrel's contents, which were tied into parcels of one hundred. Twice, the English merchant asked for one of the bundles to be handed to him. With a deft flick of his silver handled knife, he cut the cord holding the pelts together and they parted so he might examine them individually. He ran his fingers through the fur, assessing the fullness, thickness, texture, and richness of color of each. When the barrel was empty, a considerable section of the ship's deck was covered by a dense carpet of squirrel pelts.

Shipman stood silently for a number of moments in silent contemplation of the merchandise laying before him. Christina chafed with impatience but knew better than to attempt to hurry the man's evaluation of the value of the barrel's contents. Finally, he turned toward her and Christina's heart leapt into her mouth.

"It is a goodly lot, Master Kohl, one which I do have interest in purchasing. I must, however, consult with certain of my investors before I may render an offer."

Damn your eyes! Christina seethed. *Why in hell can't you just tell me now?*

The merchant continued, "If you will be so kind as to present yourself at my house in two hours, I will be fully prepared to negotiate a reasonable transaction."

Having no alternative, she acquiesced. The two men departed and Ziesolf approached her.

"Was an agreement reached?" he asked.

"Not really," she admitted through gritted teeth. "I am to go to his house in two hours to discuss the terms of sale."

"I see. Merchants everywhere want to do this little dance, designed to put their opponent off balance. He will be in the comfort of his own home, while you will feel strange and out of place. Perhaps you will feel so uncomfortable you may make a poor bargain, just so you can leave. Who knows?"

Christina cursed under her breath. "I'd already figured out as much myself; however, there's little else I could have done other than to agree. Should I have asked him to come instead to my uncle's home? Wait, wasn't I advised to not let my uncle involve himself too much in my affairs? I couldn't really order him from his own home so I could conduct my business in privacy, could I?" she asked mockingly.

"No," Ziesolf admitted, "I simply worry you are ill-prepared to bargain with this man. I have taught you how to best a man with sword, knife, and fist and you have learned well. For this fight, however, I have little in the way of experience I may pass on to you, other than what little I have observed from your father. I can only advise you to be cautious and suspect hidden motives behind any offers of concession."

She was taken aback by Ziesolf's admission. She had come to believe him to be the master in everything and always she the inept and slow-witted pupil. Now, in this instance, it was she who must take the lead. Christina resolved to meet this challenge successfully.

Two hours later, she was seated in a chair in Shipman's office. They sat across from one another in the well-lit room, with Ziesolf standing a few steps behind her right shoulder. She gawked at the parchment before her in disbelief.

"How can this be? The red and black pelts are worth at least three marks per hundred, while the grey should fetch at least six, if not seven. This was the prospective bargain you made with my father. Yet, you now offer only two marks for each!"

Shipman gazed at her with a tired smile upon his face. "I am sorry for your disappointment, Master Kohl, but you must realize the value of all merchandise changes over time, sometimes drastically. One month ago, I was able to purchase a similar cargo to yours, at the price I am proposing to you now. As a result, I have little need for additional furs. It is only out of respect for your esteemed father I even make this offer to you now."

Christina felt sick to her stomach. She had thought it would be so easy to become a grand merchant, to spend her days accumulating wealth and prestige through an enviable series of highly profitable transactions. *How could I have been so wrong*? She thought. *If I accept Shipman's offer, I will hardly make any profit at all on the commodity that comprises the majority of my cargo. Even worse, my father's partners in Lubeck will actually lose money!* It was going to be difficult enough to convince them to have faith in Thomas Kohl's young heir, but it would be well-nigh impossible if they experienced a loss in their first dealings with him!

The English merchant stared at her from across the table expectantly, a slight, disarming smile fixed upon his thin lips. *What is this man's game? Is he merely bargaining, expecting to negotiate a slightly better exchange?* "I would be willing to accept five for the grey, if you held to the agreed price of three for the others, "she ventured.

"I am afraid two marks per hundred is the very best I can do, Herr Kohl. I would advise; however, you to consider my offer very carefully. There are Hanseatic ships arriving in London every day. If I am able to procure a more favorable bargain elsewhere, I will be unable to purchase your furs at any price. Perhaps you would care for some wine while you make your decision?"

Christina fought the urge to turn to Ziesolf, to ask him what she should do. She knew that, if she did, it would confirm what the skinner probably already supposed, that the young man in front of him had no idea what he was doing. *Do I?* she asked herself. *This is more important than making one profitable sale, this is a test of whether I can truly be a successful merchant or just an arrogant girl who plays at being something she is not.*

She decided to risk everything: the sale, the returns to her father's investors, her acceptance among the skinners and mercers of London as well as by the German merchants. Forcing all fear of failure from her mind, Christina met Shipman's gaze steadily and calmly stated, "No, thank you for your kind offer of wine, but I am afraid I have no more time to spend here. I must decline your offered price for my furs as well. Such fine pelts should draw interest among the other skin merchants of London, especially those whose warehouses are not already bursting from previous purchases," she added with a tinge of sarcasm.

At her last words, small furrows involuntarily creased Shipman's forehead, although his facial features remained expressionless. He stood and bowed slightly. Recognizing she was being dismissed, Christina arose and, after a slight nod toward the English merchant, left the house the way she had entered, as no servant was dispatched to show her politely out. She sensed Ziesolf following slightly behind. When she reached the yard, she doubled over and retched her guts out, sour yellow bile issuing from her mouth onto the clean cobblestones.

"Come." said Ziesolf, "Do not give this man the satisfaction of seeing your weakness."

She drew herself erect despite immediately experiencing a feeling of lightheadedness. "Damn you, "she turned and swore at Ziesolf, although it could have also been directed through him, the walls of the house, and at Shipman. She was too sick at heart to really care. *At all of them, I suppose,* she thought wearily.

They trudged silently back toward her uncle's house. A couple of times, Ziesolf attempted conversation, but she completely ignored the man's existence. As they walked through the sturdy front gates, she saw her uncle busily supervising the unloading of a small cart into one of the warehouses that ringed the courtyard. Noticing their arrival, he gave a friendly wave and walked toward them.

Oh, God no, she thought. *The last thing I want to do right now is to have to describe the details of my failure to my uncle.*

Gerhardt Kohl seemed to be in a buoyant mood, smiling widely and clapping Christina on the back in a friendly gesture.

"So, was my nephew's first transaction with an English merchant a profitable one?"

Even in her morose state, Christina noticed something about her uncle's tone that didn't seem quite right, although she could not place her finger on exactly what that something was. She disregarded her misgivings for the moment and gave a brief summary of how the negotiations had proceeded.

An expression of sympathetic concern appeared on his jowly face.

"Hmm, yes, I have heard the arrival of several Hanseatic ships in the past few weeks has glutted the fur market in the city for the time being. That is only a temporary problem, however. If you wait a few months, the demand will return greater than ever. The wealth of this realm is inexhaustible, the desire for new garments unending. Mark my words, Nephew, you will make a profit on your goods yet." "But I cannot wait for months!" She blurted. "I must procure a new cargo for *der Greif* and dispatch it back to Lubeck or elsewhere. But I cannot begin to purchase a new cargo while the ship's hold is filled with the last. Not to mention the fact damp may eventually begin to seep into the goods, diminishing their value even more. Each day the ship remains in port, my debts will increase."

"Well, then. Why do you not just move your cargo into my warehouse for the time being, at least until the market for your furs rises?" Gerhardt asked.

Her immediate reaction was to politely decline her uncle's offer, but then she held her tongue and reconsidered. She could neither immediately sell her cargo, nor could she allow it to remain on board *der Greif* indefinitely. She had refused to move her goods into his stores previously, but her circumstances had changed since then. Now, his offer seemed generous rather than suspect, logical rather than suspicious.

She said, "Yes, uncle. Thank you for your kind offer. I agree this would be the best thing to do."

From behind her shoulder, she heard Ziesolf say, "Perhaps, Herr Frederick, you should take some time to consider other alternatives before you move your goods here. You could try contacting another of the skinner's guild to see if a better offer may be arranged?"

Christina was tired . . . and exasperated. *Perhaps. Perhaps. Perhaps. Perhaps! I cannot put things off, hoping they will eventually work out right in the end. I need to decide on a course of action that moves me forward. If I warehouse my goods, I can arrange a return cargo. It's as simple as that.* She knew Ziesolf did not trust her uncle, neither did she completely. But Gerhardt's offer was the best she had at the moment.

"No, Herr Ziesolf. I need no further time to consider my answer. We will begin to transfer *der Greif's* cargo at my uncle's earliest convenience." Gerhardt's smile broadened and he said, "Good. It is decided then. I will tell my man Richard to arrange for carts to carry your merchandise here. Please excuse me now, however, as I must return to my work."

After a few steps, her uncle suddenly turned back. "Christ's bones! I had almost forgotten. Herr Revele has sent word he will see you at Vespers this evening. Would you like me to accompany you?"

Christina gawked at her uncle, for a minute dumbfounded she would soon be confronted by another unpleasant audience, another litany of deceptions and half-truths, another person she must convince she is someone she is not. *No,* she thought, *remembering her uncle's probing questions earlier that morning. The less he hears my story, the less reason he has to doubt it.*

"I thank you, uncle, but you have done enough to assist me already. I will speak to the chief alderman on my own."

For a second, it seemed to Christina his faced hardened somewhat, then his smile returned. "As you wish, Nephew, as you wish," he said, turning and walking back toward the men at the cart.

Suddenly, she heard Ziesolf whisper, "This is dangerous business, girl. I thought we had agreed to not let your uncle become entangled into your business."

She turned and replied, "Yes, but what else is it you want me to do? Sell *der Greif's* cargo at a ridiculous loss? Let it rot on board until prices go back up? It is easy to choose the best of a number of good alternatives, but have you never had to choose the least harmful of a number of bad ones? She didn't wait for a reply. She walked into the house, went to her room, and shut the door behind her. She desired nothing more than peace and quiet until her meeting with the chief alderman.

Chapter 9

She stood outside the imposing manor house of the chief alderman not really knowing what to do next. Ziesolf had insisted on accompanying her despite her protests to the contrary.

"London has many dangers," he had warned.

"Yes, I know," she had replied sarcastically. "Cutpurses and cutthroats around every corner just waiting for poor helpless me to wander into their grasps."

"Not all of the threats may be blamed on the violent and the desperate."

His response had puzzled her somewhat. "What do you mean by that?" she had asked.

"Just that it's always good to have an extra pair of eyes," he had replied. "Besides, will you be able to find the chief alderman's house on your own?"

Christina considered whether to point out to Ziesolf he was one eye short of a pair but decided she did not know whether her intended jest would offend the man. Instead, she agreed to let him accompany her, although she made him promise to wait outside the house while she went inside.

They had arrived somewhat early as the bells at nearby All Hollows church had yet to signify the hour of vespers. She ogled the building before her in undisguised awe. It was the largest private home she had ever seen, rivaling even the rathaus in Lubeck for sheer size and architectural sophistication. This was not a half-timbered prosperous merchant's home such as her uncle's, indicative itself of prosperity and good-standing. This was a structure that must rival those of the nobility themselves.

The first thing she had noticed as she approached was the house itself fronted the street. The other necessary structures; stables, warehouses, and workshops must be hidden behind. This unusual placement of the plot's buildings focused the viewer's attention on the magnificence of the main structure. *There is little need for that*, Christina thought, consciously shutting her mouth which had been gaping wide like that of the rudest bumpkin.

The lavish use of glazed windows all along the front aspect of the house intimated a hall of large proportions rested within. The building seemed to be on fire as the setting sun reflected various hues of red from the surface of the glass, each pane like a precious jewel turned in the hand to reflect a candle flame. The entire building was made of a yellowish stone, with decorative lintels well-placed above the mullioned windows and doorways.

No thatched or tile roof crowned a building of this splendor; instead, innumerable slate tiles formed an impervious barrier to the elements. A thick wall of the same stone that rose to a height of eight feet barred rapt passersby from approaching too closely. Ziesolf crossed the street and began a conversation with two shabbily dressed men loitering there. Christina walked forward, giving no sign she knew him whatsoever.

The wall was broken by a pair of intricately patterned wrought iron gates, before which she now stood. She reached for the bell pull that hung to the side of the right gate, then hesitated. The material wealth on display before her made her feel small and unworthy. She resisted the urge to turn toward Ziesolf.

Just then, the inset gate opened and a man dressed in distinctive household livery appeared.

He bowed and asked, "Would you be Frederick Kohl?"

Christina gulped and nodded.

He quickly regarded her up and down, appraising her with slight distaste as if she were a day-old fish.   Apparently satisfied to at least a minimal degree, he asked rhetorically, "If it be your pleasure, young sir, to please follow me?"

She entered the yard, which was finely flagged with granite pavers of a similar hue to the manor's roof. The man then led her to the massive oaken front doors that arose to a height of what must have been twenty feet. They passed through a more modest inset door and into a spacious white-washed entrance hall with walls nearly covered with thick tapestries depicting what she supposed to be scenes from the life of Christ.

Before her rose a stairway constructed of a dark polished wood that was wide enough for four people to walk abreast. An intricately carved newel post depicting a hunter pursuing a stag formed the end support for a balustrade that formed the right boundary of the stairs. The stone wall along the left side was periodically interspaced with large lanthorns which cast a warm glowing light through their translucent horn panes.

She was interrupted from her contemplation of the finer details of the house when she noticed the servant had ascended the first five steps and had then turned, beckoning her to follow him. She stepped forward, climbing twenty-six stairs and negotiating two landings before she arriving at the solar chamber. As with everything in the house, the dimensions were huge, encompassing a space as large as her uncle's great hall. Everything about the furnishings indicated material wealth and personal comfort. The whitewashed plaster walls were set off with wall hangings of red, blue, and orange dyed wool, making the room seem bright and cheerful. Cushions and canvas-lined draperies were spread across benches and chairs in hues of mulberry, lilady, and applebloom. A number of tables, stools, and chests completed the room's furnishings. A massive fireplace with a carved mantel dominated the side of the room opposite the uniformly placed bank of windows.

Seated at the far end of the room on two beautifully carved chairs were who she assumed to be Herr Revele, the chief alderman, and his wife. Christina stood for a few seconds, then approached them with trepidation, as neither had motioned her forward, nor made any other gesture or sound that might indicate an invitation. When she was approximately ten feet from the couple, she executed a deep bow. The alderman made a slight gesture with his right hand, which she interpreted as an invitation to speak.

"Good eve to you, milord and milady," she began carefully, "I hope I find you both in good health."

At that, Herr Revele arose and replied, "And good eve to you, Herr Kohl. I welcome you to our home and share your grief for the loss of your father and sister."

Ah, thought Christina, he comes directly to the point. *It is obvious he has been appraised of what has occurred. Was it by my uncle or through his own sources, I wonder?*

She suddenly realized the alderman was waiting for her to speak. She had carefully rehearsed what she had hoped to say, beginning with a summary of the events that had occurred at sea. Clearly, there was no need to relate those details now.

"I thank you for your kind words, Herr Alderman. I may only hope they both sit now among God and his angels."

Revele said nothing more, only looked at her expectantly.

She continued, "Yes. Well, um, Herr Revele, I requested this audience for two reasons. One is to present myself as my late father's heir, with the intent I will assume his affairs, claiming the rights and responsibilities of a merchant of the Hanse here in England."

Revele's steely grey eyes now made a swift appraisal of Christina from top to bottom.

Afterwards, he said, "How old are you?"

Taken aback, Christina blurted out, "Sixteen years old, but . . ."

Revele interrupted her, musing, "So young, Frederick Kohl, so very young. Now you wish to be recognized as a master merchant. But we will discuss this petition in more detail at a later time. Now, you said you wished to discuss another matter as well?"

"Um, yes," Christina felt a sudden blush flush her face. "That is to inform you that, obviously, the marriage of my sister to your son cannot take place." For the first time, a slight smile creased the alderman's face. "Yes, I do see how it would be very difficult to wed my son to a dead woman, especially one whose body is missing. Ah, if only we had the corpse!" the man chuckled at his own unseemly jest. Suddenly, a voice cried, "Father!" from a corner of the room.

Turning about, Christina was surprised to see a thin, sad-faced boy rise from a chair behind her where he had been silently sitting.

Herr Revele said, "Come, Albrecht, and stop lurking about in the shadows. Say hello to our guest, Herr Kohl, from Lubeck."

As Albrecht Revele strode to the front of the room, Christina was shocked to see he was in fact a young man, probably in his mid-twenties. He was quite short, perhaps as much as a head shorter than herself. Despite the richness of his garb his garments hung loosely about his nearly fleshless body.

A full shock of hair, as pale as overworked flax, crowned his head. A face as pale as if it had never beheld the sun was dominated by a pair of huge, light blue eyes framed by white eyelashes that exerted an almost hypnotic effect on Christina. *This creature holds very slight resemblance to the handsome young man in the miniature Margarete had gloated over,* she thought with amazement. She knew she shouldn't stare at him but found it nearly impossible to look away.

The young man's father seemed to ignore her reaction, however, raising his arm and placing it warmly about his son's slight shoulders.

The alderman said, "Herr Kohl, let me introduce my son to you, Albrecht Revele. Albrecht, this is Frederick, the brother of Margarete, the girl you were to marry. I am sorry to say she is dead. It seems she drowned at sea. Perhaps she discovered the true nature of her betrothed and decided a bellyful of sea water was preferable to a marriage to you?"

Christina was shocked at the man's cruelty to his own son. She knew she should remain silent, but his harsh words demanded a rebuke.

Before she could speak, however, Albrecht said, "Please excuse my father's jest, Frederick. He has a peculiar sense of humor, one with which I am full accustomed. I will add your father and your sister Margarete to my prayers this evening."

Christina was taken aback by the contrast between the father's boorishness and the son's civility. His interjection had, however, stayed her from saying something that would have certainly had an adverse effect on her future in London. Instead, she replied to Albrecht and ignored his father's comment completely.

"Thank you for your kind words, Herr Revele. I must, however, clarify one point concerning my family's misfortune. It was not my sister Margarete who died during the voyage, it was my sister Christina. Margarete had succumbed to a fever just prior to our departure. My father then decided that Christina should take her place. It was my younger sister Christina who drowned."

She hoped she had related the convoluted tale coherently.

"So, it seems two Kohl girls chose death over marriage to you, Albrecht. That seems a bit excessive, even for you, don't you think?"

The alderman glanced toward his seated wife with a smile, as if urging her to join him in the enjoyment of his jest. She remained expressionless, however.

Once again ignoring his father's painful jibe, Albrecht said, "I will add Christina to my prayers as well, Frederick. Please have a seat, now, you have been standing far too long. May I pour you a cup of wine? It is Rhenish and quite tasty, if I do say so myself."

Christina hesitated until the older Revele gestured toward an adjacent chair. She was finding this verbal sparring between father and son tiresome. She realized, however, there was danger here as, although she was revulsed by the father's crude comments, she must do nothing to insult the man who held such power over her future fortunes.

Albrecht handed her a well-crafted cup inset with polished green stones, then sat on a nearby bench covered with an intricately woven white drape covered with ermine spots and quatrefoils. The wine was a deep blood red. She took a genteel sip, forcing herself not to just gulp the cup's entire contents in one draught to still her nerves.

The elder Revele began again.

"Well, it would seem this contract was cursed from the beginning. But a contract is a contract, don't you agree, Herr Kohl? Certainly, a master merchant of the Hanse, or even someone who aspires to recognition as such, cannot believe this is not true."

Christina was confused, not knowing exactly how to respond to such a question.

"You seem unsure, Frederick. Perhaps I need to explain myself more simply to someone so young. I often find this necessary with Albrecht, even though he is not so young anymore." He glanced toward his son who met his gaze evenly. If you made a contract with a mercer in London to deliver, oh let us say, twenty barrels of this fine Rhenish wine here."

He held up his cup.

"Now, knowing he has contracted with you, said mercer declines to purchase the cargoes of other ships, even if it is at better terms. At long last, you appear, but with a sad tale that pirates had stolen your cargo and you had not even one drop of wine to begin fulfilling your contract.

Agreed, you have been hurt by your unfortunate loss. But you must also sympathize with the mercer who has suffered a loss as well. He has no wine, even though he could have made an even greater profit through purchasing other cargoes. Perhaps he even has buyers whose demands he cannot fulfill; thus, impinging his good name among the other merchants. So, what does the mercer do?"

Christina knew the answer to this question, although she had no idea where Revele's explanation was going. "He brings a complaint before the aldermen." *Are we now back to discussing my worthiness as a merchant?* she wondered. *Is this some type of test?*

"Very good, Frederick, very good!" He congratulated her response, although she didn't understand quite why. "And, confronted with the mercer's grievance, what do the aldermen do?"

This question seemed so elementary to Christina she couldn't believe she was being asked for a response.

"They would ask to see the contract, of course," Christina replied.

If this is the extent of his questions, it would seem anyone could attain merchant status. She thought rather primly.

"Yes! Of course, of course! The contract, of course!" Revele laughed and drew a deep draught of his wine.

Christina was now thoroughly bewildered. *What is he getting at?* she wondered.

"And if the contract calls for you to deliver twenty barrels of wine, by a certain time, to a certain place, and you do not, you default on your contract and you are liable." All mirth had disappeared from Revele's voice. "Unless conditions are stipulated otherwise, you must reimburse the mercer for the damage to his trade, regardless of your own unfortunate losses." Christina's eyes began to lose focus and her stomach suddenly wished nothing more than to cover the floor with red wine and bile. She now realized the alderman's purpose in detailing his example. She asked, "I suppose a marriage contract exists?"

Revele's overstated sense of humor returned. "Ah, such a sharp lad! I thought I had wasted my example on you, but no, you are too clever not to see my point!"

He laughed and clapped his hands.

"And I don't suppose any pertinent extenuating conditions are contained in the contract," she asked rhetorically as, if there had been, the alderman would never have broached the subject in the first place. "No, unfortunately no. For who could have foreseen the demise of not just one Kohl daughter, but two? Your father was very clever, you see, he referred only to the marriage of "a daughter," and not once by name. We had discussed the one named Margarete to such an extent that the odd fact her name was not mentioned in the contract completely escaped me. Imagine that! I, the chief alderman, had almost been duped!"

His face suddenly grew serious.

"I don't suppose you have any other sisters at home, do you?"

She shook her head in the negative and his expression brightened.

"Well then, it is settled," he said, staring at her expectantly.

Still completely baffled, she asked, "What is it that is settled?"

"The contract, the contract! What do you not understand?" His mood now turned to one of impatience.

"I . . . I am sorry, Herr Revele, but I know nothing of this contract."

"I see," he said. "Well then, under the circumstances I see the cause of your ignorance. I will have a copy prepared for you. For now, there is only one salient point we need to discuss, that of the bride's dowry."

"Dowry?" she asked incredulously.

"Yes, the dowry. You see, my son was absolutely smitten by the miniature your father presented of your sister. He has done nothing but pine since he was told of her loss. Add to this the fact he has turned down the fair daughters of numerous other men of good standing and wealth, holding himself true to the one he had been promised. Can you not perceive the depth of his loss?"

Christina glanced toward Albrecht, who began to speak. His words were cut short though as his father mildly remarked, "You may go now, my son."

Albrecht's face flushed red in marked contrast to the pallor of his skin. He rose and worried his bottom lip between his clenched teeth. Again, he looked as if he were about to say something.

This time, the alderman shouted angrily, "Leave the room!"

The young man stood frozen for a few seconds, as if weighing the price of defying his father. He then seemed almost to wilt, becoming even smaller and more insignificant. Tears seemed to fill his enormous eyes and he gaped helplessly at Christina. He then shambled from the room through a side door, shutting it quietly behind him.

"Now, yes, where were we?" Revele asked. "The matter of the dowry. In the marriage contract, your father promised a gift of six hundred silver marks to accept his daughter into our family."

"Six hundred marks?" Christina said, relegated to simply repeating each astonishing fact the alderman disclosed.

So, on top of everything else, I have a debt to the most important person to me in London of six hundred silver marks! I have nowhere near that much money available to me in England, unless I sell my cargo, which, of course, I can't. By the Virgin's sweet blood, what else can go wrong?

"Yes," he continued, "That is the agreed upon sum. Now, I have heard about your difficulties in securing a suitable price for your squirrel pelts. Again, I offer my condolences."

How could he know about my meeting with Shipman already? It only occurred a couple of hours ago! Did he have something to do with the skinner's pitiful offer? Her thoughts raced wildly.

Revele continued. "It seems you are beset by calamity, young Kohl. I want you to know I am not an unreasonable man. There is a way I might help you see clear of this debt, however. What would you say to an agreement that, if you have not paid your debt to me in a fortnight, that I will purchase your furs at the current price of two marks per hundred? This will clear your family's obligation to mine and even leave some profit for you."

A bloody fortnight? She thought bitterly. *Why prolong my agony even that long?* She saw she had no chance of selling her pelts to anyone at a higher price within two weeks, or even two years for that matter, as long as the chief alderman conspired against her. With the additional burden of paying the dowry, she would certainly incur a large loss for her father's investors, even if she took not a penny for herself.

His eyes narrowed as he fixed her with a shrewd expression.

"I perceive you have no liking for this offer."

She glared back at him in stony silence, not even dignifying his statement with a reply.

"There is one other possible alternative," Revele said teasingly.

Christina's attention was immediate. "Yes?"

"I quite like you, Frederick. You seem to be a worthy young man, with both ambition and intelligence. Furthermore, you are the heir to one of the wealthiest and most respected families in Lubeck. There were several good reasons why the match between Albrecht and your sister was advantageous to both our families."

Christina's head was spinning. She had no idea where Revele's line of reasoning was now heading.

Unexpectedly, the alderman now peered intently at his wife, who had largely been ignored throughout the entire duration of the audience. She rose and went to the door through which Albrecht had exited, opened it, and beckoned to someone outside.

Christina heard a swishing of cloth, followed immediately by the appearance of a fashionably dressed young woman through the doorway. She wore a particolored cotehardie over a rich vermillion, tightly-fitted kirtle Christina believed could have been fabricated of silk. Her lustrous, dark brown hair was parted in the center and platted into two long braids that were draped in front of her ears, brought back to the crown of her head, and covered with a gold mesh crespine.

The girl moved quickly to the front of the room, followed by the alderman's wife. She curtsied to Herr Revele, though it might be better judged as a bird-like little hop. She then turned to Christina and cast her eyes downward demurely.

Christina was taken aback by the perfection of the girl's features. A high forehead, prominent and symmetrical cheekbones, and almond-shaped, sea green eyes were noticeable facets of her beauty. Christina hoped the girl had not noticed she was staring.

Herr Revele said, "Yes, she is beautiful, is she not?"

Christina flushed, though nodding slightly in agreement.

"Frederick Kohl, this is my daughter, Katharine. Katharine, this is the brother of the young woman your brother was to marry before her unfortunate accident at sea."

At that moment, the young woman lifted her eyes and met Christina's gaze squarely. Christina was shocked to realize that, what she had supposed to be an act of modesty, had merely been the other woman taking the opportunity to examine every part of her body in detail, as if Christina were entirely naked to her scrutiny.

"I am very happy to meet you, Frederick. If your sister's figure was as pleasing to the eye as yours, sir, I can only doubly mourn my brother's loss," Katharine said, her mouth pursing provocatively.

She then parted her full, red lips slightly, revealing small, white teeth that she explored with the tip of her tongue. She then laughed lightly and looked to her father expectantly.

The alderman smiled back at his daughter and turned to Christina.

"Well, it seems as if you have made a favorable impression on my daughter as well. So be it. My alternative is that we stick to the original bargain, with some very important modifications of course. You will marry my daughter, Katharine, Frederick."

"Marry? Me?" was the most intelligible response Christina could muster. "I realize this is sudden, but it does make sense. Our families will be united as originally intended. Perhaps I will even forget the dowry owed to me, that is of course if we can come to an arrangement over bride-price."

He smiled again, increasingly reminding Christina of a fox used to free range in the chicken yard.

"Therefore, you have my offers before you, Frederick. One: Pay the six-hundred-mark debt owed to me. Two: Sell me your cargo of pelts at the agreed upon price of two marks per hundred. Three: Agree to wed Katherine. Since I set a fortnight for you to pay your original debt, I will allow the same amount of time for you to make your decision. I will have one of my clerks draw up a new contract containing these additional stipulations. Will you be at the house of your uncle tomorrow?"

Christina nodded, having no other apparent recourse to propose.

Revele's daughter smiled at Christina enigmatically, then said in a throaty near whisper, "I am certain we can make each other very happy, Frederick. I know ever so many fun games we can play."

The implications of her words were not lost. Christina was certainly not prudish, but the frankness of this wanton shocked even her. She had never met a girl such as this before, although she had overheard some of her father's workmen whispering about such brazen creatures inhabiting the dimly lit upper floors of the Blue Eel Inn back in Lubeck.

Few words were spoken after this, at least none that Christina found important enough to commit to memory. Within the hour, she found herself back outside the gates once more. She turned and cast one more appraising glance at the alderman's dwelling before beginning her journey to her uncle's house. This time, however, she perceived no beauty in its architecture, only the depravity and oppression of those who lived within.

She heard the faint sound of footsteps crossing the street behind her. She assumed this was Ziesolf.

This belief was confirmed when he crossed into her peripheral vision and began walking leisurely down the street from whence they had come what seemed to have been an eternity before. Letting him get ahead approximately twenty feet before her, she turned to follow.

Damn you, Father! She thought as she took her first steps back. *How could you leave me in such a predicament?* She immediately felt guilty, however. Was it not she who had placed herself in such an untenable situation? After all, she had made the final decision to assume Frederick's identity. *I could have remained Christina.* She shuddered at the thought, imagining what life would have been like had she married Albrecht. Despite the abnormality of his physical appearance, the young man seemed to have a good heart. It seemed he was completely submissive to his father, however, a trait that was certainly not one of her virtues. *How would Herr Revele have reacted had she spoken in defense of her poor, abused husband?* she wondered. *A man such as Revele would countenance no contradiction,* she concluded. *Verbal abuse would swiftly become physical.*

She could imagine the daughter being even worse. Christina thought of how she had fought with Margarete. *That is only because she was so self-centered, although maybe I was as well,* she grudgingly admitted. She knew she loved her sister and, deep down, always felt Margarete loved her. She believed Katharine, however, would seek out new and creative ways to be cruel, to make a sister-in-law's life terrible. She was happy she was not that sister-in-law, and perhaps even more so that it was not Margarete.

Well, I can always agree to marry Katharine, can I not? She chuckled at the absurdity. No, she would be lucky if she survived with her secret intact to the day of the wedding ceremony. She imagined that, long before that time, the little strumpet would drag her into an alcove somewhere inside the vastness of the house and grope for a cock that was nowhere to be found.

Instead, I could always snap her neck and toss her down the stairs, she considered, only half in jest. *No,* she admitted to herself. *After the demise of two brides already, she was certain Revele would be very meticulous about guarding against that eventuality in the marriage contract, if only for superstition's sake. I would be right back where I started.*

Christina also dismissed the idea of selling her goods to Revele, if only to prevent him making a profit from her misfortune. She was almost certain he had somehow compelled Shipman to make such a low offer. Should she seek out another mercer, hoping Revele had not influenced him as well? It seemed to be a waste of effort as trade for Hanseatic goods centered around the council of aldermen, at the center of which was Revele himself.

The thought that the chief alderman had somehow been involved with the attack on her ships also nagged at Christina. *No one could have predicted exactly what would have happened. Any one of us could have been killed. Could the alderman have made a series of plans, each advantageous to himself, to implement whether my father, my brother, or even myself died or were taken?*

The complexity of such a scheme made her head hurt. She knew one thing with certainty, however. *If I ever find out Revele was involved in the deaths of Frederick and my father, no one in London, Lubeck, or anywhere else in the world will protect him from my revenge.*

Ziesolf drew alongside her and asked, "How went the audience with the alderman? Did he take the news well?"

Christina stopped and glared at the man in astonished anger.

She replied mockingly, "Oh, yes, it went very well indeed! He let me know I owe him six hundred marks in marriage dowry and he graciously agreed to take my cargo in payment. Alternatively, I can marry his foul daughter. Yes, everything went perfectly, thank you very much for asking!"

Ziesolf drew her into the shadows under an overhanging building, then whispered, "Although your money and goods are of great worth, it seems he values the binding the fortunes between your two families even more. Obviously, a marriage is impossible. Why did you not tell him you were already contracted to marry another? Or even that you had taken a vow of celibacy? I think it is very dangerous to permit this man to think you may be amenable to a marriage with his daughter, especially if that is truly what he desires."

She hissed at the man through clenched teeth, "It is so easy, Herr Ziesolf, for you to criticize everything I do. I understand the purpose of correcting mistakes in training to fight, I really do. One learns and hopefully does it better the next time. In this, however, there is no next time. I can only do the best I can and then what's done is done! Do I wish I would have done things differently? Yes! But it is much easier to think of better things to say here than when that damnable Revele is staring down at you. So, unless you have something useful to say, keep your damned opinions to yourself!"

Ziesolf had the good sense not to attempt any further conversation during their journey back. Christina was so deep in her own thoughts that, when she arrived at her uncle's house, she was surprised to find the elderly knight had left her company sometime before. She let herself into the house quietly and went immediately to her room, foregoing food in favor of the luxury of not having to speak with anyone. She flopped on the bed and closed her eyes, praying fervently for a better day on the morrow. Certainly, it could not be any worse.

Chapter 10

Christina awoke early. She had spent a restless night, troubled alternately by bad dreams and even worse waking thoughts. She washed, dressed, and went down the stairs and to the kitchen, where she ate a solitary but substantial breakfast of bread, cheese, and watered ale. Feeling somewhat better physically, if not emotionally, she went out to the yard and sat on the stone steps, attempting to muddle through her current predicament.

She noticed the weather was changing. There was no warmth in the air and the sky was a uniform steely grey. She could not see the sun but couldn't decide whether it was because of the denseness of the clouds or the earliness of the hour. A faint wind swirled about the yard, randomly rearranging dry brown leaves and other small debris from one corner and depositing it in the next. She had never felt more alone. Christina shivered and wrapped her arms about her knees, trying to conserve the pitifully small amount of heat her body generated.

She had been alone with her troubles for perhaps an hour when she heard the faint sound of a wagon clattering up the street outside the yard. It grew louder before stopping altogether outside the gates of the compound. They opened and a massive brown horse entered, followed by the large wagon to which it was hitched. Beside the driver, a fat, dull-eyed man with a massive hat pulled low about his hairy ears, two young men were perched upon the seat. One of these she had never seen, the other was her uncle's journeyman, Richard.

They brought the wagon to a halt in from of one of the storeroom doors, either ignoring her presence or unaware of it in the dim light. The men dismounted and the fat carter unhitched the horse and tethered it to a post nearby.

Richard said, "Will, place some blocks under the wheels. I don't want to be falling on my ass if I move one of these barrels and the cart shifts!"

The other young man hove to his task obediently. Although he was taller than Richard by a few inches, he was less muscular and clearly a few years younger. After placing pieces of cordwood fore and aft of each wheel, he moved to the rear of the cart to help the other two men remove the heavy canvas that concealed the contents within.

With the cover removed, Christina was shocked to see the wagon was loaded with what appeared to be merchandise from the cargo of *der Greif*. Christina toyed with the idea of walking over and offering to help with the unloading, especially since it was her goods. She decided to the contrary, partially because of her dislike for Richard and partly because she just couldn't be bothered.

Despite the coolness in the air, the men were soon hot and sweaty. Richard took off his tunic, his well-tanned skin glistening with perspiration. The work was heavy and the men soon became tired. As their fatigue grew, they became increasingly careless with the handling of her cargo.

Damned workmen, she fumed. *It doesn't matter where you are, they're all the same!* She had seen this tableau play out innumerable times at her father's warehouse in Lubeck. *As the men tire, the quality of their work suffers. Then you yell at them. Then they improve – for a bit. Then you feed them and give them beer. Then they improve. Then the whole cycle begins again.*

Just then, Will rolled a barrel to the edge of the wagon's bed. Instead of grabbing it and lowering it gently to the ground as they had done previously, Richard and the fat man pulled their hands away and let it crash to the stone pavement below. All three men laughed heartily and Richard began rolling the barrel toward the warehouse door.

God damn it! That's it, she thought. Christina had seen enough. She got to her feet and strode purposefully across the yard.

"Hey! What the hell do you think you're doing? What's in that barrel is worth more than your fucking miserable lives combined! Now, use some care you miserable louts or I'll stick my foot knee deep up all your asses!"

Christina felt proud of the quality of her tirade, she'd heard much milder words have the desired effect in Lubeck.

All three men started with surprise. Will glanced guiltily about and lowered his eyes, while the fat man knuckled his forehead in deference. Both men hurried back to their task.

On the other hand, Richard straightened up and ambled toward Christina. "Well, if it isn't the high and mighty young sir. Good day to you, my lord. And how are you on this fine day? It's a good 'un, isn't it? Especially for watching others do your bloody work for you while you sit idly by!"

Christina felt a momentary twinge of guilt, which was quickly surmounted by a wave of mounting irritation. These men had been given a task, presumably by their employer, her uncle. *If they are doing it shoddily then, by God, someone needs to correct them. Since no one else in authority is about, that someone is me.*

"This is your work, not mine. Now, do it right or fuck off and let your betters at it!"

A reddish tinge began at Richard's neck and slowly climbed upward until his ears were veritable beacons. The man's fury was palpable now. Christina wondered whether she had spoken too harshly to the man as the desired effect, that of returning him to perform his task more carefully, had not occurred. He glared at her, his nostrils blowing like those of an overworked horse.

"So, my better you are now, are you?" his voice raspy with emotion. "Some snot-nosed brat shows up here and thinks he's better than me just because he hid away in the cargo hold like a frightened puppy and let his family get killed. Well, there's nowhere to hide now!"

At that, Richard thrust his right arm out, placing the flat of his hand into Christina's shoulder and nearly knocking her to the ground. She cursed herself for being caught unaware. She should have anticipated that a man like Richard had only a certain amount of talk in him.

Well, if it's a fight you want, that's all right with me! she thought, the anger and frustration she had kept pent up over the past few days now overflowing like a boiling pot too long on the fire. She spread her legs a bit, gaining a better balance on the balls of her feet. She crouched slightly, bringing her fists up into a guarded position.

Although she was a bit taller than Richard, he was clearly the weightier. His broad shoulders and thick arms were heavily muscled. He squinted at Christina, then smiled. Clearly, he felt he had an advantage over the pampered youth who stood before him. He couldn't believe his good fortune that the young man was actually inviting a beating, rather than running away from it. His fists itched in anticipation of burying them into the pretty face that waited before him, just tantalizingly out of reach.

Richard took a step forward and swung wildly at Christina's head. She ducked and brought her own fist solidly into the man's ribs. She was happy to see him wince slightly from the pain of the blow. She skipped backwards, circling lightly to her right and seeking her next opening.

The journeyman came forward again, albeit a bit more cautiously. He feinted this time with his right, then brought his left hand around in a wide hook. Christina was much faster than the man, however. She parried his swing with her forearm and drove her opposite fist into his guts. This time, he let out an audible "whoosh" and moved backwards a step. She now brought her right arm forward and extended the heel of her hand forcefully into the man's nose, which crumpled and immediately flowered with his blood.

Enraged, Richard lunged forward, hoping to catch her about the waist with his arms. She danced to the side and let the force of the man's charge carry him by her. As he passed, she caught him around the neck with her arm and grasped her other bicep to lock in the hold. She tightened the pressure about his neck and brought her legs up around his body to throw her full weight on his back. He staggered for a few seconds, then dropped to one knee.

I could kill him, she thought in amazement. It had been so easy to outfight him, now she held his life in her hands. *I won't hurt him permanently*, she promised herself, *but he's definitely going to know that . . .*

The blow across her shoulders came as a complete surprise, causing her to relinquish her hold about Richard's neck immediately. She fell to the ground, momentarily stunned. Richard lay about ten feet away, gasping for air.

What had he done to her? she asked herself. Seconds later, the answer became obvious.

She peered up slightly and saw the fat man drop the large piece of timber he was holding. He swung his foot and she felt his shoe connect with her stomach. The pain made her dizzy, but she was alert enough to feel another kick from the other side, into her back.

Ah, now that will be young Will, she thought, realizing she now faced all three men. She tried to regain her feet but was knocked back down again as she felt another blow connect with her leg. With alarm, she saw Richard was now standing, albeit unsteadily, and was moving in her direction as well. She drew herself up into a fetal position, trying to at least protect her vitals from damage.

"Stop!" she heard a commanding voice say.

She felt another kick to her back, then heard the smooth sound of a sword being pulled from its sheath. She slowly began to relax as she felt no further blows.

A hand grasped her by the back of her tunic and she was pulled roughly to her feet. The three men stood before her. Will and the fat man glared at her sullenly. Richard was using a bit of sackcloth to try to staunch the flow of blood from his nose.

Before she could turn about, she heard Ziesolf's voice behind her ear say, "This is over, do you understand? You three are being paid to work, not brawl. I care not to hear who started it, your only concern is I finished it! Not get about your tasks and take care. Any more shirking and you answer to me."

The men all nodded vigorously and returned to their duties with a new-found enthusiasm.

Christina tried to turn to Ziesolf, but was pushed toward the house, him still holding her by the collar. "Thank . . ." she began.

"Quiet!" he said, in a voice that left no doubt the word was a command, not a request.

He took her to her room and closed the door solidly behind.

"What in the name of Christ's twelve holy disciples did you think you were doing back there?" Ziesolf asked.

"They were not being careful with my goods from the ship. It was only a matter of time before something was damaged or broken. I'm being offered little enough as it is, without its value being diminished even more!'

"So, you asked them to be more careful about their work, is that it?"

"Yes," she replied judiciously, "More or less."

"More or less?"

"Well," she admitted, "Not in so many words." Ziesolf sighed, "How many times do I have to tell you to be careful? To be wary of doing or saying something that might unmask you for who you truly are? And now, brawling in your uncle's courtyard, have you no sense?"

"What would you have me do then?" she remarked passionately. "You ask me to pose as a man, well then, what would a man have done under the circumstances? Would he have sat quietly by, afraid to say anything that might offend the delicate sensibilities of the loutish idiots who were destroying his property? Would he have turned and walked away? If that is the sort of man you would have me be, Herr Ziesolf, I think I would do better as a girl!"

"But there were three of them, Christina. You must have known the other two would not sit idly by while you gave their leader a sound thrashing. Who knew what they would do next, after they tired of kicking you senseless? Would they rip off your tunic and lash you with the horsewhip that was only an arm's length away? What then would happen?"

"Yes! Yes! You are right and I am wrong, as always. I am a stupid man, and an even stupider woman. Now, go please and let this stupid person clean the horse shit out of her hair."

For a few seconds, Ziesolf scrutinized her with an expression equally divided between exasperation and concern. He then left without uttering another word.

Christina latched the door behind the man. As she disrobed, she felt heartsick she and Ziesolf had again argued. *I know he is only trying to help, to safely guide me down this dangerous path I have chosen,* she thought. *But life sometimes demands that we think and do at the same time and not one first, then the other.*

Naked, she moved her body first one way and then another. She was relieved to find that, although she felt pain in several areas of her body, it was more of the dull, aching variety, rather than the sharp, excruciating sort. She would be sore for a few days, but there didn't appear to be serious damage.

I couldn't say the same for Richard, she thought with satisfaction. *His nose will long be a reminder of the hazards of being a bully.*

A sharp, insistent knock on the door interrupted her thoughts. She grabbed her cloak and wrapped it tightly around her body. She went to the door and moved to open the latch, then hesitated. *What if its Richard and his cronies seeking to pick up where they left off?* she thought, congratulating herself on her newfound caution. "Who is it?" she asked through the door.

"Chris . . . Frederick, it's me!" the concern in Trudi's voice unmistakable, even through the thick timber of the door. "Are you all right?"

"Yes, well, mostly so, "she admitted, opening the door a few inches and allowing the maid to squirm through.

She threw her arms about Christina's neck. "I was so scared! I was cleaning in the solar when Mary and Agnes rushed through the room and into the hall. I followed them to see what was happening myself. They were mulling about the door, chattering with excitement about a fight that had just occurred. I wasn't much interested until I heard one of them mention your name. I didn't know where you were but figured this was as likely a place to search as anywhere. And here you are!"

She tightened her grip as if she were afraid Christina would melt away before her eyes.

Christina yelped in pain. "For the love of God, Trudi!"

An expression of surprise crossed the young maid's face and she immediately loosened her grip.

"Oh, Christina! You've been hurt!"

She flashed Trudi a wan grin. "Um, you might say that. Nothing serious though, as far as I can tell."

Impulsively, Trudi rushed forward once more. Christina was too quick this time and stepped backwards. The back of her legs hit the bed, however, and she fell unceremoniously onto it in a heap. Both girls laughed and then Trudi wrinkled her nose.

"Oh God, Christina, you stink!"

"Well, getting rolled about in horse piss and dung will do that. Trudi, would you be a dear and fetch me a bucket of water, please? I would like nothing better than to have a good wash."

"I can do even better than that! Mary was heating water in the kitchen to do some of Frau Kohl's laundry. I'm sure she won't miss a small bucketful."

The thought of the feel of hot water on her skin was almost palpable. Christina sighed in anticipated pleasure. "That would be the best thing that's happened since we arrived here. Go now but be careful no one sees you."

Trudi nodded her head and snuck stealthily out of the door. It wasn't long before she returned, lugging a large pail of steaming water. Christina latched the door behind her, slipped her cloak off, and sat down heavily on a stool.

Appraising Christina's naked body, the maid's face flushed with renewed concern. "Sweet Mary, why didn't you tell me you've been hurt so badly? How did you get so bruised?"

"If I promise to tell you the whole story, will you not let that bucket of hot water go to waste?" Christina asked hopefully.

Trudi nodded, picked up a bit of rosewater scented soap, and began to gently wash Christina's hair and face as she started to relate the morning's events. The feel of the warm water on her skin and the sensitivity of the maid's touch made it difficult for her to concentrate on her tale, however. Soon, her sentences became breathy and marked by extended pauses, as she luxuriated in sensuous pleasure.

Trudi extended the bath downward, over Christina's shoulders and beneath her arms. The feel of the hot water on her nipples made Christina gasp as the maid softly kneaded her taut breasts with her cloth. Trudi dropped gracefully to her knees as she carefully washed her mistress's stomach, brushing lightly over the bruised areas that had now discolored her skin with dark blotches.

"I can do that," Christina objected in a small voice as the maid gently parted her thighs. Trudi ignored her, however, and Christina protested the issue no further. Instead, she involuntarily arched backwards and moved her knees further apart. A feeling of mounting pleasure coursed through her body as Trudi's cloth explored Christina's nether regions. Then another. Then another. Christina bit her bottom lip to keep from uttering an embarrassing mewling sound.

All too soon, Trudi's caresses moved to her thighs, down her legs, and to her feet and toes. The maid's eyes rose demurely to meet those of her mistress. She said, "There, we're finished. Do you feel any better now?"

Christina could only nod her head dumbly. Trudi's ministrations had left her feeling a hundred times better than she had felt earlier.

The maid got to her feet and gathered the bath items. "I will see if I can find some balm for those bruises. Will you be here today or will you be out?"

Christina, who had begun to dress, paused and looked toward Trudi unseeingly. *What will I be doing today?* She wondered. She would have liked to return to the yard to oversee the further unloading of her cargo but knew she could not risk another confrontation with Richard and his cronies. She supposed she should seek out her uncle to ascertain whether he had been in contact with any of her other potential buyers.

Well, perhaps I should just go out on my own, she thought. She felt as though she had been at a disadvantage ever since her arrival. Her initial confrontation with her uncle, her failure to make a sale to Shipman, even the disaster at the chief alderman's house all seemed like circumstances in which she was caught up, beyond her control.

If I wish to find my place in London, I cannot expect others to do it for me, she decided resolutely. Her father's account book held the names of several of her father's previous purchasers. She made it a plan to visit them, to see if she might arrange the sale of her goods on her own. *Besides,* she thought with returning good humor, *it's about time I began to find my way around this damnable city without being lost at every turn.*

It was growing dark by the time she made her way back to her uncle's house, tired, but very happy. Alone once more in her room, she recalled the events of the day with satisfaction.

She had journeyed north in the city, making several wrong turns, but eventually finding her way to the Augustinian priory of St. Bartholomew. Gaining entrance, she asked as to the whereabouts of Brother Guillaume, the one whose name her father had listed in his accounts book.

A sorrowful expression appeared on the face of the monk who had given her entrance. He said, "I am most sorry, kind sir, but Brother Guillaume passed from this earth last summer, may God rest his soul."

Is there no luck here but bad? She had asked herself in consternation. "Is there anyone who has assumed his duties?" she queried hopefully.

"The life of the priory must go on, my son, even though that of those who inhabit it do not," he replied with a benevolent smile. "I can take you to see
Brother Odo, the cellarer, if you wish."

Christina eagerly agreed and, nearly three hours later, had accepted the monk's generous offer of pottage and bread, offered up prayers for her family both living and dead, and secured a sale of four hundred weight of wax for ten pounds, sixteen shillings, and ten pence.

Although a little over sixteen Lubeck marks represented only a fraction of the value of her cargo, Christina felt happy knowing she had negotiated a good price and made a substantial profit. The sale was made even more enjoyable by the fact she had made it herself, with the help of no one. She hoped her day's dealings were a portent of better things to come in the future.

Chapter 11

Over the next few days, Christina did have some degree of success, completing three small sales at considerable profit. She also finalized a written agreement with her uncle, setting the conditions and cost for the storage of her goods in his warehouse. He had dismissed the idea of a contract as an unnecessary formality unusual between blood relatives. Christina had insisted, however, needing to know the exact state of her finances if she were to make informed decisions for the immediate future.

It was already the first week of November and the winter portended to be a cold one. She had only a week left before Martinmas, the date that traditionally ended the trading season in Lubeck. If she was not able to set sail with a new cargo by the eleventh, a return voyage would not be possible until St. Peter's day on February twenty-second. If the ship were left in harbor for those three months, its only purpose would be to accrue moorage and maintenance fees, not to mention wages for the skipper and the few trusted sailors she hoped to retain.

The vast majority of her goods remained unsold, however, leaving her with little ready cash to purchase either raw wool or finished cloth. Of course, she could sell her furs to Shipman, hoping to recoup the losses she would accrue through the potential profits she would make on her return cargo.

She knew that kind of speculation was very dangerous, having overheard her father and his friends laugh at merchants who had taken such foolhardy risks, only to lose everything including their good name. *This would be a desperate plan,* she thought, hoping she would not be forced to consider it more seriously.

Herr Revele's deadline loomed over her head as well. She had only a little over a week to provide him with her answer, whatever that might be. Christina felt as though she lived each day with an increasingly large burden on her back. Although she had the freedom of a man, it had brought her small enjoyment.

Increasingly, she longed for the days only a few months prior when her biggest concern was whether she could get away with stealing a bun from the kitchen when no one was watching or how she could avoid her chores. *These were childish decisions,* she told herself, *ones that I no longer need to consider. Even if Father and Frederick had not died, I would now be the wife of Albrecht Revele, and that would be the most worrisome of all.*

Absorbed in her own problems, Christina left the house and wandered into the yard. She sat staring at the storeroom door, behind which her goods were neatly stacked, awaiting a buyer.

"Why can't I find one? Is there no one in this foul city who bargains fairly?" she murmured aloud, knowing no one could hear, even more so no one could satisfactorily answer.

She was interrupted from her reverie by the sound of the gate opening. Richard and Will sauntered into the yard. Seeing her, they stopped and began whispering.

She sighed and rose to her feet. Since their altercation with Christina, they had given her a wide berth, she hoped as much from their fear of her fighting skills as from Ziesolf's threat. Seeming to come to some sort of agreement they purposefully strode her way.

Oh, hell! I have no heart for this! She thought morosely. She circled slightly toward the middle of the yard, however, knowing the additional space to maneuver would favor her, should they press the issue.

They marked Christina's wariness and stopped, a look of confusion spreading across their faces. They conferred again, just for a few seconds, then Richard said, "Peace, Frederick, peace. We wish only to talk with you."

Christina's eyes narrowed as she appraised the situation carefully. On the one hand, she believed neither of the young men cared a wit about honor and, despite Richard's offer of a truce, were quite capable of using it as a ruse to catch her unawares. *To the contrary, what if they are sincere?* She considered. *Should I not at least hear what they have to say? Without dropping my guard completely of course,* she added cautiously.

"All right then, speak," she replied.

They came forward a few steps. Christina widened her feet slightly, shifting her weight to achieve a better balance. She resisted the desire to curl her hands into fists, but just barely.

"Whoa," Richard said with a slightly nervous laugh in his voice. "I have no wish to fight you, especially after the results from the last time."

He pointed at his nose, which still appeared red and raw.

Christina mutely waited for the man to continue.

"Well . . .you see . . .," he began hesitantly. "Me and Will have been talking, you see, and we think you're not a bad sort actually, so we'd like to say we're sorry."

Will energetically nodded his head up and down in agreement." Richard continued, "Since it seems you're going to be around here for a while anyway, it makes no sense to have bad blood between us. We know we got off on the wrong foot, but we'd like to put that behind us now." He held forth his meaty hand to Christina.

She was taken aback by the man's offer. *Should I accept it?* she wondered. *Well, I don't see rightfully how I can't. If I decline the offer, it just means I'll always need to be wary of these two, as well as anyone who might be their allies. Better to agree, if only so there is one less thing to worry about in my life.*

She held her own hand out, still suspicious the man might grab it and resume their fray anew. Instead, he grasped her wrist strongly and, after she did the same, began to shake it up and down vigorously. Will came forward and clapped her heartily on the back, then it was his turn to shake hands. Then, there were more hands on shoulders and laughing.

Christina was astounded but couldn't stop grinning herself. She had spent so many days away from Lubeck, she had forgotten what it was like to have friends. There was Trudi, of course, whom she loved dearly. But the circumstances of Christina's deception made it very difficult to steal time to be alone with the maid. Although she still did not completely trust the motives of this pair, it was at least good to have someone to have a laugh with.

Richard then said, "Welcome then, Frederick, to the esteemed company of worthy men of Gerhardt Kohl. Or miserable louts, as some might call us." He stared at Christina with a frown on his face. After a few seconds, his face exploded into laughter,

Will and then Christina joining him enthusiastically in his mirth.

Richard wiped happy tears from his eyes and continued.

"Well then, our friend Will here came up with the idea of asking you to join us at the Nag's Head this evening. It's a bit of a celebration, you see. The boy is now seventeen years old and believes he's a man, why, he even found a hair on his bollocks this morning! What do you say?"

Christina said nothing. She had no idea as to what the Nag's Head was, but imagined that, under the circumstances, it was a drinking hole of some sort. *So, a few cups of ale in a merry place might do me good,* she admitted. *Anyway, it will be a welcome relief from sitting alone here, worrying about my troubles.*

She grinned at Richard and nodded her head in agreement.

"Great!" he hooted, slapping her across the shoulders so hard she nearly stumbled.

She frowned, but then relaxed as she realized it was just the manner of these two hearty fellows.

They ambled back toward the gate, turning to wave at her. Richard yelled, "We'll fetch you at sunset!"

She waved back and they were gone.

Alone once more, she sat down heavily on the steps, her mind twirling in amazement. The furthest thing from her mind this morning had been an encounter with her uncle's men, much less an apology and an invitation out on the town as well.

Should I actually go? She asked herself in a sudden moment of conscience. *Certainly, there could be pitfalls,* she admitted, remembering the familiar crew of young men, sozzled with cheap drink, who had been collected up by Lubeck's town watch on an eve. *Well, I'm not going to get roaring drunk,* she promised herself, *so there's little harm there.*

What will Ziesolf say? She asked, knowing the answer full well. *He would say absolutely not, the chance you will be exposed is too great. You might actually have some fun. Much better that you lock yourself in your room every evening, criticizing yourself for whatever went wrong that day and worrying about how you will err on the morrow. Well, if I'm going to do that I might as well join a monastery, er . . . a nunnery.*

She decided the easiest course of action was to not tell him she was going; thus, avoiding an argument, at least for now.

Christina made use of the day to check on the condition of her goods, periodically making somewhat guilty forays into the yard to appraise the hour through the height of the sun. She had to admit, she was anticipating the night's festivities with growing excitement. Later, as the day slipped into night, her newly-found comrades made their appearance.

Are you ready?" asked Will, producing a small wineskin and passing it to Christina.

She took a modest gulp and gave it back to Will.

Richard grabbed it and took a deep draught.

He wiped his lips with his sleeve, belched, and said, "Never pass up a free drink, Frederick. That's one of the first things you would have learned as an apprentice."

He threw the skin back to Will, who caught it deftly.

"We're off then!" he cried merrily, leading the way through the yard and out the gate.

Christina had no idea where they were going, so she clocked their progress with interest. They turned right and soon were on the street known as Watling, heading south as it cut toward the river. Between the close rows of tall buildings on each side and the blackness of the night sky overhead, she imagined they were traveling through a gaily lit tunnel leading deep into the earth. *Soon,* she thought, recalling her mother's stories from when she was young, *we will arrive at the troll kingdom and I will be presented to their king.* She peered to the left and right, trying to convince herself she saw mystical creatures moving among the shadows. She laughed aloud and Richard and Will glanced at her in puzzlement. Then, they joined in as well, although they didn't know exactly why.

Christina's reveries were broken abruptly when they turned right and she found she was staring at the great bridge of London before her. Although the bridge itself was nearly thirty feet wide, both sides were built up with a hodge-podge of structures rising to several stories above the street which cantilevered in toward each other. The soft glow of lanthorns illuminated the way, supplemented by the brilliant light given off from burning rush torches prudently kept a few feet distant from the dry, white-washed wood of the buildings.

Despite the late hour, streams of people of all social classes thronged in each direction, jostling against each other to make their way across the river. The noise was deafening, the smell of cooking meat, unwashed bodies, and wafting sewage from the water below overwhelming. As they passed the chapel of St. Thomas, built right upon the bridge, Christina felt herself grow a bit dizzy, her senses overwhelmed by the cacophony of humanity surrounding her.

After crossing the bridge, Christina realized they had left the city proper and had entered the suburb known as Southwark. This was a place she had heard of more than once, eavesdropping on the conversations of sailors on the quay in Lubeck. For it was there that they went to enjoy vices frowned upon inside the walls of London itself. Drinking to excess, prostitution, cock fighting, and bear baiting were just some of the attractions one could find along its streets and alleys.

She gulped, beginning to think she should have queried the two men more closely about their destination for the evening. *Too late to worry about that now,* she admitted to herself. Realizing she had fallen a bit behind, she hurried to catch up with her companions.

They walked down the borough's high street, passing a sprawling new coaching inn on their left. A large wooden sign with a painted green and yellow tabard hung vertically from an iron rod overhead, proclaiming the name of the establishment to those who could not read. A few doors down and another turn and they were at the door of the Nag's Head.

Compared to the Tabard, the Nag's Head was ill kept, dingy, and small. Richard pushed the flimsy door open and entered. Christina hesitated, then was pressed inside bodily by Will. As her eyes grew accustomed to the juxtaposition of shadow and light inside the establishment, her nose was assailed by a distinctive blend of sour ale, sweat, vomit, and piss.

". . . here!"

She could barely hear Richard's cry over the sounds of laughing, shouting, clinking cups, and the movement of furniture that permeated the inn's interior. She glanced to her left and saw that he had secured places at a long wooden bench along one of the blackened walls. She followed Will around a roughly-hewn support post, past a table of carousers well into their cups, and took a seat next to him.

Catching the eye of one of the girls who rushed about with their hands laden with tankards, bottles, bowls, and cups, he shouted, "Ale!" She nodded brusquely and turned toward the bar.

Christina gazed about with interest. What at first had seemed a uniform crowd of raucous revelers in the tavern, one undistinguishable from the next, now separated into distinct groups and solitary drinkers. To their left, four men seated at a table roared with laughter at a fifth's jest, beating their tankards upon the table as if they sought to drive them through the wooden surface. At the opposite wall, an older man with a sad face drained cup after cup, perhaps in an effort to erase some tragic occurrence from his memory. *Maybe he has a cargo he can't sell either,* she thought, making light of her own troubles.

Near the fireplace, at a table noticeably distanced from the seats of other patrons, three conspicuously well-dressed men conversed in low voices. They took small, measured sips of wine from their bowls, in sharp contrast to the gulping and slurping of drink by those who surrounded them. Suddenly, the man in the center lifted a surprisingly comely face and met her gaze directly. He smiled and raised his bowl lightly in salute. Embarrassed she had been caught staring, Christina quickly turned away.

Within a minute their cups arrived and they clinked them together in a comradely toast. The two men drank deeply. Christina began to take a modest sip, only to find the bottom of her cup being lifted by Will. Rather than letting the liquid spill down her face, she gulped it down, consuming nearly half its contents before he relinquished his hold on the vessel. She sputtered as she dropped it down to the table, vestiges of the liquid falling from her chin and staining her tunic.

Richard and Will hooted uproariously at her discomfort. She managed a slight grin in return.

Suddenly, Christina was taken completely by surprise as a striking young woman with enormous eyes leapt upon her lap. Up close, she discovered the woman's eyes were accentuated by heavy applications of kohl both above and below, blending into a strong line that extended slightly from the far corner of each. Rouged cheeks and painted lips made the woman's face even more arresting.

"Hello, you pretty, pretty boy," the woman remarked in a thick accent Christina presumed to be Flemish. She then leaned forward and kissed Christina deeply on the lips, the woman's mouth parting to explore that of Christina fully with her tongue. Christina was either so surprised she didn't think to resist or else the strong drink was beginning to slow her reactions. *Either way,* she admitted to herself guiltily, *the feeling isn't altogether unpleasant.*

The woman moved her head away and, taking Christina's hand, moved it inside her thin bodice and onto her ample, but firm breast.

"Perhaps you would like to go out back? Or upstairs for a few pennies more? She asked hopefully.

Suddenly, Will rose up and, raising his foot, kicked the woman roughly off Christina's lap.

"Begone, strumpet!" he shouted. "We've no time for one of Winchester's geese to break up our revelry!"

Christina was shocked by her companion's sudden brutality.

"Damn you, Will! "she said, perhaps a bit too loudly. "Have a care. You could have hurt her!"

Suddenly, the din in the room diminished markedly. A few heads turned their way with interest.

The young man glared at her, his ire rising conspicuously.

Then he laughed and said, "Peace, Frederick! I was only afraid you were going to desert Richard and me for a night of fucking. Now, that wouldn't be polite now, would it? Besides, she's had worse you know, probably even likes it."

Christina gazed carefully at the woman, noticing for the first time the dark bruises on her arms and the blackened area around her right eye only partially concealed by the kohl. The young woman gazed up at Christina, then her eyes opened wide with a look of surprise, followed by one of amusement.

Gracefully, the woman regained her feet and said to Christina, "I thank you, young sir. If you should return, please ask for me, Sybille, for a special price." She then turned and moved further into the room. Christina felt somewhat uneasy, as if the woman's words held an undisclosed meaning.

"God's blood, Frederick, "Richard sniggered, "I never figured you for a cocksman! You sly devil, you've melted that little whore's heart!"

Christina slowly realized she was no longer having a good time. *The place is too loud, the ale too watered down, and the company too ill-behaved. I'll buy the next round, then beg off, claiming I have an early appointment tomorrow,* she said to herself.

She signaled to the servant girl who had brought their drinks previously.

After quaffing the remaining contents of his cup, Richard announced, "I have to piss!" He then glanced at Will.

"Aye," the younger man agreed, "Me as well."

"Guard our seats, Frederick, and don't fill them with whores while we're out!" Richard lightheartedly cautioned.

The two men arose and moved through the crowd toward the door. Before exiting, however, they paused, Richard turning to wave at Christina while Will seemed to scan the room, looking for someone or something. Apparently satisfied, he nudged his friend and the two of them went out.

Alone, Christina sipped the remainder of her first cup of ale, idly glancing about the room once more. She realized her own bladder would soon need emptying as well. She hoped she could wait until she returned to her uncle's house, not wishing to expose herself as she sat on one of the row of public seats located outside the tavern. Neither did she wish to piss her pants; however, standing in a row of men directing a steaming stream onto the side of the building was obviously out of the question as well.

Suddenly, the five men who had been seated to her left arose as one and, surprisingly, walked to where she lounged. They stopped, towering over and staring down upon her menacingly.

She was absolutely astounded when one of them, in a voice resembling two millstones grinding together, said to her, "Get up! We don't take to the likes of your kind around here!"

Christina was totally baffled as to how she had affronted these men.

Only half-rising, she replied, "I know not how I might have offended you but, if I have, I'm sorry. Perhaps you will allow me to refill your tankards as a gesture of good will?"

"Good will! Do you hear that, Scratch?" He looked at the man who had spoken originally, then back to Christina. "We don't need your fecking good will! What, do you think we're too poor to buy our own drink, you little turd?"

Christina remained silent, realizing that any response on her part would only anger the men further. She peeked involuntarily toward the door, hoping to see Will and Richard reappear in the hopes it would even the odds slightly. It remained closed, however. *Have they stopped for a shit as well?* she thought in exasperation.

The one referred to as Scratch repeated, "Get out! Get out or I'll throw you out myself!!"

Seeing little other recourse, Christina did as she was told. As she began to walk toward the door, however, she felt one of the men's beefy hand grasp her by the back of the neck and half push and half carry her toward the door. She tried to resist, but the man's strength was overwhelming. He thrust her into the yard of the inn, shoving her roughly onto her face on the packed earth and filth.

She turned over and scrabbled on her back away from her attackers. She wracked her brain for an argument that might somehow dissuade her attackers from harming her, but nothing came to mind. Meanwhile, the men moved to surround her in a rough circle. At that point, Scratch and one of the other men drew long, curved filleting knives from about their persons.

Scratch's face contorted into an evil semblance of a smile, then said, "I'm gonna slit you open like a jack cod, boy."

Christina had never felt so frightened in her life. This was not like the pirates' attack at sea, where she had been properly armed and they had had to scale a ship's side to confront her. Nor was it like the fight in the yard against the three clumsy bumpkins. Now, she was surrounded by five armed brutes who clearly understood how to disadvantage an opponent. She felt for the small eating knife at her belt. Even that small reassurance was denied her as her hand felt nothing, it must have dropped when she fell to the ground. Of Richard and Will there was no sign, although she forgave them for their good sense in not attempting to help her against such men as these.

Her heart beat wildly, as if a crow were seeking to free itself from her chest. She felt an irrational urge to scream in terror as an unbidden image formed in her mind of Scratch holding her aloft by her chin, her guts spilling to the floor as her mermaid's tale slapped about convulsively.

She laughed hysterically at the absurdity of the mental image.

Scratch gawked at his captive quizzically for a moment, then his face hardened as he assumed he was being made the butt of a joke he couldn't comprehend. He chose that moment to take a step towards her, she was convinced, to follow through on his threat.

"Um . . . I don't believe I would do that, my good man," a voice behind the large assailant commented mildly.

The blade of a long, slim sword appearing alongside Scratch's cheek emphasized the instruction, its sharpness evidenced by a thin trace of blood that appeared along its keen edge.

Scratch grunted, then his face became engorged with rage. He flicked a glance toward his accomplices on his left and his expression changed to one of surprise. They were backing away in meek submission, hastily stashing their weapons from sight. He looked to the right, only to see a similar scene unfold. He now froze in place, uncertain of what was happening, but having the good sense not to provoke the unknown person who stood at his back until he knew more.

"Now, take a step forward and turnabout slowly. There, that's the fellow! Splendid!"

Scratch peered at the man and visibly blanched, his sparsely-toothed mouth working silently as if he wished to say something but couldn't.

"There now," the man with the sword said, still effusing what seemed like good-humor in his voice, "that wasn't so difficult now, was it?" Scratch shook his head slowly in agreement. "Do you know who I am?" The man now nodded. "And you?" the swordsman now addressed the four other men, who moved their heads in a similar fashion, only much more vigorously. "Please pay close attention then, as I cannot foresee me saying this more than once. Return to the mucky hole from whence you came and, if my eyes are ever affronted by the sight of any one of you again, you'll be enjoying a high place of honor on London Bridge. Or at least your heads will. Now, any questions?" Not one of the men uttered a word, their eyes lowered in deference. "Now, run along, before I reconsider my generosity."

Christina stared at her rescuer in amazement. It was the man who had been sitting near the fire who had raised his bowl to her. *But who is he, and how could one man have faced down the five brutes who had threatened me so completely?* She wondered.

From her seat on the ground, she carefully appraising the man who stood before her. He was of slightly more than average height, leanly built and well-proportioned. His thick brown hair was parted in the center. It fell to the sides to the level of his chin and was held in place by a rakish red velvet cap trimmed in sable. He possessed a visage that was pleasantly angular, with well-spaced eyes, a slightly upturned nose, unblemished skin, and thin lips curved into a merry smile. Over his white shirt (which might be silk or merely the finest linen – she could not tell in the light), he wore a beautifully tailored doublet, parti-colored in maroon and yellow and trimmed in marten fur. Its fashionably tightfitting sleeves were fastened with silver buttons. The hose covering his legs were of fine wool, alternately dyed pink and blue. Completing his attire, the man's feet were enclosed in leather "high-lows," slit at the instep and fitted with lappets which were hooked together. His footwear extended into extravagant points, a fine example of the cordwainer's craft. This was a man of inestimable wealth.

"Have you ever felt like a fine cow, being scrutinized oh so carefully by the farmer before he parts with his hard-earned shillings to the seller? Would you like to check my teeth as well?" the man opened his mouth wide in invitation.

Christina felt her face flush with heat at the man's jest. "No . . . of course not . . . your Grace." She added the honorific, hoping it reflected a sufficient degree of rank.

He gazed at her and his smile widened. "Well done, young sir, well done! It seems you have a wit about you, although the fact you chose here to make your merriment somewhat belies that appraisal, don't you think?"

Christina was finding it hard to know whether the man was being serious or simply mocking her. Consequently, she kept her mouth shut rather than risk offending her rescuer.

"Well, it seems you don't say much," he continued. "Interesting. That's a bit of a welcome change really. Usually young men can't stop talking, especially about themselves. Or asking for this, or wanting that, it's really quite tiresome you know."

Again, Christina held her tongue, not knowing exactly what to say.

"Perhaps getting your ass out of the dirt might help to loosen your tongue a bit. Here." He extended his hand.

She gawked momentarily at the size of the jewel in the silver ring he wore on his finger, then grasped his hand and rose to her feet.

"Thank you, your Grace," repeating her address since he had not corrected her previously.

Now it was his turn to stare. "My God," he said, his voice in an appreciative near-whisper. "Such a fine-looking lad."

He absent-mindedly used his hand to brush dirt from the sleeve of Christina's close fitting jaquette.

"Do you have a name, or must I give you one myself?"

"Frederick . . . Frederick Kohl."

He reached out and clasped Christina's right hand and drew it toward him. For a moment, she thought he was going to bring it to his lips, but he stopped short.

Still holding her hand in his, he asked, "And how does a Frederick Kohl come to find himself all alone in Southwark? Are you a naughty boy?" he smiled, but his eyes conveyed a seriousness she had not noticed before.

Again, she had no idea how to respond.

"Well, it seems I'm going to have to pry your story from you. In that case, let us return inside before we freeze to death, shall we?"

They re-entered the Nag's Head. The man led Christina to the table he had previously occupied. His companions, as with hers, were nowhere in sight. As if reading her mind, he said, "Oh, I am sure Bertram and Phillippe have found pleasurable diversion by mounting the stairs yonder." He gestured toward the back of the room. "And your fellows?"

She replied she had no idea as to the whereabouts of Richard and Will. Perhaps they had simply run away when they saw Christina being threatened. Although she couldn't fault their good sense in not getting involved, she surely could damn their cowardice. After a few sips of the strong wine that had been delivered deferentially to their table, Christina's related the events of the evening, providing a bit of her fabricated life's story as well to place everything in context.

"Frederick Kohl: apprentice, orphan, merchant of the Hanse, and man about town. You quite interest me. Now, who might you have offended so greatly as to wish your death? Certainly, it was not those five oafs who accosted you. Although they could have marked you for a bit of sport, they certainly wouldn't have risked breaking the law with open knife play, regardless that they had not a brain between them. Their actions have the smell of coin about them, mark my words."

Christina gulped, realizing the man's words rang true.

He pulled his chair closer, touching the margin of his body to hers so closely that she could discern its weight.

He then spoke conspiratorially, "Although a young man such as yourself would seem to hold little value among the powerful of London, this cargo of which you speak certainly will. Would you be so kind as to describe it to me?"

Christina began to enumerate the inventory of sundry goods she had stored in her uncle's warehouse. Before she had gotten half-way, the man's eyes widened in appreciation. By the time she had finished, he emitted a low whistle, visibly impressed.

He now peered at her intently.

For the first time since their meeting he said nothing. Again, she felt confused. *Does he expect me to say something else?* She wondered.

After several seconds, he finally spoke. "It seems what you need is a buyer, don't you think?"

Christina stifled a sarcastic retort at such an obvious statement. Instead, she just nodded her head.

"Well, would you perhaps consider selling it to me?" he enquired cheerfully.

More than a little surprised at the unexpected offer, she asked, "Um . . . and which goods in particular would you be interested in purchasing?" "Why, all of them," he replied.

"All of them?" she repeated his words, unable to believe her ears.

"Yes, of course. There is nothing you listed of which I, or my friends, would not have a need. If you spoke truly, of course, but I cannot imagine a Hanseatic merchant who does not know his cargo as intimately as his lover's thigh. Of course, we will need to negotiate a fair price, but I am sure we can come to a much more equitable agreement than the chiselers with whom you have spoken previously, don't you think?"

Again, she nodded dumbly, afraid to utter even a word that might make him reconsider his offer.

"Now," he continued, "I would advise keeping the details of our arrangement private so as not to motivate those who work against you to bring their plots forward."

She had become adept at nodding her head, as she had yet to find anything in the man's words about which she disagreed.

His smile became somewhat enigmatic and his voice dropped to a throaty whisper, "You can keep a secret, can you not, Frederick? Oh, I am certain you can. We all keep secrets do we not?"

The man's hand boldly patted her right knee as he moved his head forward so he might gaze into her eyes more fully.

Christina felt shocked, as this was the second time this evening she had the feeling someone had discerned the hidden truth about her. She decided to ignore her fears – for now, at least.

"Yes. Yes, I can certainly keep a secret," she replied with as much confidence as she could muster for the moment.

"Splendid!" he cried, returning to his previously ebullient good humor. "Well, sooner is better than later, I suspect. As this is Wednesday, perhaps you will come see me on Friday and we will work out the details. Noon, if that is agreeable to you of course?" He looked at her expectantly.

"Yes, of course! Any time you wish, your Grace!" "Good. It is settled then." He arose, as if to depart.

"But, where is it that I am to meet you?" she asked hastily, realizing she had no idea where the man lived, or even his name for that matter.

"My apartments at Lanthorn Tower would be most convenient for me." He noticed the lack of recognition in her face. "At Tower Castle," he added.

The royal castle! she thought to herself in disbelief.

She hesitated, then asked, "May I have your name as well, your Grace?"

He scrutinized her guardedly, then his expression softened as he determined no guile in her question.

"Why, its Piers, my young friend. Piers Gaveston." Gaveston then lowered his head and kissed Christina virtuously on the cheek. "I look forward to our next meeting with great anticipation," he murmured.

Then he turned and left.

Christina was so astounded by her apparent change of fortune she was unable to move for the next couple of minutes. She then lifted herself shakily to her feet and exited the tavern as well. As she made her way over the bridge, she had no thought of admiring its architectural grandeur once again. Instead, her mind oscillated between thoughts good and bad. *If Gaveston does indeed purchase my goods, I am a made man!* She thought, still unable to believe her good fortune. *I can pay my debts, purchase a new cargo for der Greif, even perhaps arrange a house of my own!"*

On the other hand, she was extremely troubled by what Gaveston had suggested. *She could accept someone trying to take advantage of her in matters of trade, even resorting to collusion in an attempt to cheat her of a fair profit. But murder?* She shuddered that someone would resort to killing her. *But hadn't Ziesolf suggested a sinister motive behind the pirates' attack that killed Father and Frederick? And he all but accused the chief alderman. What could Revele's real motive be? Regardless, I must tread lightly*, she warned herself, hoping she could separate friend from foe before it was too late.

Chapter 12

Ziesolf stared at Christina incredulously and said, "Gaveston! Dear God, what have you done?" He sat down heavily on a bench.

It was early morning and they were alone in the hall where Christina had just finished relating the previous day's events to Ziesolf. To her surprise, he had not even mentioned her unwise decision to visit Southwark, so consumed was he with the details of her meeting with Gaveston.

"What I've done is maybe saved myself from being ruined. Who is this Gaveston, anyway? Other than the man who probably saved my life," she replied dryly.

"He is the favorite of the new king, Edward II, and has been granted the earldom of Cornwall," Ziesolf replied matter-of-factly.

Now it was Christina's turn to be dumbfounded. She finally understood why the thugs at the tavern had been so easily cowed by the man's mere presence.

She sat down as well, then asked, "Well, is having such a man as a friend not a good thing?"

"He is despised by many of the hereditary barons of the land, and was hated to distraction by the old king, Edward's father. He held such ill-will toward Gaveston he had banished him repeatedly from the realm. The man walks a dangerous path. You must be careful you are not drawn down it as well, "he warned.

Christina sighed. "Herr Ziesolf, I myself well know what it is like to live precariously. Ever since my arrival; nay, since my departure from Lubeck, I have been beset by one calamity after another. Now, for the first time, good fortune may actually stand ready to fall into my lap. Better to risk Gaveston than to accept the certainty of losing everything."

He considered her words, then slowly nodded his head.

"I find I must agree with you. Go to Gaveston but do take care. There are sinister stories told about the man. It is whispered he has perverse tastes, for one. That he plies the Prince with unnatural acts, who then indulges his every whim, extending the degree of his royal patronage to extraordinary levels. Some say he has bewitched the Prince, others that he has merely corrupted him with base debauchery."

Ziesolf's words of caution left Christina with a sense of unease. *Why had Gaveston agreed to purchase her goods so readily, seeming to have small care about the price?* She realized the man must be wealthy; yet, he had no apparent reason to share his riches with her. She finally came to the conclusion those who lived at the very pinnacle of wealth and power can afford to indulge whim and whimsy. *Perhaps he views me as such, who can tell?*

Later that afternoon, she was surprised to find Richard sitting at a table in the hall, eating his midday meal. Her blood began to heat as she strode purposefully toward the man. He gazed up at her approach, an expression of guilt soon replaced by one of alarm.

He rose to his feet and said, "Good day to you, friend Frederick. How fare you?"

She resisted the impulse to do fresh damage to his nose but deferred the final decision until she had spoken with the man.

She said, "Where the hell did the two of you go last night? Why did you desert me?"

Hearing herself articulate those words only made her angrier.

He lowered his eyes and shifted his feet uncomfortably.

"Well, we passed our water like we said we was going to, then Will said we should maybe leave you alone, so's you could have your way with that little whore who seemed to like you so much. We didn't want to be in your way, you see."

The stupidity of Richard's reasoning seemed ludicrous to Christina. *To a man, though, especially one besotted with drink, who knows?* She scrutinized him closely. *His remorse seems genuine enough*, she admitted. She determined she wouldn't trust his schemes so readily in the future, although she also decided she would leave his face unscathed, for now at least.

The next day dawned beautifully, a bit of warmth in the air gave faint reminiscence of weeks, if not months, earlier. She arose with a sense of purpose and scrubbed her skin vigorously with cold water from the jug. She then opened her father's trunk that she had had removed from the ship, rifling through the garments it contained. She had originally felt fortunate they were of a similar build. Now, she felt less so.

The clothes were outdated, intended to hang loosely and comfortably about one's frame. She remembered her appraisal of Gaveston, how his garb had fit closely upon his body. She suddenly felt embarrassed. *How can I show my face at the royal palace in such garments as these? The guards will laugh at me and dismiss me as a beggar!* She threw them on the floor in disgust.

After staring at them disconsolately for a few minutes, she began to pick through them, selecting the best of the worst. *At least, the quality of the cloth is nice,* she grudgingly admitted. One other aspect brightened her mood as well. One of the best things about being a fur merchant is that one need never to want for ways to make even the dreariest clothes appear better. The houppelande she finally selected was a drab dark green but was lavishly trimmed in fine squirrel fur. Although such garments were usually left open at the front, she secured it closed with a woven girdle so as to not betray the swell of her breasts through her linen shirt. She completed her ensemble with light grey hose and modest turnshoes. Heading toward the door, she turned back, selecting a maroon woolen cap with upturned, black lapels. *Adds a bit of color at least,* she thought with satisfaction.

Somewhat confident now she would not be summarily turned away at the Tower, she made her way downstairs and to the solar. One of the maids was busily clearing the fireplace of ashes. Meanwhile, her aunt was sitting in a chair, working on a piece of embroidery, her nimble fingers making the needle seem to fly through the linen fabric. Christina laughed to herself, recalling her own lack of skill at the craft. *Well, at least I'm not going to be forced to try my hand at that again,* she though happily.

The older woman glanced up surprised, her concentration on her work had been so complete she had failed to notice Christina's entrance into the room. "Good day, Nephew. May I have Mary prepare you a morning repast?" she asked somewhat rhetorically, as she had already signaled to the young woman to do so.

"Thank you, Frau Kohl, that would be most kind of you, "She replied.

Although the woman had been exceedingly gracious to her, Christina perceived her aunt as a woman somewhat detached from the world around her. Her benign ambivalence made it hard for Christina to feel any kinship toward the woman.

She was somewhat taken aback then when her aunt queried, "Where would you be off to today then, robed in your finery as it were?"

Her mild tone belied the sharpness of her eyes, which held Christina for only a second before lowering once again to her embroidery.

Christina hesitated before responding. *Was this just an idle question, a polite way of making conversation such as asking about the weather? Or was it a subtle ploy to gain information that may be useful to her husband and, if so, how could he turn that knowledge to his advantage?* She so wished she could place her complete faith in her uncle, but somehow felt to do so would be a mistake. Outwardly, he seemed friendly and caring; however, she had a nagging feeling he had a mercer's heart, one ruled solely by profit and loss. *Any care he has for me will definitely be weighed against his own material gain.*

"Well, I am planning to seek a meeting with the chief alderman. Herr Revele had offered me certain terms at our last meeting and I wished to seek clarification on a few of the finer points."

The lie slipped smoothly off Christina's glib tongue. She hoped she had worded it in such a way that, if her uncle investigated it further, she could deny a visit to Revele had been her firm intention.

Again, her aunt's seemingly unassuming blue eyes found her own. Christina met her own gaze evenly, hopefully with a correspondingly guileless look upon her face. She believed the woman wanted to ask more, but politely refrained from further questioning. *But is it just talk, or does she have a deeper motive?* Christina wished she knew.

Further awkwardness was saved by the arrival of the maid with Christina's food. She ate as swiftly as decorum would permit. She thanked her aunt once again for her hospitality. The woman, who had put away her needlework and was now engrossed in the study of a beautifully illuminated book of hours, barely lifted her head in response.

Christina then returned to her room and fretted about for the remainder of the morning, checking and re-checking the inventory of goods contained in her father's account book, entries she had physically confirmed a few days prior. Becoming increasingly nervous, she found herself pacing the floor, consumed by thoughts upon the several ways in which things could go wrong. Unable to stand her inactivity any longer, Christina placed the ledger in a waterproof pouch, tucked it under her arm, and departed for her meeting with Gaveston.

The journey was an easy one. She made her way through East Chepe, then down Tower Street. She soon found herself before the enormous fortress complex. A massive stone curtain wall arose from the banks of a wet moat, extending both right and left until it fell from sight. Tall towers arose intermittently, surmounted by gay pennants that fluttered in the slight breeze. The entire structure reflected permanence, power, and wealth.

She suddenly felt a rush pf panic. *Who am I to seek entrance here? I'm just a girl, masquerading as a boy who had no right to be here either. What would Frederick have done if he were here in my stead?* She asked herself. She knew the answer already, however. *He would not be here at all. He would have followed through on Father's plan, accepting our uncle's offer of apprenticeship gratefully. Willing to concede der Greif's cargo for the opportunity to sit at the low end of his table. Even agreeing to a marriage with Revele's daughter, if need be. No, I am the risk-taker, the one never content to simply do as I am told. The one brazen enough to stand before a castle of the King of England and demand entrance. Fail I may, but it will not be through a faintness of heart!*

Her courage buoyed, she strode resolutely toward the bridge over the moat. Two guards in royal livery approached to confront her. Their polished polearms glinted in the sun as they moved to bar her way.

"I am Frederick Kohl, and I am here at the pleasure of his Grace, Piers Gaveston."

The two men gaped at her and guffawed, although she was hard pressed to determine whether it was because of her appearance, her voice, or something else entirely.

The shorter one said, "So, for his pleasure, eh? Well, I can believe that, I can. But we're not going to allow every jackanapes who says so to get past us, are we? We've got no orders to allow any Frederick what's-his-name to enter. Now, be gone!"

Christina felt heartsick. Had Gaveston been playing a cruel jest? Or was she simply so unimportant to such a great man that he simply just forgot to inform the sentries? Regardless of the rationale, getting inside was too crucial to her livelihood to let herself be dissuaded so easily.

"You there," she spoke to the other guard in a voice containing all the authority she could muster. "Go to Lanthorn Tower and confirm what I have said. And you," She turned to the one who had spoken, "Have a care how you speak to your betters!"

The men looked at each other in confusion. They were members of the household guard and, as such, used to taking orders. They turned back to Christina and scrutinized her once more, clocking the richness of her garb more carefully this time.

Finally, the short soldier turned to his taller counterpart, gestured with a flick of his head toward the castle, and said, "Go."

The man departed and Christina was left standing with the other guard. For long minutes she fretted about whether the man would be able to locate Gaveston. *What if he's not even here?* She thought fearfully.

After what seemed like an eternity, she saw the guard walking purposefully through the gate of the castle and over the bridge toward her.

She breathed a silent sigh of relief as he said, "You may enter, my lord. I will take you to Earl Piers posthaste, if that is your wish?" he said with a newly discovered deference in his tone.

Christina tried to keep an impassive expression on her face, struggling against the grin that threatened to explode across her lips. Instead, she gave the man a curt nod, which he rightly interpreted as a signal to proceed. She followed him through the gatehouse and across the wide wooden bridge that spanned the moat.

She marveled at the thickness of the curtain wall as they passed into the castle proper. The broad yard was a bevy of activity; the drilling of guardsmen, artisans plying their crafts, and brightly dressed nobility enjoying the uncommon warmth of the sun. All of this was set against the imposing stone background of walls and towers that reached towards the sky.

They walked down the right side of the wall, eventually coming to an entranceway with a stair that led into, what she discerned, was Lanthorn Tower. As they began their ascent, a terrible din erupted above their heads. The unmistakable sound of broken crockery was accompanied by unintelligible angry words in, what Christina believed, was the French language.

The voice was unmistakably female.

The guard's face turned ashen.

He turned to Christina and hissed, "Go back down, you fool!" his earlier politeness now forgotten in his haste to exit the tower.

They descended and moved quickly away from the entrance, a prudent thirty feet at least. They waited silently until they discerned the unmistakable sound of feet on the stairs. A few seconds later, a beautifully attired young woman erupted from the portal, her extreme rage evidenced by her pace, her deportment, and her expression. Two other women soon followed, hurrying to catch up to the first and attempting to sooth and console her. Their efforts were fruitless, however, as the other woman brushed at them angrily with her hand in dismissal. She walked briskly toward the imposing structure of pale stone located in the center of the yard, walked through the portal, and disappeared, followed closely by her ladies.

"Oh shit," Christina's companion exclaimed, absent-mindedly losing his decorum. "The Queen's in a mood again."

"The Queen?" repeated Christina, the wonderment in her voice unconcealed.

Once, when she was a little girl, she had held her father's hand as they stood in the crowd that lined the streets of Lubeck, hoping for a glimpse of Henry, Lord of Mecklenburg. Living in an imperial city that owed no obeisance to prince, duke, or margrave, she had imagined that would be the closest she would ever come to the titled nobility. Now, I share drink with earls and closely witness the unfettered emotions of queens. She shook her head in amazement at her new life.

"Right. Let's get you up there before she gets it in her mind to come back," the guard briskly remarked.

They climbed the stairs once more, coming to a finely finished door that barred their further entrance. Her escort rapped his knuckles on the wood and it opened, revealing the somewhat frightened face of a servant not too many years older than Christina.

"Master Frederick Kohl, to see the Earl," the guard made a brusque announcement.

"Yes, of course!" the servant's face brightened considerable, although Christina realized it was undoubtedly because she was not the queen. "Please come in, Herr Kohl. Earl Piers is expecting you." Christina passed through the doorway. The guard, undoubtedly relieved to shed his bothersome burden, departed swiftly back down the stairs.

She entered into a large solar, spacious and seemingly airy despite the thick walls that surrounded it. Flemish tapestries depicting scenes of extravagant courts covered the walls. The furnishings were lavish, with several matching chairs of ash and elm elaborately carved with ornamental tracery. Other seating was gaily painted in blues, reds, and yellows, with gilded decorative metal work. Multiple soft cushions were present to ease one's comfort. On the floor, two other servants worked feverishly to sweep up the pottery shards that marred the colorful carpets. The pleasing scent of chamomile permeated the room, which was kept a pleasant temperature by the glowing embers burning low in the corner fireplace.

"Ah, Frederick! So very good to see you once again!"

Gaveston spoke to her as he reclined in a broad window seat upon a plush cushion. He wore a silk dressing gown embroidered with several large peacocks. His feet were bare, his demeanor calm in sharp contrast to the royal wife who had made her dramatic departure only minutes prior.

He sprung up and walked purposefully toward Christina, catching her about the shoulders and kissing each of her cheeks in turn.

"Wine," he said simply, to no one in particular. One of the servants on the floor, however, immediately took it upon himself to fulfill his master's wishes, going swiftly to a cabinet and pouring two worked-silver cups with a deep crimson liquid.

Taking the cups in his hands, Gaveston proffered one to Christina.

As she marveled at the vessel's workmanship and obvious value, he turned his head slightly and said, "Begone now please."

She noted all of the servant left promptly, a few vestiges of pottery still remaining on the floor.

Gaveston followed her eyes to the floor, then said in a humorous tone, "I'm afraid Isabella and I don't always share the same opinion, especially when it comes to the matter of my relationship with her husband. That's why I leave the inexpensive crockery scattered about and keep the good things safely secured away." He laughed lightly at his own jest, then said, "Well, are we going to see who can hold their cup the longest, or should we drink?" He offered his cup in salute, then said, "To a very successful partnership, Frederick. May we work together ever more closely, to the pleasure of each!"

She raised her drink as well, then took a moderate gasp. The fullness of the wine startled her throat as it went down, requiring her to stifle a cough so as not to offend her host.

He observed her reaction and grinned. "It's Gascon, you know. I find it to be much more effective in countering the cold and damp of English nights than your Rhenish ferments. Now, forgive me for being such a bad host. We had agreed to talk business this day and that we shall. Please, sit."

He gestured toward a bare oak table sat with comfortable chairs to each of its four sides. He moved towards it, taking time only to grab the bottle of wine on his way to the far chair. Christina took the one opposite.

"Ah," Gaveston exclaimed, clapping his hands. "Face-to-face! Exactly how I imagined merchants would choose to haggle! Shall we begin?"

Christina took out her ledger and proceeded to inform the man in detail about the goods she had for sale. He asked little in the way of clarification, pausing more frequently to take another draught of wine. Not wishing to offend her host, she too took a moderate sip to match his deeper ones.

Eventually, she came to the end of her list.

She leaned back in her chair a bit and remarked, "Those are the goods I have for sale, your Grace. Is it still your intention to purchase them all?"

He nodded slightly.

She could not believe her good fortune still held. *Too early to congratulate yourself yet,* she admonished herself. *I have had no trouble in finding those who would gladly relieve me of my cargo, it was getting a fair return that posed the problem. How sharply will Gaveston negotiate price?* She wondered.

"I believe a price of six silver Lubeck marks per hundred for the squirrel pelts is a fair price," she ventured, choosing to begin their negotiations with the product that constituted the majority of the value of her goods.

If she could somehow come to agreement with the man over her skins, she felt a great weight would be lifted from her shoulders.

"Silver marks?" he asked. What would that be in English pounds?"

"The Italians in town are currently allowing twelve shillings, six pence for a silver mark, your Grace."

He surveyed her intently, seeking to read her veracity in her eyes rather than engage in mental mathematics. "Agreed," he said.

Christina was astonished. With that one word, she had suddenly divested herself of the majority of her cargo. She then went on, citing what she believed was a fair price for each item in her inventory. Each time, Gaveston agreed to her valuation. She now took a deep draught from her cup to mask the growing disbelief she felt must be evident on her face. She felt little discomfort now as the wine passed down her throat, only a radiating warmth spreading from her belly outward. *I wish I had chosen my garments more carefully,* she thought with a bit of annoyance as sweat began to form in the small of her back and under her arms.

"Well," he began good-naturedly. "That was much simpler than I would have believed. I had believed our bartering would have went on endlessly!"

She felt she needed to voice a reply.

"It usually does. They haggle right down to the last half-penny. Seldom is a merchant so . . . so . . . agreeable as you, your Grace," she said, recalling her recent experiences.

"Please," he smiled at her benevolently and said, "Please call me Piers. I am a but a simple man, Frederick, unused to the subtle formalities of trade." His face unexpectedly hardened. "Yes, a simple man, but do not make the error of believing I am simple-minded. You had already told me about what merchandise you had to offer while we spoke at the Nag's Head. Did you not think I might inquire of others as to their value? You quoted a fair price and I had no desire to cheat one who would not cheat me. Especially one I hold to be a friend."

His expression relaxed again into a happy one. Christina felt greatly embarrassed for having underestimated the man but relieved he had taken no permanent umbrage.

"You see, there are unseen depths to every man, knowledge and wants he keeps hidden from others," he continued. "Do you have such secrets, Frederick, ones you might be willing to share with me?"

He reached across the table and patted her hand lightly. He then filled her cup to its brim as well his own. Again, the man raised his cup in salutation to her, then drank heavily.

She was left with little recourse save to respond in kind. The wine flowed down her gullet more easily now. She felt somewhat confused by his words, but happy and at ease, in light both of the agreement they had just concluded as well as the excellent fellowship she was enjoying with Gaveston.

He rose to his feet. Knowing that to remain seated while her superior stood was an affront, she did as well, albeit slightly unsteadily. She wobbled a bit on her feet, as if the tower had somehow been supplanted to a ship at sea.

"There, there, good fellow!" Gaveston cried out in apparent concern for Christina's welfare.

He moved around the table and caught Christina about the waist.

She abruptly realized the strong drink had had a marked effect on her. She felt grateful for his assistance, thinking it would have been quite unseemly to collapse into a heap on the earl's floor. He brought his cheek closer to hers and she was able to discern the pleasant smell of cinnamon on his breath. Whether it was the warmth in the room, the wine, Gaveston's close proximity, or a combination of all three, Christina felt faint and she leaned against the man for support.

Gaveston moved to her front without relinquishing his hold about her middle. He brought his lips down to hers and kissed her, gently at first, then more deeply. His tongue found its way into her mouth, exploring it tentatively. His hand moved downward to beneath her buttocks, drawing her closely to him.

She gasped as she felt his erect manhood pressing tightly against her thigh.

Christina realized the man had seen through her disguise, revealing her for the woman she truly was. *All of his talk of secrets has really been a not so subtle allusion to the transparency of my ruse. The man has been having sport with me all along!* She thought exasperatingly.

She pushed him away and his gown fell open. His skin was pale, in marked contrast to the color of his blood-engorged cock. She realized this was the first time she had beheld a naked adult man. She fought a sudden urge to run away, frightened of what might happen next.

Calmly, Gaveston reached out to her with his hand. After a moment's hesitation, she took it in hers. Slowly, he pulled her towards him once more. She could not resist, gliding forward as if in a dream.

Is this truly what I want, this man to take my maidenhead? she considered in a fleeting moment of rationality. She knew there could be no permanence between them, that his was a world ruled by matches made for political advantage, even more so than her own. *No, if I am to give myself willingly to this man, my decision cannot be ruled by thought of future considerations. It can only be because of the passions I feel at this moment right now.* She stood frozen in indecision, her realization she did not want to give herself to this man increasingly clouded by her feelings of wanton lust.

He moved his hands inside her outer garment and across the thin material that covered the sides of her stomach. The delicious tingle from the touch of his hands greatly excited her and she hesitantly tilted her head upwards, seeking his mouth once more. She felt him lifting the back of her shirt, his touch now exploring the bare skin of her lower back. She strained against his body, urging him closer until their bodies would be fused as one.

His hands pushed her braes downward, exposing her bare ass to the open air. He alternately cupped and kneading her buttocks, igniting her passions still further. He moved one hand forward toward her sex, which she felt must be now frothing with unbridled lust.

Suddenly, he stopped and pushed her away. An expression of shock appeared on his face. Christina stood motionless, save her chest still heaving with passion. *What have I done?* she wondered. *How have I mis-stepped?*

After a few more seconds, the silent tableau was broken as Gaveston began to laugh, quietly at first, then more heartily. He lost control of himself, falling onto a small stool, then to the floor. His eyes watered as he guffawed convulsively, rolling about on the carpet and pointing toward her naked crotch.

Christina quickly moved through a series of emotions: shock, surprise, and embarrassment, before finally settling on anger.

She reached down and pulled her braes back up to around her hips, then said furiously, "Do you find something amusing about my quim, sir?"

She resisted the strong urge to kick him, realizing there was undoubtedly a heavy penalty to pay for abusing an earl thusly.

She glared at him silently until, at last, he regained a modicum of control over his emotions.

"Peace, Frederick, oh dear Lord, peace!" he cried in merriment from his position on the floor. He placed an elbow on the stool and drew himself into a sitting position. Gaveston wiped the tears of laughter from his face and said, "No, it is certainly the most splendid cunt I have ever beheld!"

Seeing her face darken even more at his jest, he added more seriously, "I certainly meant you no offense. It is just I was completely taken aback when I reached for cock but, instead, found quim." "But, what else did you expect, Piers?" her bewilderment prompting her to address him with his proffered familiarity. "Your words well implied you had seen through my masquerade, seeing me for what I truly am.

How could you possibly have been surprised by what you found?"

Gaveston chuckled and shook his head. "Oh, Frederick, or whatever your name truly is, you misjudged me as I clearly misjudged you. I believed you attracted to me, not as a woman, but as a man."

Christina gazed at Gaveston intently, a multitude of thoughts suddenly clouding her mind. *Ziesolf alluded to such unnatural behavior* she recalled. Considering the idea, however, she found she could not muster the same revulsion the knight had expressed. This man's business was his own and, as long as he visited his passions only on other who readily shared his strange desires, she did not care to condemn him as well.

Another, more pressing, consideration demanding her immediate attention, however. *Was Gaveston's ready agreement to her terms merely a ploy, one planned to gain her acquiescence to his sexual advances, then just as easily disavowed?* She realized she truly did not know this man, nor was she privy to his motivations.

She gazed at him intently, then said, "And of us, Piers? The true us?"

He appeared puzzled by her words. "I do not understand your meaning?" he replied.

"What was your intent, your Grace? Was your professed interest in my goods only a ruse to lure me here, to become your creature, have your way with me, and then discard? I cannot speak more plainly than this."

She could perceive in his eyes her words had wounded him.

"Do you not think an earl has the resources to satisfy his passions in whatever way he desires?" he asked softly. "I asked you here because I liked you, no more and no less. I was intrigued by the boy with such heart, ambition, and intelligence. Perhaps I saw a bit of myself in you, who knows? I was serious when I called you friend, as friend you remain, if you will have me as such?"

She considered his words carefully, then said solemnly, "I shall be honored, your Grace."

He sprung to his feet then, in a merry voice remarked, "Now, there is one thing I must request. The terms of our agreement must be somewhat altered."

A look of alarm flashed across her face. *What now?* She thought as a hard lump seemed to form in her throat.

"Well, I feel I must ask for additional recompense, left as I was somewhat . . . unsatisfied." He noticed her expression and laughed. "Come now, let us sit back down. I demand only you give me the parts of your story you obviously left out. Oh, and your name as well. I find it difficult thinking of you only as cockless Frederick."

She lowered herself into her chair. "Christina, my name is Christina," she said, beginning her tale again and this time omitting nothing.

Chapter 13

In London, November 1309

"What is the meaning of this? Gerhardt Kohl ran from his house and into the yard, loose bits of his breakfast still clinging to his shirt.

Christina walked over to him and said cheerfully, "Good day to you, uncle. How fare you this fine morn?"

"What are you doing?" her uncle demanded again, becoming increasingly apoplectic with each passing second.

"Why, I only seek to remove my goods from your warehouses. uncle. I deeply appreciate you allowing me to stow them here, but I have no need to impose on your generosity any further. I will of course pay the rents until the end of the month, as we had agreed."

"Yes, but . . ." the man's anger was now intermingled with a growing sense of confusion. "Where are you taking them?"

"Why, can you not see I am taking them nowhere?" Christina replied innocently, taking guilty pleasure in being purposefully evasive. "Then, who . . ." Gerhardt's bewilderment again kept him from composing a coherent question. "Who are these men?" Christina finished her uncle's query. "Why they are workhands from the royal castle yonder," she gestured broadly to her right. "I have sold my remaining cargo to the Earl of Cornwall."

"Gaveston?"

His face grew so red with rage it now threatened to burst open like an overly-ripe tomato.

"How is this possible? How could you have gained the acquaintance of such a man?"

She ignored her uncle's demand for explanation, choosing instead to simply remark, "Let it suffice to say I have met the man, and that we have come to a mutually beneficial agreement."

Gerhardt now worked visibly to gain control of his anger.

He glared at Christina and asked, "What have you done, you young fool? This is not how business is conducted here! Your rash actions will offend every merchant in London, Hansard and Englishman alike. Why could you not conduct your business as is the custom, instead of in such an unseemly manner?"

"Because I was being cheated by those who conduct business according to 'the custom!' They saw me as a ready victim; young and inexperienced, with a dire need to rid himself of his goods quickly, whatever the loss! No, uncle, I care not for this 'custom' you hold so dearly!"

He scowled at her with disdain in his piggish little eyes.

"You will find you have a need to care, Nephew. I must speak with the chief alderman about this immediately. I am sure my concern will seem inconsequential compared to his!"

With that threat voiced, Gerhardt stormed back into his house.

Christina absentmindedly worried her bottom lip between her teeth. Her earlier jolly mood now somewhat dampened. *Why couldn't he have been happy for me? I had ventured out on my own, making an agreement where previously there had been none. And at a hefty return, I might add. What merchant can criticize where profit is achieved?* She asked herself. *Must everything I do be questioned and condemned?*

She thought back to a few days prior when, returning from her time with Gaveston, she had detoured toward the moorage of *der Greif* to seek out Ziesolf. Finding him aboard, she proceeded to relate a concise version of her meeting with the Earl, judiciously omitting all reference to the more intimate details from her account. He had listened intently, although she discerned a growing sense of concern as lines of worry increasingly furrowed his forehead.

When she finished, he peered at her gravely with a thin smile upon his lips.

"I can see you are happy with yourself, Christina; a feeling to which you are well entitled. At long last you have rid yourself of your cargo and at a price even your father would feel satisfied to have negotiated."

She gazed back at the man, surprised at his unaccustomed praise.

"I am fearful; however, your immediate gain could have long-term consequences that will place you in grave danger. It is true the Earl is one of the most powerful men in the kingdom, however, in making him an ally, you have aligned yourself against other influential men. These men may seek to do you ill, not simply because you have associated yourself in trade with Gaveston, but because you represent a symbol of their darker suspicions about the man."

Christina reddened and averted her gaze from Ziesolf, perhaps equally in guilt and embarrassment.

"Please believe me I do not presume to accuse you of unseemly behavior," his words sudden and apologetic, "but it is not I whose opinion you must fear."

"I only met with the man, negotiated an agreement, and left!" She protested although, deep down, she admitted to herself her words failed to acknowledge Ziesolf's fears were well founded.

"You may be speaking the truth, but what others perceive to be the truth may be what is more important. I only say that you must take care, now more than ever," he warned.

I have no idea of what to say to please the man, she thought as she had made her way back to her uncle's house. *I have taken caution at every turn, as much as possible at least. Yet, I could not become so careful I could not act. Anyway, what is done is done. I must suffer the consequences for my actions, if consequences there are to be.*

Her mood improved considerably, however, when she later related the events of the afternoon to Trudi, now in their uncensored form. Trudi's eyes grew wide as Christina described Gaveston's amorous advances, then she laughed uncontrollably as she heard of the man's unexpected discovery of Christina's true sex. After a moment, Christina joined in the maid's merriment, the two of them holding each other close as they rolled on the bed. Wiping tears from her eyes, Trudi said, "Oh Christina, how I wished I had been there to see the expression on his face!"

Christina remembered smiling at her friend, happy that at least someone thought she was clever and daring. *At least Trudi doesn't spend all of our time together warning me, or threatening me,* she had thought thankfully.

Christina awakened from her reverie and returned to supervising the loading of her cargo. She wished to make absolute certain no damage was incurred that might somehow diminish the quality of the merchandise to less than that she had promised Gaveston. Once the task was finished, she nodded to the foreman of the workhands who, in turn, signaled the carter to urge his oxen forward. Ponderously, they began to move as Christina ran to open the gates.

As the beasts pulled their heavy burden through the gates, Gerhardt Kohl stomped down his steps, across the yard, and into the street. He said nothing as he passed Christina, the hardness of his jaw revealing his animosity toward her seethed unabated. He no longer wore his dirty shirt and bare feet. He was now dressed in fine robes more fitting for an alderman. *Or a visit to one,* she thought glumly.

What would be Revele's reaction to the news of her sale to Gaveston? The arrival of another wagon drew her attention away from consideration of the question, although she knew it would not be permanently eased from her thoughts.

She oversaw the loading of the wagon, then another, and another. As the final carter drove his load through the gates, she closed them behind him. Walking over to the warehouse door, she put her hand upon it; however, before shutting it, she took one last glimpse inside. All that remained of *der Greif's* cargo were a few loose remnants of wood and the dusty outlines on the floor where barrels, casks, and crates had once been stacked. Somehow, it made her feel sad. *For the past several weeks, I have spent my time constantly worrying about what had been stored here; its condition, its value, whether it would be swindled from me. Now, it is gone and, along with it, the burden it has placed on me.* Instead of feeling happy, however, she was gnawed by the realization she had only traded one set of concerns for another.

She had anticipated her unorthodox agreement might raise the ire of the English merchant traders. Selling directly to Gaveston, she had effectively cut them out from the transaction, negating their opportunity to turn a profit. There were clear statutes in the charter the old king, Edward I, had awarded the Hansards that forbade retail trade. After long consideration, she came to the conclusion she had not broken this convention; believing she could effectively argue the size and value of Gaveston's purchase clearly qualified as a wholesale transaction. Furthermore, no one would dispute royalty was a law onto itself and, as the King's favorite, the Earl of Cornwall clearly qualified as such. She firmly believed any dispute brought before the King would be adjudged in her favor.

Her fellow Hansards, however, were another matter. Although the Hanse was recognized as an association, the membership had always been ill-defined and amorphous. Even the question of what cities belonged was open to debate by those whose shores they visited. Consequently, the rights and privileges granted to its members were broadly bestowed by foreign rulers, often to anyone who spoke a language believed to be German.

As a result, it was left to the organization itself to police its members. Some trade outposts, such as the *Peterhof* in Novgorod, Rus', were surrounded by sturdy palisades, the merchants within burdened by strict statutes regulating every aspect of trade as well as personal behavior.

Ziesolf had told her that, up to this point, the Hansard merchants trading in London had enjoyed a much higher degree of freedom. Strong aldermen such as Revele, however, had been working hard to bring more order and control to the London entrepot. It was obvious to Christina someone such as herself, young and without reputation, who disregarded what was accepted as customary trade practices, would be viewed as a threat to his plans.

It was within the aldermen's power to impound her vessel, imprison her, and confiscate her movables and funds. There was little she could do to thwart him from effecting the first two as long as she and *der Greif* remained in London. With the sale of her goods completed, she had few physical assets beyond what clothed her.

What she did possess, however, was money and a considerable amount of it. Her sale to Gaveston had netted her slightly over seven thousand English pounds. To protect this sum from the possibility of seizure, she realized she had to place it somewhere beyond the grasp of Revele and the other aldermen.

Consequently, she had taken the prudent but unusual measure of instructing Gaveston's chamberlain to deposit her payment with the Bardi family, the preeminent Florentine bankers in London. With the Peruzzi, these two families facilitated trade throughout Europe by accepting deposits and issuing bills of exchange in return.

With representatives of the house of Bardi in dozens of cities, including London, Bruges, Paris, and Constantinople, a merchant could make purchases in another city simply by presenting the bill. This did away with the necessity of transporting heavy sacks of coin over long distances. *Or leaving it available for confiscation,* she thought to herself with satisfaction.

With Martinmas only a few days hence, Christina desired nothing more than to quickly procure a cargo for *der Greif* and dispatch the vessel back to Lubeck. There was one task, however, that was even more pressing. She knew she must pay the six hundred marks she owed to Herr Revele within the next three days or be in default of their agreement. Although there was naught she would have liked better than to send Ziesolf to the alderman with the money, she felt to do so would appear as if she were avoiding him, fearing his reaction to the news that, even now, her uncle may be conveying to him. *No, to send someone in my stead will make me appear weak and ashamed of my actions,* she decided resolutely. *This is a task I must perform myself.*

Christina took brisk action. She dispatched Ziesolf to the house of the alderman to arrange a time when they could meet. He returned quickly, informing her it was the alderman's pleasure to see her that very morning, the sooner the better. She ignored the rather ominous tone of Revele's reply, now sending Ziesolf to *der Greif* to collect up whatever members of its crew were available. Although Christina had decided she must take the dowry to Revele, she knew it would be foolhardy to transport such a large sum through the teeming streets of London alone.

She took the men to her room and they gathered their valuable burden. On the way through the yard, she saw Will, Richard, and a few other young men staring her way. She resisted a sudden impulse to waive at her acquaintances, choosing instead to walk purposefully to the gate while offering them no sign of recognition.

Although it was not a far distance to the house of the alderman, everyone in Christina's small band were tired from toting the heavy bags of coin by the time they arrived at Revele's gate. The same steward who had given her entrance previously showed her into the manor once more. This time, however, she was not led to the solar, but to the great hall.

Revele's large, ornately carved chair sat centered behind a heavy oak table that must have been over twenty feet long. The raised dais upon which the table rested caused Revele's head to be slightly above that of Christina despite the fact he was seated. He thus gazed down on her, a superior in every way, as he spoke.

Well, it seems we have had a plague of Kohl's today," he chuckled at his jest, but with no sign of mirth on his face.

Christina replied boldly, "I wish you good day, Herr Alderman. I cannot account for my uncle's visit, only that of my own which serves a more useful purpose, I venture. I have brought you the payment upon which we had agreed."

Revel's expression remained unchanged, his quick, darting eyes had already marked the bags carried by Christina's men, guessing their obvious contents. He motioned to several burly men who lounged in the shadows to the side of the hall. They took the bags and placed them on a table, behind which an elderly man sat. He quickly removed the leather ties from one of the bags, spilled its contents before him, and began efficiently arranging the tale pounds into neat stacks.

Revele said, "Please excuse me, young Kohl, for I do not mean to imply I suspect your honesty." He gestured toward the table where the man was immersed in his counting. "In business, one must learn to deal with facts only, not allowing emotion to cloud one's judgement, don't you think?"

He now flashed a grin at Christina, but one so without warmth it resembled more of a rictus of death.

"Let us be frank, Frederick, shall we?" he continued. "Your uncle came to me this morning with highly troubling news. Of course, it was news to which I had already been privy. Did he not think I would learn of your dealings with Cornwall sooner than three days hence, the fool? I must ask, you do confirm you have sold your cargo to Gaveston?"

Christina nodded and said, "Yes."

"Splendid!" he said, "I would hate to think my sources could have been so ill informed. Now, how long have you been here in London?"

"A little under two weeks, twelve days in fact."

My God, she thought to herself, *has it only been that long? It seems like an eternity!*

"And is this your first journey to London, in a commercial capacity of course?"

Christina nodded, beginning to suspect the intent of the man's line of questioning.

"Well, there we have it then, don't we?" he exclaimed. "A poor young man, beset by heartrending loss, is tossed upon foreign shores. Inexperienced and ignorant of local ways, he tries to make his way as best he knows how. A tragic story, don't you think? One that would rend the heart of any father. I shudder to imagine how my own son, Albrecht, would have fared in circumstances such as yours!"

She said nothing, her senses acutely aware the man was almost ready to spring his trap.

"Yes, poor Frederick Kohl," he continued. "When I first heard your sad story, I pitied you. I thought, 'how can I help this young man whom fate has treated so unkindly?' I offered you my friendship and the hospitality of my house. I offered to help you from your dilemma by purchasing your cargo. Why, I even offered my only daughter to you in marriage, bringing you into my very family. But how was I repaid?"

"With the six hundred silver marks upon which we had agreed," Christina answered mildly.

"No!" the alderman shouted with sudden ferocity, rising to his feet and sweeping his cup from the table with his hand.

All became deathly silent in the room save for the drinking vessel clattering about on the floor. "You repaid me with treachery! You mistook my kindness for weakness, believing I would allow my personal feelings toward you to cloud my judgement as chief alderman. To not realize your foul, scheming heart belies the innocence of your appearance!"

Christina was shocked by Revele's livid outburst. She glanced to her side and saw the alderman's men stood completely still, as if frozen by the cold fury of his tone. Even the one counting coins was motionless, his tally stick paused in mid-air.

"You devised a scheme forbidden by our agreement with the English, a fact upon which you would have been informed had you only sought the counsel of your uncle, or even myself. Instead, the decision was yours alone, unless this man here advised you?

He pointed accusingly over her shoulder towards who she inferred to be Ziesolf."

"No, Herr Alderman, my plan was mine and mine alone," she replied, seeing no advantage in sharing his ire with Ziesolf.

"Go!" Revele said unexpectedly. "Leave now!" he shouted with such force spittle flew from his lips.

The spell over his men now broken, they scrambled to leave the hall, nearly overturning the table before them in their haste. Although none of the coins were knocked to the floor, several of the carefully arranged stacks were toppled over.

Christina started to turn but halted when Revele cried, "Not you, Kohl!"

Ziesolf stared at her, his eyes silently questioning her as to what it was she wanted him to do. With a slight movement of her head, she gestured toward the door through which they had entered the hall. He acknowledged her wish with a nod of his own. He and the crewmen then left the room, leaving Christina alone with Revele.

She turned back to face the alderman squarely, having no idea what was to happen next.

Revele walked slowly to one of the huge windows in the side wall, pausing to look up and out. He stood there for several minutes, seemingly lost in thought. When he turned back to Christina, the anger on his face had dissipated, leaving an enigmatic expression she liked even less.

"It seems you have left me with a problem, young Kohl," he said, moving to where he stood only a foot before her. Without question, you have violated one of the most important provisions of our trade treaty with the English. I will soon have a never-ending line of their merchants streaming through my door, demanding your head as well as compensation. I will hear similar grievances from those of the Hanse, asking that I impose punishment upon you for endangering their livelihood. It would seem I would have little recourse but to do what they ask."

Christina blanched, fearing the worst.

"On the other hand, we are here in London at the pleasure of the King, enjoying the benefits he has granted us through his charter. What he has given, he can just as easily take away."

Where is he going with this? She wondered.

"It is whispered the current king is a weak man, paling in comparison to his father, Edward Longshanks. One of his few strengths, however, is the loyalty he shows to one man: Piers Gaveston. He refuses the man nothing, even at the expense of his own reputation with his barons. It would logically seem then that, in currying the favor of the Earl of Cornwall, you have also placed yourself in good standing with the King. Consequently, to punish you may incur the animosity of the Earl and, through him, that of the King as well."

She listened intently. *Could it be I am somehow going to escape this mess?*

"I can endure the complaints of merchants, but I cannot chance the disfavor of a king. Therefore, you are free to go about your business, Frederick, without

penalty or punishment."

"Thank you, Herr . . ." Christina began.

"Silence! I neither seek nor desire your gratitude!" His mood had turned angry again. Only this time it was of a measured and controlled variety. "Do not think for an instance I condone or compliment you on your actions. I consider only what is best for those of our confederation trading and living here. If I did not bear the responsibility for them upon my shoulders, you would even now be in prison, everything you own taken from you. Now, go, before I let those passions I hold against you to overcome the considerations of my office."

Christina had the good sense to say nothing more, as any word she uttered would only serve to provoke him further. She bowed slightly, then turned and began to walk toward the door.

"One thing more," he called out to her. She spun around to face him.

"It is a dangerous game you play. It is without question the King favors Gaveston. But it is also true that, among the other powerful men of the kingdom, he is hated beyond words. And they grow more powerful every day. Should the time ever come when they are able to force Edward to give up the man, he will be protected no more. Nor will you, for that matter. That is the time I will hunt you out and hold you duly accountable for what you have done."

He stood staring at Christina as if he hoped his eyes would cut a burning path through her skull.

Resisting the urge to run from the hall, she walked in measured steps from the room. Once outside the door, she noticed she was trembling but, whether it was from fear or relief, she could not say. They returned directly to the house of her uncle. After dismissing the sailors to return to *der Greif*, she related to Ziesolf what had occurred after he had left the hall. Christina was relieved in that, for once, he offered no critique or criticism of her actions.

"What is done is done," he said simply. He then departed, leaving her to herself.

She felt grateful to not encounter her uncle as she entered the house. The last thing she desired were more ill words. She passed her aunt as she walked through the family's solar. The woman did not even glance away from her embroidery, instead ignoring Christina completely. It was evident she had been told of what had transpired by her husband, the circumstances obviously related in the least favorable manner. *Should I say something?* Christina wondered, but the woman's severely pursed lips convinced her she should not. She went to her room, closed the door, and sat down on the bench near the unlit brazier. She felt cold, but whether it was from the temperature of the room or the loneliness in her heart, she did not know. She gathered her cloak about her.

A myriad of worries swirled in her head like a maelstrom. It was not just the threats of Revele that troubled her. She knew she had overstayed her welcome in her uncle's house and should make plans to leave, but the more pressing issue was what to do about procuring a cargo for *der Greif*. The time to make a decision was upon her. As she considered the merits of her various options, she felt increasingly incapable of focusing her thoughts. Finally, she gave in to a mounting drowsiness and, curling into a ball beneath the heavy fabric of her cloak, fell fast asleep where she sat.

Christina jolted awake, disoriented and unaware of her surroundings. She lifted the cloak from over her eyes and was amazed to see her room was almost pitch black, lit only by the faintness of the sliver of moonlight that struggled through the thick window glass. She shifted her arm slightly as a prelude to sitting up from the bench. Suddenly, she froze.

Someone else was in the room.

Christina smiled. *Surely, its only Trudi, stealing in to give me a late night snuggle.* She welcomed the thought of a warm body next to hers, tacitly reassuring her all will come right in the end. Still, she remained motionless as the dark figure made no movement to slip beneath the covers on the bed as Trudi would certainly have done. Instead, it moved stealthily about the darkest recesses of the room, a few steps at a time, crouching low to stay as concealed as possible.

At first, she had thought it moved silently, gliding over the floor as if a specter. Concentrating harder, she discerned the muted sound of padded feet upon the floor with each step. *This is not a ghost, nor is it a lasting manifestation of my nightmares. This is a real person, one whose only purpose could be to do me harm.* She scarcely dared to take a breath.

After what seemed an unimaginably long time, the lurker had made his or her way near the side of Christina's bed. She saw the glint of a blade appear in the assailant's hand, its malevolent purpose frightenedly obvious.

Christina's own hand crept toward her belt. She was somewhat relieved to find her eating knife there, although it provided small reassurance.

Unexpectedly, the figure made his final approach to the bed in a few quick bounds, bringing the knife downward in one vicious movement. He paused, however, a few inches before ramming its point through coverlet and straw mattress. The would-be murderer suddenly drew up to his full-height. Glancing wildly about the room with confusion, his eyes passed over the bench where Christina huddled without recognition or pause.

Then, with rapid steps, he left the room, pausing to gently pull the door closed after his departure. Christina heard no sound after that to provide her with a clue as to the figure's next destination.

She leapt to her feet and went to latch the door, then moved a heavy trunk against it for added security. Feeling somewhat safer for the moment, she still took the added precaution of moving her falchion to within a few inches of her ready grasp, should she find it necessary. For the remainder of the night she attempted to sleep. Her eyes would close for no more than a few minutes before some perceived or imagined sound would startle her suddenly awake, grasping frantically for her weapon before she realized she was still alone and safe. She greeted the morning sun with thankfulness, although tired and sore from the tense events of the night before.

She quickly used her chamber pot and splashed a bit of cold water on her face, its bracing effect doing little to ease her fatigue. She moved through the house without seeing anyone, although she did hear the sound of one of the maids lighting a fire in the kitchen. Christina hesitated. *I wonder if it is Trudi?* she thought, speculating if she should tell her friend about the intruder. She decided she would not, believing it would only serve the purpose of frightening her.

The city was beginning to come alive as she walked through the rain-dampened streets. She soon came to *der Greif's* mooring. Stepping lightly onboard, she was surprised to see Ziesolf washing himself with water from an oaken bucket. He was stripped to the waist as he intently carried out his ablutions, apparently unaware Christina was watching him. She noticed the several scars on his body, most notably one that slashed diagonally down his back, like a bloated worm resting under his pale skin.

Ziesolf then immersed his entire head in the bucket, swiftly withdrawing it and shaking it vigorously side to side. Water flew from the tips of his long grey hair. It reminded Christina of one of her family's dogs she had taken for a swim in the Trave. The pleasant memory brought a sudden lump to her throat.

Without turning to face her, Ziesolf said, "It happened in a skirmish with the Semigallians a few days ride from Riga. We had traveled out to survey some lands held by the archbishop on a pleasant autumn day. Believing there were no dangers in the area we rode unencumbered by our mail. We were riding through a densely forested area when they dropped from the trees, their long knives seeking our vitals. I felt his blade plough my back like a furrow as I fell to the ground. Fortunately, one of my brothers was within sword's-reach. Lucky for me that is, not so much for the unbeliever."

He glanced toward Christina and said dryly, "Now, I do not suppose you ventured out in the early hours of the morn to spy on me at my toilet, nor to hear old stories of my youth."

Although somewhat embarrassed to be discovered staring, she related the events of the past evening. "Are you sure the man's intent was not thievery? That same day, we walked through the streets of London burdened down by what was unmistakably sacks of coin. It would not have been difficult for a dishonest person to conclude there was more stored from whence that came."

"No, the actions of the man belied that notion. As he moved about the room, he took no notice of containers that may have held treasure. Instead, his sole interest was to work his way to my bedside and commit his foul deed."

Ziesolf nodded in agreement with her appraisal.

"And you have no inkling as to the man's identity?" he asked.

"None. He was tall, of average build, and he wore a cowl pulled well over his face. The light was also very dim," she replied, giving thanks to God the moon had been a wan one. *Otherwise he would have discerned my presence and pressed his attack where I lay.*

Ziesolf considered her reply and then said, "It is too dangerous for you to remain in your uncle's house. Your assailant sought you once, it would be folly to believe he will not try again, especially given the fact he believes his presence went completely undetected. You should spend your nights aboard *der Greif* from this day forward."

Although she agreed wholly with Ziesolf as to remaining no longer at her uncle's house, she was a bit more hesitant about agreeing to move back to her old cabin on the cog. She had become accustomed once more to sleeping in a large comfortable bed in a warm room such as that she had enjoyed in her parents' house in Lubeck. The thought of returning to the damp, cramped cabin smelling of rotten herring and cod juices made her inwardly groan. *I will gladly endure the discomfort for the duration of a sea voyage, but not while I have the alternative of sleeping on dry land*, she decided obstinately.

"No," she said resolutely. "I think I wish to make other lodging arrangements. Ultimately, I will look to secure a house here in London with ample storerooms below. As for now, I will try to find lodging to rent temporarily. I don't suppose you know of anywhere that might be available?" she asked hopefully.

He shook his head thoughtfully, then said, "Are you sure this is the wisest course? You would be much more secure here." He peered at her hopefully but conceded the point when she remained silent. He changed the subject. "What about the cargo? We have scant days left before we must sail, if we are to return to Lubeck this year."

"I hope to know by the end of the day," she answered, subtly implying she had some sort of plan to set in motion although really having no inkling as to how best to proceed.

"Good," was his succinct response.

Christina left Ziesolf to get himself dressed. As for herself, she departed the ship with plans for a full day beginning to coalesce in her mind.

Chapter 14

Christina spent the next hour wandering rather aimlessly through the streets of London, attempting to form her thoughts into a definite plan of action. She considered attempting to visit Gaveston to seek his counsel as well. She reconsidered, however, firstly because she was unsure whether she could gain an audience and, secondly, because his experience in the matters before her would seem negligible, if any at all.

The matter of arranging a cargo was extremely pressing. *Can I purchase goods, load them aboard ship, and have the ship set sail for Lubeck, all within three days?* she considered. Although she was extremely hesitant to admit it to herself, she thought not. Consequently, a return voyage to her home port was out of the question. She knew the crew of *der Greif* would be disappointed, however, if she offered them a hefty bonus, their good cheer would certainly return. *Much better to pay out a few pennies to the sailors than to risk purchasing English cloth that would be worthless at an alternative port such as Bruges. Even worse would be to decide to hold the ship in London over the winter.* As a result, she prudently decided a cargo of wool would be her best option. *Certainly not as lucrative as buying finished cloth or tin, but a much safer investment.*

Well then, a trip to the guildhall of the Fellowship of the Staple is the logical first step, she thought. As one of the two staple ports for all of England, London controlled the export of wool from throughout the southern part of the country as well as Wales. She vowed to visit the guildhall later in the day, now having no need to speed her purchases to meet a critical sailing deadline.

She now turned her thoughts toward her other dilemma, that of finding a place to stay in London besides the house of Gerhardt Kohl or aboard *der Greif*. There were, of course, several inns and other lodgings to choose from while she took her time making a more permanent arrangement. Many of these would be unsuitable for one reason or another. Some would be little more than a roof over one's head, and a leaky one at that. The expectation at these establishments was that several lodgers would let a room, crowding onto a bed together and sharing it further with an infestation of fleas and even larger, more voracious, vermin. Others, like the Nag's Head, were far more likely to rent their rooms by the hour, rather than the day or week.

At the thought of the Nag's Head, she suddenly recalled the inn she had passed on the High Street along the way. The Tabard appeared finely constructed and in good condition, clearly only recently built. Though she knew nothing of its clientele, it had certainly seemed less raucous than her eventual destination for that evening. She glanced up, found her bearings, and altered her course for the Great Bridge.

She soon found herself in Southwark and, a few minutes later, in front of The Tabard.

It is as I remembered it, she thought happily, *perhaps even better.* The structure rose to three stories, all straight and true and obviously built as one. The thatched roof seemed fresh and in good repair, broken only by several, evenly-spaced, dormer windows. Christina's critical eye noted this feature with approval, knowing spaces having a natural light source tended to be less damp. The inn seemed to be built as a central building and two long wings. On the fourth side, a substantial palisade rose, securing what must be a central courtyard within. Christina was excited at the possibility of living here for a time and, hoping for the best, stepped through the gateway.

Inside, the yard was a bevy of activity. Men, women, and children went about numerous tasks, all seemingly in preparation of their departure.

Christina was curious and approached a man of roughly her age. "Peace be with you, good fellow. It would seem you are leaving. Where is it to which you travel?"

"And a fine day to you, good sir," the young man replied. "Why to Canterbury, of course. We are a group of pilgrims who have traveled from Shrewsbury on our way to offer our prayers at the shrine of Saint Thomas."

He gazed at her inquisitively. "Are you not as well?"

She responded she was not, then asked him to whom she should speak about arranging a room. He pointed her toward the doorway into the common room, instructing her to seek Martin, the innkeeper.

She thanked him and walked inside the inn.

She was pleased to find the room relatively free of noxious odors, providing an indication the establishment was respectable and well kept. There were clean rushes on the floor, pleasantly scented with sprigs of lavender. Two talbots lounged by the low fire, their coats the color of rich cream. She saw a sturdy, mountain of a man wearing a leather apron busily sweeping the floor, a small pile of leaves, dirt, and spilled food before him.

He lifted his ruddy face toward her as she entered and rendered her a polite greeting.

Christina responded in kind, then added, "I take it you are Martin, the innkeeper?" He nodded.

"Good. I would like to let a room, or perhaps a suite of rooms if you have such?"

"Aye," he answered in a voice accustomed to answering such questions. "And will it be only for tonight?"

Christina paused, considering how best to answer the man's question. With the large group of religious travelers outside departing this morning, she realized she could probably have her choice of accommodation at the inn. She really had no idea how long it may take to find permanent lodging in the city, however. *Is it worth being displaced by the next crowd of pilgrims if I choose to take the room on a night-by-night basis?* she considered.

"No, Goodman Martin, I would like to secure the room for the next month."

"Well," he hesitated, now examining her more closely, "A month's a long time. Have you such coin?"

She was growing impatient. "A month's rent, all paid in advance, and no more questions."

The man appeared as though he wanted to ask more of Christina, then shrugged his shoulders instead.

"I'll show you the rooms," he answered simply, foregoing any further interrogation for now.

They went outside and mounted a staircase that led upward to a wide covered gallery. Over the next several minutes, Martin gave Christina a tour of the varied housings available at The Tabard. Most rooms were huge, containing as many as a dozen beds. Allowing two or three lodgers per bed, she imagined a group such as she had passed in the courtyard could be accommodated wholly in one such chamber. Others were smaller, with no more than three beds. All were relatively clean and well-maintained.

They passed back into the central structure and went up a small flight that was partially obscured by the end of the massive bar.

"I usually keep this one free. We oft times get churchmen or nobles passing through who, for one reason or another, prefer an inn over the places they usually stay," he said as he opened the door into a moderately-sized room.

The large window before her let in considerable light, making it easy for Christina to immediately survey the room. A wooden bed frame stood near the wall on the left, surmounted by a straw mattress encased in a well-mended hemp cover. Over this, a second mattress was placed, although she could not immediately identify its contents. *Oh God, please let it be down*, she silently hoped, although the chances of it being so were quite slim.

She sat down heavily, finding to her slight consternation the second was indeed filled with straw as well. The ropes of the bed were tightly wound, however, providing somewhat of a recompense.

A large chest for personal possessions was located by the wall opposite beside a small table set with a ceramic ewer and a brass basin. Tucked away in the opposite corner was a wooden framed box with a round hole in the top. The vessel tucked away beneath announced its obvious intent. She smiled, thinking how civilized it would be not having to squat over the chamber pot in the middle of the night.

Christina immediately liked the chamber. Regrettably, however, it was simply too small for her purpose.

Sensing her consternation, Martin grinned and beckoned her further into the room. Near the window, he turned toward the wall and opened a door that had hitherto been concealed behind a drapery. He led her into a second, larger room, that was furnished as a solar. Benches were placed about two of the walls, while an inviting fireplace and window dominated the two others. Although it was nowhere near as opulent as that of her uncle, it certainly served the purpose.

Martin opened another door that was placed opposite that through which they had passed into the solar, revealing yet another, smaller, bedchamber.

She turned to him and exclaimed, "This will do very nicely," trying to keep the excitement out of her voice.

"That will be one pound, ten shillings, paid in advance as you said."

"Including a hearty breakfast each morn, Master Innkeeper?" she asked hopefully, the emptiness in her stomach reminding her she had yet to eat today.

"Aye," he rubbed his bearded chin thoughtfully with fingers as thick as plump sausages, then added, "for one pound sixteen, that is."

"Including this morning?"

Martin grinned and nodded. He handed her an iron key then spat on his hand and extended it toward her. Responding in kind, she gripped that of the innkeeper.

In an hour's time, she was back out on the street, her stomach now delightfully sated. She whistled cheerfully as she crossed the bridge back into the city, feeling quite content with herself. *If only my business with the woolmen can be carried off so successfully*, she thought hopefully.

Christina knew the guildhall was located in the section of the city known as Chepe. Once she arrived in the borough, she queried two passersby to determine its exact location. She soon found herself before a surprisingly modest building whose purpose was clearly defined by the unmistakable woolsack prominently displayed on the hanging sign in front.

She stepped inside, proclaiming to a man sitting at a table, "Good day, God be here."

He glanced up, startled from the account documents he had been studying intently. "And good day to you, fine fellow. How may I be of assistance?"

Christina briefly detailed her intent.

The man smiled encouragingly and said, "Fortune indeed smiles upon you today! Master Butiler is working above." He gestured toward the ceiling overhead. "I will fetch him forthwith."

The clerk disappeared up the stairs at the back of the room, returning in a few moments with a man who followed energetically despite his obviously advanced age.

"I am Paul Butiler. So, it is wool you desire?"

"Yes, enough to fill the cargo hold of my cog," she explained. "*der Greif* is a sturdy vessel and she should hold some eighty-five tons."

Although the ship could carry at least five additional tons, Mattias, the ship's master, had asked to allow for additional ballast should the winter sea portent to be uncommonly rough.

The woolmonger's eyes opened wide.

He performed some quick mental calculations then said, "Roughly two hundred and thirty-three sarplar, as I figure."

Christina looked at him blankly, unfamiliar with the term.

Sensing her confusion, he remarked, "A sarplar is equivalent to two sacks, each of three hundred and sixty-four pounds. Now, this is high-quality wool, mind you, from Lemster sheep that are the finest in the land. It has been coarse combed, with the staple running about as long as your thumb. I would not normally have such a quantity this late in the season, but I have held some back this year."

Christina took a deep breath and said, "I would offer you six pounds per sack for good quality wool, and five for that of middling grade."

Thank God I had had the good sense to study my father's account book closely.

Butiler laughed and said, "Certainly you jest, Master Kohl. This past summer, I sold my best for nine, and six!"

She surveyed him evenly and smiled, "I doubt you not, but that was then. How much will this clip be worth when there is a new shearing? And if your offers were so good, how is it you still have sacks held back"

Some of the humor had now left the merchant's face. "Seven pounds, six for the good and five and eight for the average."

They bargained back and forth until they came to an amiable agreement, that is, of course, before the matter of drayage came up.

"The price then is agreed," Christina concluded. "Will you be able to deliver the wool to my ship this week?"

Butiler stared at her a bit shocked, then realized there had been a misunderstanding. "Why, that is simply impossible. The wool is not here in London, but in Ludlow some hundred and fifty miles to the northwest. Sending instructions, arranging carters, and transporting the sacks south will take several weeks at best, even if the weather holds true. If not, who knows?"

Christina was crestfallen at the man's unexpected admission. Realizing she had few alternatives, however, she agreed, which reopened their negotiations as to the additional conveyance costs. At last, even this detail was settled. For her part, she promised to pay the woolmonger half his price up front and the remainder upon delivery to her at dockside. Butiler undertook to have his clerk draw up a contract by the next day, when she could return and they could apply their respective seals.

She left the guildhall with mixed emotions. She had hoped to dispatch *der Greif* to Bruges prior to the end of November. Now, however, it appeared as though the ship would more likely weigh anchor in the new year.

I will need to let Matthias know, of course. Although they had only been in London for a few weeks, some of the ship's crew had already left, hiring on to other vessels bound back for the *Ostsee* coast, or for other, more exotic, ports. *He will need to know we need a full complement of sailors before the earliest time the wool might arrive. Meanwhile, I will offer a bonus to those who remain, should they stay to make the journey to the Flemish port.*

The thought of Matthias made her smile. He was a man of interminable age with a face as craggy as the Danish coast and skin the texture of hundred-year-old ropery. *Nothing misses his eye and the good Lord help the careless seaman who feels the furious lash of his tongue,* she now grinned openly.

Matthias had completely ignored Christina on the passage from Lubeck. He had had no cause to speak to her whilst she was a female, and what instructions that needed to pass between them in her guise as Frederick Kohl has customarily been relayed through Ziesolf.

Since arriving in London, however, she had had several extensive conversations with the man, finding him to be intelligent and level-headed. She felt assured he would have *der Greif* fully-manned, in good repair, and ready to sail by whatever date she set for its departure.

Christina broke away from her musings with sudden surprise, finding her feet had carried her before the familiar gateway of her uncle's house. She was suddenly beset by a moment of indecision, then came to the conclusion there was no better time to take her leave of her uncle than the present. There was a bevy of activity in the yard, which she ignored, and mounted the steps to the house.

Gerhardt Kohl was working at the table in the solar when she entered, much the same as she had found him on her first eve in London. He stared up at her impassively, his face betraying no outward sign of emotion.

After a moment, he said, "Congratulations, Frederick. I hear you have avoided any punishment for your rash actions, other than incurring the not inconsequential animosity of the chief alderman, that is."

"I am sorry, Uncle, if my actions have reflected any disfavor upon you. That was never my intent."

She had rehearsed her simple apology and it tumbled from her lips smoothly.

"Yes, well, it is not me who must worry about the repercussions, but you," he interjected tersely.

She ignored his somewhat accusatory response.

"Wishing to cause you no more trouble, I have decided I shall no longer impose on your hospitality. I will take my leave of your gracious household this very eve."

An expression of surprise, followed by one of anger, leapt across his plump face. When he spoke, however, it was in a conciliatory tone. "I will hear nothing of such an idea, Frederick! Come now, you made a mistake and, although it was a serious one, you have suffered no harm because of it.

All a part of life, I say. For who is it, other than our sweet Lord, who has never erred? Certainly, not me! Of course, you will continue to stay here with me, with your family!"

He had risen and moved around the table to place an encouraging arm clumsily around Christina's shoulders.

Somewhat embarrassed, Christina shrugged away from her uncle's grasp. She moved a short distance away and turned to face him. His expression now appeared so crestfallen, she felt an involuntary urge to agree to stay.

Resisting, she answered, "I am sorry, but I have already made my decision, uncle."

"But, why?" he cried, unexpected emotion obvious in his voice.

Why indeed? she asked herself. She considered whether to tell him about the intruder who had entered her room the previous night. She decided she should, if for no other reason than for his own safety and that of her aunt. "Last night, a man entered my room while I slept. He brandished a knife above my bed, obviously intent on doing me ill. He eventually left, but I have no reason to believe he will not return."

"What?" her uncle asked in an oddly measured voice, "Why did you not say something earlier? Why did you not raise an alarm immediately? Could this apparition not have appeared to you in a dream?"

"No," she stated adamantly. "The man was real, the threat as well."

"I will have some of my men sleep in the hall and ensure the door into the solar is locked as well. That should keep out any cutpurses, or varlets of murderous intent."

He chuckled, clearly not fully believing Christina's account.

Well, I have done the right thing in letting him know, she decided. *Whether he takes my warning seriously is at his own peril,* she thought, then, to her uncle she said, "Yes, those would be prudent measures; however, I have already made up my mind."

"But where will you go?" he asked, apparently finally conceding the inevitability of her departure.

For some reason she could not explain, Christina felt compelled to form a circumspect answer.

Instead of telling her uncle of her room at The Tabard, she answered evasively. "I am not really certain. For this evening, I will plan to stay on *der Greif.* On the morrow, I will seek out lodging at a nearby inn until I may procure more permanent quarters. Now, I must take your leave. I will gather a few things from my room as well as our family maid. I will send men from the ship for the rest of my belongings in the morning."

Without hesitating to invite more of her uncle's arguments as to why she should not leave, Christina walked from the solar. She found Trudi on the next floor, hurrying down the hallway with her arms full of dirty linen.

"Frederick!" the maid exclaimed loudly, giving her mistress a conspiratorial wink.

Christina smiled. She had been so preoccupied over the past few days she had given little thought to her friend. Now, she realized how much she had truly missed her.

"I am happy to see you, Trudi," Christina said in a controlled voice, just in case she was being eavesdropped upon. "Now, I have instructions for you. I need you to go to your room and change into clothes more suitable for travelling outside. Also, pack whatever it is you might find necessary for a short stay, two days at the maximum."

"But why . . . where am I . . ." Trudi seemed puzzled as she tried to voice several questions simultaneously.

The expression on her mistress' face grew warmer. "Not you, you silly goose, but we. I will be moving to accommodations of my own and will have need for a helpful servant. This is, if you know where I might find one?"

Christina could maintain her act no longer and burst into a happy grin.

It paled by comparison, however, with that of Trudi, who nodded excitedly and ran to her room as quickly as her short legs would carry her. The linens lay on the floor in a heap where the maid had dropped them.

Christina went to her room and gathered a few items of her own. In scant minutes, she heard Trudi's insistent knock. As she exited the room, Christina thought to examine the outside of the door closely.

For the first time, she noticed several small scratches at chest height, exactly where someone might attempt to wiggle a strand of wire through to lift the latch on the other side. *I almost wish I was staying another night,* she thought as they walked together down the hallway. The decision to leave had been made, however, and plans for the discovery of her assailant's identity, as well as the purpose of his attack, would have to be put off to a later time.

It took them longer to reach The Tabard than Christina had figured. She had forgotten Trudi's only glimpse of the city had been their brief walk from *der Greif's* moorage to her uncle's house. *While I have been actively exploring London, Trudi has been doing laundry and working in the kitchen,* she remembered, somewhat guiltily. *Has it only been a few short days ago when I first crossed the river myself?* Consequently, she indulged the maid's slow pace as she marveled at the sights, sounds, and smells of the city at night. At long last, they reached the inn.

Christina congratulated herself for having the foresight to procure her rooms that morning. *Surely, not even a mousehole will be vacant now!* She thought. Although the yard was teeming with people, the common room was absolutely packed, with hardly a place to stand available. In the corner, a thin man with a flute played a merry tune, accompanied by a young boy beating a small tabor. People young and old swayed to the music, mirth and cheerful talk filled the warm air.

They worked their way through the throng, toward the bar. Martin was busy, filling tankard after tankard with ale and beer and dispatching them to one of several young women who deftly delivered them to their thirsty patrons.

At last, a lull occurred in the demand for drink. Martin wiped the considerable sweat from above his brow and walked over to Christina and Trudi.

"Good eve, Master Frederick! May I fetch ye and your friend some ale?"

"Ignoring his query for the moment, she asked, "Is it always this busy at night?" remembering the din in the barroom of the Nag's Head.

Perhaps I have been a bit hasty in paying for an entire month of lodging in advance. How can anyone possibly sleep with all this racket going on downstairs?

"Oh, no!" he said, a deep chuckle arose from his barrel of a chest like distant thunder on a hot summer's night. "Do you not know what day it is?" He did not give Christina time to answer. "Why, this is Martinmas, of course! The feast of St. Martin of Tours, the patron saint of drunkards and

- 256 -

innkeepers. I don't know of which my ma was thinking when she named me!"

His infectious good humor provoked Christina to laugh aloud as well.

"Well, Goodman Martin, could I ask you to send one of your girls up to my rooms with a jug of ale and a bit of supper."

She suddenly felt Trudi tugging at her sleeve.

"Oh, master, could we not sit here to sup? It seems such a jolly place and you have been too long without merriment!"

Why not? Trudi's words rang true. It had been a long while since she had had a good time. *Which of course does not count my evening at the Nag's Head, which started well, but quickly turned to shit. Other than providing the opportunity to meet Gaveston,* she amended herself.

Both Martin and Trudi looked to her for a response. The sound of chairs being pushed across the floor caught her attention. A small table near the middle of the room was now standing vacant. She took it for a portent on what she should decide.

"Why not?" she spoke the words aloud this time. "Martin, may we please have two tankards of ale, as well as two plates of rye bread and that goodly beef there, "she gestured toward one of the servants passing by with a huge platter of steaming meat. "And the black pudding as well," she added greedily.

They quickly moved to the table before anyone else could spy it.

A few hours later, they made their way upstairs, well-sated with food and drink and thoroughly exhausted. Trudi fell into her bed almost as soon as Christina showed it to her. Christina closed her door, smiling. She went to her own room, disrobed, and had a quick wash. Getting into bed, she pulled the blanket up to her chin and stared at the ceiling. Although she could hear the last vestiges of the celebration downstairs, she was too tired to care.

As she drifted off to sleep, she thought with amazement, *This is the first time since arriving in London I have not had important tasks or unpleasant duties to which I must attend. I have no goods to sell, nor none to purchase, and no pressing need to speak with someone whom I dislike or fear. My wagons of wool wend their way toward me at their own speed, with nothing I can do to speed their arrival.* She felt contented for the first time in a long while and fell into a heavy slumber unencumbered by dreams or nightmares.

The next few weeks passed uneventfully. Christina explored the City, oft times making the acquaintance of younger merchants, such as herself. She soon knew drapers, mercers, and pepperers by name, responding to their hearty greetings with one of her own as she passed their shops and stalls. *One day soon, we will talk of business rather than the frigidity of the winter weather,* she promised herself as she passed through the Vintry. She knew she shouldn't get ahead of herself, as she had yet to dispatch her cargo of wool to Bruges, let alone have *der Greif* return and be ready for another voyage. *Perhaps I should look into procuring another ship,* she mused. She put the idea out of her mind for the present, as this course of action would certainly bring her back into contact with merchants from the Hanse.

Since her ill-favored conversation with the chief alderman, Christina had subconsciously avoided any contact with her countrymen. Although Revele had said her dealings with Gaveston would not be held against her, his subsequent threat made that hard to believe. *Who knows who he has coerced into doing me ill?* She considered cautiously. She realized, of course, that a man of his influence and means could readily bribe an Englishman or any of the multitude of foreigners in the city just as easily but hoped it less likely. *Better to give it time for now and hope his animosity moderates with time.*

She was able, however, to fill her days with pastimes other than worrying about those who might wish her harm. One day, a large, two-story wagon pulled up in the area known as Guildable Manor, located near the southern foot of the Great Bridge. Unexpectedly, a curtain parted on the upper floor revealing a stage. Her jaw dropped with amazement as, before her very eyes, she witnessed Eve's temptation of Adam and the fall of man from Eden portrayed before her.

Christina also found a wrestling competition staged in the yard of the Nag's Head quite interesting. She found herself compelled to wager a few small coins against the local favorite, a massive bull of a man inexplicably referred to as Wee Ned. She was not so taken, however, by her first experience with bull-baiting, repulsed by the essential cruelty inherent in the sport and leaving after only a few minutes.

Her time was not frittered away solely in idle pursuits, however. She also made it a point to renew her training with Ziesolf. Most mornings she would go to *der Greif* where the old knight would further her knowledge in the use of weapons as well as her unarmed body to defeat an opponent. At times, a small group of dockworkers would stray from their duties to watch Ziesolf's harsh instruction, laughing uproariously when Christina was knocked ass over tits. She was oft times frustrated as he seemed to best her without effort. A few times, however, her quickness allowed her blade to threaten his vitals, and Ziesolf would concede a grudging word of encouragement. Although these sessions left her aching and sweaty, the physical activity felt good. Although Ziesolf would never admit it to her face, she felt her fighting skills continue to improve.

One day, however, she decided to forego her time with Ziesolf. She awoke early and, taking Trudi with her, traveled northward, into the City for a day of shopping. Christina had several stops in mind, the first of these being Threadneedle Street, the primary location of London's tailors. *I will be so happy to rid myself of my father's garments,* she thought, *both for their unfashionableness and for their continual reminder of his untimely death.* She contracted for several garments to be fashioned; including two shirts of linen, a wool tunic of deepest blue, and braies and chausses. A parti-colored houppelande with woodblock prints rounded out her new wardrobe. Nor did she forget Trudi, for whom she purchased a madder-dyed kirtle. She was amazed when the tailor informed her the total for her purchases would be L3 11s 10d. *Frau Schmidt would have sewed the same for two marks, and thrown in a good hood as well,* she thought, remembering the stout seamstress who had sewed most of the Kohls' wardrobe in Lubeck. *I only hope, for this price, the sleeves are of the same length,* she giggled, recalling one of Frau Schmidt's less successful creations.

Their next stop was Cordwainer's Street, where Christina had made the acquaintance of a youthful cobbler who had just finished his apprenticeship. She ordered a pair of calf-skin leather poulaines of a relatively modest length of six inches up-curled beyond her largest toe. The grateful shoemaker promised they would be ready before the end of the month.

On their way back to Southwark, Christina made a few more purchases, including a pretty coverlet worked with a bit of colorful stitchery, another thick woolen blanket, and two bolsters. Their load seemed to grow heavier with each step. Eventually, however, they reached the yard of The Tabard.

They heaved the door open and entered the common room which, being early in the afternoon, was somewhat deserted. As she moved toward the staircase leading to her rooms, she was surprised to see that, settled unobtrusively at a small table near the fire, sat none other than Piers Gaveston, apparently deep in his cups.

Chapter 15

Christina shooed Trudi upstairs with the goods and went to see what it was that troubled the man.

Pulling up a stool, she said, "Peace be with you, your Grace. May I have leave to join you?"

He peered in her general direction and squinted. After a few seconds, a glint of recognition entered his eyes and he answered, "Well met, friend Christina! How fare thee?"

Christina was startled, both by the loudness of his voice and his reference to her by her real name. She glanced anxiously about the room and was relieved to find it deserted except for an old man and woman on the opposite side of the room who were deep in a conversation of their own. Martin stood in the yard, conversing with another man.

Relieved for the time being her secret had not been disclosed, she asked the obviously inebriated Earl of Cornwall, "Please, your Grace, not so loud!" He gazed at her and nodded his head solemnly. He took his tankard in hand and, raising it up to peer into its depths closely, then let it fall from his hand to clatter noisily onto the table.

"More ale!" he roared, apparently forgetting his vow of a few seconds before. "Christ's Nails, are the cellars dry?"

Martin rushed back into the room and swiftly poured two tankards full. He sat them on the table, offering his apologies. He returned to the yard, leaving Gaveston and Christina alone once more.

"What troubles you so deeply, your Grace?" she asked.

"Piers, call me Piers, for I may not be 'your Grace' much longer," he replied before taking a large draught.

"What do you mean?"

"It's that she-bitch, Isabella, damn her bloody eyes," He brought his drinking vessel down hard on the table for emphasis. "She incites the barons against me! She has held hatred for me since Edward's coronation. Was it I who decided to array the arms of the Earl of Cornwall alongside those of the King instead of hers? Was it I who decided I should carry the King's crown or fasten his spurs? Was it I who decided the King should sit with me at the banquet, instead of with the Queen? No, it was Edward, our sovereign, who answers to no one other than our sweet Lord himself! Who is this French child to question his choices?

Christina was stunned by the ferocity of the Gascon's words.

"It was through her scheming I was exiled to Ireland. I was made King's Regent there. King's Regent, do you know what that means? To spend my days gazing upon the most God-forsaken land on his earth and its most miserable people, that's what!"

He resumed his tirade after a brief pause to take a breath and a long pull from his tankard.

"Now she plots with that whorcson fiddler Thomas of Lancaster, 'Black Dog' Warwick, and the rest of the baronial pack of curs. She seeks my ouster, and certainly my head as well!"

Christina was left confused as to what to do to console the man. She possessed no influence and what money she had was a paltry sum compared to the vast fortunes of the country's great magnates who appeared to stand allied against Gaveston.

All she could manage to say in the form of a response was, "I am sorry, your Grace, for these worrisome matters."

Gaveston now bent his head so low to the table his chin nearly dragged in the dregs of ale that had been spilled there.

He craned his face toward her and, in a conspiratorial whisper, said, "Friend Christina, you are one of the few people here in London in whom I can place my complete trust. Pledge to me, if the time comes, I may be assured you will assist me."

Christina drew a quick breath. *What exactly is he is asking of me?* She asked herself. *This is a man with rich and influential enemies, whose wrath could not only result in my ruin, but a traitor's death as well. He is, however, the only person here in London who deemed to help me, to treat me fairly when others only sought to find gain through my loss. Can I turn my back upon him in his time of need?*

In a low voice, she asked, "What may I do to assist you?"

His face softened and he reached across the table impulsively to grasp her hand. "A time may come when I must leave London in great haste. This may be as a fugitive, with men both great and small giving chase as if hounds seeking to flush a stag from its hiding place. Throughout England there will be a hue and cry for my head. I may find refuge on my own lands, but they are distant and I must cross that of those who ally against me to reach them."

She said nothing but anticipated where the man's train of logic would next take his words. "Traveling by land will place me in great peril. Should I be able to slip from London by sea, however, I would stand a much greater possibility of being undetected. To do this, I would need a ship, one that sails under the orders of someone I can trust without question.

Your ship, Christina." He looked at her, his eyes imploring her to agree.

She had listened to his words with mounting anxiety.

Now she asked, "When will you know if you must leave?"

"How can I be sure? The intrigue at court ebbs and flows, like a great tide. My fears may come to naught and my favor with the King will remain strong. On the other hand, the barons may suddenly become emboldened. I cannot see the future, only fear it."

Her worst suspicions confirmed, Christina could only rub her head in an attempt to dispel the terrible aching welling within. *So, in essence he asks that der Greif remain at anchor, ready to sail at a moment's notice to ports unknown, and with a passenger declared outlaw by all of England. What of my wool? Should I let it rot onboard while the ship remains moored indefinitely? But what if I dispatch it to Bruges and Gaveston requires my promised assistance even as my ship disappears downriver? Damn this place! Cannot anything here ever be simply decided?*

Regretting the words that rolled off her tongue even as she said them, she told Gaveston, "Yes, should you need my help, my ship will be ready to take you wherever you wish to go."

Tears roiled from his eyes as he said in a choked voice, "Thank you, Christina, you are a friend both brave and true. I steadfastly hope you will not have reason to regret your pledge."

He squeezed her hand once more and arose on slightly unsteady feet. He turned and disappeared through the door.

"As do I, your Grace, certainly as do I," she murmured lowly, almost under her breath. She stared after him, scarcely believing what had just occurred had been real.

She threw a few pennies down on the table and trudged up the stairs, realizing her future, that only a few minutes before had seemed so promising, now teetered on a precipice not of her own making. "What you have told me troubles me greatly," Ziesolf said as they sat in the solar of her rooms the next day. "Not only for the obvious peril of incurring the wrath of the nobility through your association with Gaveston, but the chance the chief alderman may see this as an opportunity to carry through with his threats. Like Gaveston, there is little you can do save flee the city should the barons wish to strike at him through you in force. Revele, however, may mount a more clandestine attack, such as that of the assailant at the home of your uncle. It is for this possibility we must prepare."

Christina nodded, finding no fault in the old knight's assessment of her situation. Trudi was not present in the apartment, having discretely decided to take a small stack of laundry into the yard to wash in the communal tubs set aside for that purpose. *So much the better,* Christina thought. *I trust her without question, however, knowing their lives were in danger would only serve to upset her for no particular purpose.*

Ziesolf continued. "For that reason, I believe it would be prudent for me to join you and your maid here in your rooms each night."

A protest started to form in her mouth, but Ziesolf cut her off before she could vocalize it.

"Yes, I know you are able to take care of yourself and you believe you can defeat five men armed to the teeth with no more than a rusty nail held between your teeth."

They both laughed, although she then realized she was the butt of the jest.

"It is a measure worth taking, Christina. It costs you nothing and, if you are attacked, an extra blade may be helpful. Besides," he added with a thin smile on his lips, "These old bones would benefit from a night spent on a pallet in a room that is warm and dry."

Although she knew the man was joking, his words bothered her none the less. She knew Ziesolf was of advanced years, perhaps as many as sixty, and had offered to procure lodging for him at her uncle's house. He had refused, however, choosing to remain on board *der Greif.*

As to his suggestion he now lodge with her at The Tabard, she could find no fault in his logic. If she were attacked, the presence of a knight of the Teutonic Order, regardless of his age, would well serve to even the odds against her.

"Thank you, Herr Ziesolf," she answered graciously. "I will sleep better knowing you are close by."

Days passed and she received no word from the Earl of Cornwall instructing her to ready her ship for immediate departure. Her worry began to fade slightly. *Could his fears have been imaginary or, at least, greatly exaggerated through excess of drink?* She pondered hopefully.

Two days prior to the yule solstice she was sitting with Trudi near the fire in her solar when she heard a loud rapping on the door of her bed chamber. With a mounting feeling of dread gripping her heart she opened it to find one of the inn's servant wenches, her hand poised in mid-knock.

"God's day to ya, Master Frederick," she said. "There's a man come downstairs, says he has a message for ya, so Martin sent me up."

She followed the young girl down the stairs and was delighted to find, not a yeoman from the Tower, but the young clerk she met from the guildhall of the woolmongers. She quickened her step and greeted him warmly.

"Peace be to you as well," he answered. "I have fortunate news. Thanks to the uncommonly dry weather this season, the carts carrying your wool have made very good speed on the Watling Street from Ludlow. The last should arrive here in London no more than five days hence. Master Butiler hopes you will be prepared to take delivery posthaste, so as not to incur the added expense of temporary storage."

Christina thanked the man, assuring him she would call on Butiler the following day at noon to work out the details of the delivery. Early arrival was excellent news, meaning the carts had not been appreciably delayed by snow or other inclement weather on their journey south. *Why am I not happy then?* She asked herself, knowing full well the answer.

She had put off thinking about what to do about the conflicting needs of transporting a cargo and remaining prepared to effect Gaveston's flight from London. Now, the impending arrival of the wool shipment meant she could delay making a decision no longer.

She spent a troubled night tossing in her bed, finally arising early the next morning no closer to a firm plan of action. After dressing, she took a peek into the solar, only to find Ziesolf had arisen even earlier than she and had already departed. The door to Trudi's room remained closed and Christina assumed she was still asleep. She broke fast unaccompanied in the inn's common room, which become increasingly deserted in the mornings as the days turned deeper into the winter. Martin had told her to enjoy the quiet while she could as the Yule season always proved to be a busy one. Unwillingly, she was left alone with her troubled thoughts without diversion.

She exited the inn and strolled aimlessly, having no particular destination in mind save arriving at a firm decision. She avoided the quay, denying herself the diversion of a training session with Ziesolf until she had made up her mind. After a few hours, she changed her course toward her agreed upon meeting with the woolmonger, finally having decided what it was she would do.

After exchanging brief pleasantries with Butiler, Christina turned the conversation towards business.

"I assume you will send me word when your carts enter the city, am I correct?"

"Absolutely," he answered. "I take it you will be at the quayside when the carts arrive, as will I. At that time, you may inspect the wool at your leisure and we may discuss any adjustments you desire if you are unsatisfied. I do not expect you to do so, however. The quality of the wool is as we contracted and it has made the journey south without even a drop of rain besmirching a sack. You will be pleased,

Master Kohl, most certainly!"

Christina was excited as she left the woolmonger. The massive woolsacks would soon be in the belly of her ship. With little else to keep the crewmen occupied during the vessel's enforced stay in port, *der Greif's* master had closely supervised a near complete re-caulking of even the most minute of gaps between the clinkers.

Caulking clamps, or sintels, were then inserted into the planking over the caulk, ensuring the seam was completely watertight. Mattias assured her the hold was completely seaworthy and her cargo would remain completely dry, save for what moisture it absorbed from the dampness of the air of course. *Certainly, the wool will remain unharmed for the period the ship remains in port,* she thought, *and that time must be no more than two additional weeks.*

As she returned to The Tabard, Christina wondered how best she could arrange a meeting with Gaveston. *Should I simply go to the Tower gates and ask I be taken to him? Would this not draw a dangerous connection between us, should someone question why he meets with a Hanseatic merchant with a ship ready in port?*

In the end, she decided to send Ziesolf to arrange a meeting would be her wisest course of action. Later, in a less conspicuous locale, she could let Gaveston know she would hold fast to her promise, but she could not do so indefinitely. *Der Greif* would depart no later than the sixth day of January, on Epiphany morn, whether Gaveston was aboard or not.

She stepped into the inn and proceeded to her rooms. Inside, she was somewhat surprised to find Trudi was nowhere about until she remembered the maid had said she was going to the market to replenish a few things in their meager larder. *Certainly, the meals downstairs in the inn are hearty and wholesome, but the thought of one of Trudi's savory stews and a fresh loaf provokes my mouth to water.* Christina stirred the fire and lounged idly in the solar, awaiting the return of either of her two fellow lodgers.

Suddenly, Christina heard the door open and a second or two later, Trudi burst inside, excitement flashing in her eyes.

"Oh Christina!" she began, words tumbling from her mouth in a torrent. "You will never guess what happened! I was returning from the market and who should I find right outside The Tabard? You will never guess! It was Richard, your uncle's journeyman assistant! His master had dispatched him on an errand and he was just returning now.

If I would have been a minute later, I might have missed him. Oh, he's such a merry fellow, Christina!"

"Yes, the Lord sometimes works in ways we cannot decipher," Christina replied dryly, somewhat taken aback by the degree of the maid's enthusiasm.

Have I missed something here? Trudi always had a good word to say about everyone, except for Anna that is, she thought, correcting herself. *But seldom have I seen her take such pleasure in a chance encounter.*

Trudi continued without pause.

"Oh, I had forgotten to say. They are downstairs now as we speak. They . . . I mean Richard and his friend, Will. Did I mention they were together? No? Well, it matters not. We must join them for a cup of ale! Can we, Christina? Please?"

The maid's eyes grew round, imploring Christina to agree.

"Yes, of course," Christina replied, "just give me time to put my shoes back on."

A minute or two later they were downstairs. Trudi took Christina's hand and tugged her toward the table where the two young men sat. Richard glanced up and gave a cheerful wave as they approached, although it seemed to Christina as if his gaze was directed only upon Trudi. *Am I now being overly suspicious, like a maiden aunt?* She thought to herself with a smile. Will looked their way as well, although his feelings were more difficult to appraise.

Another round was ordered and the four young people talked, laughed, and joked merrily for a while, then Richard remarked, "Your uncle misses you terribly, Frederick, he really does. He often asks about you, whether you have been seen about the City, or whether there is any news of you. I know not the circumstances in which you took your leave, but you should visit him when you have the chance."

Whether it was the effects of the drink or a tinge of homesickness, she did not know, but she found herself agreeing with Richard's suggestion.

"Yes, I will certainly consider calling on him the next time I am in the City." A sudden thought occurred to her. "Has there been anything unusual you could note since my departure?"

"Not that I can recall," Will answered, staring at her evenly, "What do you mean?"

"Oh, nothing, "Christina replied hastily. "Just prying for a bit of gossip, that's all."

It seemed a bit indelicate to ask whether a muffled assassin had been noticed strolling about the house, or if her uncle had really ordered men to sleep in the hall for added security after her departure. Consequently, she bit her tongue, although she hoped the subject might arise later in the conversation.

"So," Will remarked, "Is it up those stairs yonder you have your room? It must be quite cozy, located over the fireplace and all."

"Not just that," Trudi interjected, "We have a fire of our very own as well!"

Will contemplated the chimney breast appraisingly. "Now nice," he murmured. "How very nice. It must be a pleasure, Mistress Trudi, to no longer have to clean floors and wash clothes at the house of my master. It must be a relief to not have to spend each day laboring, don't you think?"

"Yea, verily is the truth," she replied, "although there are some things I do miss from being there." Trudi glanced involuntarily toward Richard and, seeing him grinning, blushed a deep red for one of the few times Christina could recall seeing.

There are definitely some goings on about which I will query Trudi closely later, she thought. Although she was indeed happy for the maid's apparent growing affection for Richard, and he for her, she also felt an inexplicable tinge of jealousy. *She is my one true friend and confidante, if she should leave me, I would have no one who even knows my secret. Save Ziesolf, of course, but his is not the same bond I share with Trudi.*

Now feeling a bit depressed, she turned her attention back toward the conversation which, she noted with a start, was now directed towards her.

"What do you think, Master Frederick?" Trudi was asking. "Um . . . I'm sorry, what is it you were saying?" she replied.

"Richard was saying he would tell your uncle of our meeting here today. Given his earlier interests in your welfare, it is possible he may even invite you to sup, if that would be agreeable to you. Why, I could even accompany you there, should you so desire."

The plea in her voice was unmistakable.

Not knowing what else she could say. Christina said to Richard, "Of course. Tell my uncle I would be honored by an invitation."

Soon after, Richard and Will voiced their farewells and the two women went upstairs. Trudi immediately began preparations for their evening meal.

Almost bursting with curiosity, Christina could wait no longer. "So, it seems you have developed a bit of a fancy for my uncle's man, have you not?"

A wide smile appeared on Trudi's lips, then she turned her back to Christina and set vigorously to work without voicing a reply.

After a few seconds, Trudi suddenly pivoted about and exclaimed, "Yes! Yes! I like him! Is that what you wanted me to say?"

She then went on to provide Christina with the finer details of the relationship between her and Richard to date.

"Why did you not tell me of this?" Christina asked, a little hurt at the maid's unaccustomed secrecy.

"Well, you had so many worries that I did not want to bother you. Besides, I was unsure whether he was just having sport with me or if he too was developing feelings, "She added a bit shyly.

Their girlish conversation was interrupted by the entry of Ziesolf into the room. While Trudi returned to her cooking, Christina briefly outlined her plans concerning both the ship and Gaveston.

Ziesolf said, "Your decision is a sound one, Christina. I agree two weeks delay should have no adverse effect on the cargo barring, of course, a sudden unfavorable turn of the weather. As to Gaveston, I can't believe the man would have assumed *der Greif* would remain at his beck and call forever. If not two weeks, then should the ship tarry for two months, or even two years? The man's troubles with the other nobility are irreconcilable and he will certainly one day be held accountable. But even the staunchest friendship has a limit and two weeks seems a goodly compromise."

Ziesolf agreed to immediately travel to the Tower to arrange a clandestine meeting twixt her and the Earl of Cornwall, but on the condition Christina and Trudi swear they would not begin their meal before his return.

In a few hours' time, Ziesolf returned with a grave expression on his face.

"He is gone," he said simply. "He has been summoned by the King to appear before the court."

"But how can this be bad news?" asked Christina. "Is he not the King's favorite? Will he not protect him?"

"I would like to believe he will, as much as possible. The barons hold great power in the land, however, and Edward cannot risk civil war. The Queen also speaks against Gaveston and her voice holds increasing sway over the King."

"What am I to do?" she muttered to herself as much as to Ziesolf.

"Your plan remains a sound course. If Gaveston weathers this threat, he will have no need for flight. If not, he will be imprisoned or banished, neither one of which will permit him flight aboard *der Greif.* So, unless he somehow conveys you word otherwise, I believe your promise to the man is no longer valid."

Ziesolf's counsel seems sound, she thought, *although it troubles me to break a vow, especially without letting Gaveston know I am about to do so.*

"I hesitate to remind you," he continued," but should Cornwall not be returned to power at the King's side, any advantage you enjoyed through your association with him will be negated. Should the chief alderman wish to press a suit against you, he will then be under no constraint whatsoever. You must tread lightly, Christina, especially until the cargo is brought aboard."

Although she hated to admit it, Ziesolf's warning of danger afoot was too accurate to be ignored. She turned her head toward Trudi and saw the old knight's words had frightened her, but she too gazed at Christina and nodded her head in agreement. They settled down to eat in silence, the gravity of the impending situation largely dulling their enjoyment of the hearty repast before them. Each went to their beds early that evening, as all attempts at conversation ultimately turned to worrisome talk of Gaveston's possible fate and the effect it might have on Christina's plans. At her bedside, Christina offered up prayers for those who were in heaven as well as those for whose welfare she seemed to hold responsibility. The crewmen of *Der Greif*, Ziesolf, Trudi, even Gaveston in some way all seemed to depend on her. Her sleep was light and troubled.

She awoke with a start. A quiet, though insistent, scrabbling sound was coming from somewhere in the room. *Are there mice?* she thought sleepily, almost turning over to go back to sleep. As she gained her wits about her, she determined it was coming from the door. Then she came wide awake. The sound was someone trying to pick the lock!

She frantically searched her memory to identify anything in the room that could suffice as a weapon. Realizing there was nothing in easy reach, she threw the coverlet back and her bare feet thudded to the floor. At almost the same time, the door opened and she saw an assailant identical to the one who had been in her room at her uncle's house. This time, however, he had prudently placed a small lantern in the hallway behind him, taking no chance of missing his victim in a darkened room again. Consequently, both figures were readily revealed in a tableau of mutual surprise.

The assassin moved first. He shot toward Christina, his long knife before him at the ready for a killing thrust. She moved to the side, turning to go through the door into the solar. She was quick, but not quite quick enough. She felt the point of his weapon jab into her thigh, an instantaneous bolt of pain surged to her brain causing her to involuntarily cry out. She didn't stop, however, and continued her flight into the other room. Her foot tripped over something and she fell headlong to the floor, turning in mid-flight so she landed prone, but facing her attacker. He slowed now, realizing his prey was unarmed and defenseless. He began to lower himself to deliver a fatal blow, then he stopped momentarily and stiffened. He began to fall toward Christina, but she scrambled out of the way to let him hit the floor heavily instead, facedown. He remained there motionless.

From the faint moonlight coming into the room through the cracks in the shutters, Christina saw Ziesolf standing with dagger in hand. He turned wordlessly, setting to lighting a candle from the remaining cinders of the fire. He stirred them vigorously and they began to glow. From the embers, to the candle, to a lanthorn, soon the room was aglow with a soft light.

Christina turned over the man on the floor. As she started to pull the muffle from his face, he emitted a low groan. She leapt back, seeking frantically to discover whether he still held his blade. Seeing he had dropped it a few feet away, she relaxed and set to again revealing the man's identity.

As she sought to pull the last bit of cloth from across his lower face, he began to weakly struggle against her. Ziesolf knelt and held the man about the arms, rendering him motionless. Seeing his face at last, Christina was shocked to find it was Will, her uncle's apprentice. She glanced toward Ziesolf, who gave a curt nod, indicating he had recognized the man as well. Then she looked down toward the man's abdomen, where blood was rapidly staining his tunic. Christina realized Ziesolf had stabbed Will straight through and that his wound was grievous, and likely deadly. "Why?" she asked, the implication of her question simple and direct.

His eyelids fluttered open and he smiled. "Why?" he repeated, "I am spent, so do not waste my final minutes trifling with me. Unless you still seek to hide your secrets from your man there?" Christina was confused by the young man's words. "I have no idea about which you speak," she said.

"Really?" Will asked with venom in his voice. "Don't tell me you did not know!"

"Of what do you speak, man?" Christina hissed in exasperation. "Speak plainly, damn you!"

"My master had promised your father payment on the large debt he owed him; yet, he had no such funds to give. There was only one recourse for him to escape ruin. If he could not do away with his debt, then it was his creditor who must be eliminated. Plans were set in motion to make this so. The plan was flawless, it should have worked perfectly. That is until you appeared. If you had done as planned, becoming your uncle's apprentice, all could still have been well. But you demanded to assume your father's position. You possessed his accounts and contracts and demonstrated sufficient wit to understand their meaning. How long before you discovered the contract between these two brothers and recognized its significance? My master had long since defaulted on the loan, everything he owned was yours for the taking. He would be penniless, thrown to the street!"

My father was a good man, a just man. If only my uncle would have been honest with him, I'm sure they could have worked out an agreeable settlement. My uncle is family, my father would not have treated him so cruelly, she thought with tears welling in her eyes. *Killed by his own brother, as Abel was by Cain! And Frederick by his own uncle. Is there no limit to my uncle's murderous treachery?*

"But why did you become embroiled in his plots?" she asked Will. "Certainly, it is not an apprentice's duty to commit murder on his master's behalf."

He stared at her and his eyes saddened. Then he spoke through lips that were becoming awash with blood.

"Aye, I am an apprentice, but more besides. I am also your uncle's bastard and, he and your aunt having no legitimate children, a legal heir. What you sought to take from him you were also taking from me!"

He coughed and, in a sudden spasm, blood spewed from between his lips. He fell back down and remained still.

Ziesolf must have pierced a lung with his blade, she thought dispassionately. This man, to whom she had blood ties, was dying before her; yet, she could feel no pity. *He has brought it upon himself,* she thought, *would he have experienced remorse, had it been me laying there in his stead? Certainly no, he would have been gloating over what it was he had to gain.*

And what of my uncle, the man who holds ultimate blame for this tragedy? A man who sought to exterminate my entire family; yes, what of him? She thought, anger welling inside her like a raging fire. Deadly intent began to fill her soul.

Unexpectedly, Trudi's door opened. She stood in the doorway, stretching and yawning.

She glanced toward the window and asked, "Is it not morning?" Then she gazed about the room and saw Will laying on the floor. "Will, is that you? What has happened here?"

Fright filled her eyes then, seeing the blood beginning to pool around the young man's body, she stifled a scream.

Christina rushed to her friend's side and held her in a tight embrace, shielding her eyes from the sight of the man she had been laughing with downstairs only a few hours prior, now apparently mortally wounded in their apartment. She took Trudi back into the girl's room and briefly explained what had occurred, as well as the man's disclosure of the misdeeds of Christina's uncle. Trudi's eyes were wide with shocked horror. Then, a sudden thought occurred to her and she fearfully asked, "And what of Richard? Surely he cannot be a part of this?"

Christina peered at her solemnly, mulling over in her mind how she should respond. *Was it not Richard who first attacked me in the yard? Was it not Richard who, with Will, abandoned me at the Nag's Head to the band of men who attacked me?*

She then replied, "Of direct evidence we have none; however, the two were constant companions. It would seem if Will were to confide in anyone about the evil tasks he was set to, or to need help to accomplish them, Richard would be his man. I am sorry Trudi, but I am loath to trust the man ever again."

The maid looked at her with tears streaming down her cheeks. She nodded reluctantly in agreement with Christina's conclusion, although it obviously pierced her heart to do so.

She left Trudi in her bedchamber and returned to the solar. Ziesolf was swiftly wrapping the body in a blanket. Christina asked, "What do we do with him now?"

Ziesolf momentarily paused in his grim task and said, "Into the river, I say. It makes little sense to report the attack. That will only draw attention to you, something you can well do without considering the events we spoke of yesterday eve. Besides, a body with a knife wound, floating downriver from Southwark, will invoke little interest. If I can avoid being seen until I dump him, I have little fear his death will be connected to us." He then returned to his task.

Christina thought of disagreeing with Ziesolf's plan of action. *Does the man not at least deserve a Christian burial?* She thought of her own loss. *Would my uncle not feel the same grief for his son, bastard or not?*

Then her heart hardened and she caught her objections before they were voiced. *No, Will was a knave who sought to murder me in my sleep, not once but twice. My uncle was not just a willing accomplice in these deeds, but the originator. And what of my father and brother? If Gerhardt's foul scheme had succeeded as he had planned it, we all would be laying on the bottom of the sea or washed ashore, being picked over by the crabs. Who would mourn over our graves? To hell with Will and, she hoped, Gerhardt Kohl soon to follow!*

She went into her room to dress. The door was still open and the lantern continued to give off light. She retrieved the lantern and shut the door.

By the time she returned to the solar, Ziesolf had finished wrapping the body. Christina stole down the stairs ahead of her companion, keeping a sharp eye open for anyone who might still be about that late at night. With a sigh of relief, she saw no one. She motioned for him to follow her.

With Will's body over his shoulder he came alongside her. She opened the door and stepped outside. Luck remained with them all the way to the river. Ziesolf lowered the man to the ground and began unwrapping him from the blanket.

"Couldn't we just leave it?" Christina whispered, hoping to hurry the task along. "We have no need for a bloody old blanket."

The old knight continued his work without slowing. Finally, having freed the body from its covering, he pushed it with his foot as far into the current as he could reach. He then folded the blanket and placed it under his arm. He now turned to Christina and replied, "I said a body floating in the Thames would not draw undue attention. A robbery gone bad, a disagreement over a girl, even a drink knocked over by a clumsy drunk, any of these could result in a man ending up dead. But a man ending up dead, and wrapped in a blanket, is another thing entirely. No longer is it a crime of sudden passions, but now a deliberate action. Far more likely to arouse suspicions and provoke closer investigation."

"You're right," she admitted. "I'm sorry I questioned you. I'm just a bit shaken right now."

He gave her a reassuring clap on her back. They returned to their rooms in silence.

After Christina closed the door, Ziesolf turned and said, "I will scrub the bloodstain as best I can for now. Tomorrow, I will have Trudi fetch a bit of soap and I will do a more thorough job."

"Thank you, Herr Ziesolf, for everything you have done to help me. Most especially for saving my life tonight."

His normally stern face evoked the ghost of a smile. He nodded curtly and closed the door.

As she mounted her bed, she felt a twinge of pain in her upper leg. Glancing down, she saw a circle of blood on her nightshirt approximately three inches in diameter. She lifted the material to see a shallow wound where the point of Will's knife had stabbed her. *Only a flesh wound,* she thought with satisfaction, *the blood has already been staunched. A second or two later, however, and it might have been my body being rolled into a blanket.* She silently thanked God Ziesolf had

had the foresight to insist he should stay with her and Trudi. She resolved to take the man's counsel more seriously in the future, even if it ran counter to her own thoughts.

She cleaned her wound with water as best she could and wrapped a strip of cloth about her leg as a makeshift bandage, vowing to attend to it more closely on the morrow. Although a few hours of the night remained, she did not return to sleep. Instead, she spent the hours contemplating revenge on her uncle.

Chapter 16

As the sun rose the next morning, she was no closer to a decision as to what to do about her uncle than she had been the night before. She had considered several options but, in the end, found each unsuitable in some way or another.

What I know for certain is that I must do something. My uncle has sponsored at least two, and probably three, attempts on my life. He will not give up the idea simply because one assassin has been found out. If anything, the possibility his plotting has been discovered will only make him more dangerous. There is no end to desperate fellows who would be willing to stick a knife in someone's ribs for a few silver pennies. It does not have to happen while I sleep either. How easy it would be for someone with a blade to fall in behind me while I walked down a crowded street?

The most direct response to my uncle's treachery would be to repay him in kind. She weighed the chances of murdering her uncle while he slept and found them not good. *He will be doubly on guard when it becomes apparent Will has been found out. It is too great of a risk. Besides, just because he is going to hell does not mean I must be damned as well.*

What would Father do? She posed the question to herself, turning the thought over in her mind for a few minutes. *He would certainly not attempt to exact his own justice. Instead, he would attack the man where he is most vulnerable. The contract!*

She leapt out of her bed. She winced as she put weight on her injured leg but hobbled over to her father's chest in the corner of the room. She opened the lid and desperately began to riffle through the contents.

Finally, near the bottom, she encountered a stack of documents her father had seen fit to bring on the voyage to England. She swiftly scanned through them, disappointment mounting as it became apparent none made reference to an agreement between the two brothers. Reaching the end of the stack, she emptied the chest further, until there was only the wooden bottom of the box staring at her. She sat back on her haunches, considering what to do next.

Rising to her feet, she went to the table, retrieved her father's account book, and sat down on her bed. For the next few hours, she carefully scanned each neatly written entry in the thick ledger, hoping to uncover proof of the contract with her father's brother.

She found what it was she was searching for after a while. Nearly three years prior, a loan had been rendered to Gerhardt Kohl for the princely sum of eighteen thousand silver marks. She experienced no joy in this revelation, however. A line had been drawn through the entry and next to it, in her father's careful hand, had been written "settled in full."

She let the ledger fall into her lap and dropped her head back onto the bed in disbelief. *Had my uncle searched the trunk, destroyed the contract, and changed the entry himself?* Although she wanted to believe further evidence of her uncle's treachery, she knew it was not possible. She recognized her father's handwriting as his own. Additionally, the ink was faded, not fresh as it would have been had it just been written in recent weeks. *No, for some reason my father had seen fit to negate Gerhardt Kohl's debt to him,* she shook her head incredulously.

The irony of the situation made her furious. All the mayhem her uncle had caused had been to avoid the necessity of repaying a debt that no longer existed. He had murdered a man who, from the goodness of his heart, had forgiven a huge debt that would have rendered him destitute. If her uncle had only stayed his deadly hand until his brother's arrival in London, there would have been no need for bloodshed. She closed her eyes, her stomach churning at the intensity of the hatred she felt for Gerhardt Kohl.

After what seemed an eternity, she rose again and dressed. Placing the ledger beneath her arm, she traveled purposefully through the streets until she arrived at the house of her uncle. She went inside, taking no time for the courtesy of knocking on the door. She found her uncle at breakfast.

"Leave us, please," she commanded the attending servant.

The man glanced toward his master for confirmation. A look of surprise appeared on Gerhardt's face, then he nodded and the man departed, leaving the two of them alone.

"Why, Nephew, how good to see you. Richard had said he encountered you while returning from an errand and you had said you planned to call on me. I did not realize it would be so soon. Come, have a seat, and I will have a breakfast prepared for you."

He flashed his familiar, ingratiating smile that now sickened Christina in its falseness.

She remained standing.

"I have no stomach to share your table, uncle. I only wish to provide you with information that, I am certain, will gladden your heart."

He peered at her warily, his smile now becoming more guarded.

"And what might that be, Nephew?" he asked in a low voice.

"In searching through my father's accounts, I discovered a contract had been made between the two of you. A contract in which he loaned you eighteen thousand silver marks. A contract in which you agreed to repay that sum in two years' time." Her uncle's face grew pale. He rose from his seat and, still clenching his eating knife between his fingers, scowled at Christina.

He started to speak, but she cut him off.

"Yes, it seems you were heavily indebted to my father, and payment on the loan was long past due. Now, he was coming to London. Did you have the money to pay him? Perhaps yes, perhaps no. If not, what could you do? Would you be left a pauper, begging in the street for cast off cabbages?"

She paused for a few seconds before continuing.

"Did you doubt the very nature of your own brother? You should have trusted my father to do what was right. He was a merchant, but he was foremost a man of honor and integrity. He was your flesh and blood but you knew him not, uncle. He did not share your tainted heart!"

She thrust her father's ledger towards the man, opened to the page of the transaction.

"Look, damn you! See what the brother you feared so greatly did for you!"

Almost involuntarily, the man took the book from Christina. He scanned the page and found the entry for the loan. After a few seconds, he glanced upward, his mouth working speechlessly like a gaffed carp. "I . . . I don't know what to say," he finally managed.

"I'll tell you what to say, you murderous varlet!" she shouted with all the venom pent up inside her body. "Say you are fucking sorry! Say you are sorry for arranging the killing of my father and my sister, not to mention the innocent sailors who lost their lives because of you that day. Say you are sorry for the attempts on my life or, so help me God, I will have my revenge. Speak, damn you to hell!" The man's confusion now turned to anger.

"I know not of what you speak! How dare you accuse me of such monstrosity!"

She moved forward, one of her hands grabbing the wrist of his hand holding the knife, the other wrapping around his throat.

"Even now, you deny your evil deeds! I should have expected nothing less of such a coward and rogue!"

The door suddenly burst open and the servant whom she had ordered from the room appeared, along with Richard and two other men. She dropped her hold on her uncle and moved a couple of steps away.

"Is there something amiss, Master?" asked the servant. We heard shouting and were afraid you were in danger."

Gerhardt shrugged his shoulders to settle his garments back into place. He stared at Christina and managed a tight smile.

"No, everything is fine now. It was nothing more than a misunderstanding. Besides, Frederick was just leaving, weren't you, Nephew?"

Christina grabbed the ledger, spun on her heel, and left the house without uttering another word. Once in the street, she leaned against a nearby building, sickened by the injustice she felt and her revulsion for the man she called uncle. This time, she was able to control the urge to empty her stomach's meager contents onto the ground, but just barely. On unsteady legs, she began her journey back to The Tabard.

What am I to do? The question seemed to be one she asked herself constantly. *I have no confidence that, even now, he does not pose a threat to my life. Until he has my father's copy of the contract in his possession, how can he be confident I was not just lying, having annotated the ledger myself to persuade him to pursue my death no longer? He has no proof that, sometime in the future, I will not produce the actual contract, demanding immediate payment. No, things remain unresolved, only now he is certain I have knowledge both of the agreement and of his despicable deeds accomplished to negate it!"* Another wave of nausea passed through her body.

She altered her course, deciding to proceed to the quay rather than the inn. She had no desire to speak with Trudi or, especially, Ziesolf this morning. She knew the knight would criticize her for her rash decision to visit her uncle and wished to avoid any further conflict if at all possible.

She went aboard *der Greif* and decided to inspect the ship's hold to while away the time. Everything seemed clean and watertight, just as Matthias had promised. Unexpectedly a crewman stuck his head down into the dimly lit space and told her she had a visitor.

She climbed up on the ship's deck, only to be greeted by the woolmonger's clerk.

"Master Kohl, peace be with you this morning. I have exciting news for you! The wool carts have passed through Newgate and are fast approaching as we speak. Master

Butiler says they will be here within the hour. He hopes to arrive himself some time sooner."

On any other day, this news would have cheered her heart to no end. Given the recent turn of events, however, she only saw the arrival of her wool as the catalyst for a series of tasks that needed to be completed. Christina instructed Matthias to gather every crewmember he could and prepare to load the cargo. Soon, ten men had gathered on the deck. She was surprised to see one particular man amongst them.

"I did not expect you to still be here, Reiniken," she said addressing the mercenary. "Are you a sailor now?"

He contorted his wide mouth into an uneven grin. "Aye, Your Worship, aye I am. Why should I be out risking getting my liver cut out, when I can stay here, getting paid for doing naught save drinking ale and fucking strumpets?"

He laughed and rubbed his crotch for emphasis. She couldn't help but smile herself at the huge man. *He is completely without guile*, she though, *how I prefer such a lout a thousand-fold to the likes of my uncle!*

"Well, now's the time to start earning those pennies, Reiniken," she remarked. "I hope all this time spent in idleness hasn't sapped you of your strength."

He laughed again and, grabbing the man next to him with both of his meaty hands, picked him up and held him above his head for nearly a minute while the man struggled in vain to free himself. Finally, he lowered him back down to the deck.

Butiler soon arrived and, less than ten minutes later, Ziesolf appeared as well. She informed him of the imminent arrival of the shipment, mentioning neither the events of the previous night nor her meeting with her uncle. Soon, the first of the massive wool carts rolled ponderously up the street.

True to his word, the woolmonger took his time, opening the sacks for Christina's inspection. She made tallies in the ledger of the type and quality of each sack's contents. She was pleased to find they all seemed full, and that the merchant had not tried to cheat her with sacks that were light.

The men labored throughout the day as wagon after wagon brought their loads quayside. Christina arranged for a hearty meal with ample watered ale to be served to the carters and seamen alike. It was well into the night when the final load was stowed. Her men were nearly spent through the exertions of their efforts. Their faces brightened, however, when she presented each with a few pennies as a bonus for their hard work.

She and Ziesolf walked back to the inn together, each silently immersed in his or her own thoughts. Once they had settled into the solar, however, the man broached the subject Christina had been hoping to avoid. "What are your plans now, Christina?" he asked quietly.

She mulled his question over in her mind as if it had not been dominating her own thoughts the entire day

Finally, she replied, "The only thing I know for certain is that I do not wish to return to Lubeck. I cannot imagine myself being forced to be a wife, to spend the rest of my days beholden to a husband. Perhaps I should accompany *der Greif* to Bruges, beginning another life there. But how can I be certain my troubles won't follow me, even to Flanders? I realize my position here in London is precarious, but at least I know those who are my enemies."

Exhausted from little sleep the previous night as well as the tumult of the day's events, Christina went to bed, leaving further considerations for the morrow.

She arose very early and went down to breakfast alone the next day. Although she wished nothing more than to eat in peace, the common room was already filled with people. Most, if not all, were on their way to Canterbury, timing the arrival of their pilgrimage to coincide with the feast day of Saint Thomas. Noise and excitement filled the air in the crowded room, neither of which she desired to share. She ate quickly and stepped out into the bracingly crisp morning air.

Although she had not yet decided about herself, she had made definite plans regarding *der Greif.* There had been no word of gossip concerning the fate of Gaveston at Westminster, nor had there been a response to the request for audience Ziesolf had delivered. Consequently, she could see no reason why the ship should not set off to Bruges at the sign of the first favorable wind. *I will let Matthias know my decision today. Whether I will be aboard, however, may or may not be.*

Her feet carried her over the Great Bridge unconsciously now, she had traveled the route so many times. Already the streets were crowded with people; happy and sad, merry and miserable. If I do leave the City, I shall indeed miss being here. *There is a vibrancy and life about it that is unlike Lubeck,* she mused. *But dangers as well, always dangers,* she added.

She went to the ship and spoke with Matthias. He assured her all was in readiness aboard the ship and a full complement of crew would soon be aboard and ready to put to sea. She hesitated, then told him to not sail until he had received word from her to do so.

Before Christina could leave the moorage, however, Trudi appeared, waving frantically. The maid walked toward her as quickly as her legs could carry her.

"Frederick!" she shouted. "While I was emptying the slops this morning, who should I find but Richard waiting to see me. He asked me to give you this message. He needs to speak with you as soon as possible and he will await you at the Nag's Head. I knew you weren't upstairs so this is the only other place I could think of where you might be. And I was right, wasn't I?"

She gave a small smile of satisfaction.

"Yes, of course you were, Trudi," Christina answered. "Now, go back to The Tabard and wait for me in our rooms. Is Ziesolf there?"

The girl shook her head in the negative.

"Should he return, have him wait for me as well."

As the maid hurried off toward the bridge, Christina hesitated, attempting to gauge why it was Richard wished to speak to her, and why he had chosen the Nag's Head. *If my uncle has had a change of heart, would he have not summoned me to his house to let me know so himself? If he has not, would he have grown so bold as to threaten my life in a public place in broad daylight?* Completely mystified as to the reason for it, Christina warily set out for her meeting with Richard.

The Nag's Head was even more foul in the light of day than she remembered it from her previous visit. There were small piles of food, broken crockery, and other refuse upon the floor that was better left unidentified. The smell of sour ale still permeated the air. The room was cold and gloomy, despite the small fire in the hearth that burned fitfully, fueled by the few sticks of wood that had been begrudgingly placed on the grate. Two men who were obviously laborers talked with their heads close together at a table near the fire. On the opposite side of the room sat Richard, nursing a cup of ale.

Noticing Christina, he signaled to the innkeeper for two cups to be brought to the table. As she approached, she realized with a bit of a shock the table where Richard sat was the same one where she had spoken with Gaveston those many days prior.

She sat down and was about to ask Richard why they were there when the ale arrived.

He drank deeply and sat his cup down. "Good day to you, Frederick," he began amiably.

"And to you, Richard," she replied guardedly.

Why doesn't he just get on with this? she asked herself irritably, *I have more pressing matters to which to attend.*

He took another draught and again set his cup down carefully, precisely almost. His smile widened.

Is the man already drunk? she thought, considering whether she should just walk out and leave him to his drink.

"That was quite a row between you and my master. He was quite upset. I believe he even imagined you might do him bodily harm," he said.

"It is no business of yours what passes between my uncle and myself," she replied stiffly, preparing to leave before her temper got the better of her. "Oh, no, do not leave!" Richard said merrily. "I meant no offense. I was only relating what occurred."

Christina settled back in her seat, but her patience was wearing thin.

He continued. "When you were with him in the solar yesterday morning, your voices could be heard from as far away as the hall where I was busily eating my breakfast. 'What is that, I asked myself? Could someone be threatening my dear Master?' So, I ran upstairs and shooed the servants from eavesdropping at the door. I opened it and we all burst inside. And what did I see, you might ask? Why there you were, with your fingers wrapped around his neck – as if you wanted to kill him, I might say."

She said nothing, waiting for him to get to the point of his telling.

"As I said, he was frightened. You left, but he feared you may return. He asked that I spend the night in the solar to ensure he was not harmed in his sleep."

"I will not be returning to his house, not now, nor ever." Christina muttered.

Richard lowered his voice. "That may be what you say, but who knows if you speak the truth? What if you did return in the night, maybe even last night, and completed the task from which you were interrupted yesterday. Sadly, I may not have even known if you had stolen into the house, as I am a very sound sleeper."

"As I said, I will never return to my uncle's house!"

"If that is true, how is it my master now lays in his bed, throat cut, and his life's blood staining his sheets?"

He added this mildly, as if he were describing a commonplace event. "What?" Christina cried, springing to her feet. "Do not trifle with me, Richard! I find no humor in what you say!"

The two men across the room suddenly rose from their table and moved closer, their hands going to the handles of their wicked-looking knives.

Richard raised his hand and held it palm-outward. The men halted, but left their fingers resting on their weapons.

"Do you not understand, Frederick? I speak seriously. Gerhardt Kohl has been murdered, the day after you exchanged angry words with him and were seen by many with your hands upon his person. Who do you think the sheriff will blame?"

Christina fell back into her seat, her anger deflated by a growing sense of dread.

"But who could have done such a thing?"

"Why me, of course," he answered calmly.

She glared at the man, her mouth seeking to form words her amazement prevented it to speak.

"Surely you are not that thick-headed!" he grinned wildly. "When you accused your uncle of plotting to murder you, did you not hear his answer? He said he knew nothing of it! But you did not believe him. Oh, Frederick, you should have! Gerhardt Kohl was many things, but he did not have the stomach for violence. I convinced poor Will to steal into your room that night in your uncle's house, but the fool couldn't see you in the dark. I remedied that when he attacked you in your inn by instructing him to take a lantern. Little help it gave him since, as I have not seen him today, I can only assume he is now dead. So much the pity. I hope you dumped him behind the inn and not the river. You see, he could not swim!" He took another drink and laughed again.

"And . . . and my father and sister?" Christina asked weakly having already surmised the answer.

"Well, your uncle would only entrust the carrying of important messages to Lubeck with someone whose loyalty he thought unquestionable, someone such as myself, of course. When I brought your father the news of the chief alderman's acceptance of his marriage offer, I found myself afterwards in a tavern of some ill-repute. It only took the dropping of a few coins and even fewer words to set my plan in motion."

"But what did you have to gain from all of this?" Christina asked, still unable to make a final connection. "Will claimed Gerhardt had acknowledged him as his bastard, making him the man's legal heir. But what stake do you hold?" "Gerhardt and Matilda experienced much tragedy in their youth. After several miscarriages, she was finally able to birth a son who, unfortunately, died a few hours later. Three more boys were put into the ground before Matilda, thankfully, could no longer stir a child within her womb. Gerhardt, however, still had the desire to produce an heir, and set out to be doubly sure his efforts would be met with success." "You are his bastard as well," she said, finally understanding everything.

"At your service, Master Frederick," he replied with a slight bow of his head.

"But why are you telling me all of this? Surely, my knowledge of your obscene deeds is not necessary to carry them further along."

"Ah, but that is where you're wrong, Frederick, it is essential you know everything. If you did not, how could I truly enjoy the fulfillment of my plans? I have hated you since the first days I spied upon you in Lubeck, the spoiled brat of an over-indulging family. Oh, how they loved you! Then, you show up here and you are immediately provided with a room in the house and a place at my father's table while I, his heir, eat cold shoulder in the hall and sleep on foul straw! Now, you will pray for such mean fare as you wait in goal until your corpse is twisting from a rope on Tyburn Hill. I have already sent word of your crime to the sheriff, who is undoubtedly forming up men of the watch as we speak to take you into their custody. I will leave you now, Frederick, but please, do not forget me."

Although she would have gladly given her life to rip his heart out, she knew any efforts to do so would be stymied by the two men behind her. She was left with nothing to do except watch him leave the inn, followed closely by his henchmen. She placed her head in her hands, her thoughts now nothing but a black morass. Realizing she had no time to wallow in self-pity. she swiftly departed the tavern, hoping to reach The Tabard before she was found by the sheriff's men.

She was no more than halfway when she heard "Christina!" spoken in a hushed tone coming from within a copse of trees down a side street.

She immediately recognized the voice as that of Trudi. The two were soon together and they moved deeper into the shade.

Without preamble, the maid said, "Men came to The Tabard asking about you. When I told them you were not there, they grew angry and demanding I tell them where you were. I said I did not know and started to cry. That seemed to upset them and they left, vowing they would find you with or without my help."

"You must listen carefully, Trudi," Christina began. "You and Ziesolf must gather what you can from the rooms and go to *der Greif.* Most importantly of all, you must take my father's ledger. Will you make sure you carry it yourself?" The young woman nodded vigorously in assent.

"Good, that's my dear, sweet, clever girl! After you are aboard, the ship is to set sail down the river . . . "

"But what of you?" Trudi interrupted, her eyes clouding. "We cannot leave without you! I will not leave without you!"

"Hush," Christina put her hand to her friend's cheek. "We have not time for argument. Tell Matthias to moor the ship in Greenwich, that's the town we passed about twenty-five miles downriver. There I will meet you in a matter of four or five days. If I have not arrived by the end of a week, he is to sail on as planned to Bruges. Do you understand, Trudi? You must, everything depends on you!"

Trudi nodded again, then threw her arms about Christina's neck and sobbed in her ear. "I don't want to leave you!" she repeated.

Christina bent her face down and kissed the young woman softly on her trembling lips.

She lifted her head slightly and whispered, "You must. But do not fear, I will see you again in a matter of days.

Trudi tightened her grasp for a second, then grudgingly let go. Christina watched sadly as the maid began walking back toward The Tabard at a pace she hoped would appear natural to anyone watching. Soon, she disappeared from sight and Christina was left alone.

She prayed the plan to meet *der Greif* in Greenwich would never be needed. *Instead, I will try to make my way to the ship's moorage at Billingsgate undetected, sailing with her when she leaves London. I could not hint at that plan to Trudi as she and Ziesolf would have held the ship indefinitely, waiting for me to appear. This way, if I am successful, it will be a pleasant surprise. If not, there is still hope I can make the rendezvous in Greenwich.*

She pulled her hood more closely over her head and stepped nonchalantly into the street, joining the throng of yuletide merrymakers under the darkening skies. *What are my chances of reaching der Greif without being recognized?* She wondered. *There are thousands of young men who travel the streets of London fitting my general description. Certainly, the sheriff does not have the manpower to stop and question each one all across the city. Consequently, where are the places he is most likely to concentrate his search? Trudi already said men were inquiring after me at The Tabard. The ship is another obvious place they would look.* She thought for a second. *The only other place would be the bridge. A few armed men, along with one of my uncle's servants who knows me by sight, could well stymy my way across the river. But has the sheriff moved with sufficient haste to bar such a crossing already? If I move swiftly, can I evade his net before it is cast?*

She quickened her pace.

As she approached the southern end of the bridge, her heart sickened. Even though the streets were crowded, a lengthier than expected queue had formed in the approach to the southern gate tower. Men in livery were holding torches, checking everyone traveling north before they were allowed to pass. She felt certain someone who could identify her would be in their company.

Christina turned away from the bridge and began to walk aimlessly in the other direction, uncertain as to what to do next. She could not return to her rooms at The Tabard but did not know where to go in their stead. *One thing for certain, I do not relish the thought of sleeping roughly on the street,* she thought, shivering from the growing cold despite her heavy cloak. *I have no friends or even acquaintances from whom I may beg lodging for the night on this side of the river. What am I to do?*

Suddenly, she had a thought. She quickened her step and soon found herself back at the Nag's Head. *This is the last place they would think to discover me,* she smiled with satisfaction. She went inside and found the inn already full, the noise and stench now only too familiar. She avoided the man behind the bar as he was the same one who had been there earlier.

Christina approached one of the serving wenches and asked, "Where might I find Sybille?"

"You'll have to wait your turn," she replied in an annoyed voice, motioning vaguely to the side of the room with a nod of her head.

Christina turned in the direction the girl had indicated and saw Sybille sitting on the lap of a grossly fat man whose tunic sought vainly to contain his immense girth. She glanced up and met Christina's stare, but only for an instant. She turned back toward the man and pecked him on the cheek with her lips, then whispered something in his ear. He laughed uproariously and pushed her off his lap. Instead of falling to the floor, she caught her legs beneath her and stood upright. The man leaned forward and slapped her hard across the buttocks with his fleshy hand. She turned and blew him a kiss, which went unnoticed as he was in the process of draining his tankard, liquid spilling from the sides of his mouth in steady torrents.

Sybille walked gracefully toward Christina with an accentuated swing of her hips evident with each step. Christina couldn't control her curiosity.

"What did you say to that man?"

"I told him that, if I sat there any longer, I was going to have to shit on his lap," the woman said matter-of-factly. "Now, what is it I may do for you?"

Christina took a deep breath and asked, "Would a room be available upstairs - for the night I mean," she added hastily.

"But of course, my love," the woman answered softly. "That will be half a shilling, of course."

Christina dug in her purse and gave Sybille the money for which she had asked. The woman then took Christina by the hand and led her up the stairs. She was rather disappointed when Sybille opened the door to the room. It was small, rather cold, and starkly furnished with little more than a bed. *Expensive, but it will have to do,* she thought. *At least it's better than shivering outside in the night.*

She stepped inside and turned to thank the woman. She was surprised to find Sybille had entered behind her and was quietly closing the door.

"Perhaps you misunderstood my meaning. Mistress," Christina said, flushing with embarrassment. "I only seek a place to sleep for the night."

Sybille gazed at her with a smile and placed a finger to her lips to dispel any further protests before they could be voiced.

Christina panicked. "You don't understand! I . . ."

"Am a woman," Sybille finished her sentence for her. "Yes, I've known that since first we met. Men are simple, they see what they expect to see. We women, however, are much more . . . shall we say perceptive?"

Christina was stunned. The thought had run through her mind the woman had somehow suspected she was not who or what she claimed to be, but then had dispelled the idea, believing she was being overly fearful. Now she saw her suspicions had been well founded.

Sybille placed the small candle she was holding on a tin roundel designed for that purpose on the small tabletop. Its tiny flame flickered, casting overlapping shadows on the wall of the room. She moved forward slowly, until less than a hands-breath separated their two bodies. Then she reached her hand behind Christina's head and, with a slight but insistent pressure, drew it downward until their lips met.

Christina drew back from the woman's advance, frightened by her frank invitation as well as her own body's strong desire to accept it.

"Please . . . wait. I don't want . . ." Christina spoke hesitantly.

"My dear, sweet love," Sybille shook her head slightly as she moved toward Christina once again, "Allow yourself now what you clearly do want."

Their bodies now touching, Christina surrendered completely as her passions grew. They kissed softly at first, then with greater insistence, their tongues twisting and curling around each other like two writhing serpents. After what seemed forever, Sybille broke away and stepped back.

Christina's breath was ragged, she was shocked at the urgency of the desire she felt coursing through every inch of her body. She watched mesmerized as the woman let her gown fall easily from her shoulders, pooling on the floor about her feet. Her eyes traveled involuntarily down Sybille's body, marveling at the fullness of her breasts, the gentle swell of her belly, and the thicket of dark, curly hair that concealed her sex. Embarrassed at the realization she was staring, she lifted her gaze only to see the woman once more moving closer.

Without resistance, Christina allowed Sybille to remove her heavy traveling cloak, then place her hands under her tunic, drawing it over her head and casting it aside. After removing her shirt, Sybille slowly unwound the fabric Christina had wrapped around her chest to conceal the swell of her breasts. The material fell away unnoticed as Sybille cupped them in her hands, using her thumb and forefinger to gently roll each of the nipples simultaneously. An involuntary groan escaped Christina's throat as her arousal threatened to overcome her.

Still Sybille did not slow her assault on Christina's passions. Her hand moved down Christina's sides, forcing her braes down past the swell of her hips. Her small hands now gripped Christina's buttocks just as Gaveston's had those several weeks before. Just as he had done, Sybille brought her right hand around Christina's thigh, to envelope her crotch. This time, however, there was no shying away at the discovery of her womanhood. The woman probed her fingers lightly through the fine hairs to find the concealed slit, engorged and made slick from wanting.

With insistent pressure, Sybille forced her backwards until she collapsed onto the bed, causing their bodies to momentarily disengage. Christina struggled upward, until her entire body was stretched supine on the bed. With agonizing slowness, Sybille lowered herself onto the other woman's body.

Christina took the other woman's slight weight with pleasure, enjoying the feeling of their breasts meshing together. Sybille was not nearly finished, however. She moved her lips to Christina's neck, nibbling like a lamprey, but stopping just short from drawing blood. Small, enticing kisses traced a course downward until her mouth next found one of Christina's hardened nipples, sucking and biting down on it roughly. Christina cried aloud from the shock, arching her back, torn between the pleasure and the pain of Sybille's expert lovemaking.

Sybille's unrelenting onslaught of Christina's virgin body continued. Her head traveled downward, over the toned and firm surface of her belly. Finally, Christina could wait no longer. Instinctively, she grabbed the other woman's hair with both hands and thrust her head roughly into her crotch. The sensation of the initial contact between the other woman's tongue and her quim nearly made Christina pass out from its intensity. As the woman's tongue began to establish a complex rhythm, Christina began to thrust her hips in unison. Faster and faster, their movements quickened. Christina could feel a welling inside her she did not understand, only that she was powerless to stem its advance. She pressed harder against the back of Sybille's head, her thighs now gripping her tightly as well. Just as she thought she could endure no more, the licking suddenly stopped and Sybille's teeth came together lightly. Christina howled with pleasure and she pumped her hips frantically. She felt a surge issue from her quim, drenching Sybille's face with a nectar from deep within her.

For a moment, she had no power over herself as wave after wave of pleasure continued to wrack her body. Sybille moved around the side of the bed and laid down beside her. Embarrassed, Christina said, "I'm sorry, I . . . "

Sybille put her finger this time to Christina's lips, stilling her apology. After a while, they arose and climbed back into the bed together only, this time, beneath the coverlet. The temperature outside plummeted, however, that of the room grew hotter, fueled by the desire of two young bodies that pleasured each other again and again throughout the night. Under Sybille's excellent tutelage, Christina too became adept at bringing a woman's body to climax. By the time the sun rose, Christina had had little sleep; however, she definitely bore no grudge for its loss. She had also experienced no thoughts of the dangers she now had to face.

She arose and washed her face and body as best she could with ice cold water from the jug. She winced as she moved her neck, rotating it until the crick disappeared. *My body aches more now than from my hardest training with Ziesolf,* she thought happily, *although it was certainly more pleasurably attained.* She had briefly considered changing clothes with the woman, reverting to her true sex as the ultimate of disguises. She discarded the thought, however, as Sybille was almost elfin in size, smaller in stature than even Trudi.

After dressing, she stooped to kiss the slumbering Sybille, who murmured something incoherently in her sleep. "I will return to you someday, sweetest Sybille. Be it a month or a year, we shall be together again," she said to the woman softly. She turned away and exited the room, knowing the happiness she had found in the past few hours was now to be replaced by the terrible fear of being discovered.

If everything has gone as I have hoped, der Greif will already be far downriver, even perhaps already moored in Greenwich. That leaves me with no reason to go to Billingsgate. Neither do I need to cross the bridge nor return to The Tabard. That means I can avoid the three places where I would most likely be found out. With any luck at all, I can attain Greenwich in the time I have allowed myself, she thought happily, buoyed both by the seemingly good chance for the success of her plans as well as the pleasurable memories of the night before.

She considered the best means by which to depart the city. From her time residing at The Tabard, she knew there was a constant flow of pilgrims from the inn and down the road to Canterbury. *It would be simple to join one of these bands soon after their departure, concealing myself in their midst. Once clear of the city, I can break away and make my way to the river.*

On the other hand, why not just take a lighter downriver? the thought suddenly occurring to her. *There are boatmen aplenty along the river bank. For a few coins, I can make much better speed and avoid the chance any one of the pilgrims might recognize me from our time at the inn. Besides,* she thought with a grin, *traveling is so much easier on one's backside than on one's feet.*

Christina had no wish to place her life in the hands of a boatman attempting to negotiate the rapids formed by the weir-like effect of the bridge's piers on the tidal river. Consequently, she decided to walk past the Great Bridge, seeking to engage a lighterman and his boat further downriver. *After all, it's only a few more steps, isn't it?* She thought.

She gave the entrance to the bridge a wide berth by traveling up a few streets, then cutting back toward the river once she had passed. Taking a turn to the left, the Thames once more came into view. As she came closer, she saw at least three boats she felt would be suitable for her planned journey.

Suddenly, she heard a voice behind her shout,

"There he is! That's the one!"

She turned and saw three liveried men running toward her with one of her uncle's servants following closely behind.

I can surely outrun them, she thought, glancing about wildly to determine her best avenue of escape. Just as she was about to flee, however, she felt two burly arms grab her, pinning her arms to her sides and lifting her feet off the ground. Although she struggled, she could not free herself from her captor's vicelike grip. Soon, the watchmen arrived. Her arms were securely bound with a rope and she was led off, back into the city, and towards the King's justice at Newgate prison.

Her captors were in a cheerful mood, happy they had apprehended their quarry so soon after coming on watch. In a little while, they would be able to warm themselves back in the guardroom before venturing back to their appointed station.

One of them said to Christina, "So, you thought you was smart, eh? Well, the sheriff figured ya fur a runner, 'specially since that ship of yur's was nowhere to be found. So's he had us watching the boats and, sure as shit, there ya was! Not so smart after all, are ya?"

She said nothing in reply, but her heart soared at the news *der Greif* had at least made a clean escape. "Oh, yur gonna love Newgate, ya are," the man continued, obviously enjoying hearing his own voice. "Lice so big, ya can eat 'em like grapes! They make a nice popping sound when ya chomp down on 'em. Them rats will eat ya alive, too. They started eatin' one poor fella from the toes up. They'd got to his knees by the time he died, God have mercy on his misbegotten soul!"

Again, she ignored his comments, obviously intended to frighten her. *Well, I am afraid,* she admitted to herself, *but anything I say will only keep him talking.* Consequently, she chose to remain silent.

"Cat got yur tongue, eh?" the man laughed, but said nothing more.

As they passed through the streets, the crowds parted, forming up on both sides to gawk. Laughing and talking excitedly amongst themselves, they also shouted obscenities and someone even hurled a cabbage her way, missing her head by a good foot and smacking into the chest of one of the watchmen. He yelled and set off into the crowd after the thrower, brandishing his pike threateningly. Further along, Christina stumbled in a rut in the street concealed by assorted muck. She turned while falling to avoid hitting her face on the cobblestones, thudding down painfully on her shoulder instead. Prompted to rise by a swift kick in the buttocks, she struggled to her feet.

A few minutes later, she caught her first glance of Newgate, which served not only as a principal accessway into the City, but also as its main prison.

She was led up stone steps and into a large room crowded with people, two of whom were engaged in heated conversation. The one she did not know was tall and thin, richly dressed with an ornate chain of office dangling from his neck. The other she knew well: Herr Revele, the Hanse's chief alderman.

"According to the privileges granted alongside the *Carta Mercatoria* by his royal majesty Edward I in the year of our Lord 1303, the aldermen of the Hanse shall retain jurisdiction of those of its body accused of crimes perpetrated against others of its members," recited Revele in a measured voice. "As that is true in this case, I request you relinquish the prisoner to my care immediately."

The thin man, whom Christina assumed was the sheriff, glanced with indecision from Revele to Christina and back again. Coming to the conclusion further disagreement was not worth his while, he assented. One of Revele's men took the end of the rope and led her back out into the light.

As soon as they were outside, the rest of the alderman's men closed around Christina, concealing the fact she was being led away as a prisoner. They passed through the streets more quickly than she had come, while she suffered no further indignities from passersby on the crowded streets.

They walked into the now familiar yard at the chief alderman's house and, from there, into the great hall. While Revele sat himself in his chair at the table on the dais raised at the front of the room, her guards brought Christina to stand before him. He motioned for a bowl of wine and then began.

"Please understand I saved you from Newgate not because I have any particular love for you, but because it is my duty to uphold the privileges we have been granted here. Do not hope, however, that consideration of the crime of which you have been accused will be any more lenient under our laws than those of the English."

Christina nodded her head solemnly, understanding full well the meaning of the man's words. *My life hangs in the balance and this man, whom I have insulted and denied, holds sway,* she thought with regret for some of her earlier hasty words and actions.

Revele continued. "Now you will be locked away in one of my storerooms until the morrow, when a council of aldermen will hear the case and decide your fate. It is not a comfortable abode, but I suspect vastly superior to the murderer's dungeon at Newgate." The alderman grinned at his own jest, then said to the men beside her, "Take him from my sight now and lock him in the dry goods store. Oh, and allow that man to visit him, if he so desires."

Revele gestured with his hand in the general direction of his left and the two guards and Christina turned simultaneously to see to whom it was the alderman was referring. The men merely nodded their heads in assent. Christina, however, stared in shocked amazement. The man who rose to accompany her to her place of imprisonment was none other than Ziesolf.

Once secured inside, Christina threw her arms about the knight's neck and sobbed uncontrollably, thankful beyond words she would not face the ordeal of a trial for her life alone. He permitted her a full minute to release her pent-up emotions before he gently loosened her grip and stepped back.

"It is good to find you, Christina, especially so as it seems you have not suffered too greatly at the hands of the sheriff's men."

She considered Ziesolf's words and found herself in agreement that she had indeed been fortunate. Stories abounded of the cruelty and even senseless torture visited upon those held in Newgate's dungeons. She shuddered to think about what would have most assuredly occurred when they discovered she was a woman.

"When your maid informed me of what had happened, we sped swiftly to the ship. There, I found a few members of the crew and traveled onward to The Tabard, where we gathered your movables and returned to *der Greif*. I then complied with your instructions, dispatching the ship to Greenwich, there to wait until the prescribed time. At the last instant, I leapt from the deck onto the shore, that being the only way I could ensure Mistress Trudi would not insist upon remaining as well."

He paused and, reaching into his purse and pulled forth a hunk of bread and a thick slice of cheese. These he tossed to Christina, who began to eat them ravenously.

Passing her a leather flask of ale to wash down her mean, though highly appreciated repast, he continued. "I knew not where to find you, so I spent no time in trying. Instead, I knew the best way I could assist you if you were taken was to spare you imprisonment at Newgate. Therefore, I went to see the Alderman, notifying him one of his merchants was being sought by the English. I knew he could not let such an infringement on Hanseatic rights be ignored, no matter his personal bias against you. Fortune clearly favored you this morn as he had arrived at Newgate himself no more than scant minutes before you. He was just stating his claim for jurisdiction when you were brought in, sparing you even a minute in the foul cells there."

She looked at him with extreme gratitude in her eyes.

"I thank you beyond the power of words, Herr Ziesolf. From before I was born, my family has had no truer friend in the world."

Although his expression remained impassive, she could see he favored her words by a softening of the tone of his reply.

"I thank thee, Christina, both for your words and for embracing this mad scheme we have concocted. By the way, I had not thought they would discover you so quickly."

She was startled by his critical comment, then studied him closely only to determine he had meant it as a jest.

They talked on throughout the remainder of the day, Ziesolf informing her of how the next day's trial was likely to proceed as well as strategies for her defense. They had no idea of the passage of time. Finally, one of Revel's men appeared with a stale crust and a small jug of watered ale. Ziesolf took his leave at that point but vowed to certainly be present at her trial.

Alone once more, Christina's sadness threatened to overwhelm her. She took great solace, however, in Ziesolf's counsel and the fact he would be in attendance on the morrow. She gathered a few sacks together to construct a makeshift bed. Despite her fears, she fell into a deep, undisturbed sleep, realizing there was naught she could do at the moment to alter what was to come.

She awoke, not knowing whether it was night or day. Christina stretched and massaged her aching muscles, especially those of the shoulder upon which she had fallen the previous day. She then carefully went over in her mind what Ziesolf had told her, until she could recite his words by rote. After what must have been several hours, she heard the noise of someone's approach. Once more, the door opened and she was taken from the cell to her trial.

Going into the yard, the contrast between the darkness of the cell and the brilliance of the sunlight caused her eyes to water. Her vision needed to adjust once more as she was brought into the relative dimness of the great hall. The tables had been somewhat rearranged into a layout more conducive to the proceedings of a trial. Her accompanying guard motioned her to take the seat that had been prepared for her, which she did without question.

Taking a view of the setting, she saw Revele seated at the center of the table before her, flanked by two of the other aldermen to each side. Three of these men she knew by sight, having met them in passing at the house of her uncle. Her conversations with them had been limited to little beyond polite greetings, so she could expect no particular favor from them coming her way. The other man, a rotund, seemingly jolly man with a pleasant face, she knew not at all. She only hoped his cheerful appearance was evidence of a kindly heart.

She saw several people seated to the side of the room, most notably in her estimation was Ziesolf. Among the others sat her aunt, stony-faced and staring blankly at the opposing wall. Behind her sat the smirking Richard and a few of her uncle's servants. Even with the addition of several of the chief alderman's men, the vast space seemed sparsely populated.

Revele rose and began the proceedings. "Today we, the aldermen of the Hanse in London, will examine the circumstances of the murder two evenings ago of Gerhardt Kohl, a fellow alderman, merchant of the Hanse, and resident of this city. Appearing before us is Frederick Kohl, merchant of the Hanse and nephew to his late uncle who is suspected of this crime."

He paused momentarily and then continued.

"Who accuses this man?"

Richard stood up and said, "I do, Master Revele. I am Richard London, and I was apprentice and then journeyman assistant to Master Kohl, Master Kohl the elder that is of course."

"Tell us what you know about the murder of Gerhardt Kohl relating to this man," Revele instructed.

"Well, three days ago, I was working in the yard of my Master's house when I heard a terrible amount of yelling in the solar. I rushed up and saw that lot," he indicated the servants seated behind Matilda Kohl, "milling about outside the door to the solar. I opened it and saw him," he indicated Christina, "with his hand around my master's neck. He dropped his hold and stepped away as soon as we entered, the craven coward, but anyone could see he would have throttled him outright if not for us.

"Is that all?" Revele asked.

"No, not the half of it," Richard elaborated. "I thought it peculiar the boy was there at all, seeing as how my Master had banished him from his house nearly three weeks before."

"That's a lie!" Christina shouted, "I left the house of my own free will. As a matter of fact, my uncle begged me to stay!"

"Silence, young Kohl! You'll have a turn to say your piece later! Now, continue," Revele said to Richard.

"Well, as I was saying, it was clear to see Master Gerhardt was frightened by his nephew's threats. So, he asked me to sleep in the hall, in case the whoreson returned, like a thief in the night, seeking to do mayhem. I sleep very deeply, you see, but I was awakened by the noise of the hall door opening. It was dark, but I could clearly make out the face of that man there stealing back out into the night!" he pointed to Frederick for emphasis.

Christina shot upright in protest of the bald-faced lie Richard had just spoken. A withering glance from the chief alderman kept her quiet, however, and she slowly sat back down, although her knuckles were white with rage.

"But why did you not shout to wake up the servants? Did you not think to check on your master at that time, rather than wait until the morning?" Revele asked, puzzlement evident in his voice.

The questions momentarily stymied Richard, then he replied, "I . . . I didn't want to disturb their sleep. I had no idea of the hour, so I though Frederick may have just been leaving after tupping that pretty little maid of his. They're at it all the time, the maids say, with her sneaking into his room any time she can."

"So, you believed your master felt so threatened he placed you to protect his bedchamber; yet, when the man whom he feared may perpetrate violence against him passes through the house under your very nose you do nothing except turn over and go back to sleep? You are fortunate you were not apprenticed to the sheriff, as I don't believe your . . . ah . . . trusting nature would serve you in good stead."

A titter of laughter rang through the hall and Richard glanced about angrily.

"Who would have thought a man would murder his own uncle? And be stupid enough to do it the same day he threatens him with bodily harm!" Richard cried out in anger, obviously smarting from the alderman' sarcasm.

"I think we have heard enough from you, unless you recall any other fortuitous encounters with young Kohl you wish to enlighten us upon?" Richard said nothing.

The servants who witnessed the altercation between Christina and her uncle then gave their recollection of what they had seen. Opposed to Richard's embellishments, however, their testimony was truthful and to the point.

The final person to speak was Matilda Kohl.

"My husband was a man who kept his own secrets. He confided nothing in me as to any doubts or fears about his nephew, but it was plain to see there was a tension between them. They sometimes had contentious rows, starting from the very first night until the day Gerhardt was murdered. Sometimes it seemed like they got along just fine. Other days, not so well." She stated calmly and factually.

Afterwards, she addressed Christina directly, "If it was you who killed my husband, may God receive him joyfully into his kingdom, I offer you the same forgiveness shown by Christ toward those who took his own precious life."

She walked over to Christina and kissed her lightly on the cheek. She then sat back down, silently wiping at the tears flowing down her cheeks.

Revele was visibly moved by the poignancy of Frau Kohl's words.

He hesitated a few seconds, cleared his throat, then said to Christina, "Do you have anything to say in your own defense or witnesses you might call?"

Christina stood and gazed steadily into the eyes of the aldermen.

"I have much to say, Herr Revele, beginning with a declaration of my complete innocence. It is true my uncle and I sometimes argued, most especially that morning three days ago. I do regret I placed my hands upon him and humbly seek the forgiveness of his soul in heaven for that misdeed. But that is the only time I touched him in anger, I swear by God who is my witness. I left my uncle's house that morning and have not returned since. I spent the night of the crime in my rooms across the river in Southwark with two companions, one of these a member of the knighthood whose honor is unimpeachable."

The aldermen listened intently as Christina continued.

"I am not the man you seek for this terrible crime, but such a man is present in this very hall today." She turned around and saw Richard's face curl into a mask of pure hatred toward her. "I accuse Richard London for the murder of Gerhardt Kohl!"

"Bloody liar!" Richard leapt to his feet and shouted. "How dare you seek to rid yourself of your guilt by pushing it toward me, like a dog shedding its fleas? Who would believe such a lie?"

"Well," Revele said, his eyes sparkling with suddenly piqued interest at Christina's unexpected counter-charge. "It seems this story has many twists and turns. Tell me, young Kohl, how did you arrive at this conclusion? Were you hiding under your uncle's bed and recognized that man's boots when he came in to do his knife work?"

"No," admitted Christina, "I did not witness Richard murder my uncle. I did hear the story, however, from one who did."

"And who is this convenient witness?" asked Revele.

"Why, the murderer himself, Richard London," Christina said mildly, turning and pointing at the man for additional emphasis. "Yesterday morning, Richard invited me to a table at the Nag's Head in Southwark. He then confessed to this crime, as well as to others against myself, my business, and my family."

"I'm sorry, Master Kohl, but this would not seem to make any sense. Why would this man confess everything to you?" The portly alderman interjected.

"Christina contemplated her questioner and smiled.

"Because his hatred and jealousy for me knows no bounds. It was not enough for him to be responsible for sending me to Newgate or, more likely, the gallows. He wanted to ensure I knew it was him who orchestrated my ruin and that of my family. Only then could he truly enjoy the fruits of his evil deeds."

"And what say you, Richard?" Revele raised his eyebrows and peered toward Christina's accuser.

"I say this is all horseshit! He's only trying to save himself, anyone can see that." Richard glanced about, hoping to recognize support. "I've lived and worked with Master Kohl for over seven years, why would I kill him now?"

"Because you have both a motive and a ready scapegoat, "Christina replied. As Gerhardt Kohl's bastard, you could not be adjudged his heir as long as those who were legitimate blocked your way. With your master's brother already dead and his nephew, myself, convicted of his murder, his inheritance would fall to you. You would gain everything you have desired."

Revele was about to say something when Christina interrupted, addressing those who sat before her.

"Learned aldermen, I know the judgement before you is a difficult one. Two men accuse each other of an unspeakable murder; yet, there is no witness to say who is innocent and who is guilty. All other evidence is clearly incidental and provides no true insight into the actual commission of the crime." She continued. "I know I am innocent of this crime, just as I am sure of his responsibility for the committing of it. If you aldermen should acquit me through lack of satisfactory evidence, I will not be satisfied. For if I am found innocent from lack of sufficient evidence, I know Richard must be as well. This cannot be. His wrongdoings are too grievous to go unpunished."

Christina took a deep breath, trying to remember precisely the words Ziesolf had told her the previous day.

"Know ye I was neither taken in the act of committing this crime, nor have I attempted to escape your justice by fleeing from it. There is also not such evidence as there can be no denial of my guilt. Meeting these conditions, I appeal the determination of responsibility for this crime be placed into the hands of Our Sweet Lord, his decision to be revealed through trial by combat."

"What?" exclaimed Richard, dumbfounded by Christina's unexpected request.

Christina ignored him for the time being, addressing the aldermen instead. "This entreaty is based both upon our German *Sachsenspiegel* as well as English common law. Therefore, I feel I am well within my rights as the accused to request the trial be decided thusly."

The aldermen put their heads together and began to whisper earnestly

"But what of my rights?" shouted Richard, gesturing wildly. "Have I no say in this madness?"

Revele broke from his discussion with the other aldermen and, clearly annoyed by Richard's interruption, said, "Of course you have rights. If you fight and win, he will be hanged without further discussion. If you decide not to accept his challenge, however, you must withdraw your accusation of Herr Kohl, but that would leave you as the sole person accused of the crime. Should he win, he will go free." He thought for a moment, then added, "Oh, yes. Should you yield, you shall be declared infamous and stripped of freeman status. I believe those are all your rights, Master London."

Richard looked nervously about but saw no one offering any dispute to his opponent's claim. Meanwhile, the aldermen seemed to have come to a consensus.

Revele rose and declared, "Wager by combat has been requested by the defendant and, according to the ancient laws of our people and of the land, been found within his rights to do so. Consequently, both the accused and his accuser are summoned to the yard of this, my house, tomorrow at the hour of Terce, to settle the question of guilt in the murder of Gerhardt Kohl through wager of battle. May God's judgement be upheld by all."

With the postponement of the settlement of the case until the following day, Christina was escorted back to the storeroom that served as her prison. She thought back to the proceedings of the court with grim satisfaction. *Clearly, Revele didn't believe Richard's claim I had visited my uncle's house that night,* she thought. *Would he have agreed to trial by combat so readily if the case against me were stronger?*

She could not know with any certainty whether Revele's decision would have been influenced by any remaining vestiges of animosity he felt against her.

Before too long, Ziesolf was given entrance. He produced a large loaf of manchet, a half-rondel of cheese, and various other foodstuffs. Having had very little to eat over the past few days, she attacked the food ravenously. Finally, she could eat no more and set the remainder away for later.

No longer having to share Christina's attention with her meal, Ziesolf said, "I have learned tomorrow you will be fighting with a blade of which you may not be totally familiar. It is a *Hiebmesser* or cutting knife. Luckily, it is in many ways similar to the falchion which, of course, you know very well."

Christina grinned wolfishly, happy to hear she would be wielding such a weapon.

"Do not become overconfident, Christina, there are several differences as well. The blade has a single curved edge as well as a cross-guard ending in a *nagel,* or nail-like projection that will protect your knife hand. The blade is about thirty inches long and the knife weighs about three pounds."

Christina nodded, finding it hard to believe such a weapon could still be referred to as a knife.

"Now, what do you do with such a weapon?" asked Ziesolf rhetorically. "Obviously, it is designed for the slash, more so then the thrust, although you must not ignore the danger of your opponent's use of the clipped-back point. Since the *Hiebmesser* is used for menial work as well, it can be of crudely forged, making its balance poor and the strength of the blade sometimes suspect."

She scowled at this last point, fearing the possibility of the contest being decided by the skill of the smith rather than that of the combatants.

"You have not faced this man armed but can take some of the things you learned previously into this fight. Tell me, what did you notice?"

"Richard is overly confident. I am smaller than he, so he automatically assumed I was inferior to him as well, although he may have some doubts about that based on the beating I gave him," she smiled at the recollection. "He has poor balance, his punches were thrown too hard, which left him open for a counter-strike. The man is also impatient. He became frustrated and attacked wildly, seeking to overcome me by sheer weight of force."

"Yes, he has many weaknesses, but what are his advantages?" Ziesolf asked.

"Well, he weighs much more than I do. He is more heavily muscled, so I will assume he is stronger as well. I also believe his arms are longer, but I am not entirely certain this is true."

"You must also believe he is more experienced than you. Such men as he have an urge to prove they are better than others, particularly if they perceive they possess advantages in size or skill. You also must not dismiss the possibility he has fought with such a weapon as this before. But you have other advantages as well, Christina. You are faster than he and I suspect more intelligent as well. You have also been training in blade-work by one with years of experience," he gazed at her and added dryly, "Plus, as you mentioned earlier, God will be on the side of the righteous."

With that, Ziesolf rose and went to the corner of the dimly lit room. He came back with two axe handles in his hands. He tossed one to Christina, who caught it deftly.

"These are a bit shorter than I would have liked, but they will have to suffice for now. Come, Christina, show me how you can use a *Hiebmesser*!"

They sparred for over an hour. In particular, Ziesolf made several corrections in Christina's use of the weapon in defense, showing her how to use the *nagel* to momentarily catch her opponent's blade. Then, she would disengage, having a split second to press her attack before her foe had fully regained control of his weapon. By the time their practice ended, Christina was sweaty and fatigued, good signs their workout had been productive. She also felt a growing excitement, confident in her ability to defeat Richard in the upcoming combat.

Too soon, Ziesolf left her and she was once more alone. She practiced on her own a bit more, repeating the movements the knight had shown her over and over until they felt smooth and natural. She then ate the remaining food and laid down on her makeshift bed to rest. No sooner had she closed her eyes than she was fast asleep.

Christina awoke sometime in the middle of the night. She had been so tired the sound of a meager supper being delivered by one of the alderman's men had not awakened her. She relieved herself in the chamber pot that had been provided, then swiftly ate what had been left for her. She then returned to her slumbers.

In the morning, Ziesolf came and alerted her to the fact the guard would be coming for her soon. By the time the man arrived, she was ready. He led her out into the courtyard.

From her conversation with Ziesolf the previous day, Christina knew what to expect. Barriers had bent set up around the yard, enclosing a space sixty feet square for the judicial list, barring any others from interfering with the contest. Christina entered the space, followed by Richard soon after. She was shocked to see he was wearing a leather arming jacket over his tunic that would provide additional protection for his vitals, particularly against a thrust. Having no such garment herself, she was well aware he now possessed a considerable advantage. *Speed and skill, Christina, speed and skill,* she reminded herself.

The aldermen came out of the house and proceeded to a row of chairs that had been set up for them near the barrier. When they arrived at their designated seats, Revele repeated the rules of the combat and made each of the combatants swear they were neither under the influence of witchcraft nor sorcery. After their vows were completed, the chief alderman signaled and the two weapons were brought forth. *My God!* thought Christina, *that's nothing like my falchion!*

Having no other recourse, she took the weapon that was offered, feeling its weight and testing it in a series of cuts through the air. Once the *Hiebmesser* was in her hand, she realized there was some similarity to her accustomed weapon. She stepped back, now approximately ten feet from Richard, and waited for the signal to begin.

When Revele made the signal, Richard rushed forward, swinging his weapon in a series of broad, violent slashes. Having anticipated this, Christina side-stepped lightly to the right, diminishing the force of the man's attack. Her adversary followed her, however, he was too close to the barrier to swing his *Hiebmesser* effectively. She darted forward, dropping her front shoulder low to deliver a grazing cut to the outside of the man's hip which he was not able to parry. Her slash penetrated the cloth and cut into his flesh. Although it was not a debilitating wound, his hose was soon stained dark from a slight flow of red.

Christina felt good about gaining first blood but cautioned herself against overconfidence. She remembered her father had always said an injured animal was always the most dangerous.

Richard now changed his tactics completely, circling cautiously, but staying well out of the reach of Christina's weapon.

"So where is that little maid of yours, Frederick? Has she no stomach to see you die? Perhaps she is waiting for me in my bed, her heart aflutter at the chance to feel a real man's cock in her cleft!"

She felt her ire rise as the man abused her friend's honor. Christina lashed forward with her knife, but Richard was ready for her this time. He pinked the bicep on her sword arm and a trickle of blood soon began to ooze through her tunic. *Stupid!* She raged at herself for being tricked so easily, *what he says makes no matter once you still his mouth forever.*

The fight now began in earnest. Richard sent a thrust toward Christina's knee, which she parried easily with a sweep of her weapon. She then feinted a slash to his left shoulder, which she turned at the last minute to slice up across his cheek. Although her stroke lacked power, it bit deeply enough to slice through the skin and flesh, stopping only when it struck bone.

He yelped involuntarily and fell back from the shock of the pain, then went immediately into his defensive guard. It was obvious to see; however, his desperation was growing.

He again sought to press his attack. He came forward with his weapon before him, moving it like a snake as if to entice his opponent into a rash response. He suddenly moved to his left and sent a slicing blow across Christina's stomach. She stepped back quickly, if she had not, she may have been disemboweled. But his blade still penetrated her garment and found her flesh beneath.

She stifled a cry of her own, emitting instead a throaty grunt from between her clenched teeth. She moved quickly to her right, gaining distance to allow a few seconds to recover from the ache from his blow.

Richard laughed aloud. "Stop your bleating, little lamb! You can scream later as I'm cutting you into chops!"

He now made his rush, charging headlong towards her with his blade flashing furiously before him. He aimed a slice at Christina's shoulder, however, instead of parrying his blow with her blade, she allows his cut to catch on the *nagel* of her weapon. Momentarily confused as to how to disengage his knife from hers, he bulled his body forward, attempting to push her backwards through sheer brute force,

Christina stepped nimbly aside, disengaging her weapon from his with a flick of her wrist. She moved her body into a sideways crouch, throwing her weight forward onto her free hand for additional support.

The energy of Richard's momentum caused him to crash headlong over Christina's extended leg. Off-balanced, he tumbled toward the ground face forward.

Richard managed to break his fall, but was left scurrying along the ground clumsily, seeking desperately to right himself. He was able finally to regain his feet under him, however, he was left awkward and vulnerable. The man thrust his weapon outward, hoping it would keep his opponent at bay just long enough for him to once again resume an adequate defensive posture.

By this time, Christina had arisen and turned back toward Richard. Instantaneously assessing the weakness of his guard, she reacted instinctively, arcing her *Hiebmesser* through the air in a compact hacking motion. It came down hard on the hand holding Richard's weapon, neatly severing three fingers that fall to the ground still writhing like three hungry grubs.

Unable to hold his knife any longer, it clattered to the ground. He bellowed in pain and moved backward, holding his injured hand in his other.

Christina too moved away, unsure exactly what she was expected to do next. *Does Richard intend to continue the combat left-handed?* she wondered. Clearly, there did not seem to be any fight left in the man. He had made no attempt to retrieve his weapon, choosing instead to attempt to nurse his injured hand. Richard had not, however, formally yielded.

This is the rogue who is responsible for the murders of Father, Frederick, and Uncle Gerhardt, he is undeserving of either quarter or pity. Her heart was like a stone as she moved forward, ready to end the man's life who had had no compulsion against ending hers.

Richard finally glanced up from his injury and, seeing Christina's guarded approach, realized he had no other choice than to submit.

"Craven!" he hissed through gritted teeth.

For a few seconds, Christina toyed with the idea of ignoring the man's concession. She would have liked nothing better than to thrust her weapon deeply into Richard's treacherous body, twisting it until he breathed no more. She knew the rules of the combat were specific, however. She was now cleared of her uncle's murder but, if she now killed Richard after he had submitted, she would be guilty of another committed in front of dozens of witnesses. *No,* she decided finally, *the taking of his life is not worth forfeiting my own.*

One of the servants had been busily bandaging Richard's hand, staunching the flow of blood somewhat. Now Revele called the injured man forward to stand before the row of aldermen. "Richard London, by the rules of wager of combat you have submitted to your opponent. Thus, by God's good grace, Frederick Kohl is now declared innocent of the crime of which he was falsely accused by you. As punishment for your untruthful witness you are to be stripped of your status as a free man and declared an outlaw from this community, an action I will request of the sheriff that he too endorse. My men will now take you inside and, as an act of Christian charity, cauterize your wounded hand. If the sheriff agrees with our finding, you will have until nightfall to leave London forever, upon penalty of death should you return."

Before Revele's servants led Richard into the manor house, he turned and gave Christina an expression of pure malevolence. No words were spoken between the two or needed to be – the meaning was clearly understood. Christina knew she had made an enemy for life and, should they meet again in the future, no quarter would be asked or given.

"Frederick Kohl," Christina heard the chief alderman say. She broke her gaze away from her defeated opponent and walked to stand before Revele. "The good Lord has proclaimed you innocent, I will not question his decision.

Thus, you are a free man. Heed this lesson well, however. Amend your rash and disobedient ways or, next time, your fate may be far less fortuitous."

With that warning, he, the other aldermen, as well as the miscellaneous onlookers who had gathered, began to disperse.

As Christina walked toward the gate of the yard, Ziesolf met her.

He clapped her heartily on the back, telling her, "Well done! Well done! Now, let's go get you cleaned up. Your wounds don't appear too serious, at least not compared to his."

Ziesolf nodded his head in the direction of the house.

In the distance, they heard a muffled scream which, Christina surmised, could only be the effect from the cauterization of Richard's wound. Although she felt guilty, she couldn't help but take some small pleasure in his obvious agony.

At that moment, Christina saw her aunt approaching. Unsure of the woman's purpose, her trepidation mounted. She had no belly for further confrontation. Matilda Kohl came to within a foot and reached out her hands, taking those of Christina within hers.

She looked directly into Christina's eyes and said, "God's will has clearly shone you to be blameless, nephew. Forgive me for ever having doubted your innocence. My only excuse, and a poor one at that, was I was too distraught over my husband's death to see the evil treachery I harbored within my own house. Please now, come with me and accept the hospitality of my home. Let you consider it as your own, which shortly it will be, as I am soon to clutch tightly to

Christ's bosom for the rest of my life in quiet contemplation at Aldgate Abbey"

Christina was astounded by her aunt's unexpected declaration. Realizing the magnitude of the woman's offer, she replied formally. "Thank you, Aunt Matilda, for both your generosity and affection. I will accept your kind invitation, only not just yet. I have need to travel as quickly as possible to Greenwich, there to give instructions to my ship as to how to proceed. Then, having also retrieved the maid Trudi, I will return, taking residence in your sweet company as you suggested."

Her aunt nodded, patted her hand once again, and left to return to her home.

Amazed at her astonishing change of fortune, Christina looked at Ziesolf and grinned broadly, for once he met hers with one of his own. Words were not required. In unison, they turned and walked away, first to attend to Christina's wounds and then intent on finding two good horses.

Coming soon from

Lee Swanson

Her Perilous Game

In *No Man's Chattel*, a series of family tragedies and her own indominable spirit compelled young Christina Kohl to take the guise of a man, as she knows no woman would be accepted into the merchant community of 14th century London.

Christina's saga continues in the second novel of the series, *Her Perilous Game*.

Still masquerading as her dead brother Frederick, Christina experiences bitter disappointment in her life despite continued success as a merchant. Her distraction could prove perilous, as dangers both old and new arise to confront her. She is not alone, however, as the stalwart knight Ziesolf and her maid Trudi are joined by new members of Christina's budding household to assist and support her.

Increasingly, she is drawn into the world of English royal intrigue through her friendship with the much-maligned Earl of Cornwall, Piers Gaveston. Even as the King takes an army northward to battle the Scots, a number of the most powerful barons in the land remain behind, conspiring against Gaveston. When Christina learns of their plot to oust Gaveston from the King's favor, she realizes she too must journey north to warn him. At the Scottish borders, she is confronted with dire perils and unexpected possibilities that will change her life forever.

49551448R00186

Made in the USA
Middletown, DE
21 June 2019